PATERNAL INSTINCT

PATERNAL INSTINCT

J. R. MADDUX

iUniverse, Inc.
New York Bloomington

iUniverse books may be ordered through booksellers or by contacting:

iUniverse
1663 Liberty Drive
Bloomington, IN 47403
www.iuniverse.com
1-800-Authors (1-800-288-4677)

Because of the dynamic nature of the Internet, any Web addresses or links contained in this book may have changed since publication and may no longer be valid. The views expressed in this work are solely those of the author and do not necessarily reflect the views of the publisher, and the publisher hereby disclaims any responsibility for them.

ISBN: 978-1-4401-4747-0 (sc)
ISBN: 978-1-4401-4748-7 (ebook)
ISBN: 978-1-4401-4749-4 (dj)

Printed in the United States of America

iUniverse rev. date: 6/10/2009

Also by J. R. Maddux

Quileute Rising

Hunter One

For the late Lewis Babbidge
A good friend
and a patriot who served his country with distinction

FOREWORD

By
Gardner Wiseheart

Paternal Instinct, like *Quileute Rising* and *Hunter One* before it, is a smart, fast-paced thriller told in the winning J. R. Maddux style. As usual, the story is full of rich characters involved in a riveting, suspenseful plot. *Paternal Instinct*, however, has an added dimension that makes it particularly compelling and relevant. It is about the all-important role that fathers play in the lives of their children.

From intuition, experience and research we know that fathers are not just important, but critical in their children's lives. By virtually every measure of child well being, whether cognitive, emotional or social, a father's contribution to his child's development is crucial to their healthy growth and development. Having an involved, committed, caring father does more than just level the playing field. It tilts the field in the child's favor.

While *Paternal Instinct* is an exciting story about the extraordinary and heroic actions of a fictitious father, the everyday interventions of ordinary dads constitute, in themselves, a heroism that produces lifetime results. Only a few fathers will ever be asked to risk their lives for their children. But sometimes actions as simple as giving up bad habits, or bad language, or some personal time in order to be an involved, committed parent to one's child are more praiseworthy and socially significant than the adventures of any action hero.

As readers of *Paternal Instinct* are gripped by the tense storyline, and connect with the thoughts and feelings of the main character, they may come to realize that there is no line they would not cross to save their own child, whether physically, mentally or emotionally. Such a realization and commitment is what is needed in our time to protect families from the ravages that tear so many apart, and leave so many fatherless.

Gardner Wiseheart

* * * * *

Gardner Wiseheart, M.A., is an international fathering consultant and author of *Maps for Dads*, and *Doin' the Dad Thing*. He is also the founder and director of the Southwest Partnership for Fathers and Families, and lives with his wife, Carolyn, in San Angelo, Texas.

Acknowledgements

Paternal Instinct is, admittedly, a labor of love inspired, in part, by my work with struggling families in search of stable relationships. Credit and gratitude are due to the many competent and compassionate social servants who touched my life as they went about their healing errands for others. Marianne Ehrlich, Monica Clancy, Sylvia Arismendiz, Alicia Lara and Gregoria Guerrero are but a few of those whose dedication served to inspire me and remind me of the importance of family in our busy society.

Special thanks is due the late Lewis Babbidge, to whose memory *Paternal Instinct* is dedicated. His understanding of and insight into the operational workings of the clandestine services helped to drive this story's plotline, and his unflagging encouragement motivated me to write it.

Most of all, thanks to my sons, who afforded me the luxury of learning fathering through trial and error. Their personal and professional successes and persistent support of my endeavors has made the parenting journey the richest experience of my life.

Appreciation is due my several friends in the publishing industry who have encouraged my writing over the years, and especially those who have argued that *Paternal Instinct* is a story that needs to be read, and belongs in print, and to my dear wife who helped with the formatting and editing of the finished product.

Finally, many thanks to Pascal Chureau and his creation,

Fenouil, an incomparable restaurant that has afforded some entirely memorable dining experiences. While Fenouil is referred to fictitiously as the site of a family celebration late in the pages of this novel, there is nothing fictitious about either Pascal's culinary wizardry or the excellence of Fenouil's cuisine, ambience and service. A trip to the Pacific Northwest without at least one meal at Portland's Fenouil, is a delightful opportunity squandered.

PROLOGUE

Riyadh, Saudi Arabia

Buoyed by a day of highly successful negotiations, the three young American lawyers huddled at a corner table in the exotic poolside Mondo restaurant, jewel of the upscale Intercontinental Riyadh. They toasted their brand new six-year deal just agreed to with the Saudi oil ministry. Under terms they had brokered their employer—Halvarson-Brandt Oilfield Services—was to be the sole provider of certain critical downhole technology and technical drilling support to a government increasingly interested in extracting the black liquid gold from beneath its deserts in the most efficient and cost effective manner possible. Next morning, the three planned to make the thirty-minute drive to King Khaled airport and begin the first leg of their long flight home, which included a planned stopover in Amsterdam.

The Intercontinental was situated on Maazar Street, just five minutes from the teeming business district of the kingdom's capital city. Because of its prime location and appreciable amenities, it was the perpetual favorite of a wide variety of international business travelers. The hotel was, in fact, geared to just such a multicultural clientele, featuring two hundred seventy five well appointed rooms, and a multilingual staff that communicated passably in Arabic, English, French, Italian, Hindi and Tagalog. Surrounding the hotel were a hundred acres of beautiful mature gardens with the fronds of twenty-five foot date palms waving gently in the breeze, the rich scent of flowering tamarisk perfuming the air, and the deep green of thorny acacia surrounding a bubbling octagonal fountain. Also featured was a nine-hole grass golf course, a rarity in the arid deserts of the Middle East.

Scott Wells, the lead negotiator of this formidable legal team, was in high spirits, partly because of the stunning business *coup* he had just orchestrated, and partly because he looked forward with relish to some richly deserved time off, and a long awaited fishing trip with his father when he arrived stateside. Wells was a tall, good-looking, broad-faced man in his early thirties. His vivid blue eyes were rendered all the more striking by his prematurely receding hairline, and his well-tanned skin reflected his passion for the outdoors. He had two large dimples that were especially evident when he smiled, and tonight he smiled incessantly.

To his left sat Marty Logan, a product of Stanford University Law School, and a close friend as well as business colleague. Logan's wispy blonde hair, slight build and pale complexion made his appearance different from Scott's in almost every way. But his incisive legal mind and eye for financial detail proved invaluable in the hard bargaining that consumed the better part of the last several days.

Aaron Saperstein, the third member of the team, was yet another study in contrast. His skin was also darker, although not so much as a result of outdoor pursuits as of his own Middle Eastern heritage. He was short by comparison with the others, and had the powerful, compact look of a body builder, the result of hours spent in the gym and weight room. Thick, curly black hair ringed his bespectacled face, and hung loosely down over his collar. His specialty, contracts, guaranteed that every concession Scott Wells extracted at the bargaining table would find its way into the final document that the Saudi government and HB officials would sign.

All three rose eagerly to greet Faisal al-Rashidi, Saudi oil minister and his deputy, Rahim bin Qureshi. When bows and handshakes had been exchanged all around, the five sat together at the table as solicitous waiters dressed in white waistcoats bustled about providing cold drinking water and menus. The Mondo, fabled for its exquisite pan-Asian cuisine, was inevitably a dining treat, featuring not only savory Middle Eastern delicacies, but also some of the finest of China's Szechuan and Mandarin dishes, and the teriyaki and sukiyaki flavors of Japan. Patrons were of every imaginable ethnicity, some clad in sparkling white *mogasahs* typical of the Arab world, some, like the Americans, in conservative western style business suits, and some in tropic-friendly linen trousers and garish Hawaiian shirts. Tonight the three Americans were in very good appetite, and the luxuriously draped and carpeted dining room added a special elegance to the occasion.

Facing on the glistening pool, they could not see the black van with tinted windows as it pulled up slowly and stopped under the covered valet parking awning. Nor could they see the five men in desert camouflage fatigues and ski masks who jumped out carrying bulging canvas rucksacks. From the bags, each man withdrew a weapon. Three were armed with Scorpion Vz61 machine pistols, and the other two with silenced large caliber handguns. The Intercontinental, like most Middle Eastern establishments that catered to foreigners, had security guards, four of them. The intruders moved with practiced grace and swiftness, their silenced weapons quickly dispatching the four security men, and all five of the masked terrorists converging as one on the main entrance to the dining room.

The *maitre d'* intervened swiftly to block their path, and was cut down by a burst from one of the Scorpions, spewing a torrent of blood from the gaping wounds in his chest and throat and effectively announcing to the room full of terrified patrons that the restaurant had been invaded. Suddenly a fusillade of nine-millimeter bullets shattered and felled the massive crystal chandeliers, sending sparkling shards of glass flying through the air. Red and gold tapestries gracing walls and windows were similarly shredded, and diners foolish enough to rise from their meals were summarily shot down. There were periodic lulls in the terrifying onslaught as the masked men paused to ram fresh twenty round clips into their

Scorpions, while they continued moving inexorably toward the Americans and their government hosts.

As they approached the table, the short, portly al-Rashidi stood to protest, gesturing frantically and shouting in Arabic. His voice choked into silence as one of the men, armed with a handgun, put a bullet directly between his eyes, causing him to fall face forward across the table, spattering the crisp white linen table cloth a telltale crimson and scattering drinks, *hors d'oeuvres*, and silverware onto the rich damask carpet.

"Stand," shouted one of the men in English, gesturing with the butt of his weapon toward the three Americans.

Raising their hands, all three complied, whereupon their hands were manacled in front of them with leather thongs, and black hoods the texture of burlap thrown over their heads. Another withering hail of gunfire drove the surviving diners back down to the floor as the kidnappers backed out of the restaurant, made their way to an exit and hastily pushed their three captives into a side door of the idling van. In seconds they were gone, leaving behind them a surfeit of fear, death and destruction.

CHAPTER ONE

Yamhill County, Oregon. Wednesday, September 20

Dying slowly in the west, the bright red ball of sun tinted the purple haze of dusk with a halo of vivid pink. Terraced hills rolled away in every direction, festooned by the dark green of verdant vineyards as far as the eye could see. A white-tailed doe peeked shyly out from a gnarled filbert grove atop a low nearby hill. The faint mist of early evening crept up the graveled entry road that wound lazily between mottled gray stone walls that were flanked by stately aged cedars and alders. From the wraparound porch of the elegant, sprawling, European style lodge, furtive eyes swept out over the landscape, missing not a single detail of the stunning natural panorama afforded by the early evening. But these eyes were serious, intent, troubled. They were the eyes of Oregon vintner Curtis Wells.

Sleek and wiry, Wells wore his fifty-four years with distinction. Only the "crow's feet" stamped in the tanned, leathery skin at the corners of his eyes by the passage of time and the rigors of hard, outdoor physical labor, along with a slight graying at the temples of his dark, close-cropped hair betrayed his advanced stage of life. A former Navy SEAL who had done a brief stint in black ops with the Central Intelligence Agency, he abandoned that life ten years earlier to assume the management of the vineyard.

Whispering Ridge Cellars had been a struggling winery in fertile Yamhill County, a grape-growing haven just outside Newberg, Oregon. But Whispering Ridge flourished under Wells' management, and its two hundred forty-four bountiful acres annually produced some of the finest *pinot gris, pinot noir* and Riesling grapes in the western United States. The Cellars employed twenty-seven locals full-time, a dozen more part-time and still others seasonally, producing and shipping fine wines both internationally and to every part of the United States.

Curt Wells loved his business, and he loved the land. Sometimes in the early mornings he would stroll leisurely up into the terraced hills, into the vineyards, imbibe the rich smell of the ripening fruit and pick up fistfuls of the fecund, volcanic soil, allowing it to trickle through his fingers and back to the ground again. He relished the taste of good wine and the intricate and painstaking process of producing it. Although he had a full time enologist on his staff, no one knew the grapes better than Wells himself.

He and his wife, Molly, inherited the winery from Molly's father, who bought the business as one of his many investments and then, within months, suffered a massive stroke and died. It was at that juncture that Wells, with some gentle urging from Molly, walked away from the perilous and capricious world of international intrigue for the life of a country gentleman in this natural paradise. It was a decision he had not until this moment regretted.

But tonight was unlike any other. The Wells' had two children, sons Scott and Tyler. Tyler, the youngest, was an executive at a promising software firm in Seattle, and made frequent pilgrimages southward to Whispering Ridge to see his parents. Scott, nicknamed "Sunny" because of his sparkling smile and cheerful disposition, worked as legal counsel for Halvarson-Brandt, a giant corporation based in Dallas, Texas, specializing in oilfield downhole drilling support. Scott was a seasoned world traveler, frequently globe trotting to negotiate contracts, finalize patents and mediate disputes for the company. A rising legal star in his industry, he was respected and genuinely liked by everyone who knew him, no mean accomplishment for an attorney.

The troubling call had come in the late afternoon. Scott Wells and two other company lawyers had been dining at a fancy hotel restaurant in Riyadh, Saudi Arabia, after lengthy and arduous negotiations with officials of the Saudi government, when five armed, masked men stormed the place, killing eleven Saudis and taking the three Americans. At best, Scott "Sunny" Wells was a hostage. At worst, well, his frantic father could not even bear to think about that.

Rounding the corner of the replica of an old Italian winery building, Carlos Gutierrez, Wells' trusted vineyard manager, strode purposefully across the green expanse of neatly manicured lawn and up three broad stone steps to the porch where Wells sat in a weathered wooden rocker, deeply absorbed in thought, his mouth set in a thin, grim line.

"You wanted to see me, Jefe?" he said.

"Yes, Carlos, I have to fly to D.C. in the morning, and I want you to take care of things while I'm gone, as usual," Wells muttered offhandedly, his mind clearly elsewhere.

"You going about Sunny?" Gutierrez asked rhetorically.

"Yep," Wells confirmed, "'cause I'm sure as hell not going to get any straight answers from those people while I'm sitting here."

"Damned politicians," Gutierrez growled.

"Yeah, damned politicians," Wells echoed.

"We'll keep things buttoned down here," Gutierrez promised. "The grapes are growing real well. It will be a good year. You just bring Sunny home."

As Carlos walked away, Wells' troubled mind returned to his son's tenuous situation. He would go to Washington tomorrow all right, and walk directly into that swirling sea of political turmoil, petty partisan maneuvering and peddled influence. And he would meet with representatives from the State Department, perhaps someone from the White House, and maybe even some old friends at Langley. But his time with the CIA and the SEALs had taught him well that situations such as this one were often politically charged, and that what was best for hostages taken abroad was not always the highest priority of the politicians at home. He would likely be more in need of a shovel in Washington than a briefcase. About that he was confident.

Stan Blanton, executive vice-president for Halvarson-Brandt, was the first to telephone the Wells family, offering assurances that the corporate giant would use every means at its disposal to free Scott Wells and the others. Shortly thereafter, a Marvin Forrester from the State Department called to add that they were pursuing the matter at the highest levels and that the president himself would speak with the Saudi king shortly. Curt Wells was grateful, but not reassured.

Molly Wells, for her part, was beside herself with anxiety and grief, her brow uncharacteristically furrowed and the tears ever present in the corners of her sparkling green eyes. It had never crossed her mind that her son, a civilian, would become a pawn to be haggled over by terrorists and politicians. She had read the graphic and gory media accounts of the brutality directed toward American hostages in Iraq, Afghanistan and Pakistan, and the thought of them made her shudder in the early evening breeze that had begun to sweep down gustily over Whispering Ridge. The possibility that her own precious son might now face some of the same barbarous and brutal treatment left her paralyzed, numb, heartbroken. Surely the most powerful country in the world could do something. But they were able to save only a few of the others. What would happen now was anyone's guess. Curt would find out in Washington. He just had to.

Somewhere West of Buraydah, Saudi Arabia

Scott Wells and his colleagues were aroused rudely and early in the morning by their captors. Crammed together into a flat, narrow wooden cage, they had been forced to squeeze into a space so small that even turning to keep blood circulating was a collaborative three-man effort. Their heads were covered with dark hoods, and remained that way even when they were jerked roughly to their feet, led into a dusty field and ordered to urinate. This they did gratefully, while watchful guards ridiculed them in Arabic.

Next, they were loaded roughly into the back of a large, dented and dilapidated truck, and forced to lie flat, with feet shackled and arms bound tightly in front of them. They drove for what seemed an eternity, their lungs choked with dust spiraling up from the primitive roadway and the acrid diesel fumes blowing back from the vehicle's exhaust. The bruising wallop of every bump and pothole, exaggerated by the nearly defunct shock absorbers of the rickety vehicle added to the physical toll of their tortuous journey. As the parching sun soared into the desert sky, they could taste the bitter salt of their own liberally streaming perspiration. Periodically, they were offered water, carelessly poured in the direction of their mouths by their indifferent tormentors, with only a few drops finding the intended targets.

Scott Wells had little firsthand experience with loneliness, much less fear. Handsome, talented, and outgoing, he was invariably tabbed as a leader, and the life of every party. As an attorney litigating patent infringements or land usage disputes he knew the territory of uncertainty and an adversarial climate, to be sure. But he had never experienced anything remotely like this, and it dawned eerily upon him that his life to date had been a sheltered and relatively carefree one. He did not presently know where he was, where he was going, what would befall him and the others, or if he would ever see his home and family again. Not seeing his dad, mom and brother, not even being able to say goodbye properly, that was the worst fear of all. He needed to push it all down inside, use whatever senses he had available to him to learn how to survive in this new and hostile environment. His father had always taught him that change provides opportunity. So he would wait and watch for the situation to change. Then, perhaps he and Marty and Aaron, also bright fellows, could think or talk their way out of this mess. Still the truck rumbled on, north by west.

Washington, D.C., Thursday, September 21

Curt Wells' flight was long and cramped. While he could easily have afforded a seat in first class, none was available on such short notice. So he dozed fitfully while wedged into a coach class middle seat between a woman large enough to occupy half of his seat as well as her own, and an elderly priest who snored loudly and incessantly as he slept.. He jumped gladly at the opportunity to stretch his legs, even if only between the arrival gate and the cab stand. As he waited his turn, he noted that the nation's capital was unseasonably warm today, and his forehead moistened with perspiration from the tinge of humidity in the air. His first stop was the State Department, where he had made an appointment to talk face-to-face with Marvin Forrester.

Forrester, he was soon to discover, was a deputy undersecretary for Middle Eastern affairs. Never at home in the polished, marbled Washington halls of government, Wells was nonetheless squired up the elevator and into a sterile looking, sparsely furnished sixth floor conference room by an eager young aide, where he was joined by a silver-haired man in his late fifties who wore stylish titanium-rimmed glasses and walked with a slight but noticeable limp. He was accompanied by a taller and much younger man who wore a slick, expensively tailored pinstriped suit from Brooks Brothers, and had dark hair and intense, brown eyes. The older man introduced himself as Forrester, and then presented Bradley Baker, who represented himself opaquely as a White House staffer. Wells wondered cynically if that meant he was a janitor, or a presidential aide.

"Thank you for coming here all the way from Oregon, Mr. Wells," Forrester began crisply. "I know you are extremely concerned for your son's safety, as are we."

"We already know he's not safe," snapped Wells, in no mood to brook shallow pleasantries. "My question is what are *you* doing to find him and get him back?"

"The Saudis have assured the president that the safe return of the American hostages is their highest priority," interrupted Baker imperiously, as though this simple platitude would quell Curt Wells' anxiety.

"Right," snorted Wells sardonically, "except we know how the Saudis handle this kind of business, don't we? They find the bad guys and go in with guns blazing. Everybody dies, including the hostages, and they write it off as collateral damage."

"That's a bit harsh, don't you think?" Forrester chided.

"Harsh, my ass," snorted Wells. "Remember, you're talking to someone who has worked in the intelligence community and in that theater. I've seen it with my own eyes. They shoot first and then sort out the bodies. That's not my idea of a rescue."

The brusque initial exchange set the tone for the entire twenty-minute encounter in which the government men became increasingly frustrated with Curt Wells' shortage of patience, and he with their apparent lack of candor. Patronizing a man of Curt Wells' *gravitas* was a mistake, as they would soon learn.

"The president feels that we can negotiate," intoned Baker before Wells cut him off.

"Negotiate?" he said, incredulous. "So they've made contact and presented demands?"

"That's classified," snapped Baker curtly.

"Classified, you say?" mused Wells sarcastically. "So a man's own father can't know the price of his son's freedom?"

"Look, Mr. Wells," pleaded Forrester, "there's only so much we can tell you at this time. You must understand that this situation is extremely delicate. We know that you are a man of substantial means, broad contacts and considerable influence, and we hope that you won't go off half-cocked and try to take matters into your own hands. Acting prematurely and doing something precipitous and foolish before we can bring the full resources of this government to bear will only make matters worse, I assure you."

"Understand me clearly," said Wells evenly, the thinly veiled anger simmering in his acid tone of voice. "My government may be comfortable sitting on its backside while my firstborn rots in some terrorist hellhole. But I'm not! By one means or another, my boy *is* coming home, and very soon."

"What do you think you could possibly accomplish that we can't?" Baker shot back skeptically.

"That's classified," retorted Wells acidly, rising to signify that the brief, unproductive discussion was over, and having gotten precisely the perfunctory runaround he expected.

On the cab ride to the State Department, Wells had called Mark Faulkner, a former associate who now worked in the directorate for intelligence at the Central Intelligence Agency. They'd arranged an early dinner at Zorba's, an outstanding Greek restaurant in Landover, Maryland, just down the road. Maybe Mark would be able to shed some more light on an otherwise foggy and opaque picture.

Wells arrived early, got them a table and ordered up a bottle of Ballatore Chardonnay. It wasn't a Whispering Ridge vintage, but a respectable year and label nonetheless. He rose and motioned to the tall, slim Faulkner as he arrived. The two old friends shook hands warmly, and Faulkner shed his long black overcoat before sitting. Wells filled two wine glasses.

"God, Curt, I was so sorry to hear about Sunny," Faulkner began. "I know you must be in hell."

"More than you know, Mark" confirmed Wells. "But what's really frustrating me is that I can't seem to get any hard information about the situation."

"What are you looking for?" Faulkner asked warily, taking the napkin from his lap and laying it on the table.

"Who are these people? Where are they holding Scott and the others? What do they want?" Wells asked in rapid sequence.

"We're not sure exactly who they really are. Their communiqué represents them as Islamiyah al-Jihad, which nobody here or in Saudi seems to know anything about," Faulkner shared. "Where they are, we have no idea at the moment. We're working on that. But we doubt if they've left Saudi."

"Over at State they fed me nothing but smoke," Wells fumed. "They said terms had been set, that we would negotiate, but that what the kidnappers want is classified."

"That's a crock!" agreed Faulkner, leaning back in his chair. "They want that to come out in a White House press release, which it will within forty-eight hours. It's only classified so that no one will upstage the president."

"So, will you tell me?" asked Wells urgently.

"It'll land my ass in a sling if you don't keep it under your hat," Faulkner shook his head, lowering his voice as though someone might overhear. "But yes, I'll tell you, because I think you'd do the same if my kid had been taken and you sat at my desk. They want the U.S. to announce staged troop withdrawals from Iraq and Afghanistan, complete with timetables, and they want Halvarson-Brandt and a dozen other U.S. companies to agree to cut back operations in six Muslim countries to a simple support level. They also want the Israelis to release a convicted Jordanian bomber named Jamir al-Budiya from one of their prisons, that's all," he concluded, throwing up his hands in a gesture of futility.

"That's all," sighed Wells. "In other words, there is not a chance either we or the Israelis will give them what they want."

"Not a chance in hell," agreed Faulkner.

"How about a Delta Force or SEAL incursion if we can locate the hostages?" Wells inquired hopefully.

"No way," Faulkner shook his head vigorously. "And CIA has been told to stand down, except for intelligence gathering. The president and State don't want to piss off the Saudis. The way things stand, all we're going to do is talk. Any direct action is up to the Saudis, who can't find a snowball in a blizzard when they don't want to."

"Why wouldn't they want to?" Wells followed up sensing a parallel agenda and making direct eye contact with his friend. "This all looks bad on them."

"There's something they're keeping from us," Faulkner observed thoughtfully, "something they don't want us to know. I've already told you about all we do know, and a hell of a lot more than I should."

"We never talked," smiled Wells, changing the subject. "Do you like good wine?"

Over a fine dinner they chatted about family and old times, but the wheels in Wells' acute mind never once stopped spinning away. He knew the first part of what he needed to know. The rest would clearly have to come from a source outside the U.S. government. He just had to reach out, probe, sort, and think it through.

He stared out the window into the night, unconsciously rolling and unrolling a newspaper through the long cab ride back to his Arlington hotel. His normally rapier sharp thought processes were being perceptibly clouded by the growing anxiety he felt. Curt Wells was closer to his two sons than most fathers, closer than he could explain in words. He worked very hard at being a good father, even when the boys, four years apart, were small. He bathed, fed and diapered them when they were babies, allowing Molly to get her rest after delivering. He even took furlough from the Navy to make it possible. He helped both boys with their schoolwork, taught them to hunt, fish, and play sports, and ingrained in them life's most important values: honesty, integrity, justice, equality, honor and love. Most important of all—to him at least—he taught them about the unbreakable bond of being a family. When Curt Wells was threatened in the line of duty he had always been cool, fearless and decisive. As a businessman he was objective, analytical and precise. But like most who enjoyed success in the dark world of counterintelligence, Wells was an extremely internal person. On the outside he appeared to those who knew him casually as unflawed, nearly perfect. But few, except for Molly, knew him to be a chronic worrier, an obsessive perfectionist and the victim of an acute failure phobia. The reality of the man was far more complex and considerably less superhuman than met the eye. Now that his son was being threatened, Wells experienced an unnerving and paradoxical mix of rage and helplessness that was completely atypical, and he was unsure just how to process such strong and conflicted feelings. But he knew two things. First, nobody else was going to *do* anything to help his son in the near term. That seemed clear enough. And second, he *had* to do something, because if the worst should happen and he hadn't, well, he just wouldn't be able to live with that. He called Carlos Gutierrez to check on things at Whispering Ridge, and had him send Mark Faulkner a case of *pinot gris*. That night, instead of sleeping, Wells began to form a detailed plan.

CHAPTER TWO

Reagan National Airport, Friday, September 22

On the way to the airport Wells asked the cabbie to stop at a convenience store where he paid cash for two hundred dollars worth of phone cards. He needed to make a few calls he didn't want to be traceable to his cell. Once at Reagan National, he found an out-of-the-way pay phone station and made his first call.

"Hello, you old pirate," he said jovially into the mouthpiece.

"Wells? Wells?" asked the incredulous voice on the other end.

"Yeah, man, a real blast from the past," Wells said.

"I have been half expecting you to call. It's a rough situation you're in," said the anonymous voice.

"Really rough, and I may need some special help," Wells agreed.

"Just what did you have in mind, my old friend?" the voice inquired.

"Not on the phone. Where can we meet?" Wells asked.

"I'm on a plane for Washington within the hour," the man said.

"I'm in Washington now," Wells said. "How about the usual place, tomorrow at noon?"

"Very well," said the mystery man at the other end of the line. "Until then."

Hanging up, Wells walked quickly to one of the eclectic airport shops and bought two newspapers, along with a large canvas duffel bag. Stepping into a restroom and entering one of the stalls, he hastily stripped off the business suit he was wearing, emptied his suitcase and put most of its contents into the duffel. He stuffed the suit and big balls of wadded up newspaper into the suitcase. Putting on a black pullover, navy windbreaker and blue jeans, he grabbed the suitcase in one hand and the duffel in the other, and walked out. Checking in for his flight to Portland, he also checked the suitcase through, even though he had no intention of boarding the plane. Walking to the helicopter shuttle counter, he bought a ticket for the short hop to the Baltimore airport, where he rented a Ford van and headed east. It would be too early for them to have a tail on him, he thought, but he was certain that they soon would, and he wasn't taking any chances. The stakes of this game were simply too high.

From the gray sheet of sky, a shimmering sheet of drizzle fell softly, rendering the broad turnpike slick and hazardous. The wind that had shifted during the night now blew chilly and strong out of the north. He drove at a steady, but conservative speed and just over three hours later he arrived at his destination, Atlantic City, New Jersey. He paid cash for a room with a big grease stain on the lamp shade, a light bulb out in the bathroom, four shower curtain rings where there should have been nine and a commode that sounded like Niagara Falls every time it flushed. The place was entirely forgettable, which was the whole point. He'd checked in under an assumed name, and tried to get some rest before the important rendezvous with his mysterious friend.

Instead of sleeping peacefully, he was troubled by vivid and harrowing dreams. In one of them, he and Sunny were on a hunting trip in the mountains when, out of nowhere, a large, prowling cougar attacked. Frantically, the panicked father tried to beat the savage animal off, drive it away from his vulnerable young son. Just when his efforts seemed the most futile he awakened, trembling and lathered in a cold mantle of sweat. This had been a bad dream. But the chilling reality of his son's life or death predicament was entirely real.

The White House, Saturday, September 23

Seated in the Oval Office were President Norman Sloan, Secretary of State Donald Trimble, CIA Director Emmett Choate and Chairman of the Joint Chiefs of Staff General Conrad Blaisdell. The president was, as usual, first to speak.

"What do we know about these three young attorneys who were kidnapped in Riyadh?" he demanded, staring blankly at the others.

"Aaron Saperstein, Scott Wells and Martin Logan, all house counsels with Halvarson Brandt Oil Field Services. We don't know where they are or exactly who has them," Choate offered. "What we do know is that the kidnappers have made an outrageous series of demands for their safe return."

"Yes, outrageous," agreed Sloan. "I couldn't give in to them even if I wanted to, you know?"

"No one really expects you to, Mr. President," responded the old Marine warhorse Blaisdell.

"With one possible exception," corrected Trimble. "We had a predictable visitor over at State yesterday."

"And who, pray tell, was that?" the president inquired.

"He was one Curtis Wells, the father of one of the hostages," Trimble said quietly.

"So?" queried the president. "Is he somebody special?"

"We think so, sir," Trimble replied. "He's an Oregon winemaker, very rich, very influential. He can make a lot of political trouble for us if he wants to. And there's one more thing."

"And what is that?" the president wanted to know.

"He's a decorated Navy SEAL who subsequently spent some time as a covert operator for the CIA. He is extremely resourceful and very well connected in some parts of the world, including the Middle East. And he is frustrated at what he believes to be our purposeful inaction, to put it mildly. Forrester of my staff and Baker of yours both think it's possible that this Wells might try to take things into his own hands," Trimble summarized.

"He's over fifty years old by now, for God's sake," sneered

Choate. "What do you think he's going to do, invade Saudi all by himself?"

"I have no idea," shrugged Trimble. "He's not Ross Perot, that's for sure. But you should know better than any of us, Emmett, that he has certain capabilities the normal American citizen doesn't."

"*Had*," cajoled Choate, "he *had* those capabilities once upon a time. That doesn't mean he still does."

"What are you suggesting, Donald?" Sloan inquired of Trimble, waving Choate into silence.

"Perhaps that we have the FBI and the NSA keep an eye and an ear on Wells till this thing is resolved?" Trimble answered with a question of his own.

"Oh, all right," conceded Sloan, skeptical that a real danger existed. "I'll have someone call Kendrick over at the Bureau and ask him to keep track of your Mr. Wells until further notice. Now, what are we going to do about the hostages?"

"If we found them, Delta Force could do a snatch and grab. But that would make the Saudis mad as hell. They'll want to resolve this their own way," Blaisdell observed candidly.

"That doesn't bode well for the hostages, does it?" Sloan asked knowingly.

"No," agreed Trimble, "but in the end we may have to choose between trusting the Saudis to pull off a rescue or losing one of our two closest allies in the Middle East, Mr. President."

"Those are unacceptable alternatives, gentlemen. I need you to meet with your staffs and come up with some others," the president pontificated, waving his arms for emphasis.. "And in the meanwhile, if this Wells starts making waves, I want to know about it right away," he added, motioning the three advisors out of his office.

Atlantic City, the Crooked Parrot Bar and Grill

Anyone eavesdropping on Wells' call from Reagan National would have heard that his friend was headed for Washington, that Wells was already there, and concluded that the "usual place" where they were to meet was in the nation's capital. They would have been dead wrong. In Wells' days as a CIA operative, he and Zev

Shalman of Israel's Mossad frequently used the Crooked Parrot as a meeting place. It was a low profile bar just off the Boardwalk, with garish early eclectic décor that might drive a tasteful person to drink, if he didn't already. All of that was good, because the Parrot was in the business of laying down alcohol of almost any stripe in profusion, a privilege not so easy to come by in a state that takes liquor licensing seriously. The Parrot also offered some outstanding sandwiches with the usual accompaniments, and was a favorite hangout of the under thirty crowd.

Greetings exchanged, the two men found a quiet corner table in the rear of the dining area, sandwiches and drinks in hand.

"I suppose you were tailed here," Wells began.

"In the U.S.A. I always have a shadow," Shalman confirmed. "But for today I decided to lose him so we could talk privately. He is probably still tearing apart the restroom at that casino down the street trying to find me."

"Isn't trust between allies a wonderful thing?" Wells quipped.

"Ah, it is of no moment. We follow your CIA guys when they are in Israel, as well. Now I am wondering what I, or Mossad, can do for a humble grower of grapes?" Shalman cut to the chase.

"Somebody in Saudi has my son, and I want him back," Wells responded, straight to the point. "I need to know who has him and where they are holding him. Mossad knows more about what goes on in Saudi than the Saudis do, so I'm asking you. Exactly who is Islamiyah al-Jihad?"

"Do not be misled by the name," Shalman shook a bony forefinger. "This is no group of which we know. But these radical cohorts are spawned like rabbits. A few young fanatics set out on some misguided adventure and make up a name. The media shouts it all over the world and a new terror group is born. Mossad thinks this is not a large group, but just a few radicals."

"Then why would the Saudis drag their feet in trying to recover the hostages?" Wells asked.

"Does the name Tariq bin Saud mean anything to you?" Shalman asked with a wink.

"No, should it?" Wells rejoined.

"Tariq bin Saud is a nephew of the Saudi king, his brother's son, in fact," Shalman informed him.

"So what?" Wells pursued impatiently.

"Young Tariq has come under the influence of Muhammad al-Shariyah, a fanatical cleric who constantly preaches hatred and murder against America and Israel. We know that at the behest of al-Shariyah, young Tariq personally conveyed thousands of U.S. dollars donated by wealthy Saudis to the families of suicide bombers in Nablus," Shalman told him.

"What does that have to do with Scott?" Wells wanted to know.

"Maybe nothing, maybe everything," shrugged Shalman. "This kidnapping reeks of al-Shariyah. If he is behind it, he will make demands your government can never meet. The kidnappers may use this as a pretext to kill the hostages just to show that they are to be taken seriously. The royal family fears al-Shariyah because he exerts broad popular influence over the Arab masses. And if a royal nephew is in some way involved, the Saudi government will not be eager to make arrests or charges, or to spill blood."

"I see," sighed Wells, "and my government won't lift a finger because if they try to grab the hostages and a royal gets killed in the process the Saudis might alter the flow of oil from the gulf."

"Exactly so," Shalman agreed.

"You have to help me find Sunny, Zev," said Wells, an unmistakable anguish in his deep voice.

"I already have people on it," Shalman said reassuringly, "but you will have to be patient, my friend."

"The big clock is ticking, Zev. I'm afraid of losing my boy."

They agreed on a covert means of communicating before saying goodbye, then left by separate doors, Wells going through the kitchen and out the back. The first part of his plan had been set in motion.

On the drive back to Washington, Wells called the office of Oregon Congressman Denton Crouch, a second term legislator he helped to get elected. He asked for, and promptly got an unusual Sunday appointment with the representative. A second call booked a room at the Holiday Inn On The Hill. Finally, he dialed up Stan

Blanton, at Halvarson-Brandt, and arranged to have dinner with him on Sunday evening in Dallas. He was moving fast now, multi-tasking.

That night in his hotel room, Wells sat in a chair opposite the faintly babbling television set, his feet propped up on a *faux* leather ottoman, listening to the White House press conference in which the president first explained, then roundly rejected the demands of the kidnappers, reaffirming that the United States does not negotiate with terrorists. That was for public consumption, Wells knew, while the reality was that negotiations were probably already in progress. The great poker game was on, and the president had just called. Wells wished ardently that his son's life was not one of the chips on the table.

Capitol Hill, D.C., Sunday, September 24

Denton Crouch was a tall, handsome, sandy haired fellow in his early forties who had run as an independent in a liberal state. Wells liked Crouch from the beginning, along with the fresh ideas he touted, and had bankrolled his campaign and used his influence in the Oregon business and political communities to level the playing field between Crouch and the machine backed incumbent he was trying to unseat in the mid-term congressional election. Crouch's riveting hazel eyes that mesmerized prospective voters, tousled, curly blonde hair that gave the impression of vigorous youth and straightforward, progressive policy positions that appealed to the common man took care of the rest, resulting in a landslide win. So it was understandable when he rolled out the red carpet for his benefactor.

After coffee was served and they were behind closed doors, Crouch spoke in a hushed and sincere voice.

"I know you have come about your son, Curt, and I want you to know how distressed Katy and I were to hear about his kidnapping. It's an awful thing, and I know that you and Molly must be just frantic."

Concerned that his anxiety was so transparent, Wells calmed

himself and replied. "I need your help, Denton. What will it take to get the White House to move on this?"

"A good deal, I should think," responded Crouch thoughtfully. "They are not going to want to ruffle the Saudis' feathers. This one is entirely about the politics of oil."

"I don't give a damn about what the administration wants, and I care even less about the Saudis. What I do care deeply about is getting my son back in one piece. Do you have any leverage at all?" Wells asked.

"On the foreign policy front, none. But I *am* a member of House Appropriations, and have enough influence to block or fast track a variety of spending bills that *are* important over at 1600 Pennsylvania," Crouch reflected aloud. "What would you like me to do?"

"Talk to the White House. Tell them that the parents of one of the hostages, who are your constituents, believe that after all is said and done a whole lot more will be said than done about rescuing them. Find out what concrete actions they have in mind, if any. Remind them none too subtly that you will be mindful of their responsiveness when you vote in committee. Maybe that will shake them into action. If not, perhaps you can at least learn something that can help us get Scott out," Wells said.

"I'll do my best, Curt," promised Crouch. "God knows I owe you at least that."

Dallas, Texas, That Evening

The flight from Reagan National to Dallas encountered a lot of turbulence, the pitching and jostling of the plane by the rough air making sleep hard to come by and leaving Curt Wells' legs a bit rubbery as he deplaned. He was deep in thought about what he wanted to say to the people at Halvarson-Brandt, but not so deep that he failed to notice the scruffy little man in the corduroy hat who took a special interest in him as he approached the limo driver bearing a sign that read, "Welcome, Mr. Wells." They were already tailing him. But no matter, his trip to Halvarson-Brandt would be seen as a *pro forma* given the situation, and it was unlikely they would ever find out what was said there.

In the lavish, red-carpeted, tastefully draped executive dining room at Halvarson, the solid cherry table had been set with white linen and silver and the candles lit when Stan Blanton showed Wells in. Rising to greet him were Rodgers Brandt, president of the corporate giant, and another vice-presidential level man they introduced as Barton Stone. Of the three, Stone caught Wells' attention the most acutely. He had a lean, athletic look about him, ramrod straight posture and Wells could smell military painted all over him.

"Vice President Stone is in charge of security for all of Halvarson-Brandt," Blanton explained during the introductions.

They feasted on large Texas T-bones and made small talk for an hour, all three hosts expressing great dismay over the kidnapping of Scott Wells and the others. Finally, Brandt himself cut to the chase.

"How can Halvarson-Brandt be of service to you in this unpleasant business?" he asked.

"Well, first I'd like to know what, if anything, you're doing to get the boys back," Wells answered, looking him directly in the eye and propping his elbows on the table.

"If I may," cut in Stone. "We've announced a million dollar reward for information leading to the identity of the kidnappers and/or the location where the hostages are being held, and we have offered to negotiate directly with the captors regarding specific reductions of HB presence in Saudi, Iraq, Dubai, Qatar and Indonesia."

"Doesn't that run contrary to the administration's policy not to negotiate with terrorists?" Wells inquired, incredulous.

"Yes, it does, and they're mad as hell about it," grinned Brandt. "But you see, Mr. Wells, HB doesn't have a foreign policy, nor are we responsible for implementing the one put forward by the government. So, with all due respect, screw the administration. We're pragmatists here, and these people have three of our valuable assets. We want them back very badly."

"And the offer to negotiate is not capitulation. We're pretty good negotiators, and we can promise them anything. Actually delivering on those promises once they've returned our attorneys may be something else again. If we can bring them out into the light of day, our sense is that when the negotiating is done and our people are free the Saudis will exterminate them like so many cockroaches," Blanton amplified.

"I am pleased that you have a strategy, which is more than I could discern in Washington. But I'd like to back you up. When I explained my request, your human resources administrator was kind enough to put me in contact with the parents of the other hostages before I left Washington. I am organizing a little press conference to turn up the political heat on this administration. And I, too, have sources working to identify the whereabouts of the three hostages. It is in that connection that I have another question for you. Halvarson-Brandt has its own satellites, correct?"

"That's right, state-of-the-art. You've done your homework, Mr. Wells," Brandt said with admiration, realizing that Wells had discovered the fact that HB was one of the very few non-communications linked corporations to have invested in satellite technology.

"Do they have surveillance as well as communications capacities?" Wells followed up.

"Certainly," confirmed Stone, warming to the conversation. "We can look at our job sites anywhere in the world. What are you thinking?"

"I'm thinking that the hostages are still in Saudi. And the CIA isn't going to let anyone outside know what their birds are seeing as long as the administration's policy continues to be hands-off," Wells reasoned aloud.

"And you're proposing what?" Stone asked.

"I'm proposing that if I can locate the general area where they are being held, your satellite could be tasked to confirm the specific location and details of the site and surroundings," Wells explained straightforwardly.

"And what would you do with such information?" Blanton asked obtusely.

"Take my word for it. It's better for you not to know," Wells almost whispered, as knowing looks crossed all the faces in the room. "And when the FBI asks, we never talked about this."

"Right, we never talked about this," parroted Brandt, passing stern looks to his two colleagues.

CHAPTER THREE

Monday, September 25, Dallas

On the previous day, Curt Wells placed calls from his hotel room to Daniel and Miriam Saperstein in New Haven, Connecticut, and to Alex and Mary Logan in Denver. The parents of the other hostages agreed to meet him in Dallas immediately, postponing any plans they might have in order to jointly plot strategy and take an active role in attempting to secure the release of their sons. He also called Molly, and asked her to join him in Dallas. She took a "red eye" out of Portland, and was now nestled safely asleep in the bedroom of their hotel suite. The others would all be in on early flights.

Just now, he was on the phone with Carlos Gutierrez, trying to talk as softly as possible so as not to awaken Molly.

"Carlos, *que pasa*?" he asked his second in command at the winery.

"Everything is fine, *Jefe*," answered Carlos. "Fritz says that all the rain is driving the brix right off the scale. And I put on two more guys, both locals, to help get ready for the harvest."

"I'm really glad you did that, Carlos, because I need to borrow Ned and Jacob for a couple of days. Send them to the lodge down on the river. Tell them to clean it up, change the bedding out and stock the place with nonperishable food for a week, for six people," Wells instructed.

"You going fishing, boss?" Gutierrez asked, confused.

"Probably so," Wells replied tersely.

"But what about Sunny?" Carlos persisted, not understanding Wells' sudden interest in recreation.

"This is *all* about Sunny. Just trust me, old friend," Wells said.

"Okay, Boss. Consider it done," agreed Gutierrez in parting.

Curt Wells made all of his calls on his room phone, in the clear. If they were listening, and they probably were by now, he wanted them to know that they were about to be the targets of some heavy duty political pressure. And he especially wanted them to know about the fishing trip in Oregon. He smiled faintly, wondering who had eavesdropped and what they might be thinking now.

Wells was a bold decision maker, and a man of extreme guile. In the Navy, he helped plan a number of sensitive and dangerous SEAL incursions, and was known to his superiors as a top-notch strategist and tactician. They marked him for rapid promotion, and expressed real disappointment when he resigned his commission to join the CIA. In the intelligence community he was respected for the excellence of his tradecraft, his ability to confuse adversaries by doing the unpredictable and his ruthless efficiency in accomplishing even the most difficult and dangerous of missions. A former colleague had commended him to Ben Crosley, who was then director of the CIA, as "born for black ops."

These qualities were in stark contrast to those prized by his family, who knew him as a devoted husband, loving father, solid provider and pillar of the community. And they would have been equally surprising to his Oregon business acquaintances who saw him as shrewd but fair, frugal but generous, gregarious and genuinely likeable. And Wells was all of that and more.

But everything changed for him the day his son was taken. He was now a man on fire, with a desperate singular mission where failure was not an option. And he was prepared to expend his last dime, call in every marker he was owed and, if need be, give up his own life to save Scott "Sunny" Wells from his captors. And God help anyone who stood in his way.

Soon Molly was awake. Freshly showered and clad in the white terry robe provided by the hotel, she emerged with her hair wrapped in a towel, and a soft, fetching smile on her face. Wells could not help but think how she was as beautiful today as when they had married, thirty-four years ago.

"Did you get your beauty sleep?" he joked, smiling.

"That's the soundest I've slept since ..." her voice trailed off, and they both knew the event that had been triggering her insomnia. "Curt, what do you really think our chances are of getting Sunny back?"

"Oh, we're going to get him back, all right, one way or another," he said, exuding a confidence born more of a desire to allay her fears than certainty about what lay ahead.

"What do you mean 'one way or another'?" she inquired, cocking her head slightly to one side.

"Either the Saudis are going to get him back, or his company is going to ransom him, or the military is going to rescue him, or I, by God, am going over there myself to find him. Our son will come home," he said confidently.

Just then the phone rang. It was Daniel Saperstein who had arrived on an early morning flight along with his wife, and was waiting in the coffee shop.

"The other parents are arriving. I have to go," Wells said to Molly. "Can you be ready in thirty minutes?"

"No problem, if their blow dryer works," she quipped. "Shall I meet you downstairs?"

In the restaurant Wells immediately spotted Dan and Miriam Saperstein. He was short and stocky, with curly black hair, and she was petite, dark-haired and pretty. Both appeared to be in their middle fifties.

"We were so glad to get your call," Dan Saperstein said. "It just seemed like nobody wanted to do anything," he complained, throwing up his hands in a gesture of frustration.

"Right," agreed Wells. "The whole purpose of this exercise is to put political pressure on Washington to get off their hands."

"We're especially concerned about Aaron because we are

Jewish," said Miriam shyly. "If the kidnappers are Arab terrorists..."
her voice trembled, and then broke.

"I know, I know," said Wells, reaching across the table and
taking her small quivering hand between his. "It's important that
you think positively and be strong for Aaron," he continued. "We
will get them all out."

Presently a tall, balding fellow who introduced himself as
Alex Logan joined them, followed closely by a svelte blonde in her
early forties who was Marty Logan's stepmother. Mary Logan was
younger than the others by almost ten years, but she was devoted
to Alex, and extremely concerned about the plight of her stepson.
When Curt Wells saw Molly in the doorway, he rose and addressed
the group.

"Come on, all. It's time to go," he said, noting that a bellman
already had all the luggage collected and was bustling toward the
curb outside

A Halvarson-Brandt bus was waiting, and twenty minutes later
they arrived at the main gate where they were summarily waved
through. In a private conference room they were joined by Stan
Blanton and the ubiquitous Barton Stone. Once introductions had
been made, Wells began to propose a plan, speaking quietly but
confidently..

"Our next stop is Washington D.C., where I have arranged an
exclusive interview with Brady Kostner, a feature writer with the
Washington Times. After that, we'll do a press conference on the
steps of the Capitol Building. By that time, the rest of our children
will have arrived from all over the country to join us, and we'll
make a pretty damned formidable array of advocates. After we
finish answering the media's questions, we'll break up and do a
blitz of our respective congressional delegations, asking for their
support in getting the administration to act. I'll be glad to take the
lead at the press conference, but it will be important for each of you
to speak your piece as well," he said, pausing for a breath of air.

"What, exactly, are we asking for?" Alex Logan raised the
obvious question.

"Well, we're *not* asking for the government to give in to the
terrorists, because we know they're already negotiating behind the

scenes and if we urge appeasement that won't play well with the public, whose support we need. The government is supposed to have intelligence, and we know the military has rescue capabilities. What we're asking is that this administration put political considerations aside and take direct action to save the lives of our sons," responded Wells.

"Isn't there a danger in that?" asked Miriam Saperstein fearfully.

"The boys are already in grave danger, Miriam," Wells answered. "Our Delta Force and Navy SEAL units are really good at hostage rescue. They are our best chance. We just have to convince the president to use them, and deal with the Saudis' outrage later."

They discussed the pros and cons of various approaches for the better part of an hour, when Wells spoke once again.

"Our hosts here at Halvarson-Brandt have been kind enough to volunteer one of their corporate jets to fly us to D.C., so the bus will take us from here directly to a nearby private airfield where the plane is waiting."

As they filed out, they each thanked Blanton and Stone for their hospitality, and for the company's efforts on behalf of the hostages. Wells, the last to leave, grabbed both men by the arm and pulled the door closed.

"Stan, when you first called me, you said that HB would use all of its resources to get our sons out. Is that promise still in force?" he asked.

"Of course," Blanton assured him, "*Anything* we can do."

"I'm formulating a back-up plan, and if it comes to that I'll need low profile overseas transport for six. Can you arrange that?" Wells asked, staring back at him.

"Seven," said Stone matter-of-factly. "If HB is in, then I'm in."

"I know you're military," observed Wells, squinting at the younger man. "Tell me."

"101st Army Rangers, Special Ops. I was part of the advance team in Iraq before Desert Storm," Stone responded.

"Stop right there, I'm sold," Wells surrendered. "But it will be strictly freelance, and it *will* be dangerous. I'll brief you if and when we decide to go."

"Who does 'we' include?" Stone asked cagily.

"Need to know. And when you do, you will," promised Wells, before turning away to walk out the door.

A Conference Room at the Washington Times, 2:30 PM

Brady Kostner was a little man with flyaway auburn hair and bushy eyebrows. He had been in the journalism game for a long time, and when Wells offered him an exclusive with the hostages' parents it was just too juicy to pass up. Wells was counting on that. Now they sat face to face with the writer, and some of them were nervous.

"Please relax," Kostner began disarmingly. "I'd like to begin with just a little home style background on the three boys, and then we can go from there."

Kostner knew how to work his subjects, and in thirty minutes he had more detail about the three hostage lawyers than he could include in a whole series of articles. Then he got to it.

"What do you know about what's being done to free your sons?" he asked casually.

"The State Department and the White House claim not to know where they are, or who has them," Wells opened.

"And you don't believe that?" Kostner baited him a bit.

"I don't know what to believe. It's been six days. We have the finest intelligence gathering apparatus in the world, and equally great political leverage. So my question is why? Why don't we know, by now, who is holding our sons and where? We have the kidnappers' demands. The president made that clear on national television. Are we talking to them, or aren't we? And what about the Saudis? They're in the best position to know the answers. And yet they are strangely silent. We'd like to know why," Wells fired back.

"Are you suggesting that the Saudis are holding out information, or that they're not trying their best to help?" Kostner seemed incredulous.

"We're not suggesting anything. We're asking for answers," Alex Logan cut in.

"And you think you're being stonewalled by the U.S. government," Kostner remarked, a statement rather than a question.

"Well what would you think if your son was a hostage and you were told as little as we have been told?" Dan Saperstein responded, rising to get a cup of water from the cooler in the corner.

"Point taken," offered Kostner, clearing his throat. "So what do you want from our government?"

"An honest and candid appraisal of the situation, pressure on Saudi to locate our boys and the full resources of the American military if that's what's necessary to bring them out," Wells responded.

"Why not wait to see if negotiations will work?" asked Kostner.

"We tried that in Pakistan," said Miriam Saperstein, her quiet voice trembling, "and an innocent American civilian, a Jewish boy just like our son, was brutally murdered. I would like to hear the president assure me that will not happen to our Aaron."

"Hmmm," mused Kostner, "you know, don't you, that the kidnappers' demands are so outrageous that we can't meet them?"

"Perhaps not, but so far there's no indication we're prepared to make any concessions at all," Molly Wells said.

"Yes, but governments don't put those cards on the table for public view," Kostner remonstrated.

"The point here, Mr. Kostner, is that we're not just 'the public.' Thirty-two years ago I spent seven hours in labor delivering my son Scott," Molly spat, fire in her eyes. "I think that makes me a full partner in this business, and not just 'the public.'"

"You see, Mr. Kostner," counseled Mary Logan gently, persuasively, "we're not just going to make some noise here and go away. These are our children, and we are taxpayers. We want something done, and done soon, before trouble becomes disaster and our sons come home in coffins."

"Would you meet with the president if he would see you?" Kostner offered the straight line.

"Of course," snapped Wells, "and anyone else with relevant information who will be truthful and straightforward with us."

Shortly, the interview ended. Wells' external countenance remained grim, but he was smiling inside. The bait was laid, and now an invitation to the White House was all but inevitable. Kostner's morning column would make it so.

The press conference on the steps of the Capitol was more and better. Tyler Wells, a tall, handsome, articulate redhead had flown in from Seattle, as had Joel Saperstein, Aaron's erudite older brother from Boston. Callie Logan, a strikingly beautiful blonde coed from Colorado State University and her brother, Brett, a strapping college football player from Arizona State were Marty Logan's stepsiblings, and both idolized him. As a group, the families were highly photogenic, gave great interviews, and were, summarily, a news reporter's fantasy come true. They were also an increasingly embattled administration's worst nightmare.

That evening they all had dinner together at the elegant rooftop restaurant in their Arlington hotel, overlooking the gunmetal gray waters of the Potomac. They tallied up the promises, mostly empty, that they had extracted during their visits with legislators, and strategized about their next move.

"Give it twelve hours. I expect the call from 1600 Pennsylvania by mid-morning," chuckled Wells. "We've made some serious waves here today, and if this administration ignores us it'll cost them points in this week's polls. They'll call, all right."

Morning, Tuesday, September 26

Curt Wells was very wrong about one thing. He was enjoying a passable room service omelet with piping hot coffee at about eight, when his phone rang. Norman Sloan, an early riser, had already seen Kostner's feature in the Times, as if he hadn't seen enough on local and national television channels the evening before. And he had no intention of delaying contact until mid-morning. His chief of staff, Kenneth Karns, practically begged the families to attend an early luncheon at the White House. Wells graciously accepted on behalf of the group. He observed with some amusement how the people around the president had already pegged *him* as the ringleader.

Quickly caucusing with the rest of the families, Wells informed them about the call, and suggested that perhaps Alex Logan should take the lead when they arrived. If they really thought Wells was the leader, this change of strategy might throw them off balance a little. And the last thing Wells needed now was to draw more attention to himself.

The White House, 10:55 AM

After clearing security, the three families, including the children, were shown into the large, windowless Roosevelt Room by the White House social secretary, where they were told that the president was running a few minutes behind and would be joining them while lunch was in progress. They dined at the big rectangular conference table on delicious Maryland crab cakes, warm, mouth-watering croissants and a hearty lentil soup. As they were finishing, the president walked in, flanked by his secretary of state, Donald Trimble, and National Security Advisor, Ethan Ellis. The families rose.

"Please, sit," said President Sloan graciously. "Thank you for coming on such short notice. I wanted to personally brief you on our progress toward locating your sons, and assure you of this government's commitment to their safe return. I am going to ask Secretary Trimble to summarize the situation."

A large map of Saudi Arabia appeared on a portable projection screen as Trimble cleared his throat and turned on his laser pointer.

"Aaron, Scott and Martin were taken here, in Riyadh" he said, pointing to the Saudi capital on the map. "We don't believe they're still there, however, because Saudi security forces have been turning the city inside out with no results. Our assumption is that the kidnappers had been following your sons, perhaps for as much as three or four days prior to the assault on the hotel restaurant. The group Islamiyah al-Jihad is not a known terror group either here or in Saudi. So it is our assumption that a few radicals picked the name out of a hat, if you will, to lend credence to their actions and demands. In exchange for the safe return of the three attorneys, they have insisted that our government announce plans for complete withdrawal from Iraq and Afghanistan, that a group of American companies scale back operations in the Middle East, and that the state of Israel release a notorious bomber who is believed responsible for hundreds of deaths. We have to assume that the kidnappers know that neither we, nor the Israelis will comply with those demands. They will, therefore, settle for something less. The question is what?"

There was an uncomfortable moment of silence before Alex Logan spoke. "Why do you think the Saudis haven't come up with any substantive leads in a week's time?" he asked casually. Wells noted the sudden eye contact between Sloan and Trimble.

"They were as surprised as we were," stammered Trimble weakly. "They're still trying to get their balance."

"Why so surprised?" demanded Dan Saperstein impatiently. "After the Khobar Towers disaster and all the near misses involving hits on Americans, I should think they, of all people, would be alerted in advance to such a possibility."

"The government of Saudi is a staunch U.S. ally. They have extended themselves tremendously to help us in the war on terror. Riyadh, of all places, was presumed a safe haven," Trimble rationalized, sounding like an addled student explaining to a skeptical teacher how the dog had eaten his homework.

All this time Curt Wells had been silent. Pushed back from the table, with legs crossed and arms folded, he had listened with interest, but betrayed none of his thoughts or feelings. This was predictably unnerving to the government officials, who were hoping to draw him out. In truth, Wells was struggling with the decision as to whether to play the one trump card he had – the one Zev Shalman had given him. Finally, he decided.

"What do you know about the possibility that a member of the royal family might be somehow involved in the kidnapping?" he asked as casually as one might ask the time of day.

"I'd like to know where you got hold of that?" snapped Ellis, the national security advisor, the urgency of his query betraying a sudden anxiety.

"You're not the only ones with intelligence sources," Wells

replied without raising his voice. "And if I've heard it, I *know* you've heard it. So what about it?"

The silence was electric. Sloan and the other two looked as if Wells had just hit them between the eyes with a baseball bat.

"It's just a rumor," said Sloan dismissively, breaking eye contact. "We don't believe there's any truth to it."

"No?" queried Wells, looking the president directly in the eye. "Then how is it that the Saudis, who have one of the best intelligence services in the Middle East, suddenly can't find their backsides with both hands?"

"That's not fair," injected a clearly agitated Trimble.

"There's nothing *fair* about this," continued Wells. "But you know as well as I do that in a kidnapping situation—any kidnapping—the first twenty-four hours are the only twenty-four hours. After that, well, who knows?"

"Isn't it just possible," Ellis interrupted in a patronizing vein, "that because your son is one of the hostages, you're jumping to some unwarranted conclusions here? Isn't it just possible that you've added two and two and come up with five?"

"Well let's see, now, please correct me where I'm wrong. Our sons are taken as hostages, yet one full week later the most capable intelligence service in the world, our own, claims not to know where they are, or exactly who took them. The Saudis, mysteriously, have come forward with no helpful information at all. The U.S.S. Tarawa and its battle group, along with its Delta hostage rescue team, is in the Indian Ocean but has made no move into the Arabian Sea. You are telling us that you have no intention of giving the kidnappers what they want. To me that adds up to one, we're not going to really push the Saudis; two, for reasons unknown they are in no hurry to move; three, you have no intent to launch an armed rescue mission; and four, our sons are probably going to die over there. Is that about it? Because that's how it adds up to us," Wells concluded, gesturing broadly to include all the family members.

"You have no idea what the political ramifications would be of an armed intervention in Saudi," snapped President Sloan defensively.

"And you, Sir, seem to have no idea of the personal anguish we face at the prospect of losing our sons," barked the usually reserved Miriam Saperstein angrily.

The stony, silent impasse was broken by Sloan's chief of staff, Kenneth Karns, who entered the room and said in a hushed tone, "Mr. President, you and the others are needed in the situation room."

"I regret that you'll have to excuse us," said the president, rising. "But I must ask you to keep our conversation confidential, especially, Mr. Wells, your speculation about the Saudi royal family, until we have some time to sort this out."

Back at the Hotel

Before they had a chance to change into casual clothes it was all over the network television channels. Al Jazeera was playing a tape purporting to show the execution of one of the hostages. Knowing the American media would report the story, but wouldn't air the tape directly—at least not right away—Wells plugged in his laptop and got on line. In less than ten minutes, he found it. It showed a hooded man tied to a chair with a pistol held to his head by a masked gunman. As the weapon discharged, the victim's head slumped immediately forward, and he remained motionless. Wells' Arabic, though slightly rusty, was still good enough for him to understand the kidnapper claiming to have executed "the Jew."

He watched the grainy tape six more times, then walked down the hall to the room occupied by Daniel and Miriam Saperstein. Daniel answered the knock, his tear stained face conveying an unabated grief. Their son Joel sat on the bed, cradling his sobbing mother gently in his arms.

"It stands to reason," mumbled Dan Saperstein bitterly. "Arabs with guns have been killing Jews for as long as I can remember. My parents moved to New York when I was a child to get away from it. Now, death has caught up with us once again."

"I don't think Aaron's dead at all," stated Wells categorically and without preamble.

"But they said so on television," Joel Saperstein began.

"This will be hard, I know," Wells said cautiously, "but I need the three of you to watch the Al Jazeera tape with me."

"Oh, God, no, I can't," a disconsolate Miriam Saperstein wailed.

"It's the only way I'm going to know if I'm right," shrugged Wells, plugging in his laptop and booting up the saved image.

Shakily, the Sapersteins gathered around the table, trying to get close to the small glowing screen. Miriam sobbed loudly at the sight of the manacled, hooded hostage. After playing the event at normal speed, Wells slowed it down to a crawl.

"That's either a nine millimeter or a forty-five the kidnapper is holding. Either way that's one hellacious weapon. Discharged at that range, it should cause the victim's head to jerk violently away from the impact of the bullet entering the skull. Only, in this case, the victim's head slumps straight down to his chest. Also, that slug will make a bigger hole in the skull coming out than it did going in. At that range, the bullet should have exited the other side of the victim's head spraying blood, bone fragments and brain matter all over the place. Yet, in the tape, that does not occur. Now, this is where I need your help. The victim is wearing a business suit; most probably the one Aaron was wearing when he was taken. But look at the shoes."

"Boots," remarked Joel Saperstein with a knowing smile, "hiking boots. My brother never owned a pair of boots in his life. He doesn't even like boots."

Wells nodded, "Just as I thought. This tape is a hoax, and an amateurish one at that. Aaron's still alive."

"But why?" a relieved but confused Miriam Saperstein asked. "Why would they do that?"

"They're upping the ante," Wells mused sagely. "They're challenging the United States of America and Saudi Arabia because they don't think either can or will take action against them. And they might be right."

"What made you doubt the tape initially?" Dan Saperstein wondered aloud.

"Look, if I've got twenty hostages, then I might waste one just out of meanness to show that I mean business. But if I only have three hostages, then I have only three cards to play. So I might not want to give up one-third of my leverage so easily. They will likely resurrect Aaron later when it strengthens their bargaining position. Plus, the difference between kidnapping and murder in Saudi is prison and a firing squad. That might give them pause," Wells explained.

"But if I figured out that the tape's a fraud, the analysts over at CIA will have reached the same conclusion, probably even more quickly. The president will know by now, too, so it will be interesting to see how they're going to play this."

CHAPTER FOUR

Arlington, Virginia, Wednesday, September 27

At eight-thirty AM the fathers of the three hostages huddled over hot coffee and pancakes in the hotel's mezzanine coffee shop. The president had played his hand. He sent a personal note of condolence to the Sapersteins' hotel room, and then went on national television to denounce the "murder" of Aaron Saperstein and promise eventual retribution. He was lying through his teeth, and they all knew it.

"It's not at all surprising," Wells told the other two. "If the kidnappers think America believes Aaron is dead, then they will also think they have made their point and real negotiations will soon begin. If they think we don't believe it, they might execute him for real, just to prove that they're capable. And the president is likely to have the public more on his side now that we've 'lost' one. But that will only last until they see he won't act, or figure out that the 'execution' was a fraud."

"Any guess as to how long before the president will be forced to make a decision?" Alex Logan asked with raised eyebrows.

"He's already made it," Wells answered acidly. "He wants his oil."

"So, now what?" Dan Saperstein asked, clearly frustrated.

"So now we go get our boys," responded Wells.

"Who? How?" stammered the others in confused unison.

"I have a plan, I have the people, I have the resources, and I just *may* have the help of a foreign government," Wells said confidently. "But I'm going to need your help too."

"What on earth can we do?" inquired Logan skeptically.

"Can the two of you get away for a week, and persuade Joel to join you?" Wells probed, both of the fathers nodding in the affirmative.

"Good. I'll need you to come to Oregon for a little fishing trip."

"Fishing? Now?" asked a flabbergasted Saperstein. "What does that have to do with rescuing our sons?"

"All in good time, gentlemen, all in good time," Wells assured them. "Oh, and one more thing. Our government has me under surveillance, I think, and probably has my phones tapped too. So tell your wives as little as possible, and when we talk by telephone, make no mention of anything but the fishing trip. Okay?"

"But why are they listening?" Saperstein wondered aloud, squinting warily at Wells.

"Because they think I'm planning some action that will upset their political apple cart," Wells grinned.

"And they're right, aren't they?" Alex smiled back. "Well, I don't give a damn. All I want is my son back, and if you're ready to go get him, I'm with you all the way."

"Me too," confirmed Saperstein hastily. "You can count on us."

There was something in Curt Wells' demeanor that reassured them, perhaps his quiet confidence, his quick analysis, and his ability to grasp and summarize a complex situation. Whatever it was, he'd earned their complete trust and quickly galvanized them into a force to be reckoned with. He desperately hoped he was not leading them astray.

The Continental flight lifted off from Reagan National right on time despite a wet, nasty fog, and after a brief stopover in Denver, delivered Curt and Molly Wells safely back to Portland. Carlos was there to meet them in a company van, and both embraced him warmly before throwing their bags into the back and climbing aboard.

"How was Washington, Boss?" he asked.

"I need a good shower, *Amigo*. Any other questions?" Wells shot back.

"No, but this came yesterday. I think it's for you," his foreman said, handing him a FedEx express mail envelope.

"Had it been opened when you got it?" Wells asked apprehensively.

"No. It's addressed to me, just like you said it would be," Gutierrez reported.

Wells' pulse quickened as he noted the post office box return address. It was a longstanding Mossad drop. Zev Shalman had made contact. He peeled back the perforated cardboard flap and opened the envelope. Looking inside, he saw only a thin strip of paper, which he quickly removed. The solitary inscription on the paper read "28.8500 x 36.2667," which would be the latitude and longitude where the Israelis believed the hostages were being held. Underneath the numbers were the words "Al Bi'r," which would be the name of the place.

"What does it mean?" Molly Wells asked curiously, leaning over his shoulder from the rear seat.

"Maybe nothing, maybe everything," he said mysteriously, folding the paper twice and inserting it into his jacket pocket.

They landed in heavy overcast, and by the time they reached Newberg it was raining again. Carlos told them that it had rained heavily on ten of the last fifteen days. This was music to Curt Wells' ears, because just before harvest, vintners typically become nervous about the sugar content of their grapes, which is measured by a unit known as the "brix." The more rain that falls just before the harvest, the sweeter the grapes and the higher the brix count. At Whispering Ridge, twenty-two was considered a minimal count. But the mercifully wet Oregon climate normally drove it considerably higher. Carlos was right about one thing. This was going to be a good year, for making wine at least.

Washington, D.C., the Oval Office

President Norman Sloan was in rare form. The cabinet members present had seen him like this before, stomping up and down the office, ranting almost incoherently.

"These terrorist swine are making a laughingstock of the most powerful nation on earth, and it seems that I, the leader of that nation, can't do a damned thing about it. And this pissant Curtis Wells is running circles around us. How the hell did he find out about the possible involvement of a Saudi royal, or the present location of the Tarawa?"

"Unknown, sir," piped up Emmett Choate of the CIA. "I know we didn't leak it."

"It's just possible," reasoned Secretary of State Trimble, "that Wells still has contacts within the intelligence services of friendly governments. Maybe he got it from them."

"Maybe so," Sloan nearly shouted, "but if he goes public with it, we'll have the Saudi ambassador in here screaming his head off, and the public will be beating down our door demanding immediate and unilateral action."

"We don't think he'll do that, sir," said National Security Advisor Ellis. "He came to Washington with the other families and shot his public relations bolt. According to this morning's polls, for the most part we've been able to sidestep that, even with the so-called execution of the Saperstein lad. We think he's probably planning something else."

"Such as what?" demanded Sloan.

"Well, nothing immediate," said FBI Director Alfred Kendrick. "Right now, I understand he's planning a fishing trip."

"Where? In the Gulf of Aqaba?" Sloan asked cynically.

"No, he's got a lodge down on the John Day river, about two-hundred miles southeast of Portland. He goes down there for a couple of weeks every year with a bunch of his friends," Kendrick added.

"Well, get this straight, all of you. Until further notice this Wells is as much the enemy as the damned kidnappers. I want him and his family under close surveillance, and that includes his fishing lodge. I want his phones tapped and his house and office wired. I don't want him to do or say a thing without our knowing it. It's a national security issue," Sloan railed.

"It's already done, Mr. President," Kendrick promised.

"Meanwhile, get the Saudi ambassador for me. I want to talk to that mealy mouthed son of a bitch. And get General Blaisdell over here, too. I want a military option. That's one thing Wells may be right about. I'm running out of patience," Sloan concluded to no one's great surprise.

When the harried minions had all left his office, the president stabbed the green button on the intercom connecting him with his chief of staff, Kenneth Karns.

"Who's next, Ken?" he demanded.

"The speaker of the House is already here, Mr. President," came the too cheery response. "Are you ready?"

When the two entered the plush confines of the Oval Office, they were waved into richly upholstered easy chairs, while Sloan sat opposite them on the couch.

"What's on your mind, Todd?" Sloan asked Speaker of the House Brundage.

"It's this hostage thing." Brundage replied, "It's got everybody nervous."

"Tell me about it," Sloan quipped wryly. "I had the majority leader of the Senate in here early this morning, demanding immediate military action to rescue the hostages and threatening me with a resolution if I don't move."

"Please think twice about that," sighed the obviously nervous speaker, sweat beading on his furrowed brow and his necktie slightly askew. "Some of us in the House are afraid of the economic *and* electoral consequences of unilateral military action, and would urge restraint."

"Oh, really," Sloan fumed, now openly sarcastic. "That young pup Denton Crouch from Oregon was in here earlier arguing exactly the opposite, and threatening none too subtly to sit on some of our funding priorities if we don't move."

"Crouch is a lightweight. Leave him to me," growled Brundage disdainfully. "And, with respect, the Senate is wrong on this one. If the Saudis try a rescue and bungle it, we write off three Americans who presumably knew the risks of traveling in that part of the world. But the political fallout from gas rationing and heating shortages this winter would likely take us all down."

"Is that what we say to Americans, Todd? Travel outside this country strictly at your own risk? Would you like to explain that to the parents of the hostages?" Sloan snorted, putting the speaker on the spot, and hearing only silence in response.

Another fifteen minutes of sparring led Sloan back to the conclusion that while everyone was full of concerns, no one really had any answers. His feeling of isolation was growing exponentially by the hour, and with it, the degree of his paranoia.

Whispering Ridge, Oregon, Thursday, September 28

Wells climbed into his Ford pickup truck and headed into Newberg. He needed to get some supplies for the winery, and Molly had asked him to add a few things from the grocery. He had by now gotten used to his "shadow." The man had lost the funny looking corduroy hat, and routinely wore a Seattle Mariners baseball cap. But in a new development, he'd acquired an alter ego, a pretty Latina in her late twenties who was always there when he wasn't. Each drove a Chevy van, and they had established a surveillance point in the filbert grove overlooking the winery. Wells spotted them almost immediately through his field glasses. That was fine with him. If they were going to be there, it helped to know exactly where they were. He wouldn't try to lose them, wouldn't do anything at all suspicious until the time came. Then he would vanish into thin air and they would never see him again.

Outside Bailey's Super Foods Wells stepped into a public phone booth. Using one of the phone cards he'd bought in Washington, he dialed the personal cell number of Barton Stone in Dallas. When Stone answered, Wells said succinctly, "check out twenty-eight degrees, eighty-five minutes, by thirty-six degrees, point six-sixty-seven minutes. Do you have it?"

"I have it," Stone said succinctly before cutting the connection.

Within hours the Halvarson-Brandt satellite would be shooting pictures of Al Bi'r and the surrounding area. Hopefully they would strike gold.

Back at the winery, Wells was still unloading the groceries when a dark green delivery truck came rumbling up the long, winding drive, spewing gravel and mud in its wake.

"Delivery for Whispering Ridge," said the driver in a quiet, slightly accented voice, climbing down from the cab.

He was a stocky man of medium height, and he wore a driving cap pulled well down over his brow. The ruse would fool the federal agents watching at a distance, but not Curt Wells. It was Zev Shalman arriving with more news.

"Were you followed, my friend?" asked Wells as they headed into the main winery building.

"Not since San Francisco," laughed Shalman. "The fool who was shadowing me has probably jumped into the bay by now."

Holding his finger to his lips, Wells opened a heavy door, flipped a light switch and led the way down broad stairs into the labyrinthine cellars in which Whispering Ridge's finest was aging in massive oaken casks.

"The walls have ears, but not down here," he explained. "What do you have for me?"

"My sources tell me that the hostages were taken by military truck from Riyadh, in the east, to a compound near Al Bi'r in the extreme northwest," Shalman said, unfolding a tattered map of the Middle East. "That makes sense because the mosque where Muhammad al-Shariya spews his murderous bile is here, in Tabuk, just over seventeen kilometers to the south."

"Have you spoken to Tel Aviv?" Wells inquired eagerly.

"Yes," said Shalman, wrinkling his swarthy brow and stroking his chin thoughtfully. "There, I'm afraid the news is not what you had hoped. It is my government's position that the state of Israel cannot be seen to be in any way directly involved in an armed incursion into Saudi. They do not want a war."

"I see," said Wells, his disappointment apparent.

"But they do offer logistical support, intelligence cooperation and one man, with conditions," Shalman added.

"Who is that man, and what are the conditions?" Wells demanded.

"I am the man, and the first condition is that should I be killed or captured they will completely disavow me or any knowledge of my mission," Shalman said, pausing.

"And the rest?" Wells pressed impatiently.

"They insist that as a part of the incursion I find and kill Muhammad al-Shariya," Shalman sighed.

"Something for everyone, eh?" Wells chuckled. "Will al-Shariya be there at the compound?"

"My sources think so," Shalman responded.

"Good enough," said Wells decisively. "Can we stage in Israel?"

"Officially, no. But unofficially, yes. You and your men will fly into Tel Aviv anonymously and go by military transport to Eilat in the south. There we will be armed and flown by helicopter straight up the Gulf of Aqaba staying under the Saudi radar. We will helicast into the surf and make our way ashore. Our operatives will have a truck waiting to take us to Al Bi'r."

"What about extraction?" Wells inquired.

"Ah, yes, well that is a bit more complicated," Shalman began. "The helicopter will do us no good, because he can't land without risking a serious international incident. So, my operatives will conceal three motorized rubber boats into which we will load the hostages and ourselves. We must reach a ship anchored just outside the twelve-mile limit, which will take us back to Eilat. The hostages, regrettably, cannot come to Israel. Their presence would give the Saudis evidence to blame the raid on us. Sometime that afternoon we will arrange for a Finnish freighter, the Laukennen Sound, to pass through the gulf on its way up the Suez. We will transfer the hostages to the freighter, and another of my operatives, based somewhere else entirely, will place a call to your embassy in Cairo, alerting them to collect the hostages when the freighter docks in Egypt."

"The Saudis will want to question the hostages, and the Egyptians may insist on it as a condition of their departure," Wells warned.

"That is why we will all wear masks, my friend," Shalman smiled, "and no one will actually speak to the hostages except me."

"Good. What about armament?" Wells pressed.

"All manufactured in the old Soviet bloc countries – nothing of American or Israeli manufacture. Ammunition, the same," Shalman promised.

"Night vision?" Wells asked.

"The best, made in the U.K.," Shalman guaranteed. "Can you manage protective vests?"

"The best," chuckled Wells, "also made in the United Kingdom. But I have one more question. What if we get cut off from the boats, or someone gets left behind?"

"Then he, or they, will have to escape and evade through the mountains, and try to cross into Jordan. God help them," Shalman shuddered visibly.

"When?" Wells drew a deep breath,

"Soon, my friend. We both know the "execution" was a sham. But al-Shariyah is a murderous bastard, and he will not hesitate to kill all the hostages if it suits his purpose," Shalman said, a stark seriousness in his tone.

"Shall we say seven days, then?" Wells proposed after doing some quick calculations.

"Seven days, not longer," Shalman agreed.

"Here, help me load one of those small barrels onto that dolly. We have to make this look legitimate for my friends up on the hill," Wells said with a wry smile.

That evening, as the gathering shadows of dusk crept relentlessly over Whispering Ridge, Curt Wells sat alone in his office, alternately staring off into space and droodling on a lined note pad. Shalman's plan was solid, but there had been some things left unsaid between them. What they were contemplating was risky, at best. Even if they succeeded in rescuing the three lawyers, if any witness was left alive, or even a trace of evidence linked either Israel or the United States to the incursion, the foreign policies of either or both could be left in tatters and war in the Middle East triggered. That meant everyone in the compound at Al Bi'r must die. Wells was no stranger to killing. He'd personally ended a number of lives. But most of them had been trying to kill him. This could be different, and the prospect troubled him.

Shalman mentioned that the hostages were transported in a military vehicle. Did that mean they would be up against the Saudi army, or that the conspiracy went all the way to the top of the Saudi monarchy? He blanched at the thought.

And he worried about Molly. What if they didn't succeed and both he and Sunny were killed? Or, what if he got Sunny out, but died doing so? What would she do without either or both of them? He wouldn't tell anyone else what he planned to do. He couldn't. But he would have to take his son Tyler into his confidence, so that if the worst happened he could be at his mother's side. He would be busy tomorrow, but the next day he'd fly to Seattle and break the news as tactfully as possible.

Under his desk lamp stood a gold-framed picture of Scott Wells in commencement cap and gown, his beaming father with one arm around his shoulders. That was the day he graduated from law school at Princeton, Curt remembered fondly, stroking the picture lovingly, reflectively with his forefinger. No one in the world had any idea at all how much he cared for this boy, he thought to himself. But the world was about to find out.

Picking up the phone, he dialed the number of Robert "Bobby" Hammack, a former petty officer who was part of SEAL Team Seven, Wells' old outfit.

"Bobby, you old swab, how are you?" he asked when Hammack picked up the phone.

"We're pregnant, that's how we are," growled Hammack.

"That's what you get for cradle robbing," Wells chided. "Do you realize that you'll be sixty-four by the time that kid graduates from high school?"

"Yeah, yeah, yeah, but you didn't call just to make me feel old. What's up?" Hammack asked.

"Fishing," Wells retorted. "Next week, all six of us."

"We just went in August," Hammack said, sounding surprised.

"I know, but I've got the bug again, and some special incentives for all the guys. Would you mind calling them and getting them all on board for this?" Wells begged.

"Naw, I'll do it tonight – probably wake 'em all up," Hammack laughed. "Have any of us ever said no when our C.O. told us we were going fishing?"

"Everybody needs to be here by next Monday evening," Wells said. "If anyone opts out, please let me know. And kiss that sweet little Latino girl you married for me, will you?"

Morning, Friday, September 29

Carlos Gutierrez and Wells worked shoulder to shoulder almost from the beginning at Whispering Ridge. Family aside, there was no one Wells trusted more. He explained to Carlos in general terms that he was hatching a plan to free Scott and the others. But he also told him that for his own protection it was better if he knew none of the details. Carlos was going to be a key player, making contacts and running errands in which the closely watched Wells could not be directly involved. Gutierrez, on the other hand, seemed innocuous enough to the federal agents conducting the surveillance, so they let him come and go as he pleased, almost unnoticed.

It was a lazy, foggy morning, and Carlos wasn't followed as he eased one of the winery vans out the front drive and gate. Heading into the Portland suburb of Tigard, he parked in front of the low white frame building that, according to the blue on white sign in front, housed the office of Devlin Bolton, Private Investigator. Bolton was a man recommended to Curt Wells by a mutual friend. His specialty was electronic "bug" sweeps. He had state of the art equipment, and was an expert.

"My employer, Curtis Wells, requires a routine sweep of one particular room. But it must be done at exactly five PM on this coming Tuesday. He is willing to pay three thousand dollars cash, in advance," Gutierrez said quietly.

"And just where might this room be?" inquired Bolton, his keen interest obvious.

"It is in downtown Portland. I will call you with the exact location at three PM that afternoon," Gutierrez answered.

"I'll take the job," Bolton said eagerly. "Do you have the cash with you?"

"I do," replied Carlos, the hint of a smile pursing his lips as he withdrew the fat envelope from his inside jacket pocket and handed it across the cluttered desk to the overly eager private investigator.

"Here are my home and cell numbers, in case you can't reach me at the office," Bolton added hurriedly, slipping him a card with the two numbers scrawled on the back. "I'll be expecting your call."

Gutierrez' next stop was the Raymont Hotel, an old, but comfortable lodging in downtown Portland. There, he met with hotel manager Leland Geren and arranged the use of a spacious upstairs meeting room where, he said, Curtis Wells, proprietor of Whispering Ridge Cellars, would host a group of international wine buyers at a tasting. The hour would be seven thirty PM on the following Tuesday evening.

"It is most important," Carlos emphasized, "that notice of this event be posted on the hotel marquee at least three days in advance."

Concluding his business with Geren, he moved to the front desk, where he made reservations for each of Wells' special guests, complete with false names, cash prepayment for one night's lodging and an imprint of the company credit card to cover any incidental charges.

Leaving his car in valet parking, he walked out the front door, crossed the street and turned left. A block away he entered Luccio's, a restaurant renowned for the finest Italian cuisine in the city. But Wells chose Luccio's not so much for its' *Lasagne Bolognese* as for The Pit, a subterranean private dining room where even the most sophisticated external listening devices would likely be ineffective. Devlin Bolton was their insurance against internal eavesdropping. This room, Carlos Gutierrez booked in his own name for six PM Tuesday, selecting a gourmet menu for seven guests and, again, paying cash in advance. The next stage of the rescue plan had been set in motion.

Fort Collins, Colorado, Courtyard of the Morgan Library

Callie Logan sat wrapped in a long, blue, hooded coat, protection against the chill of the gusting early fall wind sweeping down from the snowy Rocky Mountains into the Colorado college town. As bright as she was attractive, Callie was extremely put off by the political sleight-of-hand the families got in Washington. There was no one in the world she looked up to more than her stepbrother, Martin, and the thought that the American government would sit idly by for purely political reasons when his life was in danger was almost more than she could bear.

In D.C. Callie was very taken with the quiet strength of Tyler Wells. They talked privately and at length about their brothers, and she knew that Scott "Sunny" Wells meant every bit as much to Tyler as her own stepbrother Marty did to her. She had talked to Tyler by phone every evening since returning to campus, sometimes for hours at a time. His voice was relaxing, almost musical to her, and she couldn't get enough of him. He was equally attracted to her, and they had even discussed a plan to spend a weekend together at a Colorado ski resort. She rang Tyler up at his place of business, MicroResolutions, and now spoke animatedly into her cell phone as students milled around her on their way to and from the large, stately library building.

"I just feel so helpless," she groused. "And those fat politicians just sit there all cozy and warm, drinking coffee in their offices. How can they do that when American lives are in danger?"

"Maybe they need a little motivation," Tyler hedged coyly. "You belong to a sorority, don't you?"

"Yes, Pi Beta Upsilon. Why do you ask?" she responded quizzically.

"Well, it just so happens that I am the regional advisor for my old college fraternity, Pi Rho Phi. I have an e-mail list of Pi Rhos all over the country, and I've been kicking around the idea of enlisting their help. I'll bet you could get a similar list of Pi Beta chapter presidents. Why don't we start an e-mail campaign suggesting a march of college students and fraternity alums on Washington next week to demand action to free our brothers?" Tyler suggested.

"What an astonishing idea," she thought aloud. "We might get several hundred students to come."

"Or even several thousand," he suggested. "Let me send you a sample e-mail. If you like it, we can both go to work and recruit some help."

Callie didn't wait. She walked straight into Morgan Library and started recruiting. Within an hour she had thirty Colorado State students signed up to go to Washington, with each promising they would recruit others.

Seattle, Washington, MicroResolutions

Tyler Wells was something of a prodigy. The youngest graduate in his MBA class, he was a masterful dealmaker and organizational strategist. On his desk was a copy of the *Seattle Times*, featuring a picture of the three families on the steps of the capitol. Further down the page, there was a zoom shot of Callie, her blonde hair blowing in the wind and a teardrop starting from her left eye and running halfway down her cheek. He had a brainstorm, picked up the phone and called the graphics department. An hour later he had Callie's picture in digitized form gracing an e-mail format emblazoned with the message, "March for Callie!" By midnight it would be on a million computers nationwide.

By midday his phone began to ring incessantly, with Pi Rho Phi members and alumni wanting details about the march. By late afternoon it was such a distraction that he changed his voice mail greeting to provide the information up front. It was only a matter of time before the wire services picked it up as a news item.

They would converge on the nation's capital on Wednesday, and demonstrate at the White House that day and perhaps the next. They would apply for demonstration permits, and Tyler would recruit trusted adult friends to coordinate the rallying points, screen out troublemakers and be certain the demonstration remained peaceful. Now, to locate some bullhorns.

Later, he called Jeff Lindblom, feature writer with the *Seattle Times*, informing him that a story was in the making. That, along with the Wells family's recent celebrity, was sufficient to bring the newsman rushing over to MicroResolutions, recorder in hand. A second call got the younger Wells a television interview on Seattle's KNIW nightly news. The snowball was gaining momentum down the slippery slope, and where it might stop, no one could predict.

Frank Chapin and Marcy Cord were befuddled by the sudden flurry of activity. They were the FBI agents entrusted with the surveillance of Tyler Wells. Federal judges had balked at wiretap requests on Tyler, and understandably so when federal agents had given as a probable cause "conspiracy", the criminal goal of which was left unspecified. But the physical surveillance didn't require a court order, and Chapin and Cord had shadowed Tyler ever since his return from D.C. Unlike his father, Tyler possessed no sophisticated intelligence or military background, and was entirely innocent of his stalkers' presence. Nor would he have cared, in view of the fact that he was planning nothing illegal. In any case, the Bureau would not perceive the method in his madness until the story hit the evening news, which it did with a vengeance. In fact, the headline for the next morning's edition of the *New York Times* would read, "Students To March for Callie," and would feature her beautiful, tear-stained face in a one-eighth page photo blow-up. Beautiful girls make good copy. Angry beautiful girls are even better.

CHAPTER FIVE

Washington, D.C., Saturday, September 29

"Like father, like son of a bitch," raged President Norman Sloan. "Who do this Wells kid and this little trollop from Colorado think they are to try to bully the United States government?"

"I suspect they think they are American citizens who have the freedom to speak their minds publicly," observed Secretary of State Donald Trimble matter-of-factly. "They'll probably muster a few hundred demonstrators, at best. They'll come, they'll march, they'll chant, they'll enjoy their fifteen minutes of fame, and then go away.

"That's about the extent of it, all right," snorted National Security Advisor Ethan Ellis with dismissive contempt.

"With respect, sirs," said Mary Ann Motley, the presidential press secretary, "I believe you should prepare yourselves for the possibility that it may be more than just a few hundred students."

"Why so?" snapped a still irascible Sloan.

"Because," Motley began evenly, "this thing is spreading by electronic mail. They're using the Greek systems, meaning that every college fraternity and sorority is getting it. Speculation is that whole businesses are shutting down to allow their employees to come to Washington, bored housewives are seizing this as a chance to get away and every malcontent in America who has a bone to pick with this administration is seeing this Callie Logan thing as a lightning rod for their particular grievance. Some estimates range at over a hundred thousand protestors."

"Can't we arrest this Tyler Wells and our Miss Logan for conspiracy, or something?" Sloan asked desperately. "They're trying to dictate our foreign policy."

"Conspiracy to do what? Exercise their constitutional rights, perhaps, or sponsor the world's biggest tailgate 'kegger'?" the press secretary fumed in exasperated ridicule of the suggestion.

Just then, the phone on the president's desk rang. Hanging up quickly, he grabbed a remote and turned on the color television in the corner of the office. Fox News had Callie Logan, Tyler Wells and Joel Saperstein on a three-way split screen in Fort Collins, Seattle and Boston, respectively.

"So, Callie, why do you want to march on the White House?" the upbeat interviewer led.

"Because they have the power to bring my brother Marty and the others home, or to make the Saudi Arabians secure their release, but for reasons of their own, they won't," she said, speaking in a firm, decisive voice.

"How many demonstrators are you expecting?" came the query.

"I have no idea. But I'll demonstrate even if I'm the only one," she spat defiantly.

"And Tyler Wells in Seattle, it's really early out there. Do we understand correctly that this whole thing was your idea?" the excited interviewer proceeded.

"Mine, Callie's, Joel's, who cares?" shrugged Tyler. "We're just pissed off Americans who are sick of governments playing politics with the lives of our brothers. And I want to say to everyone in your listening audience, if you feel like we do, join us in Washington on Wednesday and make your voice heard."

"Oh, shit," exclaimed Mary Ann Motley in frustration. "Do you have any idea how many viewers that show reaches?" she asked the others.

"And Joel Saperstein in Boston, why would you head to

Washington when your brother, Aaron, has already been killed by the terrorists?"

"First, we don't know that he's dead. We only know that the kidnappers *claimed* to execute him. That tape might be a phony, and doesn't prove anything. But second, if Aaron has been killed, then this administration had better get used to me on their doorstep. I'm giving serious consideration to running for congress in the next election," Joel said unsmilingly.

"All right, that *is* news. And there you have it. Three young citizens who mean to make a difference. Thanks to all three of you for getting up early this morning to be with us," the interviewer concluded.

Seattle, MicroResolutions, Later in the Morning

"Mr. Wells," chirped an overly cheery woman, part of the skeleton crew working the weekend shift, "there's a gentleman here to see you."

Tyler fully expected it to be either a journalist or some irate politician. He had driven back to his office from the local Fox News affiliate, and was deep into his fourth cup of coffee, fighting off the grog of a short night's sleep with the merciful help of caffeine.

"Who is it?" he growled.

"He says he's your father, sir," she responded demurely.

"Dad?" he exclaimed in surprise, snatching open the office door.

Knowing smiles were exchanged between the office personnel as father and son embraced in the doorway. Then the door closed again, as the two men faced each other alone.

Curt Wells booked an early morning commuter flight from Portland, and took a somewhat ramshackle cab from Seattle-Tacoma International airport. The cabbie was directed straight downtown, because Curt guessed that his workaholic son was hard at it, even on Saturday. He chuckled all the way from Portland as he read the *Washington Post* and *New York Times*, and paused to catch the early morning interview re-run while at the airport. He was so proud of Tyler, fighting in his own way for his brother's life.

But now he had to find a way to disclose his own darker and far more dangerous gambit.

"You didn't call and tell me you were coming," scolded Tyler. "I'd have made lunch reservations somewhere good."

"I won't be here that long," Curt Wells replied. "Ty, can we go for a walk?" he asked, putting one finger to his lips to indicate the need for silence.

Tyler slipped into his jacket with a quizzical look, and the two exited his spacious corner office without saying a word.

"Where would you like to walk to?" he inquired, bemused.

"A conference room somewhere in the interior of the building will do," the elder Wells said mysteriously.

They took an elevator down two floors, saying nothing, and entered a small conference room directly in the center of the complex.

"Do you want to tell me why all the cloak and dagger?" Tyler asked, befuddled.

"You are quite probably under surveillance by federal agents," Curt said as casually as if he were reciting the past weekend's football scores.

"What in the world for?" Tyler asked in astonishment.

"Because I am under twenty-four hour surveillance, you are my son, Sunny's brother, and now you're making noise in the media about the administration's policies. That's why," Curt explained.

"But I'm not doing anything illegal," protested Tyler.

"Right, but that has nothing to do with them trying to prove you're thinking about doing something illegal so they can detain you and get you out of circulation to keep you from further embarrassing them," Curt explained.

"They would go that far?" Tyler gasped, his father nodding.

"Just keep your nose clean, go to Washington and play out what you've started. The more you're exposed to public view, the deeper into the shadows they'll shrink. Trust me," his father counseled.

"So why are they watching you?" asked Tyler innocently.

"Because they think I'm getting ready to mount a private rescue effort," Wells replied.

"Why, that's crazy! Don't they know how old you are? You've

been out of all that for so long now." Tyler's voice broke off suddenly and his face went white when he realized that his father wasn't smiling. "Tell me you're not going to do something really dumb, Dad," he pleaded.

"If not me, then who?" Curt Wells asked quietly. "*They* aren't going to do anything, Ty."

"Dad, you just can't do this. You're one man, and damned near a senior citizen. Oh yeah, when we go hunting and fishing I see you get up early and stretch out the old muscles. I watch you rubbing those arthritic knuckles on cold mornings. You're not a SEAL anymore. You'll probably end up getting yourself killed, and Sunny too," cajoled the younger Wells, desperately seeking to dissuade his father from what seemed near suicide.

"Just simmer down and listen to me for a minute, Ty," Wells said as he put both hands on his son's shoulders. "First, I'm not going anywhere unless it's the last option. I hope to hell you succeed in Washington, and I'm very proud of you for what you're trying to do. Second, if I do have to go, I'm not going in alone. I'll have seasoned combat veterans whom I trust with me, and the support of an interested foreign government. Third, you know that I would go nuts if Sunny got killed and I hadn't tried my best to get him out. If I'm not mistaken, you're going back to Washington because you feel the same way. I'm no good at politics, Ty. I never was. I'm just an old sailor who loves his sons, both of them."

Tyler Wells had rarely seen his father so emotional. And in that moment it dawned on him that the ache in his own heart for his brother must be exponentially greater in that of his dad.

"So, why did you come to see me?" he asked, despairing of further argument.

"I came because I need you to take some time off next week, to be with your mom, in case the worst should happen." He stopped right there, knowing that more need not be said.

"Right," Tyler answered thoughtfully. "I've already taken the next two weeks off. When we're done in D.C. I'll fly straight back into Portland. Can you have Carlos or somebody pick me up?"

"Of course," Curt Wells said. "Just call and let your mom know when."

"When are you going, who is going with you and how are you going to evade the agents who are watching you?" Tyler inquired, his active mind filled with questions.

"All of that has been planned to the last detail," Curt assured him. "But to protect your plausible deniability, I'm not going to give you any specifics. As far as anybody else is concerned, I'm going fishing with the guys down on the John Day."

The two stood, faced one another and embraced once more, as though for the last time. The end game had begun, and no one knew that better than this father and son.

Curt Wells took an eleven-thirty flight back to Portland, where he was met by Molly. He wasn't ready to tell her about his plan just yet. So they talked about Tyler, his appearance on Fox Weekend News and the big event in Washington.

The remainder of the day Wells spent with Fritz Emswiler, his enologist, and Carlos, packing wine sampler boxes for the upcoming buyers' reception. An enologist is someone trained to understand the technical and chemical aspects of wine making, and Fritz was the best. He'd been with Wells almost as long as Carlos Gutierrez. Educated by the University of California at Davis, Emswiler obtained his graduate degree from one of the country's finest schools of enology. That's where he met Carlos, who was less fascinated by the technical side and more interested in vineyard, employee and business management. Carlos was an expert grower of fine grapes, and Fritz was a top-drawer connoisseur. Together, they made a great team. Wells hired Carlos first, and when he suggested they look for an enologist it was Carlos who quickly recommended Fritz. The management trio labored tirelessly together through the inevitable years of unprofitability, and finally forged a multi-million dollar a year business at Whispering Ridge. They also became fast friends, and Curt Wells would depend heavily upon them in the trying days ahead.

"Fritz, I want you to host the Tuesday night conclave. We'll have about two dozen top buyers there, so put our best foot forward," Wells told him.

"Where are you going to be?" Emswiler responded, surprise in his tone.

"Oh, not to worry. I'll be along, fashionably late. Meanwhile you can wow them with technical data about the superiority of our fruit and process. Then Carlos and I will slip in and schmooze them a little."

"Sounds like a plan," said Fritz, not realizing that the real planning would occur during the two hours before he saw Curt Wells on Tuesday evening.

Whispering Ridge, Sunday, September 30

Wells sat in his office poring over advance orders when the phone rang. "Curt Wells," he answered.

"Hello, Curt. This is Angie Dunn. I wanted to let you know that we just took Jimmy to the hospital emergency room with a broken foot. He was playing touch football with the kids again, instead of acting his age."

"Gosh, Angie, I'm so sorry. I guess that means he's out for the fishing trip," Wells sounded truly disappointed.

"I don't know," she sounded hesitant. "He'll be in a walking cast, and he told me to tell you he'd still like to come, but wasn't sure if he'd be up to the kind of fishing you're thinking about."

Alarm bells rang wildly in Wells' head. It was obvious that Specialist First Class Jimmy Dunn (USNR) had put two and two together and figured out that this was to be no trout excursion. It was also probable that the feds were listening, and they just might be bright enough to reach the same conclusion. Quickly he regained his equilibrium.

"Tell him that if he's up for it, we'll show him a good time on the river, cast or no cast," he responded jovially to Angie Dunn.

"He'll be really happy to hear that," she answered.

"And tell that old swabbie no more football," Wells quipped in parting.

He hung up the phone and stared off into space. This put a definite wrinkle in his plan. He intended to leave Bobby Hammack behind to run the fishing expedition, since his wife, Miranda, was six months pregnant. Now, Jimmy Dunn would have to do that, putting Bobby in harm's way. They were already thin, and Wells knew he couldn't go in missing both, and hope to succeed.

He also wondered how long it would take the federal agents to trace the call, find out who Jimmy Dunn was, realize that Wells was mobilizing part of his old SEAL team, and track each of them down. Now he was racing the clock, the terrorists, his own government and the Saudis, all at the same time. His odds were getting longer.

CHAPTER SIX

Salem, Oregon, Monday, October 1

Oregon's state capital was buzzing with frenetic activity. The legislature was in a specially called session to discuss a controversial measure scrapping the state's high and unpopular personal income tax, and replacing it with modest sales and personal property taxes. It promised to be a protracted parliamentary slugfest.

Curt Wells pulled into the parking lot of the old gray stone building housing the law firm of Landis, Ellsberg, Tristram and Beatty. More important matters were on his mind. He was fifteen minutes early for his appointment with Anson Landis, his personal attorney and one of the most powerful lobbyists in the state.

When the receptionist in the outer office announced his arrival, Landis himself emerged from the bowels of the elegantly furnished complex and extended his hand in greeting. Landis was wiry and tanned, with salt and pepper hair and alert, darting gray eyes. From a distance he looked a lot like Wells himself. He had served as Wells' personal attorney for ten years, and his firm also handled legal matters for the winery.

"Welcome to Salem, Navy. What brings you our way?" he asked, reflecting the gracious charm that contributed substantially to his success in persuading legislators to support causes important to his clients.

"Three things," replied Wells seriously, as they walked down a short hall and entered a' richly appointed, green-carpeted corner office with broad windows overlooking a well-planted courtyard.. "First, I want to be absolutely sure that my will is current, and I brought along a couple of additions to my investment portfolio."

"The will is just as tight as it was the day you signed it, and I will add these items to your list of assets, Curt. You're not planning on kicking off anytime soon are you?" Landis cocked a bushy eyebrow and grinned impishly.

"Not if I can help it," Wells responded. "But I do need to speak with you about a highly confidential matter. Anything I say to you is privileged, right?"

"Absolutely, so what's on your mind?" Landis inquired.

"You know that my son was taken as a hostage in Saudi Arabia, and if you've been following the news, you also know that our government isn't doing a whole hell of a lot to get him back," Wells began thoughtfully.

"We were all distressed to hear that Scott had been taken, Curt, but so much goes on underneath the table in Washington that we all assumed . . ." Landis was cut off in mid-thought.

"That's the problem, Anson. Everyone assumes too much. The president won't move because the Saudis don't want him to, and the Saudis don't want him to because a member of the royal family is probably involved," Wells revealed forcefully.

"God, Curt, I didn't know. No one did," Landis confessed.

"Of course not," Wells continued, "because the public isn't supposed to know. We're all just supposed to act like poor dumb sheep and take it for granted that everything that can be done is being done, and then one day three bodies get dumped at our embassy in Riyadh and everyone says, 'Oh, how awful, what a shame.' But I'm not going to wait for that. I have put together a private rescue effort to go in there and get those boys out. What I need to know from you is what I may be facing legally here, if and when I get back in one piece."

"Your legal downside isn't so much here as it is where you're going. Americans are constitutionally guaranteed the freedom to come and go as they please, except in special circumstances.

But if any such special prohibition were in force, it would have to apply generally to everyone, which it couldn't in this case. The government can't stop you from going over there, or punish you for it when you get back, provided you haven't violated any passport or visa laws. And hell, American mercenaries go places and fight for different causes all the time," Landis assured him.

"But over there, if you attack or kill someone, even though he is a bloody terrorist, their government could theoretically prosecute you for assault, or murder if you kill him, which they might or might not opt to do. If they wanted to push it they could even demand your extradition when you return home."

"And what do you think the chances of that being granted are?" Wells pressed.

"It all depends on whether your operation succeeds or fails. If you bring those boys home unharmed, public opinion would lynch any government that turned you over. If you fail, and the hostages get killed along with some of the hostiles, then that's shakier ground," the attorney speculated. "By the way, aren't you a little long of tooth for this Rambo stuff?"

"You sound like my family," Wells snorted. "But I can still pull my load, and I won't be alone by any means."

"You said 'three things,' Landis kept pushing.

"Yes, can you get away for a few days?" Wells asked.

"Why?" Landis rejoined.

"Because you're my size and look a little bit like me. My cover is that I'm going down to the lodge to do some fishing, but the feds have me under surveillance. I need somebody to impersonate me long enough so I can slip away," Wells explained.

"So you want me to go fishing in your place. Does that mean I have to wear that ridiculous floppy hat with all the trout flies stuck in it?" Landis laughed.

"Every damned day," Wells jibed in return.

"Oh, well, I always wanted to be a spy," Landis joked. "So, why not? The session will just have to do without me for a few days."

"I'll never be able to thank you enough," Wells said effusively. "There's a prepaid reservation for you at the Raymont in Portland for tomorrow evening. It's under the name of Bill Wilson. A man named Bobby Hammack will meet you in the lobby at three AM sharp, Wednesday morning. Don't be late."

"Holy mother, that's early," Landis offered. "I'm not going to ask why. Just count me in."

Fort Collins, Colorado, Colorado State University

CSU's student union building had been, for all practical purposes, transformed into a political protest workshop. The normally orderly common area was littered with a ménage of brightly colored, hastily painted signs. "Bring Them Home," one read, "Save Our Boys," said another, "Callie for President" touted a third, and "No Blood for Oil," protested a fourth. There were dozens more. In every corner of the building students were on telephones and laptops recruiting, making last minute travel and housing arrangements and attending to the many details that precede a successful political action rally. The buzz of animated voices formed a steady drone. Even some faculty members were pitching in to help.

The movement had reached fever pitch, and what Callie Logan, scurrying busily about the student union, did not realize was that similar beehives of activity were humming on more than two hundred campuses, and in sorority and fraternity houses all over the country. A grassroots revolution was in the making.

Tyler Wells had called to say that D.C. had formally turned down their request for demonstration permits, citing improper advance notice. But he had hastened to add that it didn't really make any difference because people demonstrated in front of the White House without permits nearly every day, and without dire consequence. He told her that he was already in Washington, that he and Joel would meet her plane the following morning, and that the three of them could spend the balance of the day planning. She couldn't exactly put her finger on it, but something about Tyler Wells made Callie feel warm all over, and she looked forward to seeing him again in Washington, as well as to completing their grand scheme. He was almost six years older than she, but she nevertheless held vivid private fantasies about what might happen between them in the future, when this nightmare they were living finally ended.

Yamhill Capital Bank, Newberg, Oregon

Before leaving Salem, Curt Wells stopped at State National Bank, liquidated equities and withdrew cash in the amount of one-half million dollars. He went through an identical exercise at Evergreen Savings Bank in Wilsonville. Now, at Yamhill Capital, he sat watching as a teller in a private room counted out another seven hundred fifty thousand and placed it in his old suitcases. When all transactions were complete, he would be carrying one and three-quarters million dollars cash in the toolbox of his red pick-up.

After leaving the bank, he stopped at Barron's office supply in nearby Sherwood, and purchased seven identical leather briefcases, drawing a curious look from the store clerk who checked him out. Stacking the briefcases neatly on his floorboards and front seat, Wells drove in a leisurely fashion back to Whispering Ridge Cellars. Later, under the cover of darkness, he removed the briefcases, along with the cash and packed a cool two hundred fifty thousand into each one. Opening the last of the briefcases, he stuffed in a newly purchased cellular telephone with four hundred prepaid minutes and unlimited roaming. His meticulous preparations were now almost complete.

Whispering Ridge, the Winery Building

It was early evening, and Wells had almost completed his nocturnal chores. A yellow glow from one of the upstairs office windows in the old Italian-styled building suggested that Fritz Emswiler was working late, poring over chemical analyses and updating his brix projection charts. A cold, clammy drizzle dampened the already saturated ground, and a thick fog was rolling in. Wells pulled up the hood on his slicker to keep the rain off his tired, drawn face. He was no spring chicken anymore, and the stress of the preceding days had taken its toll physically, as well as emotionally. He had just one more chore this evening, and it involved the man in the lighted office.

Soundlessly climbing the stairs and looking through the open door, Wells addressed the balding, bespectacled enologist. "Do you suppose that working late will make the grapes sweeter?" he asked in jest.

"Nope, these babies don't need to be any sweeter," Emswiler chirped proudly. "Both the Riesling and the *pinot* are almost off the scale. The new *cabernet* isn't far behind."

"Music to my ears," rejoined Wells.

"More like money in our pockets," chuckled the scientist.

"Ah, yes, money, that's exactly what I came to talk to you about," Wells said softly, mysteriously. "In this briefcase," he added, holding it open so that Emswiler could look inside, is a quarter of a million in cash, a brand new cell phone and a round-trip first class ticket to Washington, D.C. I hope you didn't have any big plans for the next couple of days."

"Why? Am I going to Washington?" Emswiler inquired, looking down his nose over the half-slipped horn-rimmed glasses.

"On a redeye, right after tomorrow evening's little soiree," Wells responded. "Tyler and some of his friends, quite a few of them actually, are planning a small demonstration at the White House this week. The politicians aren't going to like it much, and they may pressure the D.C. police to throw some of the protestors in jail. The leaders will have the number of that cell phone. If they land in the pokey, they will call you. And then you will use the cash to bail them out and get them back on the street."

"How much do you want me to spend? A quarter of a million smackers is a wad of bail money?" Emswiler seemed perplexed.

"Spend every last dime if you need to," Wells replied coldly. "Just keep those young people out of jail and be sure that Ty has everything he needs. You can bring whatever's left home with you, and we'll have a staff party."

"What real chance do you think they have of moving the government to go get those boys?" Emswiler queried, tipping back his squeaky black leather chair.

"Frankly, not much," Wells answered realistically. "But I want them to take their best shot."

Wells assumed that every word of their conversation had been overheard by the watchers on the hill with their powerful parabolic microphones. He further assumed that when word got back that his own private bail bondsman stood ready to intervene, the powers in Washington might not be so quick to attempt suppression of dissent via mass arrests. He had learned well in the intelligence business that what you want the enemy to know is every bit as important as what you don't want him to know. And it was a game he played expertly.

In the rustic great room of the main house, Molly Wells pitched another alder log on the roaring fire, looked out the enormous picture window over the darkening landscape and watched the drifting rain fall on the terraced hills of green vineyard. Just then, the door swung ajar and Curt walked in, followed by a cool, wet blast of autumn air.

Shivering, Molly said, "Come, sit with me."

He slipped out of his canvas deck shoes, and they curled up together on the rich leather sofa under a generous amber colored afghan.

After several warming minutes of staring into the crackling embers, she squeezed his weathered, strong hand.

"What's going to happen to us, Curt? I mean, if Sunny doesn't come home?" Her voice broke off, choked with emotion as he put both arms around her and held her tightly.

"Do you remember our honeymoon, how we danced in the rain in London?" he asked, recalling their young lovers' escapade in Piccadilly Circus.

"Yes," she said, smiling faintly. "That would be hard to forget. Ten thousand people thought we were crazy."

"Dance with me again, tonight, out there in the rain," he begged whimsically.

"Are you losing it, old man?" she inquired in mock exasperation. "It's cold out there, and we have a perfectly good fire going here."

"That's what raincoats are for, Love. Come on," he urged, easing back into his shoes.

He had put off telling her what he was going to do until the very last minute. The less time she had to worry, the better, he thought. But now she needed to know - or maybe he just needed to come clean with her- he wasn't sure which need predominated. They couldn't talk in the house. But outdoors, in the rain and the wind, the listening devices of the FBI would be impeded to near uselessness. And what looked like an outrageous aging lovers' tryst would, in fact, provide ideal cover for the difficult conversation that needed to happen.

Slipping on his raincoat, he put a Ray Conniff compact disc in the player and turned on the outdoor amplifier. That system was mostly used to clear the vineyard of workers in case of infrequent electrical or windstorms, but it would suit his purpose this night just as well. He waltzed her romantically out the door, and they whirled out into the downpour to the dulcet strains of "Dancing in the Dark." He pulled her close.

"Molly, I'm going to be gone for a few days this week," he announced.

"Right, fishing with the guys, I know," she said softly.

"There certainly are some people going down to the lodge, but the usual gang and I won't be among them," he answered.

"What are you going to do, Curtis?" she pulled away a bit and demanded sternly. When she called him by his full given name— Curtis—he knew she was peeved.

"We're going to get Sunny back," he said simply.

"What? You and that over ripe batch you consort with?" she questioned, her tone dripping with skepticism. "You're not a kid anymore, Curtis. Neither are they."

"We were the best once upon a time, Molly. And we're still in good shape, all of us. Halvarson-Brandt is going to help. We'll be in and out, neat and clean. I have to try," he said, looking directly into her eyes, which were now tearing heavily.

"If you go over to some damned foreign country, Curtis Wells, and get yourself killed, I'll never speak to you again." She stopped short, and then burst out laughing at the absurdity of her own statement. "I don't suppose it's any good my trying to talk you out of it," she conceded, resignation in her voice.

"None at all," he confirmed. "You know I have to go, and you know why. As soon as the big demonstration in Washington is over, Tyler is flying home to stay with you until I get back."

"You mean in case you and Sunny don't *come* back, don't you?" she asked petulantly.

"That, too," he confessed. "But it's not going to happen. I always come back. You know that." They held each other close and danced until the rain stopped, losing all track of time.

Later, Wells undressed and prepared for bed. He knew that this might be his last undisturbed night of rest for some time. Snuggling in next to Molly's warmth, he closed his eyes and tried to turn off his active mind. Alas, try as he might he could not drift off. Tossing and turning, he found every little noise in the house a major irritant, every glimmer of light a distraction. He wondered if his son, Scott, was getting any sleep.

Finally, despairing of getting the needed rest, he rose, slid into his worn denim jeans, clogs and an old navy blue sweatshirt and stole out of the bedroom. In the kitchen, he ate a bowl of cereal, and drank a cold Pepsi. Migrating to the recreation room, he shot pool disinterestedly on the massive green-felted slate table, then, while replacing the pool cue in the rack, fixated on the five-foot by four-foot locked and glassed in gun case hanging on the wall nearby. He focused on the Mossberg 500A pump shotgun that belonged to Sunny. Withdrawing the key from his pocket, he quietly opened the case and slid it out, feeling the heft of the powerful weapon. Holding the gun in one hand and bracing the butt on his hip, he deftly closed and locked the cabinet with his other hand, slipping the key ring back into his pocket.

Late night inclinations don't always look for logic, and even though it wasn't dirty, Wells decided the Mossberg needed a good cleaning. Part of it was because he needed a purpose during his insomnia, and the rest had more to do with having something that connected him with his son in his hands.

Stepping out into his workshop in the garage, he took care to close the door without a sound, so as not to disturb Molly. Almost lovingly he unscrewed the cap on the magazine tube and pulled the action about three-quarters of the way back so that the barrel loosened and came off in his hand. Pressing the small indented pin above the trigger assembly with a nail punch, he released the trigger mechanism, allowing it to fall free. Reaching into his well-worn cleaning kit, he retrieved a bore brush, an old toothbrush, some action oil and a partial roll of toilet paper, all tools he would need for the job. Cleaning the gun was like child's play to him. He could do it in total darkness and in fifteen minutes if he had to. Tonight, it took nearer forty-five, and he noted an actual sense of regret when at last he replaced the barrel, signaling completion of the work.

After locking the shotgun away, he read for a while. Then, about three in the morning, kicked off the clogs, lay down on the leather sofa in the great room, pulled the heavy amber afghan over him and drifted off into fitful slumber in front of the once-roaring fire's dying embers.

CHAPTER SEVEN

Tuesday, October 2, Whispering Ridge

Logistics were now all-important. Wells, Carlos and Ned Carlson were scheduled to take turns shuttling people from Portland International Airport to the winery or the Raymont. Alex Logan and his brother, Tom, were the first to arrive, flying out of Denver. Curt Wells himself met them and took them to breakfast before bringing them back to the house. Daniel Saperstein arrived around noon from Boston, having driven there from his home in Connecticut. Barton Stone was close behind out of Dallas, while Joel Saperstein would leave Washington after participating in the planning, on a late arriving evening flight out of D.C. He would bunk at the Raymont with the rest of Wells' team and Anson Landis.

As Wells mentally reviewed the schedule, a FedEx truck clattered up the drive, spitting mud from its oversized tires.

"Delivery for Mr. Gutierrez," the huffing, puffing driver announced.

Carlos helped the man unload four bulky, but lightweight boxes. Wells quickly joined them, and dismissing the deliveryman they threw the boxes onto a nearby skid and dragged them toward the main winery building. Once inside, they carefully slit the tape sealing the cartons and removed the contents. The return address on the packages read Fourteen Harcourt Downs, London, England. Each box, Wells noted with satisfaction, contained two British made MK-2 body armor vests. Reversible for day and night, each had a polyester shell filled with heavy duty Kevlar fiber, and a large zippered pocket in the middle of the chest that held a virtually bulletproof ceramic plate. This was state of the art combat protective gear. Nothing but the best for his fishing buddies, he mused. He made a mental note to ship a case of his best wine to Harry Burnham in London who, although cutting it close, came through for him yet again.

The sun was peeping out today, an autumn rarity in north central Oregon. And the wispy white puffs of cloud against the azure sky suggested a wonderful opportunity for a barbecue. Dispatched to the butcher shop, Carlos came back with a four large, fully dressed king salmon, which he then slow-roasted over a glowing, open alder wood fire. Molly took care of the rest. It promised to be a gala afternoon for the Wells' guests.

Washington, D.C., the Executive Residence

President Norman Randolph Sloan sat cross-legged in the dimly lit parlor, momentarily alone with his somber thoughts. The popular Democratic former governor of California had been drafted and nominated by party acclaim to run for the presidency. Weakened by scandal and a precariously teetering economy, the Republicans had run a predictably ineffectual campaign and Sloan was elected with a solid plurality.

The Democrats rode his coattails to a nominal majority in the House of Representatives, but the GOP retained its stranglehold on the Senate, thereby checkmating Sloan's fantasies of a smooth ride in office. His neo-liberal judicial nominees were in limbo, and his initial budget draft, riddled with pork for his supporters, was rejected by both chambers, some members of his own party bolting in embarrassment. He sat helplessly by while a genocidal tribal war raged in Kenya where tens of thousands were slaughtered. And now he faced mounting public pressure to intervene in the affairs of a recalcitrant allied government to rescue captured Americans from terrorists. Tonight, he did not feel at all like the world's most powerful leader, and wished he had *any* other job. What he did not know, could not have calculated, was that this was the calm *before* the storm.

Sloan was trapped in a cage of his own making. Understanding that the two coasts could not elect a president without solid buy-in from the heartland, he did his best to run as a moderate. But once in office, his own liberal inclinations and strong, unsubtle pressure from the left wing of the Democratic party caused him to retreat into unqualified support for abortion on demand, ever increasing taxes and the downsizing of military spending.

Predictably, the result was a sense of betrayal by the throngs of moderate voters who had supported him, reflected in a plummeting job performance rating and a unification of his conservative opposition in congress that threatened to block every presidential initiative, thwart every questionable nominee and effectively doom his presidential legacy to one of undistinguished mediocrity. Norman Sloan was living proof of the old political maxim that "you can't fool all of the people all of the time."

White House Chief of Staff Kenneth Karns and Press Secretary Mary Ann Motley entered quietly through a side door, and were invited to sit opposite the troubled president.

"You two look like morticians, and I feel like the corpse. How did we get into this mess?" Sloan demanded, looking off into space. "Better yet, how do we get out of it?"

"We need to talk about the demonstration tomorrow, sir," Motley offered anxiously.

"What about it?" snapped Sloan.

"It's going to be really, really big, Sir," Motley said somewhat timidly. "All flights into Washington today and tomorrow are completely booked. Buses and trains are sold out, too. Authorities are reporting traffic jams in seven states on highways heading this direction. Even a bikers' convention in Myrtle Beach, South Carolina, is closing early so they can all convoy to D.C."

"Bikers," the president hissed with disdain. "That means Hell's Angels, doesn't it?"

"Not at all, Sir," Karns tried to reassure him. "There will no doubt be some scruffy types among them, but the rest are just Americans who choose to ride motorcycles instead of belonging to bridge clubs or playing golf. Some of them agree with the protestors, and the rest are just joiners who enjoy a crowd and think this sounds like a good time."

"How did you find out about all of this?" the president asked Motley.

"It was on CNN, Sir," she responded.

"So how many of these 'people,' are we expecting?" Sloan wheezed contemptuously.

"Fox News commissioned Gallup to do a poll. They talked to twenty-one hundred people. Sixty-nine percent expressed solidarity with the demonstrators, and thirty-six percent said they planned to come to Washington. On that basis, if even half the people who say they're coming actually do, and the projected percentage extends to a broader segment of the population, we could be faced with a half-million angry demonstrators by tomorrow night."

"So what should I do? Should I meet with the leaders, or what?" Sloan shrugged.

"You already pretty much did that, sir, and it was unproductive. What we are recommending is that you issue a statement to the press – tomorrow would be good – stating your complete sympathy with the protestors and assuring America that those young lawyers will not be left to die alone in Saudi Arabia," Karns offered in a businesslike tone.

"How can I make a statement like that, Ken?" demanded an irritated Sloan, rising and pacing nervously back and forth. "Especially when my own cabinet tells me that unless I am prepared to intervene militarily, those boys likely *are* going to die over there."

"Maybe it's time to start looking seriously at the military option," Karns suggested cautiously.

"Have you read what Blaisdell sent over here, Ken? Blackhawks and Cobras, a Delta assault and rescue unit, possibility of a hundred Saudis dead, including a royal? That's Armageddon. We'll all be riding in horse drawn carriages again. People won't be able to heat their homes in the winter." The president was now involuntarily wringing his hands. "We get over fifteen thousand barrels of Saudi oil every day, making them our third largest supplier. Worse, they are arguably the most powerful member of the international oil cartel. If they cut back, and persuade the others to do likewise, it will be a national catastrophe."

"What about the Arctic National Wildlife Refuge, or the undersea fields off the southeast coast? We could make up some of the difference there," argued Karns weakly.

"Maybe, but it would take several years. And the party will never come behind that. Too many of them depend heavily on the environmental lobby for campaign contributions," Sloan lamented.

"It's a classic case of principle versus power," observed Mary Ann Motley, gazing off into empty space.

"What do you mean?" queried the president.

"If those boys die, and the public perceives that you let it happen without lifting a finger, you can kiss a second term goodbye. An oil shortage would lead to hard times, granted, but we stand a better chance of weathering that," she answered glumly.

"So you're both suggesting that I have no real option but to send in troops?" Sloan asked, incredulous.

"Maybe," hedged Karns. "What do CIA and FBI think? Maybe it's time you got Choate and Kendrick together for a little head-knocking come to Jesus meeting in the Oval Office."

"I think I see where you're going here," Sloan nodded. "Make the calls and tell them I expect them at the White House right after lunch."

The White House, Later That Day

The austere-faced Emmett Choate and an animated Alfred Kendrick arrived at the White House right on cue, after lunch. They sat while Sloan paced the Oval Office like a caged tiger.

"Tell me about our Mr. Wells. What do you think he's up to?" the president asked warily.

"We have him under complete and constant surveillance," Kendrick, the FBI director chirped. "We believe he has made contact with at least six members of his old SEAL team. In and of itself that is not particularly suspicious, because they're basically the group he goes fishing with."

"He's going to try it. That son of a bitch is going to try a freelance rescue," muttered CIA Director Choate.

"Why do you think that when all the evidence seems to indicate elaborate preparations for a fishing trip in central Oregon?" Sloan queried.

"I think what's troubling Emmett," Kendrick interrupted, "is that Wells withdrew large sums of cash from three different financial institutions yesterday."

"How large?" pressed the president.

"About one and three-quarter million dollars," Kendrick shrugged. "We know that part of the money is going to bankroll the demonstrations here in Washington over the next couple of days. It's the rest of it that has Emmett concerned."

"Wheew! That is a lot of cash," Sloan allowed. "But there's nothing illegal about a man withdrawing his own money or planning a fishing trip – if it *is* a fishing trip. Can't we find and detain these old SEALs? That would short circuit his plans."

"Detain them on what charge?" Choate asked. "Besides, if we're not going to send our own military in, what's the downside of letting these old fools have a go at a rescue? They're strictly private enterprise, so if they get caught or killed we simply disavow them. If they succeed, then those lawyers come home and everybody's happy but the Saudis, who can hardly blame us since we didn't know anything about it until it was all over."

"You may just have a point there, Emmett," Sloan reasoned. "We can't legally stop them from going abroad, or even from trying some half-assed rescue mission. And if it got out that we tried, we'd be the villains here at home. So, we let them go in. If they screw it up, shame on them. We can go on television and argue it was too risky and that's why we didn't try it ourselves. If they succeed, we give them a big pat on the back which costs us nothing, and move on. Is that about it?"

"That's the theory," Choate droned morosely. "But I've studied up on this Wells character, and it seems that he was one of our shrewdest and most devious operatives. He's a real wild card here, and he won't want to leave any witnesses behind, so the body count is likely to be high. The Saudis will have to blame someone if the royal nephew gets snuffed, and if it's not us it will surely be Tel Aviv. The ripple effect could still swamp our boat."

"Oh, come off it, Emmett," chided Kendrick. "You're always fixating on the dark side."

"Gentlemen, thank you for your counsel. I think we have a strategic option. But I would give a lot to know whether Wells is *really* going to mount an operation, and what his timetable looks like," the president added, looking directly at the FBI man.

"We'll stay on it, Sir. I promise," Kendrick assured him. "But unlike Emmett, I really don't believe he's going to try anything. A man like him must know by now that we're watching."

Al B'ir, Saudi Arabia

Scott Wells and Marty Logan huddled close together in the squat, windowless hut where they were confined. They had not been allowed to bathe since their capture, and they stank of perspiration. The air was stagnant and stale, and the grit of blowing sand from the frequent storms that swept through the area was matted into their unkempt hair and stuck between their teeth. The blistering heat of the days and the numbing cold wind that blew right through their makeshift jail at night meant that they were almost never comfortable. They were allowed bathroom breaks three times a day, but these consisted of closely escorted visits to a foul-smelling outhouse where they were forced to squat at ground level with their feet tightly shackled together to prevent any attempted escape. There was always a guard on the door, and periodically they had tried to start conversations. These efforts were largely in vain, since few of the guards spoke any English.

Today's sentinel appeared very young, and Scott decided to give it another try. He was used to resolving issues verbally, and thought that if he could engage one of his captors at least it might be possible to determine their agenda.

"You seem like a pretty sharp young guy. How did you get

mixed up in a mess like this?" he asked, his question drawing only a disgusted glance from his captor. "I mean, this can't be going anywhere good. You must know that."

Abruptly, and to his complete surprise, the guard whirled on him, anger burning in his sullen, dark eyes, and snarled in perfect English, "You think you know everything, American. But you know nothing. Every day our brothers and sisters are suffering and dying at the hands of American soldiers. Our people are starving while your rich companies grow fat harvesting and selling our oil. The Americans who come to our land despise our customs and defile our holy places. This must all end now!"

"Your English is remarkable," Scott said, seeking to defuse the zealot's angry rhetoric by paying him a simple compliment.

"I spit on your English, and on all things American," the young guard resumed his tirade.

"Yeah, I used to feel the same way when I was in high school," Scott jested. "But look at me. I haven't violated any of your customs - none, at least, of which I'm aware. And I haven't been near your holy places. I do work for an American oilfield support company. But all we've been hired to do is help your government get the oil out of the ground more efficiently and cost effectively. None of it belongs to us"

"My government, ha! I spit on them too," the young man continued his rant. "They are nothing but puppets of Western business interests."

"And you think that by taking us as hostages you'll get your government and mine to do exactly what?" Wells continued, pressing his luck.

"Our wise leader would see American soldiers out of Iraq and Afghanistan, and your American companies out of the Muslim lands they pollute," the young Arab said simplistically.

"I'm flattered that you think we're worth that much," Scott Wells rejoined, "but I seriously doubt whether either your government or ours will see it that way."

"Then you will die, just like the Jew," the young man hurled back.

"What do you mean 'like the Jew?' "Wells queried apprehensively. "Did you do something to Aaron?"

As the guard turned to reply he was taken to task by an older man standing just outside the door. Wells and Logan could see little more than his shadow against the sun. But they could tell that he was tall, with a long shaggy beard, and that he was slightly stooped at the shoulders, perhaps suggesting an advanced stage of life. He spoke to the guard sharply and in Arabic, obviously chastening him for fraternizing with the Americans.

Marty Logan looked at Scott Wells wide-eyed, and asked, "Geez, Sunny, do you think they really killed Aaron?"

The young guard returned to his post, his back to the door, and the two attorneys lay there shuddering in the semi-darkness, fearing now more than ever for their own lives.

The Crystal City Hyatt, Arlington, Virginia

Safely ensconced in their hotel hard by the Potomac, Tyler Wells, Callie Logan and Joel Saperstein went painstakingly over their hastily drawn but well detailed action plan. Tyler had designed and printed several hundred posters designating assembly areas and routes of march for the protestors. At each staging point a responsible leader equipped with plenty of signs and a bullhorn would explain each group's assignment, and exhort each cadre to obey local laws and cooperate, insofar as possible, with local police.

"I also had a bunch of these made up," said a beaming Joel Saperstein. He dragged out a stack of large boxes containing clip on badges that read, on the top, "Bring Them Back," and in the middle, highlighted by a big, red heart, the phrase "I Love D.C. Cops."

"They're going to want to bust our humps, right?" he asked rhetorically, the others nodding. "My thought is that if we court the police a little, they'll be a bit more lenient. And if they do arrest some of us, they'll be less likely to rough us up in the process."

"That's brilliant," Callie said approvingly. "I think you *should* run for congress, Joel."

"Tyler Wells, wrinkling his nose in a frown, said, "There's just one thing that worries me. We have no real idea how many people are going to show up for this thing. If there are too many, it might get out of control, and people might get hurt."

"We just have to get out there and preach the gospel of non-violence, guys," Callie counseled optimistically, her enthusiasm drawing knowing smiles from the other two.

After a quiet moment, Tyler said, "All right then. Callie, you and I can meet here at the hotel for breakfast at six in the morning. Then we'll brief the other organizers at eight, and head out to our staging areas. Good luck to us, and good fishing in Oregon, Joel," he added with a knowing wink that drew a quizzical look from Callie.

Tyler Wells' request to have breakfast with Callie the next morning was less about the planning, which was already substantially complete, than with the near-gravitational attraction to her of which he had become prominently and constantly aware. She seemed so much more than just a pretty face, so much deeper than the gaggle of young women who pursued him routinely seeking a good meal ticket in pants. He hated the events that had brought them here, and the danger surrounding his family hung constantly in his thoughts. But even through the pain and the fear, he still loved being with her. There was no denying it.

Whispering Ridge, Late Afternoon

Nearly three thousand miles distant, away from the bawdy bustle of the beltway, another plan was also coming together. Five hours before sundown Curt and Molly Wells, Alex and Tom Logan, Dan Saperstein, Carlos Gutierrez, Fritz Emswiler, Jimmy Dunn, and Barton Stone, along with a few hungry vineyard employees sat at wooden tables surrounding the barbecue pit feasting on the rich, smoky salmon Carlos had prepared, accompanied by fried sweet potatoes and fresh green salad from Molly's kitchen. A nice array of Whispering Ridge's finest white wines was available to chase down the food.

For dessert, Molly whipped up a chocolate infused polenta cake, using a recipe she had borrowed from a French chef who managed the Wells' favorite restaurant in Portland. Tom Logan allowed that he'd never known cornmeal to taste anything like that.

Slowly, subtly, methodically, Wells briefed each of the fishermen on his role in carrying out the necessary ruse of the coming days. All of this, he achieved under the guise of polite, quiet conversation during short respites in areas beyond the reach of the snooping, ever-present listening devices of the FBI. To all appearances, this was just a group of friends having a very good time on a lovely autumn afternoon.

As the red ball of sun began to recede toward the horizon, grudgingly yielding to the hazy onset of dusk, Curt Wells and Daniel Saperstein wandered up the gently terraced slope of the orchard to the east of the house, away from the prying eyes and ears on the hill.

"Do you really believe my son is still alive?" Dan asked earnestly.

"Yes, Dan, I do, and for all the same reasons I cited before. The tape was definitely a fake, and I just don't believe they'd give up a hostage so easily. And if they did kill him, where's the body? No, he's alive, just like Scott and Marty," Wells reasoned aloud.

"And you honestly think you can bring them out?" Saperstein pressed.

"If I didn't, I wouldn't be going. This is serious business, with a lot of big risks. My best friends in this world are going with me, and I wouldn't put their lives in danger along with my own if I didn't think we had a strong chance of success," Wells assured him.

"You said once," Dan reminded him, "that you might get some help from another government. Did you?"

"Unofficially, yes," Wells responded, tight-lipped.

"And would that perchance be the Israeli government?" Saperstein followed up, unwittingly crossing the line of need to know secrecy.

"Sorry Dan, I am bound on that point by confidentiality. It suffices that we will have significant logistical and intelligence support within the region when we go in."

Saperstein just smiled, believing he had gotten his answer.

Thirty minutes later Wells, attired in the casual chic of black turtleneck, khaki slacks and chestnut brown leather blazer climbed into his pickup and started down the road toward the main highway, and the next step on his fateful rendezvous with destiny. He smiled faintly as the white van let him pass, then, allowing sufficient distance for anonymity, pulled out to follow without immediately turning on its headlights.

Luccio's Italian Restaurant, The Pit

Carlos was waiting at the door to the subterranean room. With him was Devlin Bolton who had dutifully completed his bug sweep and reported The Pit clean as a whistle. Gutierrez called him promptly at three, and he was on the scene by four-thirty. Wells summarily thanked, then dismissed Bolton before turning to his friend.

"I'm on my own from here on in," he said with resignation. "You *are* clear about what has to happen in the morning, right?"

"Crystal!" replied Gutierrez. "I'd better get over to the Raymont and help Fritz set up."

"Good, I'll be there myself by eight," Wells promised.

Just before six, his dinner guests began to arrive, having walked out of the hotel down the street and traveled by different and circuitous routes. One had even hailed a cab and suggested that they drive around for fifteen minutes before depositing him at Luccio's. There were to be few surprises tonight. These were savvy veterans and they all knew what the game was.

Bobby Hammack was dapper, compact and athletically built, with curly brown hair and a broad, fetching smile. He and Mack Bryson, a strapping muscular fellow with a striking handlebar moustache had arrived together. The gregarious, ebullient Sean Garrity was close behind, after dismissing his bemused taxi driver, and Jimmy Dunn, replete with walking cast and cane, limped in right behind him. Marco Lopez, his shoulder length black hair flowing in a glistening mane and the tattoo of a skull and crossbones emblazoned prominently on his well-muscled forearm was next.

Denver Creel, a wiry, slender six-footer with a broad, dimpled face and expressive blue eyes arrived in a limo. He had been the team's radio operator, but was also very good with an M16A automatic rifle.

Finally, all eyes turned toward the one face they did not recognize as Barton Stone, dressed in a navy blazer and gray flannel slacks and carrying a large, brown envelope under his arm entered and closed the door behind him.

Curt Wells greeted each man warmly with a handshake and a bear hug. There was some good-natured joking about the recently interrupted football career of Jimmy Dunn. But when Stone entered, the tone turned immediately serious. Who was this stranger? And what did he have to do with the operation they were all certain they were about to discuss?

"Gentlemen," Wells broke the uncomfortable silence, "let me present Barton Stone, vice president for security with Halvarson-Brandt, the company by which my oldest son is employed. Major Stone is formerly of the 101st Army Rangers, with experience in special operations. Halvarson is providing us with significant logistical and intelligence support for this mission. Barton represents the company, and is as anxious to see this succeed as we are. You have all figured out by now that we're not going fishing – at least not the kind of fishing we usually do down on the John Day. My son Scott, along with two other Americans, has been abducted by Muslim extremists in Saudi Arabia. Thanks to Israeli intelligence and Halvarson-Brandt's satellites we now know exactly where the hostages are."

While Wells delivered his preamble, Stone busied himself taping up satellite photos around the room. The large printouts showed a symmetrical compound, walled on three sides and containing four low buildings.

"This," he said, "is the villa near Al B'ir, some forty-five miles inland from the Gulf of Aqaba. While our satellites lack the capacity for fine detail that the CIA would have, we can clearly see men being escorted from one building to the next between armed guards. In this shot," he said, pointing with a blue laser indicator, "we see a nighttime posting of guards at the four corners, with two additional sentries circling the interior. The two vehicles, visible in this shot, seem to be Saudi military transport trucks. Periodically, there have also been two private cars observed coming and going. We estimate that there are between fifteen and twenty armed men at the compound at any given time, and no women or children have been seen."

"I want to be honest with you," Wells resumed. "This operation is not sanctioned by the United States government. In fact, if they knew about it they would probably try to stop us."

"Why aren't they doing it themselves?" Mack Bryson's deep guttural voice demanded.

"Because we believe that this man, Tariq bin Saud," he said, holding aloft a picture, "a nephew of the royal family, may be involved with the kidnappers. The Saudis have told us to butt out, that they would handle it, and our government does not want to offend them," Wells responded honestly.

Oh, great!" fumed Sean Garrity. "We sure as shit know what that means."

"So, I'm going in to get those boys back," Wells said with quiet confidence. "I'm inviting you to join me. Next to your chair there is a leather briefcase. I'd like you each to open one now."

The sound of locks flipping open and cases unhinging was muffled by the loud gasps of those around the table.

"In each case there is two hundred fifty thousand dollars in cash. If you choose to go along, it's yours. I would advise you not to invest it in a single deposit unless you want a lot of ugly questions from the Internal Revenue Service."

"You hardly have to bribe us, Skip," Bobby Hammack piped up.

"It's not a bribe. It's a fair wage for the risk I'm asking you to take. We are going in harm's way gentlemen," Wells responded, his voice still measured and even. "Bobby, I didn't want you to have to go, given the fact that Miranda is with child. But 'Jimmy Unitas' here put a crimp in my plan," he said, slapping Jimmy Dunn on the back.

"If you think I'm missing this party, forget it. I'm in, over and out. Besides, where in this sorry lot would you find a point man half as good as I am," Hammack jibed, to good-natured hoots and jeers.

"Jimmy, I'm sorry that you can't go. You'd be a liability to us and a danger to yourself. But your case has the same amount in it as the others because what you're being asked to do is just as important. It's going to be up to you to run the fishing trip, make it look legitimate and keep the FBI believing we're all there fishing our hearts out instead of staging a rescue in the Middle East," Wells continued. "Some of those who are going with you may not know which end of the fly rod to use, and only one has been down there before. It's up to you to bring them up to speed and make it look like the real thing," he added as Dunn nodded glumly, disappointed to be missing out on the action.

"The FBI knows about this?" Marco Lopez rasped in horror.

"They *suspect*, and they've got me under twenty-four hour surveillance," conceded Wells.

With that admission he saw several of them begin to look nervously around, wondering if their conversation was being overheard.

"If you think they're listening now, not to worry," Wells raised his voice a bit and spoke reassuringly. "That's why I picked this place and had it swept for bugs just before you got here. They'll follow me when I leave, and are probably curious as hell about who you are and what we're saying. By the time they piece it all together, we'll be long gone. I suggest that you not use your real names or pay for anything with credit cards to make their job easier. If you need anything at the hotel, just charge it to your room. Carlos will take care of everything when he checks you out tomorrow."

"Somebody else is checking us out?" said a still confused Lopez.

"Yes, Bobby will pick you all up in a blue van at precisely three in the morning, in front of the hotel. You'll be joined by Joel Saperstein, the brother of one of the hostages, and Anson Landis, my attorney. Don't say anything to them about our operation. Later, when we switch vehicles, Barton and I will join you and the two of them will take our places." Wells hoped he was doing a good job of explaining his intricately laid plan.

"We'll meet out near my place, and drive to a prearranged airfield where a Halvarson-Brandt corporate jet will take us to

Dallas. There, we'll load onto a converted Boeing 727 cargo jet and after a brief stopover in Baltimore, fly to Amsterdam, and from there on into Tel Aviv. In Tel Aviv, a friend of mine will lead us to a military transport plane that will take us to Eilat, near the Israeli-Saudi-Jordanian border. I asked you all to bring your passports. Hold onto them for now, but we won't be going through customs. At Eilat, we'll be outfitted and armed, get updated intelligence and board a Mossad helicopter for an after hours helicast into the gulf. When we hit the beach in Saudi, more Mossad will meet us with a truck that will get us to Al B'ir. A Mossad operative will be going in with us on a separate mission of his own."

"May we know what that mission is?" Stone piped up.

"Certainly," Wells answered. "He's going in to assassinate Muhammad al-Shariya, who probably is behind the kidnapping. And while we're on the subject, you all need to understand clearly that we are in a 'no witnesses, no prisoners' situation. No one walks away but the hostages and us. Clear?"

All nodded grimly as his meaning set in. They were going to raid the compound, rescue the hostages and kill everyone else. That's how it had to be, and to a man they understood why.

"I have to be somewhere else in a few minutes, and the best Italian dinner you've ever eaten is about to be served with my compliments. Keep the talk light, because I can't vouch for the wait staff," Wells said in parting.

As the door closed behind him, Stone took down the surveillance shots and talk turned to fishing. They took turns reminding Jimmy Dunn about the odds and ends of keeping a trip running smoothly. Waiters in white coats soon bustled in with bread, salad and wine. Among them, dressed in a black skirt and blouse under a white apron, was an attractive Latina with no apparent function. Stone and Bryson spotted her at the same time and reached the same conclusion. The FBI had arrived fashionably late, and the whispered alert quickly circulated around the table guaranteed both her total frustration and a surfeit of grossly embellished and intentionally risqué fishing tales.

Meanwhile, at the Raymont just down the street, Wells slipped in right at the end of Fritz Emswiler's technical presentation to greet, mingle with and schmooze nearly two dozen buyers from all over the world as they tasted and savored Whispering Ridge's finest. Carlos and Fritz busied themselves filling out order forms, while Wells spewed a seemingly inexhaustible stream of humorous anecdotes and small talk. At ten, he was still huddled in the corner with a Canadian and a New Yorker, and still talking wine. A half-hour later, Fritz and Carlos finished packing up the display, and Wells said his goodbyes, following them wearily out the door with the FBI watching every mystifying move.

CHAPTER EIGHT

Whispering Ridge, Wednesday, October 3

Nacho, Carlos Gutierrez' Golden Labrador grumbled as the foreman pulled on his boots, a light sweater and denim jeans. The illuminated dial on the nightstand clock said half past two in the morning. In half an hour Bobby Hammack would be picking up Wells' raiders at the Raymont, and everything at Whispering Ridge would have to be in place by then. Gutierrez could see the light on in Curt Wells' study and wondered in passing if the man ever slept.

Wells met him at the maintenance barn, and together with Barton Stone, they packed the van for the fishing excursion. Alex Logan, his brother Tom and Dan Saperstein brought down their bags the evening before, and they were quickly hoisted aboard. Shortly they, too, joined Gutierrez, Stone and Wells for the final preparation. Jimmy Dunn, who had stayed in the guest apartment over the winery building, came limping along in his heavy walking cast, his cane rattling the gravel in the drive as he crossed to the barn. Wells brought out a thermos of hot coffee and some plastic mugs, and they all drank heartily while they finished packing and made small talk.

"It's three-fifteen, you'd better go, Carlos," Wells reminded his foreman.

With that, Gutierrez hoisted himself into the cab of the diesel truck loaded with wine casks and crates of empty bottles, and began to back the big rig out onto the apron.

"Where's he off to so early?" Alex Logan asked.

"He's going to be the key to a little diversion," Wells smiled knowingly. "He has a small surprise in store for the Federal Bureau of Investigation."

Atop the hill the watcher was alert, too. He had donned the funny looking corduroy hat again, and was peering down through night vision glasses at the goings on below, the soft green light in his scope bathing the activity in an eerie luminescence. He was alone this night. The Bureau higher-ups were quite convinced that Curt Wells was doing business as usual and preparing to go fishing. No trouble there. But the fishermen certainly seemed to be getting an early start today, the man thought to himself.

A light, wispy ground fog blanketed the vineyards, lending a ghostly aura to everything visible. Carlos Gutierrez was hardly noticeable as he coaxed the big diesel a quarter mile up the narrow drive and into a turnout, sheltered by a grove of alders. He had never turned the lights on and now he switched the engine off, took a long draw on his steaming cup of java, stroked Nacho's ears and waited.

At the Raymont the pickup went as scheduled. Bobby Hammack, Mack Bryson, Marco Lopez, Sean Garrity, Joel Saperstein, Denver Creel and Anson Landis were wedged in tightly, some of them sitting on the flak jackets Carlos packed there the previous evening. Hammack drove the blue van abruptly off the road and into a copse of trees a scant hundred yards before the turnoff to Whispering Ridge. There he, too, shut down his lights and engine, and waited.

The fishermen climbed into the white van parked in the barn next to the main winery building, and at precisely four AM Wells backed it out, dropped it into gear and gunned the engine, spinning his wheels in the damp gravel. This action sent the FBI agent on the hill sprinting to his own white Chevy van and into a hectic descent via the skinny spit of moist dirt pathway that led down from the hilltop observation point. His tires slipped and slid in the loose earth and gravel, once nearly careening him off the road and into a shallow ravine. Pleased by his timing, he emerged onto the entry road just in time to see the taillights of Wells' van as it sped away. Turning off the parking lights he needed to make his way down the steep hill, he wheeled onto the road and began his discreet pursuit without benefit of illumination.

He was just gathering speed when the cumbersome diesel winery truck lurched out of nowhere, slid across the road in front of him and mired its front wheels in the sodden earth on the far shoulder, completely blocking the thoroughfare.

"Damn," the Bureau agent swore, stomping on his brakes and hastily exiting his vehicle, which slid to a sudden stop less than ten feet short of the oversized truck.

Wildly waving his badge and credential, the agent shouted, "FBI, move that damned thing right now."

Being bilingual allows one to practice selective understanding, just as many practice selective hearing. Carlos Gutierrez, whose English was in actuality impeccable, suddenly did not *"habla Ingles."* Feigning ignorance regarding the stranger's frustration, he inspected his truck, sunken nearly to the axle and shrugged in mock helplessness. It would be a full and exasperating twenty-five minutes before the truck could be moved far enough to let the law enforcement officer's vehicle proceed.

During that time, Curt Wells made his scheduled rendezvous with the blue van and planted his floppy fishing hat, festooned with a myriad of trout flies, directly on Anson Landis' head as the latter, along with Joel Saperstein, switched vehicles with Wells and Stone. The fishermen set out east by south with Landis at the wheel, while the SEAL team headed due north for Interstate 84 and the quick trip to The Dalles where the Halvarson Lear awaited.

On the verge of panic because he had lost Wells and his party, the FBI agent called for help and promptly got it in the form of a Bureau chase helicopter, the fog be damned. The proud chopper pilot clucked his tongue and smiled with satisfaction as he reacquired the white van southbound. What neither he nor his relieved superiors could possibly know, was that Curtis Wells was no longer in it. In fact, he and his men had, for all practical purposes, vanished into the morning mist.

D.C., Near the Washington Monument

Callie Logan stood on an impromptu podium, hastily constructed of plywood and four-by-fours. Behind her loomed the timeless white spire of the Washington Monument, while framing the sea of faces before her was the Ellipse, and further on, the White House. She had no idea how many people were in the crowd, although she guessed it to be hundreds. In reality, it was nearly four thousand.

The sun was well into its inevitable ascent, and the autumn air was crisp and brittle. It was a good day for a demonstration. Dressed in blue jeans, a Colorado State sweatshirt and a warm blue knit jacket, she picked up the bullhorn, her blonde hair ruffled by the hint of a breeze.

"Welcome to Washington, brothers and sisters," she began enthusiastically. "Thank you all for coming. We're here to send a message, am I right?"

A deafening roar of affirmation greeted her question, as the crowd broke into a rhythmic chant of "Cal-Lee, Cal-Lee." She wasn't used to public speaking, and the response left her momentarily bewildered. At length, she raised both hands to quiet the crowd, one hand still clutching the bullhorn.

"Our message is, 'Bring them home!'" she said, triggering another roar and a new chant, this one reiterating her own words. The chanting went on for a full two minutes before she raised her hands once again for quiet.

"There are people moving among you passing out signs and buttons. We want to space the signs out, rather than bunching them all together, and we want everyone to take and wear a button, until we run out of them. The signs tell the president and those around him that we want our brothers back home again. And the buttons tell the Washington police that we appreciate them and mean them no harm. We're going to march to the White House in a few minutes. Our goal is to join up with the groups marshaling elsewhere and encircle the place. We want lots of noise. The police may intervene, and even arrest some of us. Don't fight them. They're just following orders and doing their jobs. If they take you to jail, let them. Someone will be along soon to get you out, provided you haven't resisted arrest," she said, pausing for effect. "Are you with me?"

Again, a raucous chorus of ebullient support resounded throughout the park.

"We've designated some people as organizers. They'll be providing signs, passing out water and helping you with any problems you encounter. You'll recognize them because they'll be wearing one of these," she added, pulling an electric blue muffler from around her neck and brandishing it high in the air. "Let's get our message across, and let's keep it peaceful," she admonished.

Tyler Wells recruited over fifty adults of both sexes to act as organizers. They were to oversee the various areas in which the protest was taking place, intercede with police when possible, and help weed out troublemakers. Each of them had the number of the cell phone clipped to Fritz Emswiler's belt, and similar numbers for Callie and Tyler. One of them took the bullhorn from Callie now and began to bark instructions, dividing the large crowd into smaller units. In thirty minutes they were moving across the Ellipse, advancing on the White House.

On the opposite side of the White House, in Lafayette Park, a similar scene was unfolding, orchestrated by Tyler Wells. His group quickly linked with another that had been massing in Franklin Park and yet another coming from the National Mall, and soon the overflowing chain of humanity spilled out onto Pennsylvania Avenue chanting, "Bring Them Home, Bring Them Home."

The Secret Service was also out in force, ringing the White House and its grounds. Washington Metro police, obviously staffed for trouble, stood outside the fence armed with hardened plastic shields and rubber truncheons. President Sloan hibernated in the richly paneled second floor study, pretending that nothing was happening while the crowd outside continued to swell. As the seething mass of humanity exceeded the space available in the capitol area, and the police reached the limit of their patience, Tyler Wells saw an ugly scenario brewing.

Marching up and down the front line of demonstrators on Pennsylvania Avenue, he counseled cooperation with police. The strategy he and others had mapped out earlier was an amoebic undulation in which demonstrators gave way to police advances while, at the same time, others further down the line pushed forward. The crowd manifested no intent to actually enter the grounds of the White House, and absent physical resistance to the officers provided scant grounds for arrest.

By noon, the bikers arrived from Myrtle Beach and over three hundred of them began circling the complex, their powerful engines roaring above the chanting crowd. When Tyler and Callie finally linked up, she told him that CNN was projecting that the demonstrators would likely number four hundred thousand by the day's end. Both agreed that such a turnout exceeded their wildest dreams.

As he moved away from her, and in the direction of the National Mall, he found himself suddenly flanked by two very large men in dark suits. One grabbed him somewhat roughly by his right arm, and jerking him none too gently toward a parked car growled, "National Security Agency, Mr. Wells. Come with us."

Brady Kostner's Office, The Washington Times

The rumpled reporter was munching on the remainder of a ham and cheese on rye, while leafing through the day's mail. Disinterestedly, he opened a business-sized letter postmarked the previous day in Washington. What he read sent him reaching for his nearly spent bottle of Coca Cola. He needed it to keep from choking on his sandwich.

"Dear Mr. Kostner. You should check out the possibility that Saudi Arabia and the United States government are not trying to rescue the American hostages because Tariq bin Saud, a nephew of the Saudi royal family is one of the kidnappers."

The letter was signed simply, "A Knowledgeable Friend." Kostner beat a hasty path to the office of Gardner Fitzgerald, his senior editor, excitedly showing him the letter.

"Interesting theory," mused Fitzgerald. "And it would certainly explain a lot of things that otherwise seem inexplicable."

"My thought exactly," Kostner concurred, "but I hate to go out on a limb without some kind of confirmation."

"We just can't," confirmed Fitzgerald. "But I'll tell you the fastest way to get it."

"How's that?" Kostner asked, puzzled.

"Call the White House. Act like you know more than you do. Tell them we're going to run the story. If they start foaming at the mouth you'll know we're getting too close to the truth," Fitzgerald smiled, tilting back in his soft leather chair with visions of a juicy international political scandal dancing in his head, as Kostner ran off on his errand of verification.

In minutes, the reporter was on the phone with the White House, asking to speak with presidential chief of staff Kenneth Karns about an urgent matter. The latter, sure that this well known scribe was calling with reference to the rampaging demonstration, and sensing an opportunity to blunt criticism of the president, temporarily exited a meeting with some lower level staffers in order to take the call.

"Mr. Kostner, so good of you to call. While we certainly honor the demonstrators' right to free speech, we ... " he stopped, interrupted mid-sentence by Kostner.

"My paper is preparing to run a story naming royal nephew Tariq bin Saud as a possible co-conspirator in the Saudi kidnapping, and attributing the lack of action by the Saudis and this administration to the politics of oil. Would you care to comment?" Kostner said succinctly.

"Well, uh, why, you can't do that," Karns stammered in alarm. "There's no proof ..."

"So, then, you're denying it?" Kostner pressed.

"We just have no comment about it, that's all," Karns rasped, momentarily regaining a semblance of equilibrium. "You have to understand, Brady, that this is a very delicate situation. You know I can't tell you ... " he blathered, as he was interrupted again.

"I think you just have, Ken. I think you just have."

The letter, written by Curt Wells and mailed by Tyler from Reagan National, had done its inevitable work. And the ripples from this new stone cast into the political pond were sure to rock President Norman Sloan's already beleaguered raft.

A Windowless Room, Somewhere in D.C.

Tyler Wells did not know Washington very well. The speed of his virtual abduction served to confuse and bewilder him, and he did not think to notice where the so-called NSA agents were taking him, assuming it would be a well-known government building. It wasn't. Instead, they entered an undistinguished building with a brownstone front that was several miles away from the noisy protest going on around the capitol. The men silently declined to answer his questions about why he was being detained, or where he was being taken. Once inside the building, they took him to an elevator, reached the third floor, entered the anteroom of a drab, unmarked office, and then the room where he presently sat.

The room had no windows and only the one door as a means of ingress and egress. The walls were painted a uniform pallid yellow, and there were no pictures or posters on them. In the room were a heavy table and four uncomfortable wooden chairs, one on one side of the table and the other three facing. His escorts parked him in the single chair and left him there, telling him only to "relax." He was unrestrained, as he had been during the entire ride, and his first, and entirely predictable move was to rise, walk to the door and turn the knob. No cigar. It was locked from the outside.

Presently, he heard the deadbolt unlatch, and one of the men entered with a tray of sandwiches and a small, iced cooler full of soft drinks.

"Thought you might be hungry," he said tersely while exiting and relocking the door.

About that, the man was right. Tyler Wells hadn't eaten since his early morning breakfast with Callie Logan and he was ravenous. Doubting that food looking so appetizing was drugged, he began greedily wolfing down a roast beef on whole wheat, quenching his thirst with a cold Pepsi, a preference he shared with his father. Just as he finished a second sandwich, he heard the deadbolt slip out of the hasp again, and three men entered the room. These were new faces. He had not seen any of them before. They nodded toward him, and each sat in a chair across the table from their nonplused captive.

"My name is Jernigan. I'm with the National Security Agency. This is Crowe, FBI, and that's Hanson," the man in the center chair said.

"I didn't catch who you were with, Mr. Hanson," Tyler said mockingly.

"That's because I didn't say," Hanson responded flatly. "Let's just say I'm an interested party."

"Interested in what?" demanded Wells, his ire rising. "Are you interested in restricting free speech, in unreasonable seizure or just in playing fast and loose with my constitutionally guaranteed rights in general?"

"We just want to talk a bit," Jernigan interposed.

"So, talk. I'm listening," Wells replied, obviously not mollified.

"Where is your father, Curtis Wells?" Jernigan droned in a flat monotone.

"Ask him," Tyler retorted, nodding toward Crowe. "His people have been following both of us all over the place. Or don't you talk to your people in the field?" he inquired snidely of Crowe, who remained silent and impassive.

Jernigan was a stout man with a stern, expressive face that reminded Tyler Wells of the late Johnny Cash. He shifted in his chair and spoke again.

"We have reason to believe that your father is planning some kind of operation, and we'd like to know more about it," he said casually.

"My father's a wine maker, not a surgeon," Wells sneered.

"Right," said the man called Hanson sarcastically. "He's a wine maker who has recently mobilized elements of his old Navy SEAL team for a so-called fishing trip. To me, that stinks, even without any fish."

"So put a clothes pin on your nose," Wells shot back. "He's been fishing with those guys since before I was old enough to hold a pole. They're all like my uncles."

"If they're going fishing in the Middle East, they're trolling for a boatload of trouble," Crowe added.

"Middle eastern Oregon," Wells responded cagily.

"Say what?" Jernigan snapped.

"They're headed, by now, for a lodge on the John Day River. That's in east central Oregon," Wells clarified. "I'm sure you have people following them there. Why don't you pick up the phone and call them?" he followed up peevishly.

The FBI man looked away toward the ceiling and rubbed his eyes, realizing that both Tyler and Curt Wells had made the surveillance teams assigned to them, and wondering if they were that sharp or the Bureau people involved that inept.

"Do you understand, Mr. Wells, that if your father launches an armed incursion into Saudi Arabian territory he can be charged with crimes both there and in the U.S., and that if you knew in advance what he was doing you can also be charged as a co-conspirator?" Jernigan chided.

"And so if the wolf steals the chicken and the cow sees him doing it you're going to kill the cow?" Wells mocked.

"You think this is funny?" Hanson leaned forward and spat, his eyes full of disdain and his face florid.

"I think you're all learning impaired. You remind me of the three stooges," Tyler Wells shot back angrily. "My father is fifty-four years old, and his fishing buddies aren't that much younger. They were all SEALs once and they're proud of it. When my brother and I were little, they used to sit around the fireplace down at the lodge and bore the hell out of us with their war stories. But they're old men now. They fish, and they tell stories. They don't try to relive their glory days by mounting half-assed rescue missions. And if they did, I'd be first in line to talk them out of it. The fact that the three of you actually believe something sinister is going on is laughable," he concluded with conviction, hoping to convince them.

"So you know nothing about any plan to rescue your brother?" Crowe pressed.

"This is what I know," the younger Wells said slowly, thoughtfully. "The president of the United States is sitting on his fat ass doing nothing, and he'll undoubtedly continue to do so until my brother

95

and the others turn up dead. Then he'll say what a shame it is that three *more* Americans were killed by terrorists whom we can't seem to identify or find. I also know that I have a demonstration to run that's designed to light a fire under this administration. So you need to either charge me, or let me go – right now! I'm not answering any more of your stupid questions without an attorney present."

"It is not our intention to charge you with any crime at this time," Crowe confessed. "We were simply hoping that you'd be reasonable and help us to avert something that has 'disaster' written all over it. You may leave whenever you like. Lunch is on us. Take a sandwich with you if you wish. There is a car and driver in front of the building who will take you wherever you want to go. Here is my card. If you change your mind, or come by any information you think we should have, please call me at one of these numbers."

They watched as he rose, walked straight out the door, summoned the elevator and climbed aboard. Their mood was pensive, puzzled. They were anything but unanimous in their reading of Tyler Wells.

"He doesn't know squat," Hanson said abruptly.

"Of course he does. The father and son are close. If Wells senior is planning something, the kid knows about it," Crowe responded.

"Then again, there's a chance he's telling the truth," mused Jernigan. "And he may be right. This may just be an old guy going fishing with his friends to get his mind off of something he hates, but can't do anything about."

Tyler successfully left them befuddled, and no more knowledgeable than they were before they snatched him off the street. His feigned ignorance and belittling of their suspicions worked like a charm. They'd seriously underestimated him. and were just as surely underselling the capacities and resources of his father.

The stone-faced driver dropped him off near the National Mall. They had stripped him of the headset and earpiece that connected him to Callie and the other organizers by means of a wireless network. When they returned it to him, pieces of it were damaged, obviously by intent, and it was quite useless. He struck out for Pennsylvania Avenue at a trot, looking for Callie's flowing, blonde hair and an update on the progress of the demonstration. As he slowed to a walk, a large, middle-aged man in a charcoal suit blocked his path. From the outside breast pocket of his rumpled jacket hung a leather wallet with the gold shield of a D.C. Metro police detective prominently displayed.

"Tyler Wells?" the sallow faced fellow barked gruffly.

"Yes," Wells replied, taking a step back and squinting at the man's credentials.

"I have a warrant here for your arrest on charges of conspiracy to conduct an unlawful demonstration and inciting to riot. You have the right to remain silent. If you give up the right to remain silent, anything you say can and will be used against you in a court of law. You have the right to an attorney. If you desire, but cannot afford an attorney, one will be appointed for you by the court. Do you understand these rights as I have explained them to you?" the man asked.

"I understand my rights," Tyler snapped. "Do you understand the repercussions of false arrest?"

In a flash, a squad car pulled up, and two uniformed patrolmen jumped out, cuffed his hands behind him and, pushing down hard on his head to guarantee he would not bump it on the frame of the car, shoved him in and slammed the door shut. With a loud squeal of rubber on pavement the car sped away.

The White House Press Room

"Ladies and gentlemen, the President of the United States," crowed Press Secretary Mary Ann Motley as the Washington press corps rose to salute the commander-in-chief.

"Thank you, ladies and gentlemen of the press," Sloan began, a broad and engaging smile on his face. "I have a brief statement, and then I'll entertain a few questions. As you all know, we are currently besieged with upwards of a half million demonstrators who are concerned about the safe return of American hostages recently taken in Saudi Arabia. I want to assure them, and the entire nation, that no one is more concerned about the safety of these Americans than I. Our intelligence services are continuing to make slow progress in ascertaining the whereabouts of the hostages. When that location is known with certainty, the appropriate authorities in Saudi Arabia will be notified, and it is our expectation that prompt action will be taken to free those being held. Until then, we must all continue to hope and pray that those who are still alive will remain so until such time as their release is secured."

Sloan paused and looked up, indicating the conclusion of his prepared remarks, and his readiness to take questions. A doughty-looking woman on the first row stood up, her hand waving for the president's attention and the great folds of flesh surrounding her bejowled face flapping as if in a strong wind.

"Mr. President," she said in a gravelly, irritating half shout, "will you authorize an American military rescue mission when the hostages are located?"

"We will make that offer to the Saudis, but since this crime transpired on their soil, and since they are a close ally it will ultimately be their call," Sloan replied evasively.

A male voice from deeper in the chamber followed up. "What do you say to the allegation that a nephew of the Saudi royal family may be involved in the abduction, and the charges that you already know where the hostages are but have not moved to rescue them because you fear Saudi economic reprisal?"

The story was spreading like wildfire through the press corps even before Kostner dropped the bombshell in print. Sloan, quickly on the defensive, struggled to retain his customary plastic smile, while shaking his head vigorously.

"I'd say that's a lot of groundless speculation," he answered. "When it comes to protecting our citizens, economic considerations are not in play."

"So you're saying that you would order the military in if the Saudis agreed, even if a member of the royal family should be involved?" another male inquisitor badgered.

"I am not prepared at this time either to announce or foreclose *any* option," Sloan responded cannily. "And I would ask you ladies and gentlemen to be responsible about spreading defamatory speculation that could damage our relationship with a trusted ally, absent the proof to back it up."

Verbal sparring continued for another ten minutes, with the president yielding little ground or helpful information. The hastily arranged press conference had clearly been a stunt to placate the growing horde of protestors, and it fooled neither them nor the seasoned political wags of the Washington press contingent.

D.C. Metro Lock-Up

Tyler Wells was doing a slow burn. The off-the-books federal detention, closely followed by police arrest could not, he knew, be coincidental. He made his one call, to Fritz Emswiler's cell phone, and was assured that Fritz would soon be on the way, an attorney in tow.

Wells was placed alone in a room with what he guessed to be a two-way mirror, and bars on the windows. It contained a green metal table that was bolted to the floor, and three matching chairs that were secured to the table by heavy steel chains. It was clearly a place where criminals, some of them probably dangerous, were routinely interrogated.

By and by, a tall, slim man with a gold detective shield, thinning brown hair and deep creases across his forehead and between his eyes strode in.

"Are you Tyler Wells?" he asked brusquely.

"What's it to you?" Wells responded in kind.

A sardonic smile crossed the detective's lips, further emphasizing the permanent creases in his aging face.

"Have it your way, smartass," he rasped. "But you're going to sit here until you talk to me, even if it takes all night."

Pacing for a moment he turned to Wells, who by now was seated in one of the chairs. He was about to speak when the door burst open and a local assistant district attorney stepped through, accompanied by a small, compactly built, bespectacled black man. Taking the detective by the arm, the assistant D.A. squired him out the door, leaving Tyler Wells alone with a man he had never seen before in his life.

"Quentin Sharpe, attorney at law," said the man, extending his hand. "More specifically, I'm *your* attorney."

"What's going on here?" Wells blurted out, his pent-up frustration evident.

"What's going on is pretty much unvarnished police harassment, Mr. Wells," Sharpe rejoined. "The organizing a demonstration without a permit charge will go away. They didn't charge any of the dozen or so groups who demonstrated here last week without a permit, and I have convinced the district attorney that if they press that charge we will hit them with a discrimination suit. The other specification, inciting to riot, is basically about six bikers who ran through police lines and then resisted arrest. When I pointed out to the district attorney that you had never met any of these gentlemen, and were in clandestine federal custody at the time of the incident, he saw the handwriting on the wall. We'll have you out of here within half an hour, as soon as the paperwork is processed. I initiated an off the record chat with a precinct police captain, and he seems to think the order to have you picked up came down from the White House. We might be able to use that information later, but for now I have a couple of the other organizers outside waiting for you, and I don't want you to be alone again for the remainder of the demonstration where they might be able to pick you up again."

The National Mall, Washington, D.C.

Tyler Wells was completely exhausted, and his voice was almost gone. Demonstrators continued to ring the White House, demanding raucously that the president act immediately to save the hostages. But young Wells was simply spent. He sat quietly on the pavement sipping bottled water, his back against the concrete base of a light pole.

"What's the matter, big boy? Are you all worn out?" asked the soft, fetching, but somewhat hoarse female voice.

He looked up and straight into the warmth of Callie Logan's broad smile. She appeared as tired as he felt. Momentarily she sat down beside him, and he recited for her the tale of his federal detention and interrogation, police arrest and eventual liberation. She shook her head in amazement. "That is one frightened man in there," she said, pointing in the direction of the White House. "This thing is a lot bigger than we are now, you know?"

Unable to speak further, Callie moved close to Tyler and cuddled against him. He put both arms around her and pulled her even closer. They sat together entwined for a long time. And they thought about their missing brothers. Callie's heart ached, but Tyler's strong arms around her made it feel as if he had always been there, and she wondered if he always would be.

By day's end, the demonstration, now well out of the control of its organizers, would peter out, with the demonstrators returning to normal lives. But something had changed for many of them here. They now knew what it was to get involved in the process, to make themselves heard, to try to make a difference. There was a quiet but palpable power in the solidarity they felt with the siblings of the hostages. They would go home, but continue to write or call their congressmen. The White House would shortly be flooded by organized e-mail campaigns, and prodded to remember what had befallen the young lawyers. It was sound and fury, to be sure. But this time it signified something very real.

An HB Boeing 727, Somewhere Over the Atlantic

At twenty-eight thousand feet the big General Electric jet engines throbbed with a numbing hum as most of Curtis Wells' team slept. They had not been long in either Dallas or Baltimore. In each place they picked up tools essential both to their assumed identities and their ultimate mission. Outfitted in blue Halvarson-Brandt field coveralls and hard hats, they looked like just any other oilfield support crew as they boarded. The documents they kept secured in long cardboard tubes were not oilfield topography charts, but satellite surveillance photos and maps of the Al B'ir area, as well as the roads leading there from the coast where they would go ashore. Their innocent looking rucksacks contained body armor and tactical gear, all of foreign manufacture, and a quantity of carefully packed, lead-shielded Semtex plastic explosive.

Wells collected their passports, wallets and other forms of identification when they boarded, and consigned them to a locked metal ammunition box for safe keeping, They wouldn't need them to get into Israel, but they might need them to get out of wherever they ended up if things went awry. Once they were away, Bobby Hammack sat down beside Wells and spoke in a quiet voice.

"Why'd you really leave the Navy for the CIA anyway, Skip. I always wanted to ask you."

"A lot of reasons, I guess," Wells answered, seeking to put into words something he'd never really faced himself. "I guess I was just tired of having responsibility for the lives of other men in dangerous situations. With every successful mission we ran, the odds of somebody not making it back from the next one went up. I guess I'm just a worrier, and the worry finally got too heavy to carry. You jokers came to mean too much to me."

"And it was different at the agency?" Hammack wondered.

"It was," Wells confirmed. "I was pretty much a lone wolf operator there, most of the time without the benefit of official cover. The only life I had to risk was my own. It was a lonely life. I couldn't even talk to my family about what I really did. It got old. I suppose I just really missed my old team," he smiled, leaning his head back against the bulkhead.

While the others slept, Wells, Hammack and Stone sat in the lighted forward section of the cabin, the maps and satellite photos spread in front of them, and began to fine tune the extraction plan.

"What concerns me," Wells confided quietly, "is the unknown number of variables. All evidences suggest that the hostage takers are Islamic militant thugs. But, then, where did they get the Saudi military vehicle? If elements of the Saudi regular army are in on this, we could be walking straight into a buzz saw."

"It's definitely worrisome that we're short on intelligence. Don't the Israelis have eyes on the ground around Al B'ir?" Stone replied.

"Yes, some, and I hope to get an update in Eilat before we go," Wells confirmed.

"So I gather you are committing us at this point," Stone said with a raised eyebrow.

"Yes, and no," Wells answered ambiguously. "The Israelis are monitoring the political situation in the U.S., and the movement of the Tarawa and its battle group. If it looks like the president is prepared to order American forces in, then we'll stand down and give him a chance to do that."

"And if the Saudis try to move first?" Hammack pressed.

"Then we try to beat them to the site," Wells countered grimly. "I think you know why."

CHAPTER NINE

The Oval Office, Thursday Morning, October 4

"Greetings, Mr. Ambassador," offered President Norman Sloan, warmly welcoming the seasoned diplomat who represented Riyadh to the U.S. government.

"I believe you know Donald Trimble, my secretary of state, and Emmett Choate, the director of central intelligence," the president continued, the ambassador's polite nods indicating that he did.

"We want to talk about the plight of the Americans taken hostage in your country – specifically about the progress your intelligence service has made in locating them and the plans your government may have to rescue them," Sloan added.

"Ah, it is a very sad thing. But alas, try as we may, we have yet to locate the hostages," whined the ambassador, rocking back and forth from one buttock to the other in his chair.

"Emmett, give this man some help, will you?" commanded the president, winking knowingly at his DCI.

With that, Choate shoved a large manila folder across the coffee table toward the Saudi, then sat back to await his reaction. Opening the envelope and removing the sheaf of celluloid contents, the ambassador let out a loud sigh, realizing that his weak attempt at subterfuge had been exposed.

"What are these?" he asked, playing dumb to the last and trying to forestall the inevitable.

"They are satellite photographs of a compound near Al B'ir in the northwestern part of your country. That's the place our combined intelligence services believe our men are being held," said Choate in a low, even voice. "But, if I may be frank Mr. Ambassador, we do not believe this can come as a complete surprise to you or your government. Yours is one of the finest intelligence services in the Middle East. Knowing what we do, we must believe that you have also known about this compound for some time," Choate followed up, ever the president's stalking-horse.

"What we don't understand sir, is why your forces have not yet moved against the terrorists. Could it have something to do with the involvement of young Tariq?" Sloan bore in.

"Mr. President," the Saudi exclaimed in *faux* affront, "I had hoped we would never speak of such delicate matters. You are accusing the son of the king's brother."

"We're not talking about anything that hasn't already made the newspapers in every major capital of the world," chided Secretary of State Trimble. "And while we might understand the king's reluctance to jeopardize his nephew's life, we face mounting political pressure here at home to bring this matter to a conclusion."

The ambassador slumped in his soft chair, looking for all the world like a helium-filled balloon whose contents had slowly ebbed away, collapsing him into nonentity. After a few moments of tense silence, he spoke.

"Our people in Riyadh are trying to reach the foolish young man through, as you Americans say, a 'back channel.' Their hope is to persuade him to extract himself from this unfortunate business before it becomes a complete catastrophe."

"What do you think the chances are of persuading him and, more importantly, how much time are you prepared to allow?" the DCI queried.

"On both counts, I don't know," shrugged the deflated Saudi diplomat.

"Then let me help you," the president said patronizingly. "I have ordered the U.S.S. Tarawa and its full battle group into the Red

Sea. Within twenty-four hours our ships will come to anchor in international waters, just off your coastline. Aboard the Tarawa is a detachment of our elite Delta Force commandos. They specialize in rescue missions like this one. With regret, I must inform you that unless, within the next forty-eight hours, Riyadh moves to recover those American hostages, I will reluctantly order our forces to do so. I offer you three options. One, you can move on Al B'ir yourselves. That is what we would really prefer. Two, you can invite us to do so, with the full blessing of Riyadh. Or three, your government can simply turn a blind eye while we go in and execute the rescue. But one way or the other, our men are coming home within the next two days.

"Mr. President, Mr. President," the ambassador agonized repetitiously, vigorously wringing his hands, "I fear for the state of relations between our two nations should you invade our territory and inadvertently kill a member of the royal family."

"That danger has not eluded me, sir. But I have run out of time – and options. If you have another proposal, I will be happy to listen," Sloan conceded.

Stroking his silver beard thoughtfully, the Saudi finally replied. "Let me consult with my government. Let us talk together about how to resolve this very ugly business in such a way that we may all preserve our interests."

"I shall await your government's reply with great interest," the president said, rising to indicate the end of the meeting. "But don't take too long, Mr. Ambassador. Don't take too long."

Tel Aviv, Israel, Ben Gurion Airport

Wells' warriors, looking convincingly like past their prime oilfield grunts, deplaned, and passed through neither the terminal itself, nor Israeli customs, but were shepherded by plain clothes operatives across the tarmac to a waiting propeller driven military transport aircraft where they loaded their gear quickly aboard. Zev Shalman was waiting inside, and greeted Curtis Wells with both a firm handshake and warm embrace before turning to the pilots with a whirling hand gesture indicating the order to take off.

"What news from my homeland?" asked Wells as soon as the plane was in the air.

"Your president has summoned the Saudi ambassador, who subsequently made several urgent calls to members of the royal family, including both the king and the king's brother. Also, our own intelligence tells us that the Tarawa has moved into the Red Sea," Shalman told him.

Sloan is trying to pressure the Saudis to go in," snarled Wells. "We have to assume that he's also given them the intel about the location of the hostages. There will probably be a deadline."

"That means time is short," observed the Israeli.

"Very," Wells agreed. "Assume the Tarawa is in strike position by midday tomorrow. The Pentagon isn't going to want that battle group sitting out there in the open where any fanatic with a motorboat and some Semtex can make a run at them. Not for long, at least. So the deadline is probably tomorrow night."

Quickly agreeing, Shalman added, "The Saudis will, of course, cave. They must. That means they will move against Al B'ir sometime between now and tomorrow night."

"That's it, then. We have to go tonight," said Stone who had now moved forward in the aircraft to join the conversation.

"Hey boys, we're in the deep shit now," shouted Bobby Hammack gleefully when he saw Curt Wells nod agreement.

While his men were primed for action and enthused about the mission, Curt Wells himself harbored a few nagging doubts. Two knuckles on his right hand were even now afflicted with the swelling induced by osteoarthritis. Although he worked out regularly, he knew that he could no longer run as fast, swim as far or even shoot as straight as he did in his SEAL days. Moreover, he suspected that the same was true of the rest. The fine physical, instinctual mental alertness and the clockwork tactical movements of the SEALs were all ingrained in men for a purpose. That purpose was to keep themselves – and each other – alive in situations where that outcome was anything but automatic. As he looked aft at the five familiar faces, he thought about the twenty-one successful missions they had completed together without a single casualty. He thought, too, about the many hours of fishing, hiking and hunting they had shared in the intervening years. It was, however, those intervening years that worried him. It had been twelve years since they had gone into combat together. What if they really were too old, too slow? What if one of them hesitated to pull the trigger, or forgot the battle plan? What if their survival instincts were not what they used to be? What if he got them all killed? What if he got killed?

Banishing his demons temporarily, he also thought about his son, Scott. What must he be going through at the hands of his captors? What would happen to him if the Saudi security forces invaded the compound at Al B'ir in a random hail of gunfire? What did it mean that these old men were his last, best hope of surviving, *if* they could get there first? Some of the others slept. But Curt Wells could not. Nor could he evade the realization that his flight from responsibility for the lives of others was, in the end, flight from himself. That weight seemed even heavier now.

Later, the Compound at Al B'ir

A door burst open, as Scott Wells and Marty Logan, unaccustomed to the bright cascade of sunlight that now flooded their prison, held shaky hands over their eyes.

"You, up," the young guard snapped at Logan.

As Logan got to his feet, the muzzle of an AK-47 was jammed into his back prodding him out the door. An improvised blindfold of black cloth was tied over his eyes, and he was pushed and pulled by unseen men in front of and behind him as he stumbled across an open area between the buildings. He heard another door open, tripped over a raised doorstep but was prevented from falling by his captors. Soon he was forced down into a creaky wooden chair and the blindfold removed. As his eyes adjusted to the dim light he saw a video camera with single, tripod-mounted spotlights on either side. A large, older man with a long, graying beard grabbed him by the hair, jerking his head to a position where he was looking almost straight up, and into the man's face.

"You will read this statement for the camera, infidel," the man barked harshly.

Logan looked at the sheet of paper placed in front of him as once again his eyes struggled to adjust. As near as he could tell, it was a propaganda statement decrying the evils of America and begging the president to negotiate for his life and that of Scott Wells. He closed his eyes and bowed his head.

"You will read now," snarled the older man, jerking his head up by his hair once again.

The two spotlights glared as the green light on the front of the camera flickered on, indicating that tape was rolling. Logan looked into the camera, a vacant smile on his face, and spoke.

"We, the people of the United States of America, in order to form a more perfect union, establish justice, ensure domestic tranquility, provide for the common defense ..."

Logan's recitation of the opening words of the preamble to the Constitution was cut short by the butt of a Kalashnikov rifle slamming forcefully into his right jaw, sending vivid shockwaves of pain shooting up into his head and downward as far as his shoulder, and causing the room and its occupants to spin crazily out of focus. Semi-conscious, he was dragged from the building, presumably by the same two who had brought him there. His awareness was confined to the throbbing pain in his jaw, and the gritty dust of the courtyard that choked his airways, matted on his profusely sweating body and dimmed his half open eyes. Kicking open the door of the makeshift cell, the men lifted him a few inches off the ground and pitched him into the room where he fell heavily in a disheveled heap.

"You," the younger of the two men shouted at Scott Wells, "up."

Once again the ritual was repeated and Wells, blindfold securely in place, was herded indelicately across the open yard toward a destination he could not see. Seated in the same rickety chair he, too, was confronted by the graybeard, who began by backhanding him across the face, striking him hard on his left cheek.

"Did you see your compatriot, infidel?" the man barked haughtily. "If so, you know what befalls those who do not do as they are told. We have a message prepared for your president. When I order you to do so, you will read it in front of the camera. Do you understand?" he emphasized the question by poking Wells sharply in the chest with his forefinger.

"I understand what you want me to do," Wells affirmed.

Again, the lights came on, the small green light flickered and the big man slapped him hard on the back of the neck.

"Read, infidel dog!"

Wells cleared his throat, looked straight into the camera, and began to speak.

"Fourscore and seven years ago, our fathers brought forth on this continent a new nation, conceived in liberty and dedicated to the proposition that all men are created equal."

There was a moment of disbelieving shock on the part of his captors as the utter defiance of their hostages fully sank in. Then a blunt instrument smashed into the side of Scott Wells' face, and his world went mercifully black.

Two hours later he awoke with a throbbing ache in his head and neck, the darkened room zooming in and out of focus. He was aware that he had been unconscious, but he had no idea how long he had been that way. Rising to his knees, he crawled to the basin of dirty water his captors had provided and splashed it liberally over his face, head and the back of his aching neck. Only then did he become aware of an animalistic groan from the opposite corner of the cell. It was Marty Logan. He lay curled up in a fetal ball, his swollen jaw badly discolored and his face a mask of pain.

Crawling to his stricken companion's side, Scott spoke in a low voice.

"Marty, it's me, Scott. Are you okay?"

It was a dumb question for a smart lawyer, but amid the grog of his own injury and concern for his friend and colleague, it was all that would come out. Getting up slowly, and moving tentatively on rubbery legs, he got a gourd full of water from the basin and poured it on Marty's face and head. He took a handkerchief from his own pocket, gently wiping away the caked dust from Logan's face and hair and trying to get a better view of his injury.

It was a strategy they'd agreed upon. They would refuse to

become instruments of the militants' propaganda nor, if it came to that, would they beg for their own lives. The Constitution and the Gettysburg Address were Wells' idea. Now he could not help but think how easy it was to have noble, brave ideas, yet how hard to pay the price for those ideas and how much harder see others you care about pay that price as well. For a long time the two of them lay there motionless, comforting one another through mere proximity. But both realized that hopes for a happy resolution to their captivity were rapidly ebbing away.

Central Oregon, the Lodge on the John Day

The fishing trip was progressing nicely. It was crisp, fall weather, but it was mostly sunny, and while they all wore heavy jackets and waders to protect them from the breezes and the cold water, they were having a blast. All of them took avidly to flyrodding, and with the likes of Jimmy Dunn and Anson Landis as instructors, were routinely throwing back the little ones.

Taking turns cooking, cleaning and chopping firewood, they had all the appearance of a group of fast friends enjoying the great outdoors and worshiping the gods of nature. There was an appropriate amount of ribbing and laughter, but when the flies were tied on and they scattered to their various fishing locations, everything got serious.

Truth to tell, their mood was already serious, for they all either knew or had guessed what the men they were impersonating were trying to do, and how much hung on the success of both. And they also knew that they were not alone. High on a bluff above, they could see two pitched navy blue tents. Sometimes they could see the flicker of lanterns at night, and occasionally the odor of whatever the FBI agents were cooking would waft down to them. But the accommodations were strikingly unequal. While the fishermen below stayed in a warm lodge in comfortable beds, or with their sleeping bags piled on either side of the see through central fireplace that heated the place, the agents above shivered in cramped tents, with little makeshift heaters they couldn't leave on all night. While they dined on fresh caught trout, smoked bacon and fluffy flapjacks with warm maple syrup, the FBI team ate whatever they could heat up out of cans.

Alex Geddes, the agent in charge of the surveillance team, was not a happy man. Peeved that Wells had initially given him the slip at Whispering Ridge, he joined the team belatedly, and was focusing on the man he believed to be Wells through his field glasses. The craggy bluff from which the surveillance was being conducted rose far too steeply and was too treacherous to accommodate a Bureau mobile unit, and that had left the team of watchers not only shy of amenities, but also somewhat technologically challenged. They were forced to conduct their surreptitious business the old-fashioned way.

"Call for you, Alex," said a tall, dark-haired agent, handing Geddes a cell phone.

"Geddes here," he said into the receiver.

"Alex, this is Assistant Director Grady Friese in Washington. The director wants an update on the surveillance. What's happening there?" said the all too cheerful bureaucrat on the other end, sitting in his toasty office and sipping hot coffee.

"They're all still down there," Geddes reported. "We see them coming and going from the river, usually with full stringers of fish. There are six of them, just like there are supposed to be."

"And Wells too?" questioned Friese.

"Yeah, he's there too. We always recognize him by his floppy hat with the trout flies on it," replied Geddes.

"Have you gotten the photos of all six yet?" Friese persisted.

"Right, we have digital images, but no hard copy," Geddes complained.

"So, I assume you've made positive facial ID on all six," said Friese.

"Well, uh, not exactly," Geddes answered haltingly. "You see, it's chilly here and when they come out, they're all bundled up and wearing sunglasses. We watch them through the binoculars and keep a head count, and we observe whether anyone leaves. No one has left so far, so we know that everyone who came in that van is still here. And we don't have electronic surveillance capacity here yet."

"But you can't say with one hundred percent certainty that these six are Wells and his old SEAL buddies?" asked the suddenly concerned assistant director.

"They all match up to the physical descriptions, and we think we know who was in the van. The only way to know for sure is to go down there and talk to them, and that's going to be hard to do," reported Geddes.

"Why will it be so hard?" asked Friese naively.

"What am I going to do? Shall I knock on the door of their lodge and take roll? Shall I take our digital images and ask them to line up so we can be sure each of them is accounted for. They already know we're watching them. How much more obvious do you want us to be? We don't really have any probable cause – none, at least, that would stand up in court – for searching or detaining them. Impersonating a retired Navy man is not a crime, so long as they're not applying for veterans' benefits," Geddes whined.

"Special Agent Geddes," Friese intoned imperiously, "the president wants to know for sure that we're watching the right men. I know you'll find a way to give him that assurance - *today*. Call me back when you have something to report."

As contact was abruptly broken, Geddes raised his field glasses and scanned the campsite below. Nothing was moving. How was he going to give Washington the assurance they were seeking? Then an idea came to him.

Moshe Dayan Military Command, Eilat, Israel

Wells' commandos sat in the squat metal building, huddled around a crude *papier mache* mock up of the Al B'ir compound. Curt Wells spoke in hushed tones as he outlined their battle plan. Shalman had just heard from his contacts in Saudi Arabia that the Tarawa was nearly in striking range, several hours ahead of time. Threatened by imminent U.S. military action, the Saudis were marshaling their own security forces at a military encampment twenty kilometers northwest of Ha'il. Israeli intelligence estimates were that a dawn strike against Al B'ir was likely in order to preempt direct American intervention. Given the clumsiness of such Saudi rescue attempts in the past, the Israeli operatives gave the hostages less than a twenty-five per cent chance of surviving the incursion.

"We'll leave here in less than four hours by chopper, flying low over the Gulf of Aqaba under the Saudi radar, and helicast into the surf here, about ten clicks north of Tabuk. We'll have to hike about two clicks inland to a road, here," Wells said, indicating a spot on the map. "Zev's Mossad guys will meet us with a truck that's been rigged to look like a Saudi military transport. They'll drop us less than two clicks from the compound, and we'll hump it on in. It will be dark, so we'll need our night vision gear. Clear so far?" he asked, pausing, as heads nodded all around.

"There are four buildings and one small shack which, we think, doubles as a station for on duty guards and a communications center. According to the eyes on the ground, there are five or six guards on duty all the time. One or two stay in the shack and man the radio or whatever form of communication they're using, while four walk patrol. They patrol in an 'x' pattern, pacing the compound diagonally, circling outside the buildings, re-entering the main courtyard and then reversing the pattern so that they virtually pass each other in the middle. The best time to get them will be while they're on the outside, between the rear of the buildings and the desert. We'll use silencers and knives, keeping it quiet all the way. Zev will eliminate one of the guards with his silenced sniper rifle. Denver, you, Marco and I will take the other three. Bobby, you and Mack will take out the guard shack and disable their communications, then set up a defensive perimeter to the northeast just in case the Saudis should arrive ahead of schedule."

"Question," said Bobby Hammack. "Where are the hostages?"

"We believe that two of them, probably Scott and Marty Logan, are in this building about thirty meters from the guard station. Aaron, if he's still alive, is being held separately, probably in the building next door. The long, low building at the end is where the terrorists seem to eat and sleep. They'll pose the greatest danger, so while Zev, Bart and I go for the hostages, Sean, Denver and Marco will break into the barracks, frag the place and then hose it down room to room. Remember, if there are survivors, and they make us as Americans, the international ramifications will be enormous," Wells said earnestly.

"The firefight has to be over in five minutes. If it isn't, we stand a chance of losing the hostages," he added emphatically.

"There will, of course, be guards with the hostages," Stone cautioned.

"Correct," agreed Wells. "The two buildings where we assume the hostages are being kept are very crude, just oversized outbuildings really, with no windows. We doubt the doors have mechanical locks, and so we have to depend upon surprise to break in and kill the guards before they can harm the hostages. The way we have it figured, there are only about seventeen men in the compound at any one time. That leaves five or six man shifts. So the hostages won't be watched directly by more than one or two at the most, and some of the terrorists will likely be asleep. We just have to be quick and sure. And those of you who will attack the big building can't start shooting until we've secured the hostages and taken out their guards. Clear?"

"Clear," six voices affirmed in chorus.

"Look at this picture carefully," Wells said, holding up a tattered photo of an Arab with a long gray beard. "This man is Muhammad al-Shariyah, who we think masterminded the kidnapping. Our Israeli friend here," he continued, patting Zev Shalman on the shoulder, "has the unique mission of dispatching him. But if you run into him first, kill the bastard on sight. Just like everybody else, he dies. Shoot him one extra time just to be sure!"

"What about this Tariq character?" Bryson inquired. "Do we kill him too?"

"I'm afraid so, if he's there" Wells answered. "His death will cause the biggest stir, but he also poses the biggest threat to us, since he is possibly the best educated of the lot and might be able to identify us to the Saudis."

"Let's hope Allah is well-stocked with virgins," Creel snickered. "If they get seventy apiece in paradise there's going to be a serious run on girls in the morning."

"That's if they *go* to paradise," chided Garrity. "Personally, I was planning on sending them the other direction."

"One more thing," added Wells. "If I go down, Major Stone will assume command. The hostages are the first priority, then our own wounded, if any."

"Weapons," announced Shalman unceremoniously, sliding two wooden crates out from under a low table. "Brand new AK-74 assault rifles, thirty round magazines, fire up to six hundred fifty rounds per minute, effective range, five hundred meters. These were manufactured in Bulgaria and designed to accommodate 5.56 NATO ammunition. There are six extra magazines for each weapon. Sidearms are mix and match Tokarev 7.62's and Glock 26's. We have silencers and night sights for the Glocks. Each man will have four fragmentation grenades, two smokers and one phosphorous. All the weapons are untraceable and none are manufactured in the United States or Israel except for this," he sighed, proudly holding up his Israeli made Galil SR 99 sniper rifle with telescopic sight and silencer. "This is for longer distance work."

The old soldiers sounded like a bunch of giddy children around a Christmas tree as they fondled the weapons, sliding out the magazines and checking the actions. Wells distributed the body armor and Shalman handed each man a set of night vision goggles. The equipment was state-of-the-art, just as the wily old Israeli agent had promised. Then he raised his hands for quiet and spoke again.

"My mission, as my friend Wells told you, is to kill Muhammad al-Shariyah, who masterminded the kidnapping. Our agents have seen him at Al B'ir, although he doesn't always stay there. If you see him first, kill him and save me the trouble. If he is not at Al B'ir, well, that will be my problem," he said solemnly.

"Put any remaining personal identifiers in here," Wells said, producing the rectangular metal ammunition box. "They will remain at Eilat and you can collect them when we return. We go in about three hours, so get your gear stowed in the chopper. We'll hit fast, snatch the hostages and kill everybody else, in and out. Everybody comes home."

Early Afternoon, the John Day River

Alex Geddes was a solid veteran FBI field agent, but he was no woodsman. His silly corduroy hat kept catching in the low hanging branches of the brushy young cedars, and though he was trying his best to be stealthy, a deaf man could have heard him trampling the twigs and leaves of the forest's floor a hundred yards away. He'd decided that the best way to see if Wells and his men really were the men they were watching was to go down and confront them. Suddenly, as he advanced on the lodge, he heard a voice with a soft drawl coming from behind him.

"You just freeze right where you are, mister. Are you lost or somethin'?"

Geddes turned slowly around to find himself looking directly down the twin barrels of a shotgun held by Jimmy Dunn.

"Uh, yes, er, I mean, no," Geddes stammered. "I'm looking for Curtis Wells."

"Who shall I say wants him?" Dunn inquired skeptically. "Easy now," Dunn added as Geddes reached into the outside breast pocket of his jacket to produce his FBI badge and credential.

"Special Agent Alex Geddes," he said, holding the badge out for Dunn to inspect.

"F-B-I, as I live and breathe," Dunn remarked with a distinct sarcasm. "And just what would you be wanting with Mr. Wells? He's kind of busy right now," Dunn said, his words oozing a skepticism bordering on contempt.. "You see, trout fishing is a religion with him. Just like you wouldn't want somebody messin' with you while you're in church, he doesn't take much to people who interrupt his fishing. Maybe I could tell him what you want." Dunn's voice trailed off.

"Just who are you?" Geddes demanded, trying desperately to regain control of the situation.

"My name is Jimmy Dunn, and I would be the one tellin' you that unless you've got a warrant, Curtis Wells ain't gonna give you the time of day," the old sailor barked defiantly.

"I can get a warrant, if that's what it takes," Geddes promised unyieldingly.

"You know," mused Dunn aloud, "I don't think so, since you've got no probable cause to believe any crime is being committed here. But if you do get one, if I was you I'd show up at the front gate and present it all nice and proper, so's I didn't get a load of double-ought up my backside. Just now, I'd be obliged if you got your clumsy feet and skinny ass back up that trail and out of here before I get nervous and decide to shoot me a trespasser."

Frustrated in his purpose, and never having made face-to-face contact with Curtis Wells, Geddes wheeled and moved away, muttering under his breath. But his little sortie accomplished one thing. The man wearing a cast on his foot and wielding a shotgun was definitely Petty Officer James Dunn, USNR. He quickly pulled out and looked at the electronic picture he had received to verify it. If Dunn was here, there was a better than average chance the others were as well. And that, Geddes decided, is what he was going to report to Washington.

Washington, The White House Situation Room

"Please sit," President Norman Sloan said to his cabinet members absently as he entered the room. "Emmett, give us an updated situation report."

The DCI shifted uncomfortably in his chair, cleared his throat and spoke slowly.

"Intelligence – both satellite and ground – indicates that the hostages are still at the Al B'ir compound. The Saudi security forces seem to be marshaling an assault force in a location that is about an hour distant by helicopter. Everything we know suggests they plan to hit the compound in the morning," Choate said.

"Where is the Tarawa battle group now, Admiral?" Sloan turned to his senior naval advisor.

"In position, in international waters off the Saudi coast," the gruff admiral replied.

"Who is in command there?" Sloan persisted.

"Rear Admiral Garth Mahorn," came the response.

"Can I talk to him?" the president wanted to know.

"Yes, Sir, he's standing by right now," came the answer.

"Good. Put him on speaker," ordered Sloan.

A static click followed by a low hum filled the room.

"Admiral Mahorn, this is the president. Can you hear me?"

"Five-by-five, Sir," Mahorn replied.

"Good. Admiral, I want you to prepare your hostage rescue team for an extraction. If things go according to plan, Saudi authorities will notify us that the hostages are safe, and your people will be given Saudi permission to go in and pick them up. Should the Saudis fail to act promptly, your mission will be a different one, along the lines prescribed in your earlier operating orders. Do you understand?" Sloan asked, wanting no unclarity between them.

"I understand, Sir," Mahorn confirmed.

"But you are to undertake an uninvited rescue incursion into Saudi territory only if and when you receive that order directly from me. Are we clear on that point?" the president asked emphatically.

"Crystal clear, Sir," came the muted response from the carrier.

"Thank you, Admiral. We will be in touch," Sloan promised, breaking the connection.

CHAPTER TEN

The Gulf of Aqaba, 1900 Hours GMT

Shimmering below them were the blue-green, placid waters of the Gulf. They rode in virtual silence, each man alone with his thoughts about the operation to come. They were clad in reversible battle dress, the black side out, for it would be dark when they hit the beach. Zev Shalman rose and moved purposefully toward the cockpit.

Their chariot of chance was an American made Blackhawk UH-70. Wells found it amusing that a machine the Americans had sold the Israelis was now being used to frustrate America's confused foreign policy. The chopper's powerful 2000shp engine moved the craft effortlessly through the still night air. Hovering just sixty feet above the water to stay under the radar. They gave the Tarawa battle group a wide berth, so as to arouse no suspicion, but that was easy since the American ships were moored over fourteen miles out, and slightly south of Tabuk. They might be picked up by the sophisticated American surveillance gear, to be sure, but since they did not approach or threaten the ships in the armada, would most likely be written off as a harmless commercial flight. The Saudis, on the other hand, would never see them coming at this altitude. Shalman returned and bent close to Curtis Wells.

"Surveillance says that the Tarawa has not moved for hours.

They have a squadron of armed fighter planes on the deck, but that appears to be solely defensive. There is no visible activity above decks," he said.

"The Tarawa is a trump card for the Saudis to see, not for Sloan to play. He's badgering them into moving on Al B'ir. Can your people patch into our comm link if they do launch an assault force?" Wells inquired.

"Absolutely," Shalman assured him.

"If and when they do, we'll stand down. Otherwise we go. Do you agree?" Wells asked.

No further words needed, Shalman gave a single, meaningful nod.

"Ten minutes to insertion," the pilot shouted, looking back at the huddled commandos behind him.

The White House

Norman Sloan looked out across the north lawn where massed demonstrators besieged his seat of government throughout the day prior. He wondered what other presidents might have thought about such a volume of dissent, and how they would have chosen to handle the current crisis. Given the choice, his preference was to come out of this mess a hero to the nation that elected him. But the more he thought about what was playing out in Saudi Arabia, the more he feared that he stood to be universally blamed for the deaths of the three Americans. It was a lose-lose situation for him.

A knock on the door signaled the imminent entrance of his chief of staff.

"Kendrick says that Wells and his men *are* on that river in Oregon, sir," Ken Karns reported.

"I guess that's good," Sloan mused. "But I confess that a part of me is disappointed. I found myself hoping that somebody with a semblance of competence would try a rescue, but as the head of our government, my hands are tied. I guess Wells decided against trying it. I'm afraid that what's about to happen over there is more like an execution than a rescue."

"We have to hope for the best, sir," Karns counseled.

"What do I do to keep this from happening again next week, Ken? What's our guarantee that these nut cases aren't just going to keep on kidnapping and bombing and murdering until they get what they want?" the president reflected bleakly.

"I guess there are no guarantees, Mr. President," Karns shrugged.

"No, there aren't," Sloan responded decisively. "So what can I say to the American people to assuage their fears about traveling abroad? Do I say, 'oh, we'll send in the military to get you out *unless* we would offend one of our allies by doing so – or *unless* it threatens our flow of oil'? Is that what I say to them?"

"You can't say that, Sir?" the chief of staff cautioned.

"That's ironic, Ken," Sloan shot back. "I can't say it, but everyone with a lick of sense knows it's true. I wonder what the Saudis would really do if I gave Delta Force the green light?"

"But you already promised them time to resolve this on their own," Karns protested. "They would react badly if you reneged."

"Of course, you're right. The problem is that I feel like I've made a deal with the devil, and wasted the lives of three innocent Americans in the process. I'm not sure how I live with that," Sloan said, pacing again.

"Presidents have to make difficult decisions, and sometimes the national interest supersedes the interests of individual citizens," Karns philosophized.

"Uh-huh," Sloan said, almost under his breath. "I think I'll let you explain that to the three mothers at the funerals."

Whispering Ridge, Oregon

One of the mothers, Molly Wells, tried to stay busy, hurrying about household chores, putting fresh linens on Tyler's bed and becoming absorbed in a cookbook. Anything would do, if it kept her mind from the deadly danger surrounding her eldest son and her husband. But nothing really seemed to work, and she found her mind straying not only to their predicament, but to what Miriam Saperstein and Mary Logan might be thinking and feeling just now. She thought about calling them, then realized she couldn't because of who might be listening.

Like most mothers, she didn't really think of her sons first of all as young men. When she thought about them, their faces as babies and as toddlers were the first visions to appear. The memories of their happy childhoods came rushing back like a flood. The cuts and scrapes, the ball games, the report cards, the first prom. They would always be children in her mind.

She was a strong woman, and when Curt was gone on extended assignments, she was always able to protect them, listen to them, advocate for them. Then, when at long last he came home, they bonded again as a family and it was like he'd never been away. The boys worshiped their father. She knew that, and it was okay, because in a way she worshiped him too.

She had been an eighteen-year-old waitress in a truck stop near Leesburg, Virginia, when this handsome young sailor, all dressed out in his Navy whites, had ambled in and ordered breakfast. At the time it seemed to her that he was drinking an awful lot of coffee, but then it dawned on her that the coffee refills were just a pretext for conversation. He came in again, and again, and conversation soon led to the first date. She never again looked seriously at another man, nor he another woman. They quickly became true soul mates. Fourteen months after they married, Scott was born. What a day that was. The first time Curt held the baby she laughed at him because he acted as though he was handling something breakable. She was flabbergasted when he requested a leave from duty to care for Scott while she regained her strength, and at the conscientious vigor with which he took to fatherhood. It was a time of happiness, of bonding, of one family's joy.

Even though Molly knew Curt was in a dangerous line of work, she never thought much about what she would do if the worst happened. She was close to the wives of the other SEAL team members, but no one talked about the dark side. They always just supported one another, and eventually welcomed their men home again.

After he joined the CIA, he rarely spoke about his work, and she didn't pry, didn't really want to know. They never were in a situation he didn't seem to know how to handle, and her faith in him was complete. They rarely fought, but when they did it was usually over some dangerous or open-ended deployment. Somehow she just knew he would always come home, because he just had to. And he always did.

But she had a different feeling about this job - this most important mission of his entire life. He was older, maybe mellowing out and slowing down a bit. If he, or the others with him had lost their edge, if they were just a hair slow to react, the slightest bit indecisive, if they couldn't see or hear as well, or move as fast as they used to, well, this time could be the last.

No! She couldn't entertain that, couldn't think it, couldn't feel it, couldn't doubt him. He would come home. He would bring Scott and the others home. She would will it so, and he would do it. He would do it for her, and for his family. At seven, she would pick Tyler up at the airport. Tyler was strong. He would help her to be stronger even than she already was.

The Blackhawk, Just Off the Saudi Coastline

When the green light came on, Wells didn't have to say a word. Everyone was up and ready, and at about eight feet above the lapping surf they jumped, one at a time, feet first. They were a scant twenty yards offshore, and the water depth was just three to four feet. In less than five minutes they were on the beach, forming a crouched semi-circle in the failing light, facing inland. Their eyes swept the terrain in every direction for any sign of danger, but nothing moved.

As soon as they hit the water, the chopper pivoted and headed northwest, away from the coastline and the ominous American armada. Now, Wells ordered a weapons check, and directed Creel to connect and activate the wireless electronic network by which they would communicate with one another. Silently indicating their direction of march by a hand signal, he ordered Bobby Hammack to move out on the point, with the others following at safe intervals.

They moved slowly, cautiously, and in about an hour were a hundred meters west of the road where Shalman's contact was supposed to be waiting. Shalman knelt alongside Hammack, and taking a small flashlight from his pocket, emitted a single, short beam of light. Presently, he was answered by two longer flashes.

"Come on," he said, "this way."

He led them across a shallow ditch and up the short embankment on its far side. There, among some scrubby bushes, was a truck with a camouflage tarpaulin thrown over it. A man got out carrying some kind of automatic weapon and said something to Shalman that the others did not understand. Then, suddenly, there was another man, also armed and behind them. These were obviously skilled covert Israeli operatives who were taking no chances. Shalman pulled back the tarpaulin exposing the cargo hold of the truck.

"In," he said simply, motioning to the others.

They climbed aboard, and immediately the truck's engine roared to life as the big vehicle rumbled away down the bumpy road. Each man strapped his night vision goggles on, the lenses resting on their foreheads, and checked headsets to be sure they were all working properly. It was almost completely dark outside and there was no one else on the road.

When they turned east toward Al B'ir, Zev Shalman faced Wells, who was sitting next to him in the back of the truck. "We'll be close in just over an hour. If you have second thoughts, there is still time to go home," he said gravely, staring out into the night.

"Not without Sunny," Wells answered quietly. "We're going all the way."

Mack Bryson, sitting on Wells' other side grasped him firmly above the knee and squeezed gently, affirming the support they all owed and willingly gave this man who had led them into and safely out of danger on so many occasions gone by. Little else was said as the truck bumped and jostled its way along the uneven, pitted thoroughfare that passed for a road.

At twenty one hundred hours GMT, the truck ground to a halt. The driver got out and motioned to the men in back, and they were soon moving away from the road on foot. The truck and the Israeli agents opted to venture no closer to the compound now, but promised, once the danger was eliminated, to appear on site to extract the team, along with the hostages.

Twenty-four hundred hours came as Wells and his men reached the site. Hammack inched his way slowly to the top of a large dune where, with his night vision goggles, he could look down on the compound. He stared for a full two minutes through the infrared lenses that bathed everything in an eerie pale green, then motioned for the others to stay where they were. He crawled back to Wells and Shalman and whispered.

"We've got a little surprise, fellas. Instead of four guards prowling outside, they've got eight. That means there's never a time when somebody isn't in that main yard between the buildings," he said. "That'll make it tougher."

Wells motioned to the others to retreat back down the dune so they could re-think the strike plan.

"We've got eight outside, instead of four. And we don't know who's in the guard shack. If we don't take them all down quietly, we could lose the hostages. So here's what we'll do. Bobby, you're going to have to take the guard shack and whoever's in it by yourself. We'll wait until four of the guards are outside on the perimeter. Mack, Denver, Sean and Marco will each take one – knives only, no sound. Bart and I will screw the silencers onto our Glocks and crawl down close enough to take out two of the guys in the yard, while Zev sits on the side of this dune and picks off the other two with his silenced Galil. As soon as we know all eight guards are down, Bart and I will go straight for the hostages, while Marco, Denver, Mack and Sean assault the garrison. If they've got more than we expected outside, they may have more than we expected in there, too. Bobby, when the guard shack is neutralized, look sharp and back up whoever looks like they need it. Zev, hump it down the dune after you do your two in the yard and help us get the hostages. Everyone clear?"

Heads nodded. "On my 'go,'" added Wells, before slithering away into the night, with Stone so close the two looked attached.

Timing was going to be everything, Wells knew. No matter how long it took, they needed to wait until at least four of the guards were patrolling out of view of the open area between the buildings. Since these were not highly disciplined soldiers, trained in precise and regular movements, their pattern would likely be ragged, uneven. And the longer the intruders waited to attack, the greater the chance they would be discovered, or that someone would inadvertently make some noise that gave them away.

It took nearly thirty minutes for Wells and Stone to work their way into position, about twenty feet deep in the shadows outside the perimeter, but well within range for the Glocks. It was hot and sticky this night, and both men were sweating profusely. Zev Shalman took considerably less time to find a suitable place of concealment on the down slope of the big dune, and now he moved the crosshairs on his night scope slowly from one pacing guard to the next.

At 0115 hours they got their first break. Four guards moved into the empty alleys between buildings and toward the outer perimeter in virtual unison, while two leaned aimlessly against the building housing Scott Wells and Marty Logan, and two stopped dead center in the open yard to chat and smoke. Wells signaled to Stone to take one of the smokers, while he targeted the other.

"Go in five seconds on my mark," Wells said softly into the microphone on his headset, "mark."

Counting slowly and to themselves, he and Stone assumed firing positions. Only a split second separated the soft pops of the silenced Glocks, and the two smokers fell dead on top of one another. Shalman dropped the guard nearest the hostage building with a single head shot, and when the third, sensing that an attack was in process, began to run for the main barracks, he caught a round squarely between the shoulder blades and dropped quietly into the dusty, sandy courtyard.

Meanwhile Creel, Lopez, Garrity and Bryson, their field knives in hand, soundlessly eliminated their assigned targets as they passed behind the buildings. There had been almost no sound, and eight terrorists were stone cold dead.

Looking cautiously about, Stone and Wells first trotted, then broke into a sprint in the direction of the hostage building, while Hammack stealthily approached the guard shack. Quietly, the latter grasped the makeshift handle and eased the door open. A single guard sat in front of an older model cellular phone on a wooden table. Hammack was on him in a second, cutting his throat in a single, practiced move. Nine down. So far, so good.

Commandos are trained to expect the unexpected, and just as he got ready to exit the guard shack, out of the corner of his eye Hammack saw another terrorist leaving the outhouse, zipping up his pants as he went. Suspecting nothing at first, the man stared at the ground as he walked in the general direction of the barracks. As he passed the partially open door he asked, in Arabic, if everything was quiet. Hammack considered not answering, but knew instinctively that doing so would surely invite further inquiry.

"Yalla hala'am," he said in a muffled voice, indicating all clear.

The terrorist took four more steps before realizing that he didn't recognize the voice coming from inside the shack. The words were right, but something was amiss. Unholstering a sidearm, he wheeled and headed back in the direction from which he had come. When he pulled open the door, he caught a full four round burst in the chest from Hammack's unsilenced Kalashnikov, killing him instantly, but alerting the rest of the complex that an attack was in progress.

With that the door of the hostage house opened and a man burst through the aperture, firing wildly into the night. Stone, already behind him shot him cleanly behind the right ear, dropping him in his tracks. By the time Wells rushed in, the other guard inside had retrieved his Scorpion and trained it on the menacing figure rushing through the door.

Curt Wells froze momentarily, seeing that the terrorist had him dead to rights when suddenly a large bulky figure hurtled out of the shadows leveling the guard with a wicked cross body block. Separated from his weapon, the guard flailed wildly to regain his advantage when he caught a 7.62 slug from Curt Wells' Glock right in the belly. Screaming in pain, he pitched to the floor, writhed momentarily, then lay still. Scott "Sunny" Wells' high school football training had just saved his father's life.

Seeing Scott bound and bruised caused an enormous surge of grief to rise within Curt Wells. He wanted to run to his son, cut him free of his bonds, put his arms around him and never let go. But he could not. This was not over, and for the sake of his men and the hostages he had to remain focused, anonymous, professional. Saying not a word, he motioned with his gun for the hostages to get down.

Meanwhile, Shalman broke into the building next door, hoping to find Aaron Saperstein. Instead, he found what looked like an empty single room, no guard, and no hostage. With his flashlight in one hand and Tokarev in the other, he swept the room. Seeing nothing, he was about to join the battle outside, and then he heard a low moan. Shifting his light quickly in the direction from which the sound had come, he saw a twisted body in a darkened corner. Approaching, gun at the ready, he pulled away a small tarpaulin under which lay the tightly manacled, but very much alive Aaron Saperstein. Saperstein whimpered as the light assaulted his eyes, held his hands up defensively over his face and curled tight into a fetal ball.

"It's all right, son. You're going home," Shalman said gently.

At first, Saperstein did not react, could not seem to comprehend what was happening, or move on his own. As Shalman ran the light up and down his body, he could see why. The young man had been severely and repeatedly beaten, and had massive bruises on his face, neck, arms, chest and legs. He was wearing nothing but shorts and a sleeveless undershirt. Zev Shalman gritted his teeth and cursed. He had seen this too many times before. Withdrawing his field knife, he slashed through the shackles that bound the young lawyer.

"Can you stand? Can you walk?" he pressed.

Saperstein nodded affirmation, but when he tried to stand collapsed again in a heap. Lifting him gently, and getting one of the younger man's arms around his neck and shoulder, Shalman got him up, and together they shuffled out the door and toward the other hostage building.

By now, a furious firefight had begun at the barracks. As soon as the shooting started, Lopez and Creel had lobbed fragmentation grenades through uncovered windows and into the building, killing or wounding everyone in the main dining area. But others

129

in the sleeping quarters, had roused, armed themselves and begun a steady patter of automatic weapons fire. Kicking in the flimsy door, Lopez and Bryson stormed inside, hosing the interior and everything that moved with a withering barrage of bullets. From the outside, Creel and Garrity returned fire from any window with an active sniper. Opposing fire had almost completely died away when a single shot ripped through the night, tearing into the flesh of Creel's left thigh, and sending him down with a grimace and a cry of pain. Hammack, who had sprinted across the compound to join the battle, saw the lone remaining sniper on the roof and nearly cut him in half with a long burst from his Kalashnikov.

When Shalman reached Wells, Stone and the other two hostages, he found them staring at one another in silence.

"Aaron?" said Scott Wells, appalled at the bruised visage of his friend.

"Help him," ordered Shalman, motioning Wells and Stone out of the building, and transferring Aaron's weight to Scott and Marty Logan.

At that moment, two vehicles rolled into the compound. One, Curt Wells recognized as the truck that brought them here. The other was a beat up old panel truck and both he and Stone swung their weapons instinctively toward it from the doorway.

"No," shouted Shalman. "It's one of ours."

Re-entering the building, he spoke to the three hostages, mincing no words.

"We have come to rescue you," he said, stating the obvious. "You need to go outside and get into the black panel truck you see there. Get into the back and lie down. Do not attempt to speak to the driver."

"Who are you, and where are we going?" Scott Wells asked shakily.

"It is better for you not to know who we are. And wherever we are going is better than here, yes?" Shalman asked rhetorically.

Just outside, they saw the two masked intruders who entered their building standing watch. Hesitating, Scott Wells stared for a long moment at one of the masked men standing guard. There was something about him, something very familiar. There were also several similarly masked men dragging bodies from the open courtyard into the now quiet barracks building. Marty Logan tugged urgently at Scott's arm, and together they made for the truck, dragging the stricken Saperstein with them.

As they got in and closed the rear door, Shalman motioned to Curtis Wells and Stone.

"We need to be out of here in five minutes," he said. "It will be best if we burn the buildings and the bodies, burn everything."

Wells, nodding agreement, started off in the direction of the barracks, then turned to Shalman.

"The guard inside is still alive. He's gut shot, and I think he's the royal nephew."

Frowning beneath his mask, Shalman turned on his heels and headed back into the hostage building again. Approaching the wounded terrorist, he turned him over, appraised his wound and spoke.

"You are going to die, my young terrorist friend. The blood from your abdomen is black. That means a bullet has penetrated your liver. If you tell me what I want to know, I will end your suffering mercifully. Otherwise, I will leave you to Allah's mercy," his voice trailed off as Tariq bin Saud moaned.

"Where is Muhammad al-Shariyah?" Shalman demanded harshly.

"Tabuk, he is in Tabuk. Go there and you will die, American," spat the dying young royal, nearly delirious with pain.

"Very well," sighed Shalman. "May you find peace with Allah, my foolish young fellow," he added quietly, just before putting a bullet from his Tokarev into the man's brain.

Hammack found two partially full five-gallon gas cans, and dousing the buildings liberally he and the others set them ablaze with the phosphorous grenades. Into the main building, Bryson pitched the satchel of Semtex with a fifteen second time fuse detonator attached.

The White House Situation Room, Washington

"What is it?" asked President Sloan, as he entered the room, still buttoning a rumpled sport shirt.

"We thought you should see this, sir," said DCI Emmett Choate. "This is being shot in real time by one of our birds over Al B'ir."

On a large monitor they could see the buildings of the hostage compound engulfed by flames shooting forty feet into the air. A major explosion rocked the biggest building. Small figures stood around two vehicles, apparently watching the conflagration.

"The Saudis?" Sloan asked soberly.

"We don't think so, sir," said the laconic Choate. "They are apparently still staging in Ha'il."

"I specifically told Admiral Mahorn to wait for my order," snapped Sloan irascibly.

"It's not us either, Mr. President," said General Conrad Blaisdell. "The Tarawa is all buttoned down."

"Well, if it's not us, and it's not the Saudis, then who the hell is it?" National Security Advisor Ethan Ellis demanded.

"Curtis Wells, that's who," smirked Sloan, shaking his head.

"But Wells is fishing in Oregon," Chief of Staff Ken Karns reminded them.

"Want to bet your job on that, do you, Ken?" Sloan cracked sarcastically. "I think Kendrick's FBI people have some explaining to do."

"If it is Wells, he's decided to leave no evidence and no survivors," Choate said. "Look at that place burn!"

"I wonder if the hostages are alive or dead?" Ellis mused distantly.

"I wonder if the damned royal nephew is alive or dead?" Sloan barked, raising his voice.

"If he was there, I'd say the chances of him having survived are nil," Choate opined. "You know you're going to get a call either from Riyadh or from the Saudi ambassador here, don't you?"

"No shit, Sherlock," intoned Blaisdell snidely.

"It'll take the Saudis some time to get there, and even more to figure out just what happened. There won't be much left to work with. They've been shadowing our battle group, and they'll know we haven't launched anything. They're going to be even more confused than we are," Choate observed analytically. "I hope Wells has an extraction plan."

"Well of course he has an extraction plan, Emmett. Do you think he's just going to hang around there and wait for the Saudis to pick him up?" Sloan demanded impatiently.

"The question is, what are we going to do?" Blaisdell sighed.

"Absolutely nothing, that's what we're going to do. We have to wait until the hostages surface, *if* they do," Sloan said. "The ball is really in the Saudis' court now."

"What if they apprehend Wells and his people before they get out?" Ellis sounded worried.

"Based on what we know of Wells at this point, I'd say that if he doesn't want to be caught, the whole Saudi security service won't be able to find him," chuckled Choate.

"I'm glad you find this amusing, Emmett. I have a headache," said the president as he rose to leave the room.

The Inferno at Al B'ir

The whole compound was consumed by flames as Zev Shalman approached Curt Wells.

"Get in the truck and go. When you get to the coastline our men will show you where the boats are. Get into them and head straight out to sea. It is imperative that you get as far out as possible before daylight," he said, a sudden urgency in his demeanor.

"Where do you think you're going?" Wells asked, believing he already knew.

"Your mission is complete, my old friend. But mine is not. I must go to Tabuk, find and kill al-Shariyah," Shalman replied fatalistically. "Take this locator," he said, handing Wells a compact black device the size of a remote garage door opener. "When you get well offshore, push the red button to activate it. Keep moving out to sea and our ship will find you."

Wells stared at Shalman in silence for a moment. This was a man who had gone to extraordinary lengths to help him save his

133

son. Now he asked to be abandoned to his fate, an Israeli assassin in a hostile Arab state. Furthermore, while Wells knew and trusted Shalman, he did not know the anonymous drivers of the getaway vehicles. What guarantee was there that if they were stopped they would not choose to save their own lives and leave the hostages to the wolves. He had come this far to see his son safely out of danger. He could not leave the final leg of the journey to chance, or to strangers.

"No," he said firmly. "You know the terrain, the drivers, the people on the ship, and I don't. You go with the hostages, and I will go for al-Shariyah."

"I cannot ask that of you, my dear friend. It is my duty," Shalman protested.

"You didn't ask. I volunteered," Wells replied. "You just get my boy safely out of here. Al-Shariyah will be dead by dawn. Tell me how to find him."

Shalman hesitated, then took a map from his pocket and began to draw on the blank side. "Take the jeep over there," he said, pointing to one of the terrorist vehicles. "When you get back to the main road, follow us in the trucks until the road branches. Take the left branch and it will lead you straight into Tabuk. Park well on the outskirts. You will be less than a hundred meters from al-Shariyah's mosque and home when you enter the town."

All the time Shalman was talking he drew a precise diagram of the street where al Shariyah lived and all of the buildings on it.

"There are, or used to be, large sand hills here, and here," he added, indicating two different spots on the crude drawing. From one, you will have a clear view of his house. Just remember, he will have bodyguards, probably a lot of them. From the other hill you will have a clear view of the mosque. If he delivers the morning call to prayer in person, you might be able to get him then. You'll need this," he said, handing over the Galil.

"Afterwards, don't make for the sea. An hour after the Saudis figure out what has happened here, the coastline will be swarming with patrol boats and there will be soldiers watching the coast everywhere. The Jordanian border is just less than ninety-nine kilometers due north of Tabuk. That's about sixty-two of your miles. When it's over, take the jeep and drive north into the Hijaz. Get rid of the jeep. Stay to the east side of the escarpment, and make your way on foot. Do not go down into the valley. The area around Wadi Aziz is full of al Qaeda, and when news of al-Shariyah's assassination is circulated, they'll be after you, too. Remember, there are over eight thousand Saudi troops based in the region. They will be alerted. If you can cross over into Jordan, you should be safe. Head due west to the Israeli-Jordanian border. Keep the locator I gave you. I have another one like it. And when you get near the Israeli border, activate it. We'll find a way to get you out."

Creel's wound, while not life threatening, was nevertheless serious and bleeding profusely, and while Wells and Shalman talked, Garrity and Bryson cleaned and bound the thigh as best they could and helped him into the truck. He could not walk far on his own.

Hammack, along with Lopez, Garrity and Bryson approached Wells, their intent looks of concern covered by the masks they wore.

"Are you sure you want to do this, L.T.?" Hammack asked. "We'll go with you. Just say the word."

"I'll stand a better chance alone. I never got you jokers killed before, and I'm not about to start now. You get the hostages out and to safety. Trust Zev, and keep your heads down. I'll see you back in Israel."

CHAPTER ELEVEN

Saturday, October 6, The Outskirts of Tabuk

As Wells approached Tabuk he saw no overt signs of life. Entering the town with headlamps off, he parked the jeep quietly behind one of the dunes Shalman drew on the impromptu map, noting that the blowing sand had drifted in such a way that the two dunes were virtually fused by a slightly lower ridge. Climbing to the top of the sandy hill, he flipped down his night vision goggles and scanned the deserted streets. It was all just as Shalman had described it, every building, every street, every alley.

Muhammad al-Shariyah's house was a modest one, befitting a Muslim holy man. It was white, with a stucco type exterior that had been blasted even whiter by the continual winds coming off the gulf. There was a half story above ground level that Wells guessed to be the sleeping quarters. Near the front entrance on two low benches sat guards armed with automatic rifles. Wells deduced that if there were rear or side entrances they would be similarly guarded.

The two sentries in front appeared to be dozing. Wells gave passing consideration to circling the house, killing all the guards, breaking in and dispatching al-Shariyah in his bed. But one thing field operatives learn, those, at least, who live to undertake subsequent missions, is the studied art of patience. Eliminating the guards, particularly in their current semi-comatose state, would be child's play. The downside was that Wells had no idea who else was inside the house, how it was laid out, or which room al-Shariyah himself would be in. No, storming the house would be reckless, foolish. Wells was in full tactical mode now, alert to every sound, every movement, continually processing options. He would watch, and wait, and when Muhammad al-Shariyah showed himself, an opportunity would arise to do what had to be done. Wells was not, by trade, an assassin. He and his men always executed missions with as little shooting as possible. And while he was with the CIA he left the wet work largely to others. But the vivid memory of the brutalized hostages, one of them being his own flesh and blood, canceled out any compunction he otherwise might harbor about killing Muhammad al-Shariyah.

Sliding part of the way back down the dune, Wells lay flat on his back, stared up at the stars and partial moon, and wondered about his recently liberated son and whether he would ever see the green arbors and gentle hills of his home again.

The Gulf of Aqaba, 0430 Hours GMT

They had been on the quiet waters of the gulf for over two hours. The rubber boats were found undisturbed under camouflage netting near the shoreline. Shalman removed his ski mask, loaded the three hostages into one of them and took the lead. Bryson and Hammack assumed responsibility for the wounded Creel, and Stone, Lopez and Garrity manned the third craft. High tide had come and gone, and as the water ebbed rapidly back out to sea the purring outboard motors churned easily through the salty brine. At one point they saw a single Saudi patrol boat, shut down the motors and drifted. But their low profile against the lapping waves made the small black boats nearly invisible in the night, and the danger soon passed.

Shalman had activated his locator about fifteen minutes earlier, and now the pick-up vessel was in plain sight. It was a sixty-foot fishing craft driven by powerful twin diesel engines, and it headed right for them even though they were technically inside the twelve-mile limit. Easing his boat alongside, Shalman urged Scott and Marty up the ladder, then, with the help of a crewmember, got Aaron Saperstein aboard as well.

Descending back to the water, he directed the others to follow suit. When Creel was safely aboard, Shalman spoke in a loud whisper to Hammack and Bryson.

"Scuttle the boats. Make sure everything goes down. We don't want to leave any telltale signs."

Hammack and Bryson slid quietly into the water, their field knives slashing at the rubber craft. The boats began to take on water immediately, and slowly slipped beneath the surface leaving no visible trace that they ever existed.

"Hurry up," called Shalman over the side. "They've picked up a Saudi patrol boat on radar, and from the speed with which he is approaching they think he's seen us as well."

In less than a minute, Hammack and Bryson had scaled the ladder and the ship's captain gunned the nimble craft westward at high speed. The Saudi gunboat was now clearly visible, its running lights flickering against the horizon. But its captain soon slowed his pursuit, realizing that at the respective speeds of the boats, the intruder would be in international waters long before he could close and board. It was still too early for news of the massacre at Al B'ir to have leaked out, so there was no reason for him to press the matter.

The former hostages were hustled below decks, where an Israeli doctor began administering first aid. Food and drink were on the way, they were promised, and then they were to remain in their cabins and try to sleep. They were given loose-fitting military fatigues to replace their filthy, damp and uncomfortable clothing.

Tabuk, Thirty Minutes Before Sunrise

An hour earlier, Curt Wells saw a light go on in an upper level window, probably just a candle or small oil lamp, he thought. He took this as a sign that al-Shariyah was stirring, and it helped him to decide on a strategy. At most mosques, the *imam* has a *muezzin* who chants the five daily calls to prayer. But Shalman told Wells that al-Shariyah was an early riser who, as an example to the faithful, often preferred to deliver the early morning *adnan* himself. So, when he was in residence, he would rise, walk to the mosque, perform the *wudhu* – the ritual ablution or washing – then scale the steps to the minaret to deliver the day's first call to prayer.

Wells was counting on al-Shariyah's spiritual vanity holding to form on this day, and during the night repositioned by negotiating the ridge to the other dune depicted in Shalman's crude drawing. It was not as high as the first one, nor was it as close to the house. But it still afforded a distant view of the cleric's residence and a clear line of sight to the minaret. All he had to do now was wait.

Just before sunrise, a tall, slightly stooped, gray-bearded man exited the house and began walking slowly in the direction of the nearby mosque. He was trailed by two armed guards who looked thoroughly bored and disinterested. Wells could take him right now, but there was no hurry. Once he ascended the minaret, al-Shariyah would be completely alone, and totally vulnerable.

Fifteen minutes that seemed an eternity ticked by. Wells hefted the Galil, played the scope back and forth across the narrow balcony where he expected his quarry to emerge, and concentrated on normalizing his pulse and breathing. At length a narrow door opened and the tall graybeard that was al-Shariyah emerged. Moving near the railing of the small porch atop the mosque, he bowed to the east, cupped his hands to his mouth and began the wistful Arabic wail Wells had heard on so many mornings when he'd worked in this part of the world.

"Allah is great! Allah is great! I testify that there is no god but Allah. I testify that Muhammad is the true prophet of Allah. Come to prayer. Come to the good. Allah is great! Allah is great! Prayer is better than sleep. Prayer is better than sleep."

Wells zeroed in on his head, releasing a breath completely, his finger caressing the trigger of the sniper rifle. Completing the *fajr*, al-Shariyah bowed again to the east. As his head came up and steadied after the second bow, Wells squeezed off a single, deadly shot. The silenced weapon made hardly more than a muffled plop, and would not attract the attention of the guards stationed outside the mosque. Instinctively, al-Shariyah grasped his right eye - the one Curt Wells had just put a bullet through. As blood gushed between his fingers, he keeled over backwards like a tree falling in the forest. It was a clean kill shot. Of that, Wells had no doubt.

Slowly, cautiously, Wells slid down the hill on his back, creating no profile against the tinge of first light, and no sound. He crawled most of the hundred or so meters to the jeep, and laying the rifle casually on the rear seat, started the engine and drove away to the north. The entire mission was now complete, and al-Shariyah would no longer be able to instigate brutality and murder in the name of his god. Now came the hard part. Curt Wells was a foreign infidel assassin, still in possession of the murder weapon, and deep in the heart of a fully mobilized Islamic country. He had to find a way out. And he had to do it right now.

The Gideon Bar Lev En route to the Suez

With the hostages sleeping peacefully below decks, Bobby Hammack and Mack Bryson decided to stretch their legs on deck. It was a beautiful morning, with waves of gulls skimming the blue water in search of a late breakfast. The commandos unmasked in order to enjoy the sun and the wind on their faces. They were still sailors at heart.

Bryson was puffing away on his pipe, the delicious aroma of cherry blend tobacco wafting up into the air and then away on the sea breeze. They spoke little of the raid at Al B'ir, yet they shared a relaxation that had not been present since they'd departed Baltimore for Israel. So engrossed were they in the open water and their own small talk that they failed to see the figure moving quietly in behind them.

"Uncle Bobby? Uncle Mack?" came the astonished cry of Scott Wells, who never was very good at following directions and had decided to explore the ship on his own.

Both men spun sheepishly to face the young man they had known since he was a child. The ruse was over, and now one of the hostages had lost the edge of deniability he might need in Cairo.

"You weren't supposed to find out," Hammack offered despairingly. "We blew it, The L.T. will kill us."

"My dad?" Scott pressed on. "Is he here too?"

"He's not here now," Bryson said guardedly, "but he was at Al B'ir – the place you were being held. That was him you saved with your tight end routine."

"Who else is here?" Scott inquired, still incredulous.

"Sean, Denny, Marco – all of us except Jimmy," Hammack confessed.

"And you planned this whole thing and got us out," the younger Wells reasoned aloud, still trying to get his mind around it all.

"Actually, your old man planned and bankrolled the whole thing," Bryson said, "but you're not supposed to know it."

"Why on earth not?" demanded Scott, his mouth agape.

"Because when you get to Cairo, our embassy, the Egyptians and probably the Saudis are going to question you hard about who rescued you. We came because the president was afraid to piss off the Saudis and wouldn't move. That's when your dad called us. If any of those people find out for sure it was us, somebody's going to get in big trouble," Hammack remonstrated.

"I see. That's why you wanted us to stay below decks, so we wouldn't find out," Scott reasoned aloud. "Well, I never saw you. And the others wouldn't know you if they did. The only man who spoke to us in English had a Russian accent and nobody wore any uniform. We have no idea who rescued us," he concluded with an impish grin.

"But I do have just one more question. Where *is* my dad? Can I at least see him?" he asked.

"Uh, I'm afraid not," Bryson replied. "You see, he's still in Saudi."

"You *left* him there?" Scott demanded in disbelief.

"He insisted, Sunny," interjected Hammack. "He stayed to take out the man who set the kidnapping up in the first place. When he's done, he'll come out."

"And just how will he do that?" Scott Wells pressed, alarm in his tone of voice. "Don't you think the Saudis will have something to say about that?"

"Not if they can't catch him," Bryson added confidently. "Scott, your old man's the shrewdest SOB I know. He got us in and out. He got you out in one piece. He'll find a way."

Scott Wells stared out over the water, trying feverishly to process the revelations he had just heard. He fought to suppress the fear he felt for his father, the man he admired and loved more than any other in the world, but found the euphoria of his liberation evaporating into desperate concern.

"You say we're going to Cairo?" he broke the silence again.

"You are. In an hour or so we'll transfer you and the other two to a Finnish freighter. They'll take you up the Suez, where people from the American embassy will meet you," Hammack instructed him, engaging his eyes. "Please be careful what you say to them."

"And where will you be?" Scott asked as he turned to go below.

"We're going back to Israel to wait for your dad," Hammack said, "for as long as it takes."

Al B'ir, the Smoldering Ruins of the Compound

Elite commandos from the Saudi army swooped out of the sky in roaring helicopters, spraying automatic fire indiscriminately as soon as they hit the ground. Racing to the smoking rubble they saw bits and pieces of charred human remains. The ground forces were only minutes behind them, and armored troop carriers quickly circled the perimeter.

Their commanding officer, a colonel by rank, jumped out of one of the vehicles and strode assertively up to the commando team leader.

"Is everything secure, Major?" he asked in Arabic.

"The buildings are all completely burned down and everyone inside is dead, sir," the commando leader answered.

"And the hostages?" came the follow-up.

"Unknown, sir. They may also be dead," the junior officer replied.

"Who could have done this?" the colonel demanded, irritation in his tone.

"The Americans," the two men said simultaneously, exchanging knowing looks.

Trudging back to his vehicle, the colonel got on the radio, reporting to his superiors what he had seen and what he and the others had concluded.

"No, no, no," barked the annoyed voice on the other end. "We have been watching the American ships constantly. The only planes that have left went on security patrols and returned. We tracked them all the way. And no boats or helicopters have been launched."

"Who, then?" asked the colonel, bemused. "Could it have been the Israelis?"

"I hardly think the Zionists would risk war over the American hostages. We will contact Washington and see what they know."

The Road North

Driving like a bat out of hell, Curt Wells covered the distance from Tabuk back to Al B'ir in a flash. Before reaching the town, he went off road to avoid any unpleasant encounters, nearly getting stuck in a sandy hollow, and clearing the area more than twenty minutes before the Saudis' ill-timed commando sortie. Soon he was climbing, as the road turned slightly west into the Hijaz and safety, he hoped.

Al Hijaz is a mountainous area flanked on the west by a fertile coastal plain of arable land that is nourished by the run off from a few trickling streams and the infrequent rain shower. To the east lay lava flows of dark-colored, hardened basaltic rock, and beyond them, the arid wastes of An Nafud, a barren and treacherous desert. Wells planned to follow the mountain road as far north as possible, making his way eventually to the extreme northwest part of the kingdom and Haql, a seacoast town near the Jordanian border. There, he would attempt to cross over into Jordan, and then west toward Israel and refuge. It was a sensible gambit in theory, but it was doomed from the beginning by circumstance.

About forty-five clicks up the steep, narrow and rocky road that was, once again, hardly more than a goat path, Wells stopped at a switchback, climbed out of the jeep and took out his field glasses. There, just before the northernmost descent from the Hijaz he saw the first roadblock. Those manning it were heavily armed, but wore no uniforms. That meant they weren't regular army or Saudi security forces, and that left only one possibility, he reasoned. These were hardcore al Qaeda gangsters, probably based at Wadi Aziz and alerted by allies in Tabuk about the slaying of their spiritual leader, and maybe even about the attack on Al B'ir. They would know that the assassins must escape either to the west, by sea, or to the north, through the Hijaz. Since there were virtually no natural harbors between Duba and Haql, it was a safe bet that their quarry was headed north by west through the mountains.

While Wells watched them, pondering his next course of action, he heard, off in the distance, the whir of rotors. It was the sound of a fast approaching chopper. He pulled the jeep in under a large rock outcropping, and quickly hid himself from view. As the helicopter appeared from the east he put the non-reflective glasses on it and saw that it was a Saudi military aircraft. They, too, were looking for him. It was now nine hours since the hostage rescue, and three and a half since the shooting in Tabuk. It hadn't taken them as long as he would have wished to organize the hunt.

With several thousand troops at their disposal the military was already swarming the coastline and the border with Jordan. And combined with an unknown number of murderous al Qaeda foot soldiers, the sheer numbers made his original escape plan untenable. He would have to find another way.

"Think Wells, think," he said aloud to himself.

Where wouldn't they expect him to go? There was only one answer. He couldn't go back south, because Al B'ir and Tabuk would now be teeming with armed hostiles. He couldn't go west, because even if he made it to the sea he had no boat and the Saudi navy would be all over that anyway. Since he couldn't continue north, that only left one possibility - east, into An Nafud. They would never expect him to go there. He would give Wadi Aziz a wide berth and head into the desert, later to turn north again in search of a remote and unpatrolled crossing into Jordan. But this plan was fraught with many grave problems of its own. He needed to ditch the jeep, and right away, and get out of the mountains as soon as possible. There were few, if any useable roads eastbound, and they would be heavily patrolled. So he would have to make the tortuous climb down, cross the lava flows and long dried up wadis, and make his way into the desert in hundred-and-ten-degree heat, and on foot. And even if he made it, he would have to cross the broadest part of the Jordanian kingdom to get to the border with Israel. His odds of survival had been slashed by half.

Washington, The White House

Norman Sloan huddled in the situation room with his senior advisors. The mood was serious.

"All right, Ken, run it down for us," he said to his chief of staff.

"There were no survivors at Al B'ir, and the hostages seem to have vanished into thin air. Muhammad al-Shariyah, a noted radical Muslim cleric in the nearby town of Tabuk was assassinated early this morning. The two events may or may not be connected. The Saudis seem to believe they are," Karns reported.

"Bastards," snorted CIA director Choate. "The Saudis know very well that al-Shariyah planned and bankrolled the kidnapping. That's why they're so quick to connect the dots."

"The real question," piped up Donald Trimble, secretary of state, "is who are the Saudis blaming?"

"They're being very cautious, very measured at this point," Karns responded. "The ambassador has asked for a meeting with the president, and that's scheduled for tomorrow. He'll be looking for confirmation or denial of our participation."

"And I'll give it to him. We had nothing to do with it," Sloan snorted.

"His next question," Trimble mused distantly, "will be what do we know about who did. How are you going to handle that one?"

"I may tell him the truth and say that we think it might have been a rogue operation put together by relatives of the hostages, but that we have absolutely no proof of it."

As they continued to bat the possibilities back and forth a telephone in the middle of the table rang loudly. Karns picked it up.

"Mr. President, it's Clarence Howell, our ambassador in Cairo asking to speak with you."

Looking mystified, Sloan took the phone.

"Ambassador Howell, good to hear from you. What can we do for you?"

"Mr. President, about three hours ago we received a telephone call from a man with a heavy accent - we believe it was Spanish. He told us that a Finnish freighter, the Laukkenen Sound, would soon be docking at a port on the Suez, about an hour from here, and that the three American hostages taken in Saudi would be on it."

"And so?" Sloan demanded impatiently.

"We sent a diplomatic limousine to meet the ship, and sure enough, the three hostages were disembarking. We scooped them up and they're on the way back here now. One of them is reported to be in pretty bad medical condition."

"This is important, Ambassador," Sloan prompted, "Were there any other Americans with them?"

"No," Howell replied decisively, "just the three of them."

"Did your people question the crew as to how they came to be aboard?" Sloan demanded.

"Yes sir," came the reply. "They claim that they were hailed by an unflagged vessel when they slowed to approach the canal, and that the three Americans were transferred by shore boat."

Muting the call, which he had long since put on the speaker, Sloan turned to his DCI.

"Can you get people from your Cairo station over there to debrief the hostages?"

"Right away, sir," Choate answered, rising and striding to another phone in the corner of the room, engaging in a short, animated conversation in which he did most of the talking.

"Ambassador, what do you plan to do with the hostages?" the president inquired.

"Well, we thought we'd debrief them and then get the Navy to fly them out to Ramstein for complete physicals and medical attention. The Saperstein lad is going to require some patching up first, though."

"I hear you, Ambassador," Sloan said. "I think it will be best to keep them separated until they have been debriefed."

"I agree, sir. We're accomplishing that right now."

"Very good, Ambassador Howell. Thank you for calling, and please keep us posted."

Sloan rang off, stood and smiled broadly.

"He did it. That magnificent bastard Wells pulled it off," he observed almost gleefully.

"Maybe, but where is he?" Choate wondered uneasily. "If he and his people are still in Saudi and get caught by the army or, God forbid, al Qaeda finds them first, they'll torture the hell out of them and try to link them to us before they execute them in the most painful way imaginable."

"Shall we have Admiral Mahorn and the Tarawa battle group stand down?" Trimble asked hopefully.

"Not so fast, Don," snapped Sloan. "We still don't know for sure exactly what has happened over there. And even though Curtis Wells may be a son of a bitch, he's still *our* son of a bitch, and I'm not going to let them torture him for doing what we probably should have done anyway. Let's keep the Tarawa on alert for now."

"One thing we can certainly do is shut down the Bureau's surveillance on the John Day. I think that cat is now fully out of the bag," the DCI chortled.

"Agreed," Sloan smiled knowingly. "Ken, please notify the joint chiefs to keep the Tarawa in place, and tell Kendrick to call his dogs off in Oregon. Tell them to discontinue surveillance on the rest of the family, too. It no longer serves any constructive purpose."

CHAPTER TWELVE

Cairo, the American Embassy

The three weary Halvarson-Brandt attorneys were given sleeping quarters within the embassy compound. The American doctor who examined them urged that Aaron be admitted to a Cairo hospital for treatment and observation, but he had refused, saying that he wanted to stay with his comrades.

Scott Wells reclined on a comfortable single bed, staring at the bland white ceiling and walls. He had wolfed down the hearty beef stew, freshly baked bread and dates provided by the embassy, but he couldn't seem to get enough to drink. While in captivity, water rations had been sparse and available only at irregular intervals. He, like the others, was suffering from extreme dehydration. He dozed into a fitful sleep, only to be awakened by a sharp rap on his door.

"Enter," he said.

The door opened and a wiry little man, about five-nine and weighing a scant one-sixty, according to Wells' best estimate, entered smiling.

"Martin Sage, Central Intelligence," the man said simply, extending his hand.

As they shared a handshake, Wells was surprised at the strength of Sage's grip. He eyed the smaller man cautiously.

"What can I do for you?" he asked somewhat suspiciously.

"I've been assigned to debrief you and find out exactly what happened. When we've finished, I'll explain to you what's next, and how we plan to get you home," Sage said with a warmth that seemed genuine enough.

"Where would you like me to start?" inquired Wells.

"Let's start at the hotel restaurant in Riyadh," Sage replied before being interrupted by another loud knock on the door.

Sage rose to open the door and found himself face to face with the impressive physique and bearing of Barton Stone, Halvarson-Brandt's chief of security who had flown in from Israel by private jet.

Introducing himself, Stone said, "I'd like to sit in on the debrief. It's been approved by the White House."

As they spoke, Sage's cell phone chirped. He answered, turned away from Stone, walked to the far corner of the room and carried on an inaudible conversation, while Stone spoke quietly with Scott Wells. Momentarily Sage rang off and returned.

"You're right. It's been blessed at the highest level," he conceded disapprovingly. "I assume you two already know each other."

"Yes," Scott Wells responded, "we've met several times during our mutual employment at Halvarson-Brandt."

"Okay, then, back to Riyadh," Sage prompted. "You were dining with Faisal al-Rashidi and his deputy, Rahim bin Qureshi, is that correct?"

"That's right," Wells confirmed. "And then these masked Arabs broke in and started shooting the place up."

"How do you know they were Arabs?" Sage wondered.

"Because we saw them unmasked later and even talked to some of them. They were Arabs all right," Wells said with absolute assurance.

"Then what happened?" Sage resumed his questioning.

"Rashidi jumped up and started screaming at them in Arabic, and they shot him dead," Wells reported.

"What did Qureshi do?" Sage inquired.

"He just sat there. I guess he was scared spitless just like the rest of us. When the shooting stopped, the five guys grabbed us and started herding us toward the door. They had it all planned out. A black van was waiting right outside. They pushed us into it, hooded us up so we couldn't see anything, tied our hands and feet and drove off," Wells continued.

"Who knew where you'd be dining?" Sage asked matter-of-factly.

"Just the three of us, the maitre d' who took the reservation, Rashidi and Qureshi. I don't know who else they may have told," Wells answered.

"The maitre d' is dead. That pretty well rules him out as an accomplice. How far in advance did Rashidi and Qureshi know?" Sage probed.

"That's kind of funny now that I think about it," Wells said, scratching his head. "We were originally supposed to meet at another place, further downtown, but Marty got a little nervous about getting all packed for our flight, so we made the reservation at the hotel restaurant instead."

"Then you called Rashidi?" asked Sage.

"Yes, I mean, not exactly," Wells stammered. "Before I got the chance, Lloyd Kerolyan in Dallas called to congratulate us on making the deal and to ask us what our plans were. I told him that we'd just changed dinner locations and that I had to inform al-Rashidi. Stan said not to bother, he had to talk to him anyway right after we hung up, and he'd let him know. Since they showed up more or less on time, I guess that's what he did."

At that, Sage and Stone exchanged long, pensive stares.

"Did you talk to anyone else at all? It's important," Sage pursued.

"No, no one at all," Wells assured him.

"So then what happened?" asked Sage.

"They put us in a rickety old truck and we drove for hours - no food and very little water. They took us to this compound and locked us in a nearly empty building with no beds. But they gave us blankets and a pitcher of foul tasting water. Later, they took Aaron away and put him somewhere else. One of our guards later told us they'd killed him. From the looks of him, I'd say they beat him up pretty badly. They tried to make us videotape anti-American crap, and when we wouldn't, they beat Marty and me too." Wells stopped, involuntarily stroked the tender spot on his neck and jaw, walked to the night table and swallowed two entire glasses of water, one right after the other.

"Did any of them talk to you?" Sage queried.

"Except for the old bearded guy that told us to read the videotaped statements, only that one guy who sometimes guarded us. He was pretty young and seemed to hate the Saudi government more than us," Wells responded. "But he spoke very good English."

"Did he look anything like this," Sage asked, pulling a black and white glossy photograph from his shirt pocket.

"His beard was a little longer, but yeah, I'd say that's him," Wells confirmed.

"The royal nephew," Sage said to Stone who just nodded.

"We're almost done here, Scott," Sage assured him. "Let's talk about the rescue. Who were the guys that raided the camp?"

"Beats me," Wells lied smoothly, his flat affect yielding not a trace of his deceit.

"They didn't talk to you at all?" Sage was incredulous.

"Just one guy. I think his accent was Russian," Wells mused.

"Russian?" gasped the astounded CIA agent.

"Yes, we tried to talk to some of the others, but they wouldn't say a word to us," Wells said.

"And all of the bad guys died in the firefight?" Sage was looking for confirmation.

"I guess so," Wells shrugged. "I didn't see anyone moving. The shooting had stopped and all the buildings were on fire."

"And on this boat that picked you up, did you talk to any of the crew?" Sage inquired.

"No, they were speaking some other language I didn't recognize. The guy with the Russian accent gave us all our instructions. They fed us, gave us the clothes we were wearing when we got here, patched Aaron up the best they could and made us stay below decks until the shore boat transferred us to the Laukkenen Sound," Wells summarized.

"And on that ship did you talk to anyone?" an exasperated but doubtful Sage asked.

"Sure. Those sailors were really nice guys and most of them

spoke some English. They all asked us who we were and where we were coming from. Pretty much the same as you," Wells concluded.

"When did you last see your father?" Sage demanded sharply, hoping that the question out of the blue might rattle Scott Wells enough to cause a stumble and an admission. The strategy was anticipated, and ill fated.

"I think it was about a month ago. He was passing through Dallas on business, as I recall. We had dinner at Angelo's," Wells replied. "Why?"

The dinner reunion he mentioned had actually happened, and he figured Sage might check it out. But he gave not a word, a facial tic, a gesture or a hesitation that would suggest he had really seen his dad more recently, at Al B'ir.

"Okay, Scott, thanks for talking to me. I'll have to ask these same questions of the other two. You'll all bunk here tonight, and in the morning a U.S. Navy jet will fly you to Ramstein, Germany, where the military medics will give each of you a thorough physical exam. Next stop, Andrews Air Force Base in Washington, D.C.," Sage told him.

Stone gripped Wells' shoulder reassuringly as the two men rose to leave. Outside the door, Stone and Sage stopped and locked eyes.

"Are you thinking what I'm thinking?" Sage said.

"Devious minds tend to think alike," Stone concurred. "I'll work the Dallas angle beginning immediately."

"Excellent. I think our Saudi friends might benefit from a chat with their Mr. Qureshi, but that depends on what you find out," Sage cautioned.

"I'm on it," Stone said over his shoulder as he hurried to a phone.

Dallas, Texas, Halvarson-Brandt Headquarters

Although it was nearly six PM in Cairo, it was just before nine AM in Dallas. Maggie Furlong, Stone's deputy was running a comb through her long, auburn hair that, for whatever reason, seemed to be in full rebellion this morning. When her desk phone rang, she put down the mirror and picked it up immediately.

"Maggie, it's Stone," came the voice on the other end.

"Where are you? How are you?" she demanded.

"I'm in Cairo, I'm fine, and more importantly, Scott Wells, Aaron Saperstein and Marty Logan are here with me," he said.

"Thank God," she sighed deeply.

"Yes, thank God. Maggie, I need you to do something for me discreetly, and right away," he said hurriedly.

"Name it, Boss," she answered.

"Can you get into our phone logs without attracting a lot of attention?" he asked hopefully.

"Of course. What's up?" Her curiosity was piqued.

"Let me narrow it down for you. I need you to identify every number Lloyd Kerolyan called on September 19th and 20th. I can't tell you why yet, but I'm in one hell of a hurry," he added.

"I should have the information within the hour. Should I call you?" she asked.

"No, I'll call you back when I can," he said, ending the conversation abruptly.

His next call was to HB vice president Stan Blanton. After assuring Blanton that both he and the hostages were in one piece, he posed a question.

"Was Lloyd Kerolyan involved in the deal with the Saudis?"

"No, but he'd sure like to be," Blanton said, laughing. "Why do you ask?"

"What do you mean, 'he'd like to be'?" Stone pressed, ignoring Blanton's question.

"I mean that he's approached me three separate times since the kidnapping, suggesting that someone from HB needs to get over to Saudi and keep the deal from falling apart. Each time, he volunteered to be the one to go," Blanton said.

"Did that strike you as odd?" Stone asked.

"Not really," said Blanton. "Lloyd's a motivated climber and always wants to be where the action is. Actually, I've about decided to send him."

"No, no, don't do that. Not yet, at least," Stone said assertively.

"What are you not telling me?" Blanton asked acutely.

"I don't know anything yet for certain. It's just a hunch. Give me a couple of days," Stone replied.

"All right, but I don't like it in the dark, Stone. Call me soon," Blanton instructed before hanging up.

Halvarson-Brandt's telecommunications system was 100% state-of-the-art digital. It logged every incoming and outgoing call by number, extension and length of conversation. It had an automatic feature whereby, with the punch of a button, executives could record their calls, if they so desired. Stone was counting on Maggie's telesleuthing to shed some light on the suddenly troubling events preceding the kidnapping.

Early Evening, the Eastern Escarpment of Al Hijaz

When the army helicopter cleared the area, Wells pushed the jeep into a deep gorge. The rock overhang made the wrecked vehicle impossible to spot from the road. Next, he donned some Arab garb he had seized at Al B'ir, a loose-fitting ivory-colored *thobe* under a flowing, black *mogasah* that had gold trim. On his head, he wore the traditional three piece Arab headgear composed of the *thagiyah*, or skull cap, the *gutrah*, a shoulder-length head covering worn over the cap, and the *ogal*, or decorative band to hold the *gutrah* in place. The *mogasah* included a cotton sash at the neckline that could be pulled across his face to protect him from the wind and blowing sand or, alternately, to obscure his identity. He buried his boots, donning instead a pair of leather sandals that one of the dead kidnappers had been wearing. Conveniently, they were just his size. Into the fabric belt binding his *thobe*, he stuck the Glock. He removed the sound suppressor and stuffed it into his canvas bag, along with his mostly full canteen, some energy bars, a few dates, his field glasses, night vision gear and several extra magazines. He debated about whether to ditch the Galil, but didn't relish the thought of going against a group of armed terrorists with nothing but the Glock. The rifle was already broken down and in a soft-sided case with a carry strap, so he threw the bag over one shoulder and slung the gun case over the other just before starting the steep downward descent.

Climbing down was rigorous, but he found that by sliding down the prehistoric lava flows and following a series of dry riverbeds, he could make it quite nicely. Three hours after sunset he sat atop a twenty-foot dune looking down on Wadi Aziz, the place Zev Shalman had advised him to avoid at all costs.

Physically, Wells could pass for a middle-aged Arab. His deep tan and several days' growth of salt-and-pepper beard combined with his purloined apparel would render him unremarkable on the streets of any Arab town. His Arabic was authentic, if rusty, and if he could infiltrate the town, steal a vehicle and make his escape he could be at the Jordanian border by morning.

Wadi Aziz wasn't much. There was a ramshackle guest house where one could sleep if he didn't mind keeping an eye open and fixed on any possessions of value, and an eatery of sorts that provided strong coffee, fresh bread, dates and a lukewarm stew of vegetables, garlic, lamb or goat and who knew what else. Further east was the lagoon and two deep wells that tapped into the natural aquifer. It was this water source, more than anything else that drew travelers of An Nafud to Wadi Aziz.

But Wadi Aziz and other desert way stops like it were also the equivalent of the wild, wild west. Malcontents, revolutionaries, zealots and those on the wrong side of the law were constantly in and out. Wadi Aziz was a known hangout of al Qaeda, and government officials seldom came here, and never without a full complement of armed soldiers.

Wells squinted through a night vision monocular at five men gathered around a weathered truck in front of the diner. All carried automatic rifles, and each had a toughened, grizzled look about him that said he could use his weapon, maybe even liked to use it. Wells pondered briefly trying to take them all out and stealing the truck. But even if he could get them all before they got him, it was likely they had friends inside, and the commotion of the firefight would alert the whole oasis to the presence of an intruder.

He shifted his gaze eastward, toward the water. Near the waterhole he saw a sizeable group of Bedouin camel herders,

Rwala by the look of their apparel. This gave him an idea. He reached inside his canvas rucksack and withdrew the thick belt he had taken off when he changed clothes. Unzipping the top of the hollow strap, he began to peel off gold sovereigns worth about two hundred American dollars each. He had twenty-five of them. His CIA tradecraft had taught him that gold was a universal language unto itself, and so he had come prepared to buy his way out of trouble if he had to. If he could manage to purchase a camel from these Bedouins, that would be his transportation and well worth the risk of entering the town. Camel riding requires some skill and is not for neophytes. But Wells had ridden them before. In fact, he and Zev Shalman once rode camels out of Syria while being pursued by an army patrol somewhere in his dim, dead past.

Scrambling down the dune he moved quickly, skirting the huddled buildings of the little outpost, and headed toward one of the wells. As he approached, he chanced to look down at the ground and suddenly shrank back in horror. Perched there, not eight inches apart, were two large scorpions, inevitable inhabitants of the desert. Wells was a man who had routinely faced down enemy guns, bluffed his way through maximum-security checkpoints in hostile countries and evaded assassins bent on ending his life. None of those things frightened him. But, for whatever reason, scorpions did. He'd been stung once, in Dubai, but it wasn't the pain so much as the hostile sight of the coiled sting waiting to strike the unsuspecting passerby that sent chills right through him. Giving the nasty little creatures a wide berth, he closed his eyes momentarily, as though to banish their visages from his mind, and then moved on. Finding no one at the nearest well, he lowered the bucket and filled it. He drank, threw some water on his face and filled his canteen to the brim. As he turned, he was challenged by a swarthy, stocky Bedouin who demanded to know who he was and what business he had there. Marshaling his best Arabic, Wells inquired as to whether he might have an audience with the headman. He knew from experience that he would have to negotiate his business at the top. So why not start there? The man squinted at him momentarily, then turned and beckoned him to follow. As they approached the herd, the man turned to him again and told him gruffly to wait.

In a moment he heard a booming voice say, "I am Masar. Who are you?"

Turning, he saw a giant of a man, perhaps six-feet-five, and weighing at least two hundred fifty pounds. Wells understood immediately why Masar was the headman.

"I am but a humble traveler," he answered, bowing in deference. "I come in peace to negotiate a purchase."

"Bah! I have nothing to sell," growled Masar.

From beneath his *mogasah* Wells produced a fistful of the gold sovereigns, causing the Bedouin's eyes to widen. He also allowed the outer garment to hang open far enough so that Masar could see the Glock in his waistband. This was just in case the other man had ideas of killing him and taking his gold pieces.

The sight of the gold wrought a miraculous transformation in Masar's disposition. Smiling broadly, he invited Wells to walk into the herd of camels with him. Wells would choose one, and then the haggling would begin in earnest. He spied a sturdy looking female Dromedary that appeared, according to Wells' best guess, to be about three years old, although with camels it would take an expert to know for sure. She stood over six feet at the shoulder and probably weighed a thousand pounds. He approached her and stroked her chin and ears. In return she nuzzled him gently. It was love a first sight, if one believes in that sort of thing.

"Five gold pieces," Wells opened the bargaining. No point in being cheap.

"Ten." came the avaricious counter.

They haggled for the better part of twenty minutes, Masar insisting that Wells was trying to steal his prize camel, and Wells countering that the Bedouin would leave him destitute. When stalemate seemed to have been reached, Masar pointed to the soft-sided case in which Wells carried the Galil.

"What's in there?" he demanded.

Obligingly, Wells unzipped the case and showed him the components of the well-made rifle. Masar smiled again, and pondered for a moment.

"Five gold pieces and the gun," he finally said.

As much as Wells didn't want to give up his only means of long-range self-defense, he was buying in a seller's market. He looked from the Galil to Masar, and back again.

"You are too shrewd a businessman, Masar," he conceded.

"But the rifle and five gold sovereigns seems a fair price. Will you include the riding blankets and bridle?"

"Yes," shouted Masar gustily, seizing his new toy and snatching the five gold pieces from Wells' outstretched hand.

In another twenty minutes, Wells had readied and boarded the camel, which he immediately named Maybelle, and they trotted off together into the night. Camels are wonderful creatures. They secrete many gallons of liquid and have to drink seldom. They don't break down or get flat tires, and while they aren't as fast as horses, they have much more staying power. An adult camel can lose up to forty per cent of its body weight to dehydration, and still function, and can travel over fifty miles a day through the arid deserts. Spread out before them under the moonlight were twenty-five thousand square miles of the trackless waste that constitutes An Nafud. Wells found himself hoping against hope that Maybelle was an outstanding example of her species, because they had miles to go before they could sleep.

The Gulf of Aqaba, The U.S.S. Tarawa

Admiral Garth Mahorn was a tough and seasoned naval commander. By now he knew that the hostages were safely in Cairo, but that his orders were to keep his battle group in place until further notice. That didn't mean that his ships would simply sit at anchor, inviting some terrorist nitwit with a rowboat and some explosives to make a run at them. So the ships were constantly on the move, re-positioning and running drills.

What Mahorn didn't know was just who had rescued the hostages nor what had become of the extraction team. The battle group's sonar had been pinging away constantly, and had detected no submarines in the area but their own. Only a few fishing boats and the occasional cargo ship bound to or from the Suez had appeared on radar. And while he couldn't definitively rule out the possibility that one of these had picked the team up right under the Tarawa's nose, there was no evidence to suggest they had, either.

No, Mahorn was inclined to think the rescuers were still in Saudi Arabia and, if they were, would move expeditiously northward toward the friendlier environs of Jordan or Israel. Not knowing what might yet be required of his battle group but sensing that the action was probably north, he began to ease his ships in that direction.

The capacity of a full naval battle group is awesome, to put it mildly. First there are the escort destroyers and the inevitable guided missile frigates. Then there is the aircraft carrier itself, with a full complement of state-of-the-art fighter-bombers, usually Super Hornets, sundry reconnaissance aircraft, transport and attack helicopters and a moderately sized ground strike force including elite teams from the Navy SEALs or the army's renowned Delta Force. Beneath the surface lurked a nuclear-powered submarine, carrying both conventional and thermonuclear ordnance. The prospect of the havoc this group could wreak upon an enemy was a deterrent nearly equal to its actual striking power.

Garth Mahorn couldn't read all the fine print yet, but he was convinced that the headlines were screaming that the president of the United States thought this battle group might still see action here. Mahorn wanted to be in the best position possible if and when that order came.

Eilat, Israel

As the sun set and nightfall settled over the Israeli military outpost, the concern of the rescue team turned to serious worry. It was several hours since their return, and still no word from Curt Wells. Commandos are generally a fatalistic lot. They go in, execute their mission and come out. Every now and then one of them gets killed. But because many of their operations are top secret, their families never find out what really happened. This was different. To these men Curt Wells *was* family. Denny Creel sat with his heavily bandaged leg elevated as Bobby Hammack and the others stood, or paced in the metal building that served as a mess hall.

"We should go back in and get the L.T.," suggested Marco Lopez.

"You're right, we should," agreed Bobby Hammack. "The problem is that we don't have a freaking clue as to where he is by now."

They were all thinking that one over when Zev Shalman approached.

"We are making arrangements to take you back to Tel Aviv in the morning. From there, Halvarson-Brandt will fly you home," he told them.

"Not a chance," said Hammack, spinning around to face him. "We're going nowhere without Curt Wells."

"I understand and share your concern. But you must also try to understand my position. You cannot stay here for long. Information has a way of leaking out, and if the Saudis discover that we are harboring the men who destroyed Al B'ir, they may see it as grounds for war. My government will simply not permit it."

"Then take us to the border with Jordan and dump us," Mack Bryson said stoically. "We'll find the L.T. and make our way out through Jordan."

"And put the Jordanians in the same position now held by Israel? I hardly think you'll be welcome there," Shalman argued. "And what are you going to do with *him*?" he continued, pointing to the wounded Creel.

"It seems to me that all of these half-assed governments, Saudi, Israel, Jordan and the good old U. S. of A. can think of a thousand friggin' reasons to let good people die, but not one to go in and get them out," a disgusted Sean Garrity snapped.

"I guess maybe it's not as simple as we think, Sean," mused Hammack distantly. Shalman nodded agreement, glad that at least one of them could understand his uncomfortable position.

"Why can't it be *just* that simple?" demanded an unappeased Garrity.

"We wait here, or hide out in the desert until the L.T. activates his locator, and then we go in and get him. That man has saved every one of our butts more than once. And now we're going to fly out and leave him twisting in the wind? I don't think so!"

There was a long, quiet spell, and then Shalman spoke.

"We wait until noon tomorrow. No longer," he said with finality.

"Wells is a dear friend of mine, and we, too, have saved each other's lives on more than one occasion. But after noon tomorrow it is out of my hands. He is on his own."

A quiet gloom hovered over the group as they dispersed to their improvised sleeping quarters. Bobby Hammack was last to leave, and as he did so, Shalman met him at the door and said quietly, "A moment, please."

"What's up?" Hammack asked.

Shalman handed him a black box with a retractable antenna, and a set of keys, as Hammack looked at him quizzically.

"This locator is keyed by GPS technology, as is the one Wells has. When the green light flashes, he is ready for extraction. The locator will show you exactly where he is. Later tonight, behind this building, there will be a truck, painted for desert camouflage, enough desert fatigues for you all, some food and water and plenty of extra ammunition. Steer clear of the roads. Leave the wounded man. I promise that I will see to his safe return to America. *Shalom*," Shalman said before turning away and disappearing into the darkness.

No further conversation was necessary. Shalman had delivered the speech he had been ordered to give even though he knew these men would never leave while Curt Wells was missing. Before dawn, the commandos, minus Denny Creel, disappeared into the desert, where they would wait for Curt Wells' signal. They would wait until hell itself froze over if that was necessary.

CHAPTER THIRTEEN

Cairo, Egypt, the American Embassy

Scott Wells heard a voice, or did he? It was way off in the distance, or was it? Groggily he fought back the clinging cobwebs of unconsciousness, suddenly aware of the need to respond, to wake up.

"Mr. Wells, please wake up, sir," the woman was saying.

"Huh, who?" Wells mumbled.

"You've been asleep, and we have visitors who want to speak with you," the woman said.

"Give me a minute," he said sleepily, rubbing his tired eyes. "Who wants to talk to me?"

"It's a colonel from Saudi Arabian Intelligence, a Mr. Kadir, I think," said the somewhat flustered duty officer.

Scott Wells was expecting this. He was warned by both Stone and Martin Sage that the Saudis might want to question them all, preferably before they left the Middle East. They would be looking for help in identifying the perpetrators of the Al B'ir massacre. Wells resolved in advance that no matter how hard they pushed, he wouldn't give them any. And he was the only one of the three who had a clue as to who the rescuers were.

After donning a blue tee shirt provided by the embassy that said USA in bold red and white letters across the front, he threw some water on his face, wiped it off with a towel, slicked back his hair and walked out into the hall where he was joined by Marty Logan and Barton Stone. Stone demanded that he be allowed to attend the interrogation, and met with little resistance from the tired-looking Saudi colonel.

They were shown to a conference room where, through the skylight, Wells could see that it was getting light. Logan and Wells sat across a large, sturdy conference table from Kadir, while Stone eased a chair to the end of the table, where he could observe all three of the others.

"You are the American lawyers who were held hostage at Al B'ir?" Kadir began.

"We were being held somewhere in Saudi Arabia, but we never heard the place called by name," Marty Logan answered.

"And the men who rescued you are the same men who killed everyone else there?" Kadir demanded, an edge to his voice now.

"We don't really know," Wells responded.

"There was a hell of a lot of shooting, and then this guy with a Russian accent told us to come out of the building where we were being held and get into a truck. We saw some bodies, and buildings on fire, that's all."

"Russians?" shrieked Kadir, incredulous. "You want me to go back and tell my people that you were rescued by Russians, and that it was Russians who murdered the royal nephew?"

"We don't actually much give a damn what you tell your people," an irked Logan shot back.

"We're telling you exactly what we saw and heard, nothing more, nothing less. And by the way, what in holy hell was this royal nephew doing there anyway?"

Averting his eyes, Kadir dodged the question and said, "So you know nothing at all about your rescuers? You wish me to believe that you didn't talk to them on the way to the coast, or on the boat that picked you up?"

"Oh, we talked to them a lot, all right," Wells rejoined. "They just didn't talk back to us, except for this one guy who spoke English with what we all agreed sounded like a Russian accent."

"What did this 'Russian' look like?" snorted the frustrated Saudi.

"He was about five-ten or so, salt-and-pepper hair, maybe weighed a hundred and eighty, real dark eyes," Logan volunteered.

"What is this 'salt and pepper'? I do not understand," shrugged the Saudi, looking at Stone for help.

"He means that the man had some gray hair," Stone smiled, "and some that wasn't so gray."

"Could you identify this man from a picture?" Kadir asked hopefully.

"Maybe," conceded Wells.

With that, Kadir reached into a folio he had laid on the table, and withdrew four sheets of colored photographs. Each page had eight pictures on it, four across the top, and four across the bottom.

"Do you see him here?" Kadir inquired, shoving the photos across the table at Scott Wells.

Wells leafed casually through the virtual lineup, and there, on the top right hand corner of the third page was a picture that caused his heart to skip a beat. It was a picture of Zev Shalman. He hurried on, not dwelling on the page, and then said decisively, "Nope, he's not here."

Next, Kadir slid the pictures in front of Marty Logan. As Logan reached the third page, he felt a shooting pain in his right shin where Scott had kicked him hard under the table. An unsubtle message had been sent and received.

"I don't see him, either" Logan finally said, pushing the photos back at his inquisitor.

"These men on the first boat that picked you up, they did not speak to you either?" Kadir pressed.

"No, only to each other, and in a language we didn't understand," Logan replied.

"More Russian?" asked a skeptical Kadir.

"No, it was something else," Scott answered.

"And would you recognize it if you heard it again?" Kadir asked doubtfully, obviously wearying of the inquiry.

"I doubt it," Logan opined. "You have to understand, Sir, that we were pretty much out of it. We'd been starved, beaten, threatened, denied water, and then ended up in the middle of a gun battle.

Strangers kidnapped us and more strangers took us away from the kidnappers. We're lucky we can remember our own names."

"I will need to question the Jewish man," Kadir said to Stone.

"I'm afraid that's out of the question," Stone said. "He's been severely beaten, and is on around the clock medical watch. He's in no shape to answer questions, and he'd just tell you the same thing if he could."

"Very well, then," sighed Kadir. "I suppose we are finished here."

"May I have a word with you privately?" Stone asked as Kadir was packing his folio.

"Of course," Kadir said. Then he turned and quietly dismissed Wells and Logan.

When the door closed behind them, a serious faced Stone said, "Is it possible, in your country, to determine who received an incoming call to a government ministry on any given day?"

"Of course. We are not as far behind America technologically as you might think. Why do you ask me this?" Kadir looked puzzled.

"I have a troubling theory that a highly placed official in your government and a management level employee in my company may have conspired together to facilitate the kidnapping that set up the unfortunate events at Al B'ir. The only way I can prove that theory is if you can find out who at the oil ministry in Riyadh received a call from America that originated at this number and extension within these time parameters," Stone explained, handing Kadir a business card with a series of numbers scribbled on the back.

"It will, of course, be necessary to make this inquiry most discreetly, so as not to arouse suspicion," he added.

"Of course," Kadir smiled.

"The difference between your government and mine is that our intelligence apparatus is not bound by individual rights to privacy, and we do not get bogged down by, how do you say it? Red tape?"

"How long?" Stone inquired directly.

"Hours at most. Here is the number in Cairo where I can be reached. May I assume that if I confirm your theory, you will then fully share it with me?" Kadir asked cunningly.

"You may, indeed," Stone answered as both men rose to leave.

Washington, The White House

For his meeting with the Saudi ambassador, the president chose the warmer, less formal environment of the Roosevelt Room. Replete with comfortable sofas, overstuffed chairs and opulent tapestries, the room held a less intimidating aura than the Oval Office, commonly seen as the seat of presidential power. Originally scheduled for morning, the meeting was delayed well into the afternoon so that the ambassador could consult with others in the Saudi government regarding the delicate situation surrounding the kidnapping and rescue of the three American hostages. As the ambassador was shown in, Norman Sloan rose, greeted him warmly and suggested that they be comfortably seated. He noted that the ambassador, usually seen in a western style suit, had chosen native Arab dress for this meeting. An indication of things to come, perhaps.

"Mr. President," the Saudi diplomat began, "I come to you today with great heaviness in my heart. My government and I believed your assurances that you would not intervene in our internal affairs. And now, alas, the royal nephew has been killed, and I fear there is much to repair between us."

This was, of course, a pathetic bluff born of a desperation to get Sloan's admission that he had used the Tarawa battle group as a decoy, then sent in commandos from some other venue.

"Mr. Ambassador," Sloan responded without hesitation. "We know that you were monitoring our battle group. Tell me. Did your military or intelligence services at any time see any of our aircraft, ships or ground forces violate the Saudi territorial limit or homeland?"

"No, we did not," conceded the ambassador dolefully, "but the killing at Al B'ir ..." his voice trailed off as Sloan cut in.

"That was not the work of anyone connected with my government, on my honor and on my soul."

"Who, then, Mr. President? Who?" begged the other man.

"That is a matter that is less clear," Sloan began tentatively. "We believe it could have been mercenaries hired by the father of one of the hostages, but we have no proof of it."

"And if you should obtain proof," asked the Saudi with narrowed eyes, "would you agree to extradite him to the kingdom to stand trial for murder?"

"You're assuming it was murder," Sloan hedged defensively. "What if he or his hirelings simply went there to extract the hostages and fired their weapons in self defense? When criminals caught in the act of their crime die violently, the principal burden imposed by international law is irrefutable proof that anyone intervening fired first and with premeditation. Would your government be prepared to offer such proof?"

"Not at this time," conceded the ambassador. "But investigators are still working on the case. Do you at least know where this man is at present?"

"That's another problem," Sloan answered grudgingly. "At this time we do not. And the matter of extradition would be tricky, at best. You see, while to your government this man might be a villain, if he has rescued the hostages he will be a folk hero to the American people. If I simply hand him over to your government without ironclad proof that he committed a crime, I would be throwing away any chance for re-election, while facing a virtually certain congressional rebellion."

"And what if this man, or any of those who assisted him were taken while still in my country?" the ambassador pressed, looking for any kind of concession.

"That would be quite a different matter," Sloan replied, staring off into space, a cold remoteness in his voice. "Americans who violate the law in foreign lands are routinely prosecuted and punished there. So long as the proceedings are just and the offer of proof reasonable my government would probably look the other way."

"It is a Curtis Wells about whom we are speaking, is it not?" the Saudi asked, watching for Sloan's reaction.

"Where did you get that information?" demanded Sloan.

"While our intelligence apparatus is not a match for your CIA, neither are we without our sources," came the reply.

"It may, in fact, be Mr. Wells," the president agreed. "But, again, we don't know that and we don't know just where he is."

"My government thinks it probable that he is still in the kingdom," the ambassador mused with a sardonic smile. "If so, let us hope that we apprehend him soon, and without further loss of life so as not to exacerbate the situation between us."

"Why do you think Wells is still in Saudi, if he ever was?" Sloan said doubtfully.

"Our security service believes the kidnapping may have been orchestrated by a radical cleric known as Muhammad al-Shariyah. Within hours of the slaughter at Al B'ir, al-Shariyah was assassinated in Tabuk, nearby. This goes beyond hostage rescue. It is a revenge killing. Who else but a man of Wells' motivation would do such a thing?" the ambassador posed the question.

"Your suggestion is not without its logic. But it's still guesswork and circumstance. In my country it would be thrown out as nonevidentiary," Sloan argued.

"But your Mr. Wells may not be in *your* country," the ambassador reminded him edgily, rising to signal an end to his somewhat contentious visit.

CHAPTER FOURTEEN

Northern An Nafud, Pre-Dawn, October 7

Wells and Maybelle had traveled all night. Bright, twinkling stars in a canopy of deep indigo had lighted their way and the endless landscape of enormous rolling dunes reminded Wells of a vast expanse of tempestuous ocean. The plan was to travel in the cool of the night and rest during the blistering heat of the day. Wells' hand held GPS system convinced him that they were still tracking in the right direction and were now less than fifteen kilometers from the Jordanian border.

First light, however, revealed another new and potentially deadly menace. He wondered why the sun wasn't more evident when he first noticed the towering, ominous cloud moving in from the northeast. It was a notorious An Nafud sand or dust storm. Driven by winds gusting to fifty miles an hour, it had stirred the great Syrian Desert into sandy clouds that towered thousands of feet into the air. Such storms were, Wells knew, both dangerous and powerful, with the capacity to pick up and move entire dunes and blanket everything in their path.

He estimated that the storm would be on them in less than an hour, and that he must immediately find a place to wait it out. Trying to ride through it would be suicidal. He spotted a long, low ridge of reddish sand, not unlike ten thousand others they had passed since leaving Wadi Aziz. He liked this one because it ran north and south, and was low enough, about ten feet high, that it would not bury them too deeply if the storm did, indeed, move part of it. Urging Maybelle to the west side of the dune, he dismounted and coaxed her into a reclining position. Camels are not only good for riding. They make excellent shelters against storms such as the one they now faced. When he was sure she was comfortably settled in, and had scoured the area thoroughly for dreaded scorpions, he secured the sash so as to protect his face, laid down facing west and cuddled as close to the big desert animal as he could get. Soon, he fell into a fitful, troubled sleep.

0745 Hours GMT, Cairo

Stone rose early. Tossing and turning the night away, he hoped for an after hours call from Kadir. But his patience was only rewarded with silence. He was once a consummate military officer commanding a unit in one of the world's elite fighting forces, the U.S. Army Rangers. Most figured him for a "lifer," career military who would one day wear the stars of a general officer. But on one fateful day his wife drove off base on a common everyday errand and never came back. Her car was rammed head on by a drug-crazed teenager who also lost his life in the accident. That changed everything for Stone.

He became distant from his men and the other officers, almost reclusive. He sought grief counseling, but nothing seemed to help. Fate had punched a big ugly hole in his life, and he didn't know how to put things back together again. Finally, sensing his declining effectiveness, he resigned his commission and left the service.

But Stone was gifted with an extremely acute intellect, and had a penchant for being able to see the bigger picture. He decided to enter the sometimes-complex world of corporate security and went to school to learn loss prevention, lock and alarm systems, digital surveillance, high tech lighting and executive protection. He was recommended to Stan Blanton at Halvarson-Brandt by a mutual friend, and soon thereafter became director of security for one of the world's largest and most diverse corporations. Later, based on performance, his position was elevated to the vice presidential level.

In a few months' time Stone remodeled the entire HB security apparatus, insisting on uniform, layered protection at HB facilities worldwide, instituting a rigorous training regimen for all security personnel and developing an exemplary executive protection protocol for HB bigwigs, especially those traveling abroad. He blamed himself in part for what had happened to Scott Wells and his colleagues, although there was precious little anyone could have done to prevent it. That was why he insisted on accompanying Curt Wells' raiders on the perilous rescue mission.

He splashed some water on his face and toweled off just before the phone on the nightstand buzzed loudly. He picked up the receiver.

"Stone here," he said with anticipation.

"It is Colonel Rashid Kadir, Mr. Stone. I am sorry it has taken so long for me to learn what I needed to know. It is important that we meet right away."

"Just say where and when," responded Stone.

"I prefer to meet somewhere other than one of our embassies," Kadir said mysteriously.

"How about the coffee shop at my hotel in one hour, then?" Stone proposed.

"Satisfactory," confirmed Kadir. "Oh, and one more favor, please. Could you contact Mr. Sage of the Central Intelligence Agency and ask him to join us?"

"I will attempt to do so," Stone promised.

Kadir continued to receive nonstop updates from his operatives in the field at Al B'ir, as well as those at his home office in Riyadh. They told him of spent cartridges from Soviet bloc weaponry and badly burned corpses. The notion that one of the liberators spoke English with a Russian accent was totally mystifying to him. Maybe this Stone fellow could help him make some sense of it all.

For Stone's part, he was unsure what Kadir thought he knew, but it must be dynamite, he surmised, as he picked up the phone to call the number Sage had given him.

He showered, shaved and arrived at the coffee shop within

thirty minutes. Sage was already there, and with a half empty cup of coffee. Kadir, dressed in civilian clothes, joined them shortly. They huddled at a table in the back of the room, talking in hushed voices.

"I have much to tell you," Kadir promised. "Will you tell me first what you know, and to what conclusions it has led you?"

Stone cleared his throat, leaned forward and began deliberately.

"When Mr. Sage was debriefing Scott Wells, he asked who else knew about the dining plans for the evening of the kidnapping. Wells mentioned having talked to a man in our Dallas office, a Mr. Lloyd Kerolyan, and telling him that the plans had actually changed and that he still had to notify your ministers. Kerolyan volunteered to pass on the information for him since he had to call Minister al-Rashidi anyway. That didn't sound right to me, so I called my second in command in Dallas and asked her to look at the digital phone logs to find out if and when Kerolyan made that call. He did. The call went to the Ministry of Oil in Riyadh, extension thirty-seven, and lasted twelve minutes. After the kidnapping, Kerolyan repeatedly approached HB executives volunteering to travel to Saudi to hold the deal that had been struck together. Something about that didn't smell right to me either. That's when I asked you to find out who was at extension thirty-seven," he concluded.

"You are a very astute man, Mr. Stone. Now let me tell you what we have uncovered. Extension thirty-seven is *not* that of the late Minister al-Rashidi, but that of his deputy, Rahim bin Qureshi. We confirmed his receipt of Mr. Kerolyan's call. Immediately after the completion of that call, Qureshi made a call on his personal cellular phone. We have the records. It was to a man in Tabuk who is a known close associate of the late Muhammad al-Shariyah. Thirty minutes later that man made a call from his home to Tariq bin Saud, the royal nephew. Less than two hours after that, the kidnappers struck."

"Let me see if I can connect the dots," cut in Sage.

"No need, Mr. Sage," Kadir smiled.

"We have already arrested Qureshi, interrogated him most harshly and charged him with complicity in the kidnapping of the

Americans and the murder of al-Rashidi. He admitted everything. He and Kerolyan were planning to sidetrack the agreement made between al-Rashidi and the Halvarson-Brandt attorneys. They would then renegotiate the deal on terms slightly more favorable to Halvarson. Kerolyan would receive a ten million dollar kickback over time, and with Rashidi out of the way Qureshi would be in a position to feather his own nest, as it were. Qureshi is not really an ardent al Qaeda sympathizer, but used al-Shariyah to set up the murder of Rashidi and the kidnapping of the Americans. In turn, al-Shariyah used his influence over Tariq bin Saud to trigger the event itself, which he thought to turn to militant propaganda advantage."

"What a tangled web we weave," mused Sage. "But I have an idea. We don't know and may never know who hit the compound at Al B'ir. Our president has assured your ambassador that it wasn't us. But the kidnapping and bloody rescue have caused a certain amount of tension between our two countries. So maybe we can spin what we know in such a way that there's something in it for everybody."

Stone and Kadir looked at Sage quizzically.

"We've got bad guys in Saudi, right? Qureshi and al-Shariyah. And we've got a bad guy in America, Stone's Mr. Kerolyan. Am I correct, Colonel, in the assumption that there was no love lost between al-Shariyah and the house of Saud?"

"That would be putting it mildly," Kadir laughed wryly.

"But al-Shariyah was a populist leader, and so while there will be cheering in the palace, there will also be some public mourning, yes?" pressed Sage.

"I suppose so," Kadir agreed with open disgust.

"What if, instead of making al-Shariyah out as a martyr, you take the evidence that you and Mr. Stone have gathered and make him a criminal, a conspirator who died as a result of his nefarious involvement in the kidnapping? And what if, instead of painting Tariq bin Saud as a rogue royal turned terrorist, you were to conclude that he was an innocent dupe of al-Shariyah who died in the crossfire at Al B'ir, possibly even trying to save the hostages?"

"Just so," enthused Kadir.

"In that case, the royal family saves face and Tariq becomes the martyr, al-Shariyah loses face even in death, and the issue of who actually did the killing at Al B'ir and Tabuk begins to recede into the shadows. If you can arrange for your FBI to deal with Mr. Kerolyan, preferably rather publicly, we can announce a joint investigation between American law enforcement and Saudi security."

"Right on," said Sage, looking from Stone to Kadir and back again. "I'll make a call and put both of you in touch with a high ranking FBI official."

"There is one, how do you say it, loose end, I believe," lamented Kadir.

Stone and Sage stared at the Arab intently, waiting for the other shoe to drop.

"We believe that the leader of the raiding party at Al B'ir may have been a Mr. Curtis Wells, the father of one of the hostages. We further have reason to believe that he may still be somewhere in the kingdom. If so, and if he or any of his accomplices is apprehended, our plan will fall apart like a house of cards and the focus will be back on Al B'ir," Kadir fretted.

Martin Sage squinted at Kadir like he was considering whether to share something. Finally, he spoke.

"I know Mr. Wells, Colonel, even served with him for a time. He is ex-CIA and he is tough, smart and resourceful, speaks good Arabic and knows the culture, geography and customs of the region as well as any Arab. If he *was* behind Al B'ir, and if he *is* in your country, he will be *very* difficult to find, and even harder to take. You might want to consider leaving well enough alone."

"I understand, but your president did not seek to dissuade us from pursuing any aggressor within our borders, and our military is even now pressing the hunt in the area between Tabuk and the Jordanian border," Kadir assured them. "If I try to call them off, too many questions will be raised."

"Even so, I believe we should proceed with our new strategy. If circumstances change, we may have to re-think it," Sage observed calmly. "Let's stay in touch, Colonel. You can reach me at the embassy in Cairo. What about you, Mr. Stone?"

"I'll accompany our three employees to Germany, and then home. I want to be there when the FBI nails Kerolyan," he smiled.

Whispering Ridge, Oregon

It was nearly six in the evening as Molly and Tyler Wells sat glued to the big screen television set in the den. Both had been sleepless and on pins and needles for many hours. News had just broken that the hostages were safe. The networks had shown pictures of the three leaving the American embassy in Cairo for the flight to Ramstein. Scott walked normally and smiled broadly in the pictures. But still no word from Curt Wells.

As they watched continuing coverage, most of which was sketchy and short on detail, the telephone rang. Reaching behind him without taking his eyes off the screen, Tyler picked up.

"Hello, brother," came the most welcome sound he had ever heard.

"Sunny?" Tyler gasped, hardly believing his ears. "Then it's true, you're okay?"

"All three of us" Scott assured him, "although Aaron has been beaten up pretty badly."

"In the TV shots it looked like you and Marty had bruises on your faces, as well," Tyler remarked apprehensively.

"A rifle butt will do that to you, brother," Scott replied soberly. "But that's all behind us now. Can I talk to mom?"

Without answering, Tyler handed the phone directly to Molly.

"Oh, my dearest Scotty, you have no idea how I have prayed for this day," she said, glistening tears staining her cheeks.

"Then I guess praying helps, Mom. I'll be home in three days," Scott added eagerly.

"You mean back in America?" she asked.

"No! I mean right there at Whispering Ridge. I'm going to take a couple of weeks off, and if I have my way about it, I'll spend every minute of that time with the family I almost lost," he answered emotionally.

"Have you seen your father?" she asked warily.

"I can't talk about that now, Mom. We'll talk more when I get there," he said soberly.

"But he's all right, isn't he? Tell me your father is all right, Scott," she demanded.

"I *really* can't talk about it now. I believe in dad, and you have to believe too. Everything will work out for the best," he said over static on the line. "I have to go now, Mom. Hug Ty for me."

Scott's call was as perplexing as it was exhilarating. Clearly, he was well. And he knew something about the condition or whereabouts of Curt Wells but wouldn't or couldn't share it on the phone. What did that mean? Had Curt been killed, and was Scott waiting to break the news to her in person? Finally, all of Molly's great strength and resolve dissipated into the disconsolate abyss of total uncertainty. She laid her head on Tyler's shoulder and wept aloud.

An Nafud, the Leeward Side of a Large Dune

Curt Wells was fully awake now, his senses assaulted by the raging tempest around him. The swirling winds churned the sand into an impenetrable veil through which nothing at all could be seen. He dared not even look to the northeast, the direction from which the wind was blowing, for the gritty bombardment would be sure to blind him even more. The giant dust cloud blocked out the sunlight so completely that even though it was nearly midday, it was as dark as night.

This storm was costing him precious time. Zev Shalman and his own men would doubtless be waiting somewhere near the Israeli-Jordanian border for him to make contact. But it was likely that they, too, would be blinded and hampered by a storm of this size. And he was paralyzed. All travel under these conditions was out of the question. He just needed to wait it out. But would that be hours or days? His sole comfort came in the knowledge that those who were hunting him would be equally frozen in time by the elements. They couldn't move either, their communications would be malfunctioning and perhaps their thirst for the pursuit somewhat slackened, although he doubted the latter.

He huddled closer to Maybelle, closed his eyes and thought about his family far away. He imagined Molly, his soul mate, languishing in the green hills of Oregon, waiting and worrying. And had Scott really made it to safety? Was Tyler at Whispering Ridge, and could he offer his mother the strength and consolation she needed until his return?

Wells was a seasoned veteran of many combat and covert intelligence-gathering missions. His life had been in jeopardy more times than he could even count. Yet he had never seriously thought about dying, about what it would be like. Now he found himself fighting back a foreboding avalanche of fears about whether this desert might prove his sandy grave, about whether he would ever see his family again, about how and if he would ever get to a place where he could be extracted. His thoughts were troubled, transient. Only the relentless, driving wind and grit remained constant.

The White House Situation Room

Gathered at the table were Chairman of the Joint Chiefs General Conrad Blaisdell, DCI Emmett Choate, FBI Director Alfred Kendrick and Secretary of State Donald Trimble. They all rose as the president entered.

"Sit," Sloan said, gesturing for them to resume their chairs. "Emmett, this is your meeting. What do you have for us?"

"A way out of this Saudi mess, perhaps," Choate responded.

"Please, we're all ears," Sloan retorted.

"Our agent in Cairo who debriefed the hostages, working with the security director from Halvarson-Brandt and a colonel from Saudi intelligence, may have uncovered a conspiracy involving Saudi's deputy oil minister and a management level Halvarson man. They believe that the two worked together with al-Shariyah and his thugs to orchestrate the kidnapping," Choate reported breathlessly.

"Why on earth would they do that?" the president wondered aloud.

"The oldest reasons known to man," Choate rejoined, "money and power. You see, Kerolyan, the HB man was apparently to get about ten million dollars in kickbacks over a period of time. He learned where the three lawyers would be, then called Qureshi who, in turn, tipped off al-Shariyah. The latter then green lighted the snatch."

"What does Qureshi get out of it?" the secretary of state inquired.

"What he's going to get is a firing squad, or worse. What he wanted, and thought he had within his grasp, was to succeed the oil minister, al-Rashidi," Choate filled in the blanks.

"So the murder of al-Rashidi was always part of the plan," marveled Sloan.

"Apparently so," Choate nodded," and that's where our opportunity arises. The Saudis aren't just pissed about the royal nephew. They're pissed that al-Shariyah is being celebrated as some kind of half-assed martyr, and that one of their own government guys was involved in this mess."

"So how does that help us?" asked General Blaisdell impatiently.

"My man in Cairo has suggested a joint Saudi-FBI investigation. We arrest, try and convict this Kerolyan, while they arrest, try and probably execute Qureshi. He's already been arrested, probably tortured, and admitted the whole thing, including Kerolyan's and al-Shariyah's roles," Choate explained.

"So they get an American's head - Kerolyan's - *and* they discredit al-Shariyah publicly while cleaning out a rat's nest inside their own oil ministry. It has a kind of intriguing appeal to it, but how does it mollify the royal family?" Secretary of State Trimble pressed.

"That's the best part," Choate gloated.

"By putting the full blame on Qureshi, Kerolyan and al-Shariyah, they can paint Tariq bin Saud as an innocent dupe, claim he was a bystander who got caught in the crossfire at Al B'ir."

"*Ergo*," Sloan extended the reasoning, "the focus on Al B'ir fades into the background and the conspiracy, heroically uncovered by a joint Saudi-American investigation comes front and center. The royals save face and everybody wins."

"That's the theory," Choate offered, "but there *is* one complicating factor."

"Tell us," ordered the president.

"It's Wells," Choate mused morosely. "They, and we, think he's still in Saudi, and they're trying like hell to find him. If they do, and if they kill him or put him on trial, the whole mess blows up again."

"Why would Wells have stayed behind in Saudi?" Blaisdell wanted to know.

"The way our agents over there have pieced it together, he led the raid on Al B'ir himself, then stayed behind alone to knock off al-Shariyah. After the hit at Tabuk, things got hairy and he went on the lam, most likely didn't get out of the country," said Choate.

"I don't suppose we have any idea *where* in Saudi he might be," Sloan said hopefully.

"As a matter of fact, we do," Choate responded.

"We think it's unlikely that he made for the coast, because that's the focus of the Saudis' search. But he's probably up in that northwest quadrant somewhere, waiting to sneak across the border into Jordan. That whole area's blacked out just now by a mother of a sand storm."

"So what should we do?" Sloan asked, looking around the room.

"For now, there's nothing we *can* do. The storm has everything shut down, and the Saudis are ultra sensitive to any transgression into their territory. So we wait, hope he makes it into Jordan, and then try to work something out with the Jordanians that would allow us to go in and extract him quietly," Choate recommended.

"I don't like that!" Trimble said. "Word will get out and it will look like we were complicit in the Al B'ir thing. The whole fire will flame up all over again."

"Don't you think," the president reasoned aloud, "that a guy as smart as Wells has some exit strategy of his own?"

"Yes, I do," agreed Choate. "But with Saudi security and al Qaeda after him, he may just be overmatched."

"Come again, al Qaeda, you say?" asked Blaisdell.

"Yes, General," Choate humored the man, "northwest Saudi is an al Qaeda hotbed. Muhammad al-Shariyah was Usama bin

Laden's own spiritual advisor. Every extremist thug in that part of the world with an AK-47 will be hunting Wells by now."

"What about the other men in the Al B'ir raiding party? What happened to them?" inquired FBI Director Kendrick.

"Unknown," Choate shrugged. "According to the hostages they got out at the same time. But they weren't on the freighter. Where they are by now, God only knows."

"If, as we have surmised, they are part of Wells' old SEAL team, they won't be far from where Wells is. You can take that to the bank. Those men live by a code. No one gets left behind," the general reminded them.

"Good God, that's just what we need, a bunch of gun-toting over the hill vigilantes provoking an armed conflict in the Middle East," Trimble snarled.

"Oh, I hardly think they're out to take on the Saudi army," Sloan chuckled.

"It's a better bet that they'll lay low and try to intervene only if and when Wells makes it to his extraction point, wherever that might be. General, I still want to keep the Tarawa in place for another forty-eight hours. If push comes to shove, I want the intervention option on the table. If our solution hinges on the Saudis not capturing Wells, then we have to do our damndest to see that they don't, and hope he's really as good as he has seemed to date. Kendrick, I want you to set up this joint task force with the Saudis right away. And get a short leash on this guy Kerolyan. I don't want to lose him."

"Yes, Mr. President," replied Kendrick meekly as they all rose to go.

CHAPTER FIFTEEN

An Nafud, Near Sundown

As is typical of great desert sand storms, the winds began to quiet as day began its inevitable retreat into night. Wells dozed off and on, and as he came fully alert he saw, or thought he saw something move nearby. Was it just his imagination? No, there was definitely something out there. Not thirty meters from his position there were shapes, a lot of them. As his eyes adjusted to the dusty, fading light, he realized that what he was seeing was the silhouettes of about thirty camels, all bedded down like Maybelle. Slowly it dawned on him that a group of Bedouin travelers had encamped there to wait out the storm, blissfully innocent of his presence nearby.

Wells remained motionless, not wanting to give his location away prematurely. Bedouins can be very territorial about whichever stretch of sand they have laid temporary claim to, and the last thing he needed was an altercation with these nomads. Like the group at Wadi Aziz, they looked to be Rwala. As he stood contemplating his next move, an inspiration struck him. He got Maybelle to her feet, and led her casually toward the Bedouins who were stirring now themselves. As he approached, he saw the silhouette of a very large man, covered from head to toe as protection against the storm. Could it possibly be? Yes, by God, it was Masar, minus about half of his earlier entourage. These desert dwellers must have split off from the rest of the group, possibly become lost in the storm and then bedded down almost on top of Wells position without seeing him, or he them. He hailed the big man.

"Greetings, Masar the Mighty," he smiled. "May Allah continually smile upon you."

The big Bedouin was momentarily astonished, as Wells had been, and looked as though he were seeing a ghost.

"*Salaam,*" he said, opening his hands and bowing slightly. "From where did you come, traveler?"

"I was riding out the storm right next to you and your people. Because the dust was so thick, I guess we couldn't see each other. But now I come with a question," Wells answered.

"Ask what you will," Masar said, narrowing his eyes and regarding Wells cautiously.

"Where are you going, if I may ask?" Wells inquired.

"North, to Wadi Rum," Masar smiled. "We have some camels to deliver before we rejoin the rest of our band."

"Wadi Rum is in Jordan," Wells observed, "and to get there you have to cross the border."

"The Bedoui have no borders. The desert is ours, and we come and go as we please, like the wind," Masar boasted.

"And the border guards don't bother you?" Wells pressed.

"Sometimes they stop us and ask us where we are going, nothing more," Masar shrugged.

"Then I have a favor to ask, and if you agree to what I propose, I will make you a rich man," promised Wells.

"My ears burn," Masar smiled. "Say more."

"Let me ride with you into Jordan. Then we go our separate ways. I will give you fifteen more gold sovereigns, and when we part I will return the camel to you," Wells bargained.

Masar became suddenly mistrustful.

"What trouble do you bring?" he asked cautiously.

"I will tell you the truth. I am likely being sought by Saudi security forces and by some bad men from Wadi Aziz. They may be pursuing. I will be much safer after we cross the border. Should they accost us on the way, I will ride away alone, so as not to put you and your people in harm's way," Wells promised.

"Fifteen gold pieces and the camel for safe conduct, eh?" Masar sought confirmation.

"That is my offer," replied Wells.

"I must speak with the others," Masar said, gesturing for Wells to wait where he was.

Ten nervous minutes passed, and then Masar returned.

"It is agreed," he said. "We journey now, while the wind abates."

"I am at your command," Wells sighed in relief.

In ten minutes they were moving. Wells figured that at this pace they would reach Jordan before first light. He mixed in among the Bedouins so as not to attract special notice, but soon Masar, hungry for conversation with this beneficent stranger, motioned him to ride forward.

"You know that the Saudis and those who live in Jordan have no use for each other, do you not?" he asked.

Wells nodded, recalling how Jordan maintained strict neutrality when Iraq threatened the kingdom during the first Gulf War, and how the Saudi royal family had never quite forgiven them.

"I know little of what goes on in Riyadh and Amman. To the Bedoui all rulers, governments and politicians are shit of the camel. Is it so in your country?" Masar inquired with a broad smile.

Wells chuckled aloud, and then said, "Yes, Masar, in my country the politicians are mostly camel shit, too."

By 0400 hours they neared the border without having seen another living soul. Masar again motioned to Wells, and they dismounted and climbed to the top of a ten-foot dune. In the desert there are no roads, only well worn pathways frequented by those pursuing the shortest distance between two points. The storm had sanded this one over heavily, and the only indicator of its existence was a checkpoint, manned by four Saudi soldiers on the near side, and a similar number of Jordanians on the other. Wells pulled out his night vision monocular and studied the checkpoint. He could see that there was no fence between the two countries, only yellow markers protruding from the sand at seventy-five meter intervals for half a kilometer on either side of the guardhouses. Seeing that Masar was curious about the night vision gear, he handed over the monocular so the big Bedouin could have a look. Masar peered for a few moments, then turned, a broad smile on his face.

"It is like day, except green," he marveled.

"How do you normally cross?" Wells asked.

"We never go near the soldiers unless we must. Sometimes if they have nothing better to do they will run after us and scold us for not stopping. But they are always careful not to anger us. They know that my men are armed, too," Masar responded.

"So, I guess we just pick a spot a couple of hundred meters down from the guard houses and ride across in the dark, eh?" Wells asked, hoping it would be just that easy.

As Masar was considering this, Wells looked back toward the checkpoint and saw movement, two trucks pulling up and stopping. He continued to watch as a group of heavily armed, non-uniformed men got out.

"From Wadi Aziz?" Masar speculated, looking back at Wells.

"Probably," Wells agreed.

"So, we wait a bit, let them cross over and disappear. They will probably head straight for Wadi Rum. Then we cross. If they are looking for you, you will have the advantage since they are in front of you instead of behind," Masar observed.

"Maybe so," Wells mused, teasing out the possibilities of what lay ahead.

An animated conversation was in progress at the checkpoint. Clearly, neither the Saudi nor Jordanian guards were enthused about allowing this gun-toting riff raff to cross the border. The other side of the coin was that they were outmanned and outgunned, and probably didn't feel strongly enough about it to risk a shootout. Finally, the driver of the lead truck reached inside his fatigue jacket and pulled out a wad of folding money. He counted off a few bills and then, more reluctantly, a few more. With that, the gate opened and they passed through to the Jordanians, where the process was repeated. In a few minutes, all that could be seen of them was their taillights fading away into the dusty night. Fifteen minutes passed, and then Masar motioned to his men to mount their camels and get the herd ready to move.

At one of the yellow markers about a hundred meters west of the guardhouse, they began their crossing. All was going well, and the lead elements were nearly in Jordanian territory when a spotlight sliced through the dusty darkness, and a husky voice, amplified by a bullhorn, instructed them in Arabic to stop where they were. In less than three minutes, two of the Saudi border guards were on them, guns at the ready.

"Who are you, and why do you not stop at the check point?" one of them demanded.

'We are Bedouins, herders of the camel," shot back Masar indignantly. "My people lived in and traveled these sands for centuries before your yellow markers and check points. Border guards never stop us because they know we mean no harm to anyone. Leave us to go our way in peace."

"We are looking for a man, perhaps an American?" the guard persisted. "Have you seen such a man?"

"The sands have filled the skies for many hours, my friend. There could be a thousand Americans in An Nafud - a million - and neither you, nor we would ever see them," Masar answered.

"These are my people," he said gesturing broadly. "Do any of them look like Americans to you?"

The guards made a cursory pass through the Bedouin ranks, one stopping not five feet from Wells and Maybelle.

"Very well," snapped the lead guard, "be on your way, and next time stop at the check point as you are supposed to do."

The caravan moved on without challenge from the Jordanians.

Riding alongside Wells, Masar smiled. "I think you are famous, my friend."

"Infamous is more like it," Wells grunted in reply.

Two hours passed. The wind had begun to blow again, and swirling sands were making visibility difficult.

"Wadi Rum in about one hour," Masar commented. "It is best if you leave us before we get there."

Wells nodded, "I guess this is as good a time and place as any. I cannot find the words to thank you for helping me."

"It was our joy," the gregarious desert dweller responded, "but there is one thing."

"What is it?" Wells asked, wondering anxiously what was coming.

"I do not think our bargain was a fair one," Masar asserted with a stern look.

People in this part of the world live to bargain, and Wells had suspected all along that they might not yet have reached the bottom line. The problem was that he had little left with which to bargain.

"Fifteen of your gold pieces, my camel and your gun for safe passage?" Masar asked quizzically, dutifully unstrapping the Galil and handing it back to Wells. "I think before you get to wherever you are going, you will need this more than I," he smiled.

"Your beneficence is overwhelming," a flabbergasted Wells blurted out, accepting the rifle gratefully. "What else can I leave you as a token of our friendship?"

"The night eye, perhaps?" Masar said hopefully.

Wells fumbled briefly in his rucksack withdrawing the fifteen gold pieces and the monocular, then handed them to the smiling Masar. He dismounted, stroked Maybelle on the nose and handed the bridle to Masar before walking westward, soon to disappear in the wind whipped curtain of sand.

Jordan, October 8

What he didn't know was that a second convoy of al Qaeda, about twenty-five men, had crossed at the checkpoint not forty minutes behind him. While the first group headed northwest, toward Wadi Rum, this second group paralleled the border, due west. If Wells and his men were still in the mountains, this force would be waiting when they tried to cross into Jordan. If not, they would execute a pincers movement with the reinforced group leaving Wadi Rum, trying to catch the assassins making for the only other conceivable safe haven, the Israeli border.

Wells stopped to rest in the lee of a big dune, inventorying his resources. He had the Galil now, with forty rounds of ammunition, plus the Glock with three extra magazines. He still had his night vision goggles, and a scope for the Galil, if he needed it. Masar's men had filled his canteen to the top, and he had some energy bars and dates to eat. Looking at his GPS, he concluded that he was about thirty-five kilometers from Israel and a possible extraction. That was a very long way in this desert, he knew. Soon he was moving again, trudging through the sand as fast as he could go.

The distinction between the Great Syrian Desert, An Nafud and the Negev - the latter shared by Israel and Jordan - may be meaningful to cartographers. But when one is surrounded by them there is no obvious difference at all. They comprise a single unrelenting ocean of sand, blistered mercilessly by a fiery orb of sun, and swept harshly by winds that seem to come from and go to nowhere in particular. It was on this waterless ocean that Curtis Wells was but a solitary lifeboat, alone and adrift.

As the sun approached its zenith, the heat approximated one hundred twenty-five degrees Fahrenheit and the skies began to clear. Though Wells had drunk regularly, and in small sips, his canteen was nearly empty and he had stopped sweating, a telltale sign of impending heat prostration. He kept his face covered against the unkind elements, but he could tell that his lips were starting to crack and blister. Soon he began to feel nauseated, his muscles cramping and knotting painfully.

"One foot in front of the other," he mumbled to himself aloud as he thought about Molly, Tyler, Scott, the endless green vineyards of Whispering Ridge and home.

In the desert, both the eyes and the mind play cruel tricks. Wells knew it because he had watched men dying of thirst stagger desperately toward what they believed to be a life saving pool of water, only to see the mirage vanish into the merciless heat and barren sand before their very eyes. The optical illusion of mirage is caused by light rays crossing air layers of different densities. The level of dense air just above the surface of the desert refracts the light in such a way as to cause a mirror effect of something that is much farther away than it appears. Thus, what looks, in a mirage, to be nearby is, in fact, many miles away, below the horizon.

In Wells' experience, mirages constantly lured one away from the intended direction of travel. Even now he could see the simmering promise of thirst-slaking water to the north, away from where he needed to go. But he knew that it was just an illusion, made all the more real because it was a siren offering of what his mind and body craved.

It felt as though the heat was crushing him in an inescapable crucible of torment, and as he walked on he had the sensation of growing shorter and shorter. In fact, the sandy floor of the desert was rushing up to meet him. Soon he fell face first into the hot sand, unable to walk another step, his consciousness coming and going. He had underestimated the power of the desert and overestimated the flagging resiliency of his aging body. He had no idea how long he had lain there when he heard a hoarse, cheery voice croaking at him in some of the worst Arabic he'd ever heard.

Opening his eyes he saw a sprightly little man in his sixties, with a mane of white hair and an equally white beard bending over him.

"I say, are you all right?" the man asked in a clipped British brogue.

"You're British?" Wells asked weakly.

"By heaven, that I am," the man responded. "And you, unless I miss my guess, are either American or Canadian."

"Canadian," Wells lied. "Where did you come from, and what are you doing out here?"

"My name is Andrew Parker-Smythe, and I am an archaeologist. I spent the night at Wadi Rum, and now I'm headed into Israel. What about you?" the man answered.

"I ... I'm lost," Wells stammered.

"Well, this is a bloody damned poor place to be lost, if you don't mind my saying so," Parker-Smythe observed. "Come, let us get you into the Land Rover and put some cool water on your face and head."

Assisted by the old archaeologist, Wells rose, first to one knee and then, shakily, to his full height before stumbling toward the vehicle. Was this actually happening, or was it some kind of hallucinatory fantasy induced by the suffocating heat?

Sitting in the passenger seat of the Land Rover, Wells reclined on the head rest and allowed his kindly rescuer to trickle water from a fresh canteen over him. In a few moments he was feeling better. Looking over his shoulder into the back of the vehicle he spied what looked like an ice chest.

"What's in there?" he asked, half expecting it to be full of old bones and broken pottery.

"Soft drinks, and more water." Parker-Smythe responded, quickly exiting the driver's side and opening first the rear door and then the chest.

"Pepsi Cola," Wells gasped, "I must be dreaming."

"Not at all, old fellow. Would you like one?" the older man asked.

"At least one," Wells answered as he popped the top from the aluminum can and began to drink.

"Not too fast, now," Parker-Smythe cautioned. "Your body needs to adjust and rehydrate slowly."

"You say you're going to Israel?" Wells asked, still sipping the soft drink.

"Yes, I'm supposed to meet some colleagues at a dig there," came the reply.

"Can I hitch a ride for part of the trip?" Wells asked, trying not to sound as though he was begging.

"Of course, of course," Parker-Smythe smiled. "I'm glad for the company."

The old man fired up the four-wheel drive vehicle as Wells loaded his gear, and soon they were moving west. Wells dozed between snippets of conversation, then came suddenly alert, as though prompted by a sixth sense. As they chugged along the dusty road which was hardly more than a well-worn path in the desert, Wells saw, in the distance what appeared to be a roadblock.

"Stop the vehicle now!" he snapped, conveying a sudden sense of urgency that startled the other man.

Parker-Smythe did as he was instructed, and Wells climbed up on the hood and took out his field glasses. What he saw made his blood run suddenly cold. Less than a mile ahead, a group of heavily armed non-uniformed men had set up an impromptu checkpoint. Wells thought it more than probable that they were al Qaeda, and that they were looking for him. Hastily he hauled his meager belongings out of the Land Rover and moved to the driver's side.

"You must go on without me," he said, an urgency in his voice. "Those men up there are probably looking for me. For your own safety it is better if you have not seen me, know nothing of me. Now go!" he said.

"But what about you?" protested Parker-Smythe. "I mustn't just leave you out here in the desert."

"I'll be fine. Just drive on as normal," Wells instructed. "I don't think they'll harm you."

Within ten minutes he found out just how wrong he could be. He watched through the glasses as the men manning the roadblock stopped and searched the Land Rover, forcing Parker-Smythe to get out and stand with his hands on his head as they did so. When the search was over a small man, who appeared to be the leader approached Parker-Smythe and began questioning him, gently at first, but then becoming progressively more animated. Suddenly he pushed Parker-Smythe hard in the chest with both hands.

What unfolded next was a nightmare seen by Wells as if in slow motion. Two of the men fired long automatic bursts, flattening all four of the Land Rover's tires. A gun appeared in the hand of the al Qaeda leader. He pointed it at Parker-Smythe's head and continued talking animatedly. Then, without warning, he pulled the trigger, the automatic bucking in his hand. Since light travels faster than sound, Wells saw the blood, bone and brain matter explode from Parker-Smythe's shattered skull before he heard the report of the heavy caliber hand gun. Wells winced as Parker-Smythe collapsed in a heap, dead before he fell. A terrible thought forced its way into Wells' consciousness. Was this his fault? Was he responsible?

In a flash the guilt and uncertainty gave way to a simmering white-hot rage. These bastards had just murdered an old man whose only crime was to be alone on a desert road, white, western and a non-Muslim. To them he was simply more fuel for the fires of hell. But now, Wells vowed silently, they would pay and pay dearly for their atrocity. He would personally administer a primer on what hell was all about. The surging adrenaline rush within him compensated quickly for his weakened condition as he moved smoothly and easily on his deadly errand of vengeance.

He assembled the Galil and slid the scope into place. Running low, and sometimes crawling, he inched his way toward the murderers, who were now talking and laughing among themselves. At two hundred yards, he crawled to the top of a large dune that stood perhaps eighteen feet high. Carefully, he brought the crosshairs to bear on the smallish man who had shot the archaeologist. His heartbeat normalized, his breathing slowed as he gently caressed, then pulled the trigger. The man's head literally blew apart as the heavy slug blasted through, entering above one ear and exiting below the other. In the moment of his death, Wells thought with some satisfaction, he may have known what the innocent old man he just murdered had felt.

The five others at the roadblock were at first stunned, confused. Where had the shot come from? Who had fired it? Was he targeting them next?

As a second man fell, followed ten seconds later by a third, they knew the awful truth. They were being hunted - hunted by an expert sniper who neither wasted ammunition nor did anything to give away his position. Desperately, they sprinted for the truck. But one of them did not make it, Wells' shot severing his spine just below the neck. The two remaining men leaped into the truck, and the starter began to grind. Patiently, Wells sighted in and fired. The glass in the driver's side window exploded, and the man at the wheel slumped lifelessly forward. The other man immediately fled the truck, taking care to keep it between him and the direction of the deadly shots. Five shots, five kills. Not bad. Either Wells had lost none of his acumen as a marksman, or his senses, sharpened to a razor's edge by the sudden adrenal surge and a healthy dose of moral outrage had taken over, rendering his concentration nearly superhuman.

He now had a decision to make. If he pursued the lone remaining killer and hunted him down, he would waste valuable time and be drawn away from the direction he needed to take toward safety and home. If he didn't, and the man had a cell phone, he might alert every al Qaeda foot soldier within a hundred miles to Wells' presence. The latter, he concluded, was a chance he would have to take. He was now within three kilometers of the Israeli border. He turned away and moved off into the hot, dry expanse of sand, stopping momentarily to activate the locator given him at Al B'ir by Zev Shalman. Would anyone be listening?

The Gulf of Aqaba, 1600 Hours

Rear Admiral Garth Mahorn was a veteran naval commander familiar with the Middle Eastern theater from service in Desert Shield, Desert Storm and the Iraq war. It was a special reassurance to the president that Mahorn was the man in charge in the Gulf, because he knew Mahorn to be calm, cool, collected and to perceive the broader implications of whatever action had to be taken. Mahorn was on the bridge, staring out over the unruffled water and smoking his pipe when a voice blared over the speaker.

"Admiral, this is comm. There's something we think you should see."

Mahorn sprang from his chair and strode from the bridge, handing operational command off to one of his senior officers. Tapping his unfinished pipe on the railing and spilling its still glowing contents over the side, he headed for the bowels of the ship. Entering the spacious communications complex, he saw the officers there rise and salute.

"Stand at ease," he barked. "What's this that I should see?"

A set of double doors opened and the admiral was escorted inside, where once again everyone rose.

"What's going on?" he asked Petty Officer First Class Kevin Brenneman, the senior technician on duty.

"About fifteen minutes ago we picked up the beeping signal from a locator, one of ours, we think," the officer reported.

"And . . .?" Mahorn encouraged him to continue.

"We traced it to a spot in the Jordanian desert," Brenneman said.

"So what's an American with a military issue locator doing in the Jordanian desert, and why should I be concerned about it?" Mahorn pressed.

"Who and why is anybody's guess, sir," Brenneman responded haltingly, "but you'd better take a look at this."

He pointed to a large screen and a series of thermal images denoted by green blips.

"We started tracking the locator and used the satellite's thermal imaging capacity to pin down the source of the transmission. This is what we found," Brenneman concluded, waving one hand at the oversized screen.

"Walk me through it, Petty Officer," Mahorn said, wanting to be certain he read the panorama playing out before his eyes correctly.

"The signal is coming from this figure, one lone target who is apparently double timing it through the desert toward the Israeli border. The problem is this group closing on him from the south, and this even larger group converging from the north. He's being hunted by a large force, Sir," Brenneman said with an unnerving confidence.

Garth Mahorn processed what he had seen and heard for all of twenty seconds, then asked, "Given the pace of everyone on the field, what are the target's chances of making it into Israel before his pursuers close?"

"Zero, Sir," came the expected response.

"Right. Get me the president, right now!" the admiral said.

CHAPTER SIXTEEN

Washington, The White House, 5:10 AM

Norman Sloan was a light sleeper. Although the thick drapes on the windows of the bedroom in the presidential residence were still closed, he sensed that the beginning of day was near. He was in the nether world between sleep and wakefulness when the phone on the nightstand rang shrilly.

"Yes," he said, talking into the receiver in a low voice so as not to awaken his wife.

"I understand. Ten minutes, in the situation room."

He trotted through a cursory shower, then pulled on a velour sweat suit and hurried out of the residence toward the situation room, deep underneath the White House. The two burly secret service agents accompanying him opened the double doors for him, and he entered the secure room to find General Conrad Blaisdell and DCI Emmett Choate waiting.

"Bring me up to speed," he said, motioning for them to sit.

"At 1600 hours, the communications boys on the Tarawa picked up the beeping of an electronic locator, probably American military issue. Using satellite imaging, they found a lone target being pursued by a large and presumably hostile force through the Jordanian desert toward the Israeli border," Blaisdell summarized succinctly.

"Wells," said Sloan decisively.

"Probably so," agreed Choate.

"The people aboard the Tarawa say the forces are converging on him from two directions and that he hasn't a snowball's chance in hell of making it out."

"Who is chasing him? Jordanian military? The Saudis?" Sloan demanded.

"The Jordanians have no significant forces in the region. We're not sure they are even aware of what's happening," Choate answered.

"And no way it's the Saudis," Blaisdell added. "They'd be risking war to be operating that far inside Jordanian territory."

"Then who the hell ...?" Sloan stopped mid-sentence. "He's being chased by al Qaeda, isn't he?"

"That is our conclusion, sir," confirmed Choate.

"The question is what, if anything, are we going to do about it?" Blaisdell stated the obvious.

"What *can* we do?" asked Sloan nervously, looking for ideas.

"If we contact the Israeli military post at Eilat, we're pretty sure we can get their permission to overfly," Blaisdell said.

"If so, I'd send a Blackhawk in to get him, with a couple of Cobras riding shotgun," he added, referring to the military's premiere attack helicopters. "The problem is Jordan, and what they will or won't allow."

"The hell with Jordan, call the Israelis and get those birds in the air now, General. I'll call the king of Jordan and have a heart-to-heart. I will not have *any* American hunted down and slaughtered by those fanatical al Qaeda bastards when I have military capability in position to prevent it. Is that perfectly clear, gentlemen?" Sloan finished.

"You are clear, sir. I'll ring up Admiral Mahorn. The call to Eilat will go down better coming from him," Blaisdell said, rising to go.

"Emmett, stay while I talk to the Jordanians, will you?" Sloan requested.

Jordan is a small country, about the size of the U.S. state of Indiana. It shares borders with Saudi on the south, Israel on the west, and with Iraq and Syria on the north and east. Ninety-three per cent of its inhabitants are Sunni Muslims, which makes it surprising that Jordan was one of the first of the Arab states to make peace with Israel, and that its small but excellent intelligence service partnered so effectively with the U.S. in the war on terror. The explanation is that Jordan is also a poor country, not endowed with large oil reserves like some of its near neighbors, and without a great deal of arable land. In other words, Jordan desperately needs trading partners, and so making nice with the U.S. and the European Union is paramount. The president of the United States was about to plumb the depths of the Jordanian king's commitment to nice.

Soon the red phone in the situation room rang, and Ken Karns, White House chief of staff informed Sloan that King Abdullah was on the line.

"Hello, Excellency," Sloan purred into the receiver.

"Mr. President, what an unexpected pleasure. To what do I owe this honor?" the king asked.

"A troubling situation exists, and decisions must be made. I hate to disturb you, but there isn't much time," Sloan started.

"Tell me of this troubling situation," the king said, seeming sincerity in his voice.

"There is a lone traveler, an American we believe, in your desert region between Al Aqaba and Ma'An, near the Israeli border. We further believe that he is being pursued by a large force of al Qaeda who plan to execute him. We have asked the Israelis to permit our helicopters to overfly the southern end of their territory in order to extract him. My question to you is, will you grant my helicopters permission to land and extract this man from Jordanian soil?" Sloan concluded.

There was a long, troubled silence on the other end, muted voices whispering in the background. Then the king came back on, his voice strong, deliberate, unwavering.

"Does this have anything to do with the recent nasty business in the kingdom of Saud?" he asked perceptively.

"We don't know for sure. But that possibility exists," Sloan confessed reluctantly.

"Jordan cannot, Mr. President, present ourselves to the Saudis as aiding and abetting men who have spilled the blood of their citizens," he said.

"I understand, majesty. That is why we do not ask you to send forces to intervene, nor do we propose to make a ground incursion into Jordan. We know that you have no use for al Qaeda, nor does the house of Saud. We ask that in the name of friendship you simply allow us to retrieve this American, whoever he is, from your midst," Sloan hoped he didn't sound like he was begging which, in fact, he was.

There was more silence on the other end, followed by more whispering.

Then Abdullah said, "I spit on these al Qaeda devils. They kill without discrimination, and they recruit our children to become killers. There will be killing in the desert today no matter what you and I do or do not do. I know it. But because I despise these sons of jackals, and in the name of Jordanian-American friendship, we will look away. Please, kill them *all*!"

"Your military and air force will stand down, then?" Sloan wanted to be certain.

"They will, Mr. President. Let us speak no more of this unseemly thing. I look forward to my trip to Washington next month," Abdullah brought the call to a conclusion.

"As do I, Excellency, as do I," Sloan said with all the genuineness he could muster.

As quickly as he hung up one phone, the DCI handed him another, saying that it was Admiral Mahorn on the Tarawa.

"Did you get clearance from the Israelis, Admiral?" demanded the president.

"With some stipulations, yes," Mahorn responded.

"What stipulations?" Sloan pressed.

"We can overfly, but we can't land in Israeli territory. If we can protect our man until he crosses into Israel, the Israelis insist that they be allowed to make the extraction. I think they're concerned about what the Saudis might think." the admiral reasoned.

"So am I," Sloan said uneasily. "Admiral, these are your orders: overfly Israel, locate the target and do whatever is necessary to protect him until the Israelis can make the extraction. And Admiral, kill every one of those terrorist scum in the process, if you can."

"I read five-by-five," Mahorn responded. "My birds are in the air as we speak."

The Negev, Eighteen Hundred Meters From the Border

Special operators all have a certain bearing about them. The lean athleticism, the penetrating, restless eyes constantly scanning everything and everyone in sight, the relaxed, calculated manner of speech, the ability to blend into any environment anywhere in the world - those are the telltale marks. But they all have one more thing that makes them a breed apart. It's a sixth sense, an ability to smell and feel danger even when none is evident. It was that sense in Curtis Wells that was claxoning loud alarm sirens in his head.

He couldn't see or hear his pursuers. But he knew they were nearby, nonetheless. He could see Israel from the small dune where he sat. But he knew that to make a dash for it would likely provoke a blistering fusillade of gunfire that would result in his death. He had seen two scouts from the group of hunters to the north nearly forty minutes ago, moving south by west. And he had heard what he took to be a single gunshot to the south shortly afterwards. Whether it was an accidental discharge or a way of alerting the other group to the presence of their compatriots he did not know. But he knew that they were moving in on him from both directions. Did they know for a certainty that he was there, or were they assuming it?

It was at least two hours until sunset, and another hour until the dark of night. Logically, the thing to do was to hide somewhere, taking up a position he could defend, and hold them off until the pitch black of night provided cover under which he could simply melt away. There were just three problems with that, but they were, in a word, gigantic. First, the storm had blown itself out and a three-quarter moon would shortly be lighting up the desert night. In other words, dark wasn't going to be all that dark. Second, in the woods or the mountains one can easily hide behind a fallen tree or in the hollow of a sunken riverbank. But in the desert there are no trees, no rivers, nothing but the eternal sands. A dune providing cover from one direction leaves the unfortunate hider exposed from the other. Third, he doubted they were going to wait until dark to close their noose around him. If they had him bracketed, why take the chance of losing him in the night? What Curt Wells desperately needed was some help.

But about one thing he was clear. He wasn't just going to sit around and wait for them to come for him. His version of the redoubtable bayonet charge would be to seek one group out, taking out as many of them as possible before their reinforcements from the other direction arrived. But which group should he go for? The group to the north, he reasoned, was the one he had seen crossing from Saudi into Jordan. That would be about twenty-five men. And they would certainly have picked up reinforcements at Wadi Rum. Were they forty now? Or fifty? Attacking that large a force by himself, and without grenades or a mortar would be suicide, he knew. So, it had to be the southernmost pursuers. But how many men did they have? How were they armed? Would he have any chance at all against them? These were potentially lethal unknowns, but in this particular case he decided that the devil he didn't know was probably preferable to the one he did. Staying low, he began a gradual movement to the south. He buried his rucksack in the sand, removing only his night vision goggles and the extra magazines for the Glock. Stuffing them into the soft-sided case in which he carried the Galil, and keeping the rifle barrel well out in front, he began to move in on the hunters. Soon enough they would become the hunted.

Archangel Flight Approaching Israeli Territory, 1730 Hours

"Archangel One to Eilat command, do you read?" came the voice of Colonel Stuart Reddick, USN, over the radio.

"Moshe Dayan Military Command to Archangel leader, we read you five-by-five," came the reply.

"Archangel flight requesting clearance to overfly and commence Operation Desert Rescue," Reddick followed up.

"Permission granted, but you must not land in Israeli territory," the voice said.

"Roger that," Reddick said quickly. "Will you have rescue personnel on the ground at the border?"

"We will do what is necessary Archangel leader. Good luck."

"Copy that," Reddick signed off.

Reddick was a career military pilot in command of a shiny new Blackhawk helicopter, the U.S. military's paramount means of conveying troops into hot zones and bringing them out again. And this hawk had teeth, with two side-mounted Gatling guns and an assortment of air-to-ground missiles that caused any enemy to think twice about firing on her. But the real muscle of this mission was the two AH1-Z Super Cobra attack helicopters. Armed with twenty-millimeter Gatling guns that fire three thousand rounds a minute, along with air-to-surface Hellfire missiles, these birds of prey were awesome killing machines. Archangel Bravo, flown by Captain Godfrey Bridges, and Archangel Charlie, piloted by Captain Jack Kraft closed up the formation as the choppers headed inland and toward the Jordanian border.

Jordan, Inside One Thousand Meters from Israel

Al Qaeda is truly fortunate to have leaders like Usama bin Laden and Ayman Alzawahiri to do their thinking. Because the great majority of their foot soldiers are stupid, stupid, stupid. A common saying in the U.S. military is that "any one of ours is worth ten of theirs." Wells put the actual ratio at more like one to thirty. The thought brought a wry grin to his face as he sighted in the Galil.

He had managed to worm his way inside a hundred meters from the southernmost group, and lady luck had smiled on him because he counted fewer than twenty men. Apparently he had eaten into their number back at the roadblock ambush, and they had no immediate source of reinforcements. His crosshairs were even now playing back and forth across the body of the single survivor from the roadblock. Taking his time, he waited until he had a good head shot, then fired. His bullet entered the man's eye, tearing away a huge chunk of the back of his head upon exit. He had taken them completely by surprise. Some of them didn't even have weapons in their hands.

Three more men went down before someone figured out the direction from which the shots were coming and screamed in Arabic for others to fire back. A hail of automatic fire was launched in the direction from which the first deadly shots had come, but they did nothing except stir up sand and churn the air, because Curt Wells was long gone.

He made the decision to flank the group on the west, toward Israel, so that every time he changed positions he would be a few steps closer to safety. He sighted in and fired twice more, taking down two more terrorists. This time they reacted a bit more quickly, and their return fire narrowly missed. Again he scuttled right, hoping they would not divine his tactic until it was too late.

Deliberately, and with deadly accuracy, he cut down three more men, his fourth shot narrowly missing another because he was forced to scramble to avoid return fire. Then he realized that the fire he had most recently fled had not come from the direction of the group he had engaged. Looking over his shoulder, he saw thirty more armed hostiles slogging through the sand toward him as fast as they could move, periodically spraying wild bursts with their AK-47s as they ran. He guessed that this was finally it. He said his prayerful goodbyes to Molly, Scott and Tyler, drew the Glock and cut down the lead elements of the attacking mob.

Suddenly, out of nowhere, heavy automatic fire began thinning the ranks of both groups of al Qaeda soldiers. Moving toward him, laying down fire to cover one another were Bobby Hammack, Mack Bryson, Marco Lopez and Sean Garrity. Like Wells, they had lost few of their combat skills, and their fire was proving increasingly deadly to the overmatched fanatics. Out of breath as he reached Wells' side, Hammack spoke urgently.

"C'mon Skip, we gotta go. There's fifty more of them just over that big dune. The odds suck!"

Needing no persuasion, Wells rose and they all headed for Israel, then hit the dirt as one when bullets rained down around them.

"Some of 'em got in behind us," growled Bryson, disgusted at having allowed this to happen.

"We have to keep going," Wells said quickly. "Better to take them on than the guys coming up from behind."

Together they rose and formed a crouched skirmish line, laying down a withering barrage at those who threatened to deny them escape. The tactic proved effective, as many of the enemy died and the rest were compelled to flatten themselves in the sand to escape the same fate. Looking over his shoulder, Wells noted that their pursuers were gaining ground, since they were taking no fire. As they came within range, the five commandos were again forced to the ground, hot lead flying over their heads like a swarm of angry hornets. Well, they had almost made it, hadn't they?

With a sudden deafening roar the choppers from the Tarawa emerged out of the lowering dusk, unleashing thousands of rounds of lethal cannon and machine gun fire and blasting all the enemy positions with surface-to-air missiles, including one Hellfire that wiped out at least fifteen al Qaeda in a single, brilliant fireball.

"Yee-haw, the U.S. Navy has arrived," Bryson shouted, pumping a fist skyward.

Amply covered by the blistering fire from the choppers, the five made their way past the orange and black pylons that demarcate the border. Another helicopter, not American, swooped out of the sky, and the friendly face of Zev Shalman greeted them.

"Welcome to Israel, gentlemen. Get in. You'll like our hospitality better," the Israeli said.

Then he picked up the microphone and went air-to-air with the Navy choppers as his own bird lifted off.

"Well done, Archangels," he said jovially. "We'll take it from here."

Waggling acknowledgment, the three Navy birds wheeled and headed west, back toward the Tarawa. Wells and Hammack both looked back onto the Jordanian side where the ground lay littered with what looked like nearly a hundred very dead bodies, and nothing was moving.

They had flown for only a few minutes when the pilot spotted the truck, sitting right where Wells' men had parked it. Swooping quickly down, they dropped off the two Israelis who had been riding shotgun for Shalman so that they could drive it back to Eilat. Alone, their voices challenged by the racket from the bird's swirling rotors, Shalman turned to Wells and spoke.

"So, are you well, my friend?" he asked.

"Better now," Wells smiled.

"You make a very convincing Arab, you know?" Shalman teased.

"Yeah, I can hardly wait to get rid of this garb and into a comfy pair of jeans and a tee shirt." Wells rejoined.

"There will be time for that, and some food at Eilat, but not much more," frowned Shalman.

"How so?" Wells asked, thinking his longest day at an end.

"We fly you back to Tel Aviv tonight, and from there Halvarson-Brandt will take you to London where they have made reservations for you, under false names, of course, at a five-star hotel. There you'll rest a bit, and then travel via commercial flights to various different destinations in the U.S. It wouldn't do to have you all showing up in the same place now, would it?" the wily Jew smiled.

"No, I guess not. Where am I going?" Wells inquired.

"You, my friend, are going to Dulles International Airport in Washington. There is a man who lives in a white house there who wishes a word with you. My government has to make concessions sometimes, too," Shalman shrugged.

The Oval Office, Two in the Afternoon

The president sat in the power chair opposite the fireplace. On the sofa to his right sat his DCI and the secretary of state and to his left sat the chairman of the Joint Chiefs of Staff. Soon they were joined by Ken Karns, White House chief of staff and Director Kendrick of the FBI.

"So, they got Wells and his men out in one piece?" Sloan directed his question at the old general.

"Safe and sound. Actually, his men were already out and went back for him, as I predicted," the general responded with a smug satisfaction.

"And did we draw blood?" the president persisted.

"A lot of al Qaeda blood," Blaisdell assured him. "We estimate their casualties at 100%."

"We killed them all?" asked a horrified Donald Trimble.

"Every last one," confirmed Blaisdell gleefully, and we did it with joint Jordanian-Israeli approval. Those particular fellows won't be blowing up any more civilians. Truth is, according to our people on the scene, Wells and his men were holding up their end of things pretty well until our birds arrived. Maybe we should see about getting those old guys back into uniform."

"I hate to be the dark cloud on the horizon," interjected the FBI man, "but according to Justice we have some significant problems with the Kerolyan prosecution."

"What kind of problems?" Sloan asked, cupping his hands to his forehead.

"We know the guy's dirty, but it seems that everything we have is circumstantial. Justice doesn't think it's enough to convict," Kendrick said.

"Even with Qureshi's direct testimony?" an incredulous Sloan demanded.

"That's the crux of the problem, Mr. President. We don't *have* Qureshi's direct testimony. Justice doesn't believe, nor do I, that the Saudis are going to allow him out of the kingdom to testify, and since his information was obtained under torture it probably would be inadmissible in a U.S. court anyway. If our whole case is built on his testimony and Kerolyan doesn't have the right to confront his accuser, well ..."

"I hear you," Sloan muttered softly. "But if we can't nail him, our deal with the Saudis will go south in a hurry."

They sat in silence briefly, and then Emmett Choate made a suggestion.

"There may be another way," he said slyly.

"We're listening Emmett," the president waved his hands for the DCI to continue.

"The Halvarson-Brandt security chief, Stone, I think is his name, told the Bureau that Kerolyan is hot to go to Saudi and firm up their deal. So, why not encourage them to let him do that?"

Choate said with, his straight face masking the mischief in his suggestion..

"Are you suggesting what I think you're suggesting?" asked the secretary of state disapprovingly. "It's monstrous."

Kendrick of the FBI was now nodding and smiling, and began to reason aloud.

"Kerolyan goes to Saudi. We, the FBI, and HB turn over all the incriminating evidence to them, and the minute he steps off the plane they arrest him. They put him on trial using our evidence and Qureshi's testimony, he's guilty and he gets a firing squad. What a shame!"

"And we're well within our rights not to lift a finger, since he will have been arrested in a foreign country for criminal acts committed there. Will HB go along?" the president asked hopefully.

"I think so. They're really pissed at the guy," Kendrick answered.

"All right, make the call," ordered the president as they rose to leave.

"We get our hostages and their rescuers back, they get an American's head for the royal nephew, not to speak of cleaning out their own rat's nest, the oil keeps flowing, and everyone's at least somewhat happy.

Dallas, Twenty Minutes Later

Barton Stone and Stan Blanton stared at each other across the table as the FBI director spelled out the White House suggestion on the speakerphone.

"You want us to feed him to the wolves, eh?" mused Blanton.

"He's done that to himself," Kendrick corrected. "Only in Saudi, the wolves can bite him, while here, they can't. You understand, of course, that this conversation never occurred."

"Of course not, Mr. Director. Give us a short while and we'll try to cooperate," Blanton promised.

As the phone went dead, Stone spoke quietly.

"Give Kerolyan the go ahead verbally, but not in writing. Tell him we're short on air transport at the moment and you want him to take the first commercial flight and charge it to his company credit card. Later, if he claims HB sent him to Saudi, we'll deny it and say he went on his own in order to protect the fruits of his crime. Our hands will be clean, and he will get what he deserves."

"What if he tapes me?" Blanton fretted.

"Let him. We'll remove his phones the minute he leaves, and sanitize everything. Something tells me he won't like his severance package," Stone quipped with grim irony.

"Won't he get suspicious when he can't reach Qureshi?" Blanton worried.

"The Saudis will fix it, probably have some lower level bureaucrat tell Kerolyan Qureshi's away in Vienna on OPEC business but will return by the time he gets there," Stone theorized.

"I have to tell you that this makes me a bit uncomfortable. But it seems like the only way, and the guy's sure got it coming," Blanton said.

"If it was up to me, I'd send them the asshole's head in a box with an apple in his mouth. But for the record, I never said that," Stone replied caustically.

CHAPTER SEVENTEEN

Tuesday, October 9, London, England

They flew for much of the night aboard one of Halvarson-Brandt's well-appointed Lears, arriving at London's Gatwick airport. Checking in at the sumptuous Beresford Arms, overlooking Hyde Park, each man went straight to his room and to bed. Seven hours later, they sat together at a table adorned with white linen, fine silver and crystal, in a private dining room. It was to be their last meal together before going their separate ways. The first flights began leaving in just over three hours.

Most of them brought but a single extra outfit, and they were all casually, but neatly dressed. For his part Wells wore a long-sleeved navy blue shirt, open at the collar and a freshly pressed pair of tan chinos.

He'd provided the Beresford's finest beef Wellington, caviar and a well-ripened champagne. When all the glasses were filled, he rose to speak.

"I want to propose a toast," he began emotionally. "To another successful mission, to our next *real* fishing trip, and to the finest group of men with whom it has ever been my privilege to serve," he said, raising his glass.

Clinking the goblets gently together they drank the toast. Then Wells continued, "I want to thank each one of you from the bottom of my heart for putting it on the line to save my son's life. That would go for Molly, too, if she were here."

Then Bobby Hammack rose to another toast. "And here's to the finest C.O. any outfit ever had. We wouldn't have missed this one for the world, L.T."

Again they drank. Then it was Marco Lopez' turn.

"I want to offer a toast to Denny's new wooden leg," he said as they all burst out in laughter at Creel's newly acquired cane.

There was more drinking, and a lot more laughing before a uniformed chauffeur informed them it was time to leave for the airport. Zev Shalman made sure their passports were stamped and waiting for them at Tel Aviv, but they'd have to clear customs one at a time at Heathrow. Some shook hands, others hugged. They all knew this was one they would never forget. Then they departed, leaving the dining room empty and still.

Creel flew out first, on a British Airways flight bound for New Orleans. There, his brother was scheduled to pick him up and drive him to Baton Rouge to stay until he was recovered. He had no family outside the men he was leaving and his brother, so he'd enjoy some good Boudin hospitality before eventually returning to his home in St. Louis.

Lopez left last, flying non-stop to LAX, and the others would trickle into JFK in New York and Chicago O'Hare. Wells, of course, was headed for the nation's capital.

It was nearly four PM in London, but still early morning in Oregon. After clearing customs, Curt Wells found a phone, and using one of the cards he had purchased when his odyssey of danger began, he dialed a familiar number. On the second ring a male voice he recognized answered.

"Hey," he said casually, "can you get us tickets for the Seahawks-Raiders game in two weeks?"

"Dad? Dad?" Came the incredulous response. "Where in the world are you? Are you okay?"

"Yes, Ty, I'm just fine," he said to his youngest son. "Put the phone on speaker so your mother can hear me/"

"Curtis?" came Molly's question that carried both exhilaration and a world of relief. "Is that really you?"

"In the flesh," he responded. "Are the home fires still burning?"

"For you, always, my love," she cooed like a schoolgirl. "Where are you and when will I see you?"

"Just now I'm at the airport in London. After our hop over the pond, I have to make a quick stop in Washington, then home to you. What do you hear from Sunny?" he asked.

"We've talked to him three times. The first time was from somewhere overseas, Germany, I think. And then he called again from Dallas a couple of times," she responded.

"Dallas?" he marveled. "I figured he'd be there with you by now."

"He told us that you might still be in Saudi, and that he wasn't coming home until he'd pulled every string he could to be sure you got out safely. Like father, like son, I guess," Molly said with what he imagined to be a proud smile.

Momentarily they called his flight for boarding, and he had to hang up. Her voice still made him tingle all over, and he could hardly wait to see her again.

As soon as he was off, Molly dialed Scott's new cell phone to tell him the good news. After that brief and happy conversation, Scott called Stan Blanton to see if a company Lear could fly him to Washington to meet his father. The answer was a quick and emphatic "yes."

On his way out of the building, Scott ran into Barton Stone.

"On your way to a fire?" Stone ribbed him.

"No. Dad's coming home," Scott shouted over his shoulder.

"He's all right, then?" Stone asked animatedly, turning to follow him out. "You know, your dad is one hell of a leader," he offered.

Scott stopped dead in his tracks, a sudden realization dawning as to how Stone would know what kind of leader the senior Wells was.

"You were at Al B'ir too, weren't you?" he gasped.

"That's classified," Stone answered with a wink and a smile.

"Good enough," Scott smiled in return, "but I owe you."

"No you don't," Stone said, "It was your old man's show all the way. I was just along for the ride."

Washington, D.C., Early Evening

As Curt Wells was clearing customs, a tall, balding, hawk-nosed man in a blue customs uniform seized his passport and motioned him into a room behind the counter. He was expecting this. It was the government's way of reminding him that he'd crossed that ephemeral line between what the law demands and what current policy expects.

"You are Curtis Wells?" the man said blandly.

"I am," Wells answered, giving him nothing more than requested.

"According to the stamps on your passport you are coming out of Tel Aviv by way of London, is that correct?" his inquisitor pressed.

"If that's what it says, then that must be where I've been," Wells gave a flip answer.

"May I inquire as to what business took you to Israel?" the agent continued.

"You can ask, but I don't have to tell you," Wells replied, becoming irritated.

"You think this is funny?" the agent demanded.

"No, I think it's boring as hell. Fact is, I didn't take anything illegal out, and I don't have anything illegal on me now. My passport is duly stamped and you can't touch me. You know it. I know it. So what the hell are we doing here?" snapped the agitated Wells.

As things heated up, two dark suits entered the room and flashed United States Secret Service credentials.

"We're here to escort this man to the White House on the president's orders," one of them said curtly to the customs agent, opening the door and motioning Wells out at the same time.

As they walked out of customs and cleared the knot of travelers, Wells looked down the concourse and saw a solitary figure sprinting towards them. There could be no mistake about who it was. Scott Wells had been there waiting, and as father and son met and embraced the world seemed to stand still around them. During the tense days of the hostage standoff, Scott's picture had routinely run in the newspapers and on television. A news photographer saw him on the way in, put two and two together and now his shutter whirred as he took the reunion pictures that had Pulitzer prize stamped all over them.

Urgently, the Secret Service men tugged at Curt Wells, trying to keep this from turning into a media circus.

"Come on, Mr. Wells, you have an appointment," one of them said quietly.

"I'm his attorney. Where he goes, I go," interjected Scott assertively.

"Then let's all please go," the other Secret Service agent pleaded. "This is going to get out of control if we don't."

They hustled through the growing group of onlookers and jumped on a motorized cart that headed toward the airport exit marked "private cars." Climbing into a big, bulletproof limousine, they sped away toward Capitol Hill. Within two minutes the lucky newsman was on the phone to his editor, and in a few minutes more, the White House press corps was on alert.

By the time they arrived at the White House it was nearly six PM, eastern standard time. But by Curt Wells' body time it was the next morning. At their efficient best, the Secret Service whisked them into the White House and a receiving foyer. There, the head of the detail informed Scott that he would have to wait, because the president desired a private meeting with Curt Wells.

Once he had cleared a metal detector and undergone a thorough body search, the elder Wells was led through a dizzying maze of hallways and stairwells, arriving finally at a long and elegantly appointed hall leading straight to the Oval Office. Inside, presidential receptionist Brenda Phillips, asked him politely to wait. Obediently, he did as he was told, glancing nervously around at the simple elegance of the place and gaining a sense of why it was so intimidating.

He thought about this conversation all the way from London to Washington. He wasn't sure what was on Norman Sloan's agenda, but he was confident it would include a dressing down for making his own foreign policy and taking matters into his own hands. He was prepared to cut Sloan some slack on that score, but he didn't want to be patronized by idle threats. Momentarily Brenda emerged from inside.

"The president will see you now, Mr. Wells," she said demurely.

He walked into the big office to find the president staring distantly out the window at the venerable sights of the city. As he entered, Sloan turned, half-smiled, and invited him to sit on one of the big couches flanking the blazing fireplace, while he sat in one of the leather chairs beside him. Curtis Wells was now alone with the most powerful man in the world.

"Let's get some ground rules straight between us," Sloan began, not beating around the bush. "I don't want you to bullshit me here today."

"You don't patronize me, and I won't lie to you, deal?" retorted Wells.

"Deal," Sloan agreed with that thin smile Wells had seen on his face before.

"You know, Wells, that you have pretty much run circles around this government as well as the government of our Saudi Arabian allies, and you damn near made a shambles of our foreign policy."

Curt decided in advance to draw Sloan out, keeping his own counsel as long as possible, so he simply nodded, inviting the president to get it off his chest.

"Justice tells me that there's very little we can charge you with, and politically we wouldn't do it anyway because when this gets out, you're going to be a national hero. But you knew that already, didn't you?" Sloan asked with a tinge of sarcasm.

"I'm no hero, sir," Wells offered deferentially. "I'm just a father who loves his son so much that he couldn't let him die over there."

"The Saudis would like to extradite you for the killing of the hostage takers at Al B'ir. Does that surprise you?" Sloan followed up.

"Nothing surprises me anymore," Wells shrugged, "but I'm not overly worried because I know this administration will never go along with it."

"And why, pray tell, wouldn't we?" Sloan played the devil's advocate.

"Because you want another term, for one," Wells quipped. "And without eyewitnesses or good forensics their case would be the thinnest kind of circumstance. You send me to face a kangaroo court and a firing squad over there and you couldn't get elected mayor of Dubuque. Am I way off base here?"

"No," Sloan sighed, "you're pretty much right on the mark. Governing, Mr. Wells, is about making hard choices. My reluctance to send our military in after those hostages was not meant as a personal slight to you and your family. I acted or, in this case, declined to act on what my senior advisors and I felt was in our nation's best interests."

Wells considered this for a moment, and could not help but note that Sloan seemed to feel some need to justify himself. He knew where this was going, and he knew, too, that he could never agree with the president that it was in the best interests of the country to allow its citizens to be tortured and killed in order to appease a foreign government. So he decided to change directions.

"And I felt compelled to do what I thought best for my family," he said evenly. "It seems like we're just two men who did what they thought was right for those to whom they felt responsible."

There was a prolonged and pregnant silence between them, until finally Sloan spoke again.

"As president, I should be mad as hell at you for taking matters into your own hands. But in light of how things turned out, personally, I can't help but admire what you've done. I don't suppose there's any chance of drawing you back to Langley?" he added wistfully.

"Zero," confirmed Wells, "but it was nice of you to ask."

"What's next for you, then?" Sloan hooded a look of concern. "You know that from the time you walk out of here, and for the foreseeable future, the press is going to be all over you. What are you going to say to them?"

"Very damned little," Wells promised. "I have grapes to harvest and wine to make."

"Good!" exclaimed the president. "I think it will be best for all of us that way."

The two men made some small talk, rose and shook hands, and then walked out of the Oval Office together.

The same limo that had brought them to the White House was waiting under the portico with the passenger doors open. Scott, using his cell, thoughtfully made them reservations at a nearby hotel, and was already in the vehicle with Curt right on his heels when a horde of reporters came boiling out of the White House. Secret Service agents did their best to hold the gaggle at bay, but as the cameras flashed they shouted a barrage of questions at Wells.

"Did you just see the president? What did you two talk about? There's a story out there that you led the group that rescued your son. Would you like to comment? Were you in Saudi Arabia? Don't you think that maybe you've crossed the line here?"

Wells ignored all the questions but the last one. It was so stupid that it made his blood boil. He stopped dead in his tracks, turned and faced the reporter who had shouted it.

"Who are you?" he demanded.

"Maury Zimmerman, *New York Sentinel*," the short bespectacled man answered.

"Do you have children of your own, Maury?" Wells asked coldly.

"Uh, yes, two," came the reply from a reporter suddenly on the defensive.

"If, God forbid, someone snatches one of them and makes demands for his or her safe return and if, in your heart of hearts, you believe your child is about to be killed, then I want you to call me up collect, and explain to me exactly where that line is that demarcates what you would and would not do to get him or her back safely, Maury. If you consider the scenario for a moment, I think you will have answered your own question," Wells said acidly, getting into the limo and slamming the door behind him.

Wednesday, October 10, D.C.

Father and son slept too little, wolfed down a hotel buffet breakfast too fast and caught a cab to National airport where they were booked on a Continental flight that was to terminate in Portland after a brief stopover in Denver. They spoke little of either the daring rescue or Scott's time at Al B'ir. There would be plenty of time for that. Both could hardly wait to get home.

All of a sudden, Curt Wells was acutely aware of his age. His body hurt all over. His hamstrings were screaming from all the double-timing through the soft desert sand, he was still suffering the after effects of dehydration, even though it seemed to him that he had been drinking constantly, and his shoulder ached from the repeated recoil of the sniper rifle he had wielded so expertly.

"So this is the beginning of old," he muttered to himself.

With the pressure lifted, the politics and the press far away, both men slept most of the way to Denver, awakening only when the 747 jumbo jet touched down on the runway. After a couple of cups of black coffee, the conversation turned to the ordeal of the last two weeks. The large bruise on Scott's cheek was healing already, but Curt noticed it and ran his hand across it gently.

"How'd you come by that?" he asked, pretty sure that he already knew.

"They told me to read a propaganda statement on camera and I recited the Gettysburg address instead," Scott chuckled.

"Had to be a hardass, huh?" Curt remonstrated.

"My mom and dad didn't raise any traitors, that's all," Scott teased in return.

"Is that what happened to Marty's face, too?" the Curt followed up.

"Pretty much," Scott confirmed.

"Except I think he recited the preamble to the Constitution, or something. Speaking of Marty and the Logans, how do you feel about a new daughter-in-law?" he changed the subject.

"A what?" inquired a flabbergasted Curt Wells.

"I've been on the phone a lot with Tyler since I got back in the country. He says he's in love with Callie Logan and plans to ask her to marry him, maybe as soon as next week," Scott reported with his broad trademark smile.

"This is some kind of practical joke, right?" Curt asked in an exasperated tone.

"I think it's the real deal, Dad. You'll just have to ask Ty," replied Scott.

"You bet I will," snapped a thoroughly nonplused Curt Wells.

Oregon, That Afternoon

As Curt and Scott walked off the plane and passed through security, there were loud cheers from about three dozen well-wishers who'd assembled to welcome them home. Molly rushed to embrace them, with Tyler close behind. Looking around, Curt saw Fritz Emswiler and Jimmy Dunn, riding in a wheelchair pushed by Anson Landis, along with a variety of Yamhill county friends and neighbors. Press people were there, too, but they were uncharacteristically polite and settled for what footage they could take as the group moved off toward baggage claim.

Flanked by his tall, handsome sons, Curt made his way through the crowd waiting at the carousel and claimed the single bag he'd taken with him, along with what he had jokingly said must have been three weeks worth of Scott's dirty laundry in two oversized duffels.

Carlos was waiting in a van curbside, and as the family, plus Emswiler and Dunn piled in, he gunned the engine and wheeled out of the airport southbound for Whispering Ridge. There was a lot of laughing, some talk of the harvest that was now well in progress and the orders that were piling up on Curtis Wells' desk. No one mentioned the ordeal the older Wells men had just endured. There would be plenty of time for that later, and the emotion of this moment was unbridled joy.

Curt had handled the reunion well. His world was suddenly in balance again with all the people he loved most safe and at home. What he did not anticipate was the deep surge of emotion he felt as the van wheeled off the main highway and onto the tree-lined approach to the winery. Between the trees he glimpsed the rolling hills of green vineyards that stretched almost as far as the naked eye could see. There were moments in An Nafud when he was not sure he would ever see this sight again, and the combination of the rolling green and cool, moist air brought a deep gratitude welling to the surface, and a teardrop to his eye. Curt Wells loved his family, and God, how he loved this place.

The Logans and Sapersteins all returned to their respective homes for reunions of their own. Jimmy Dunn was booked out on a flight the next morning, but just had to stick around and see his old friend safe and well again and hear the stories about how the team performed in Saudi. Tyler was delighted to see his brother and father, but Curt thought he seemed a little pensive. It was time for a father and son talk.

After a good spaghetti dinner, the crowd began to break up. Early evening found Curt and Tyler Wells sitting on the wraparound porch in comfortable wooden rockers, facing one another.

"Well, you pulled it off," Tyler sighed. "I was afraid I'd never see you again."

"There were a few moments when I wasn't sure either, Ty," said the father. "It turned out to be a lot hairier than I anticipated over there."

"Sunny said our uncles helped. Are they all in one piece, too?" Tyler asked.

"Denny caught one in the leg, but the medics said it's healing well and the round didn't hit bone," Curt replied. "I think this was our last fight."

"Why didn't you let Sunny know it was you getting him out?" Tyler wondered aloud.

"Because we thought the Egyptians, the Saudis and the CIA would likely question them in Cairo, and we needed to give Scott the same plausible deniability I tried to give you. We didn't want to open ourselves to extradition and prosecution by the Saudis if they took a dim view of what we had done," Curt explained.

"But it's all over the papers that it was you." Tyler blurted out.

"Me, not the others," Curt Wells smiled, "and the political consequences for the president if he agreed to my extradition are just too great for him to bear. I'm not worried about that. But from what I hear, I went away for a few days and my son lost his mind. Tell me about you and the Logan girl," he added, changing the subject with a sly grin.

"Yeah," Tyler let out a deep breath, "well it just sort of happened. We were in Washington together, we spent hours on the phone and … I love her, Dad. I know we haven't known each other very long, but I'm not some twenty-one year old and both you and mom always said I'd know when the right one came along. I know I've found her."

"Have you considered the fact that you're a few years older than she is?" Curt queried.

"We've talked about it, but it really doesn't matter to either of us," answered Tyler. "I want to ask her to marry me."

"Can you do anything else?" the senior Wells asked bluntly.

"What do you mean 'can I do anything else'?" Tyler did a double take.

"I mean do you honestly believe that you would be so miserable without her that this is the only course of action open to you?" Curt pressed.

Tyler didn't answer right away, clearly processing the ramifications of his father's question. Finally, he spoke.

"No, dad, I really don't think I can do anything else," came the answer.

"Then propose to the girl," instructed Curt Wells, "Beg her if you have to, because that's exactly how I felt about your mother. By the way, does your mom know yet?"

Tyler Wells nodded sheepishly, a broad grin lighting up his face.

"I'd like to invite the Logans here for the engagement celebration, if that's okay with you," he added.

"Of course, it's fine. When?" Curt Wells asked.

"How about Thanksgiving weekend?" Tyler asked.

"That's fine. It will give me a little time to get my head back into the business and get this place ready for guests."

Rising, they began to amble back toward the house, Curt lagging a bit with a slight limp.

"Are you all right?" Tyler expressed concern.

"I'm fine," Curt muttered. "I just found out that my youngest son was right about something he told me awhile back."

"What was that?" Tyler inquired.

"I'm getting too old for this commando crap!" Curt growled.

CHAPTER EIGHTEEN

Whispering Ridge

Wells read with interest about the Saudi arrest of Lloyd Kerolyan. President Sloan, when questioned by the media about whether the U.S, would intervene, explained with overdone sincerity how Americans arrested on foreign soil for crimes committed there would simply have to pay the piper. How, Wells wondered, would Sloan have reacted if things had not worked out so well in An Nafud and if *he* had been captured? But he would shed no tears for Kerolyan. As far as he was concerned whatever the Saudis wanted to do to the man was just fine by him.

The days literally flew by now, with the harvest near completion and the winery humming along as the sweet grape juice was fermented and blended into fine wine. Carlos and Fritz had been right. This was going to be one of the best vintages ever.

And Wells himself was a cause *celebre*. Enough details about Al B'ir and the slaughter in the Negev had filtered out that America was now convinced that Wells was behind it all. And with every "no comment," or declined talk show interview the legend was embellished. The bloggers were speculating about how Wells had single-handedly dispatched over a hundred terrorists while bringing the hostages home. His home phone had rung so often that he changed the answering message on the machine to include a press and media disclaimer.

One day, however, in a weak moment, he absent-mindedly picked up on the first ring while he sat at the desk in his study. The voice on the other end almost prompted him to hang up.

"Mr. Wells, this is Maury Zimmerman with the *New York Sentinel*," said the caller.

"No interviews, Maury. Not even for the *New York Sentinel*," he groused offhandedly.

"There is no line!" came the baffling response.

"Pardon?" Wells responded, scratching his head.

"At National you told me that when I could explain where the line was that I would not cross to save my children, I should call you. I thought very hard about it, and then I understood why you did whatever it was that you did. There is no such line. I want you to write a book with me," Zimmerman said.

"I've told all you press guys that I'm not going to discuss what happened in the Middle East," Wells complained wearily.

"I don't want to write about the rescue," Zimmerman said, a calm sincerity in his voice. "I want to write about what it means to be a father. About two weeks after I talked to you in Washington I made an appointment with a guy in Baltimore who works with young dads. I spent a day with him and he gave me a crash course in fathering. The more I listened to him, the more I felt I understood you. You see, there are kids out there on the streets without fathers because their dads are in prison, or on drugs, or split from their mom, or spend all their time working, or just don't have a clue what a dad is supposed to do or be. Nobody's going to listen to me, but right now you're a national hero. If you help me tell the story I know that a lot of men will pay attention."

"I don't know, Maury, I'm no expert on parenting," Wells demurred.

"I don't think it's so much about what you know as it is about what drives you that's important," Zimmerman offered. "It's about what a father's love will do for his kids."

"I can't get away right now. This is our busy season here at the winery. Could you come out here?" Wells asked, warming a bit to the concept.

"I'll be on a plane tomorrow if you say so. You name it," an excited Zimmerman enthused.

"How about next week?" Wells asked. "I'll only be able to give you a couple of hours a day, but if you think we can do some good, then I guess I'm game to give it a shot."

"Next week then," Zimmerman said. "And thanks for your willingness to humor me on this."

The hours and days became a blur as Curt Wells pored over advertising copy, filled orders, scheduled appearances at wine shows, signed off on payroll, fretted with cantankerous machinery and did all the other trivial but vital things that made Whispering Ridge Cellars so successful. Periodically he thought about Maury Zimmerman's call, but hadn't a clue what he would say to the man when the time came.

He was also planning his youngest son's engagement party, aiming for the night after Thanksgiving. Tyler had asked, and Callie, with her parents' blessing, had said yes. The whole Logan family would join the Wells tribe for a great Thanksgiving feast, followed by the formal announcement party the following evening.

For that occasion, Curt Wells selected Fenouil, an upscale continental restaurant in the Pearl District off downtown Portland. He reserved one end of the upstairs dining area and arranged to meet with Henri, his good friend who was part owner and executive chef, to go over menu and wine selection. This was a big deal for Tyler, and Curt wanted to make it extra special.

Downtown Portland, Early the Following Morning

It was a part of his daily ritual. After reciting the morning prayer, Anan Barghouti would walk the four blocks from his one-bedroom apartment to Starbuck's, order a tall coffee, usually decaf latte, and begin his copious reading of the local paper. Born in Lahore, Pakistan, Barghouti had been an al Qaeda "wannabe" who idolized Usama bin Laden. Adjudged too bookish by the militants there, he was nevertheless trained in terrorist tactics and sent to America on a student visa. But his only involvement with the network was as a courier, conveying funds from the *hawaladars* - private untraceable bankers - in Vancouver, B.C., and San Francisco to cells planning terrorist acts or just hiding out in Portland and Seattle.

The plain truth was that the hardcore al Qaeda soldiers thought Barghouti somewhat effeminate, and unlikely to perform bravely in combat, and so had relegated him to the more menial tasks of supporting terror. This bias was not lost on Barghouti, and he longed for the chance to wage active *jihad*, and prove himself as brave as any of the others.

He read with disgust the media announcement of the upcoming engagement celebration by the Wells family, and the big party planned for Thanksgiving weekend at Fenouil. The U.S. was not the only place where the father, Curt Wells, had become well known. His adventures in Saudi had caused ripples as far away as the mountainous regions of Afghanistan and Pakistan, and *fatwas* had been issued there and elsewhere ordering his death in grim recompense for Al B'ir and Muhammad al-Shariyah.

A *fatwa*, or religious edict, is a pronouncement by an Islamic cleric decreeing its subject to be the will of Allah, and thus an exception to the normal Muslim code of behavior. Herein lay the greatest moral weakness of Islam. Ethical absolutes could be subjectively set aside by clerics with political agendas, justifying anything at all, including mass murder. Clerics in Iran issued *fatwas* demanding the death of an award-winning author because, in the view of some clerics, he had denied and disgraced the faith. It was even rumored that some clerical moron in Saudi had approved bin Laden's use of nuclear weapons against America, although he had thoughtfully capped the body count at ten million.

But for Anan Barghouti, a promising synchronicity leapt out at him from the pages of the *Tribune*. This was his time, his chance to avenge the deaths of many brothers and prove himself a true warrior of the faith. Yes, he would visit this Curtis Wells. He would do it when he was distracted by his great celebration, and he would strike a decisive blow for Islam. To the Wells family, the book was closed. In the mind of Anan Barghouti, the deadly epilogue had yet to be written.

CHAPTER NINETEEN

Whispering Ridge, Monday of the Following Week

Maury Zimmerman arrived from New York on the previous evening. Eager to get started on their joint writing project, he took a taxi out to the wine country, appearing at Whispering Ridge promptly at nine o'clock AM. Wells expected him, and the two retreated to Wells' private office to talk. With legal pad and ball point pen in hand, and a digital pocket recorder rolling, Zimmerman dove right in.

"I don't really know where to start with this," he confessed, "so I'm just going to ask some random questions and you can say whatever comes to mind. Let's start with the reunion at National airport, and the picture that just about everyone's seen of you and your son embracing. That was an emotional moment for both of you, I know. Some fathers hug their young children, but the sight of two grown men hugging like that begs the question. Do you always do that?"

Wells chuckled before responding. "You mean do I always hug my grown sons when I haven't seen them for awhile? I guess the answer to that would be yes. Sometimes families today seem afraid to touch each other. Our family has always been expressive that way. Let me show you something."

Rising and walking to the maple bookshelves that occupied

an entire wall of his study, Wells reached up and plucked a photo album from one of the higher ones. Returning to his desk he opened it and flipped through the pages. Soon he pushed the book across the desk toward Zimmerman and pointed to a black and white photo in the upper right hand corner that showed a younger Wells embracing a strapping young man in full football regalia.

"That was the day Sunny's high school football team won the district championship. He caught two touchdown passes in that one," he said proudly, before turning the page.

In the middle of the next page was a color shot of him with his arm around a tall red-haired boy.

"Molly shot this one right after Tyler's basketball team won the state title. Ty had just limited the state's leading scorer to six points. What a game that was. You see, I've been touching my boys with affection since they were newborns. I know that a lot of kids go through phases when they don't like an overt show of affection from their parents, but children need to be touched. I read somewhere that a doctor did a study on some kids who were deprived of touch from birth, kids who were wards of the state. He compared them with another group that were touched regularly from birth on. He had pictures proving that the brains of the children who had been touched were significantly larger and more developed by age two than those of the ones who weren't. I guess maybe a lot of fathers don't touch their children when they're little because they seem so fragile, and by the time they're older it doesn't seem natural anymore because it hasn't been happening all along. The truth is that Sunny and I might have hugged each other in that airport even if there hadn't been any kidnapping. But I won't deny that it was a special moment," Wells sighed, now staring mistily out the window.

"What would you say was the most important thing in your relationship with your sons?" Zimmerman followed up.

"Communication," Wells replied without hesitation. "I always tried to keep the lines of communication open. Molly and I counseled them against under age drinking, but I made a deal with them that if they ever got caught up in it and had one too many, or were riding with someone else who did, they could call me and I would come pick them up at any hour of the night, no questions asked, no judgments, no lectures, no punishment. I think that set the tone, and opened the door for us to have conversations about drugs, love, sexual responsibility, money and a lot of other things some kids won't talk to their parents about. But the lines of communication have to be set up and nourished by the parents, and they have to be free of negative judgments and criticism. If kids don't feel supported and trusted they aren't going to talk."

"Whoa, let's back up a minute," Zimmerman said. "You run a winery, right? You make and sell wine for a living. And you're telling your kids not to drink?"

"You bet I did!" exclaimed Wells. "Alcohol in any form is not for kids. In quantity, it kills brain cells, and drunk driving is a leading cause of death among teenagers. The wine we make here is for adults, to be consumed with meals or on special social occasions. And it is meant to be sipped and savored, not swilled until one falls into a drunken stupor. We don't market to kids, and if you'll check out the list of contributors to Mothers Against Drunk Driving you'll find that Whispering Ridge is annually among the top donors."

"Principle ahead of profit, eh?" Zimmerman smirked.

"Yeah, that's Curt Wells, that's how I live," came the response.

"Did you spank your sons?" Zimmerman wondered aloud.

"I think I might have popped Tyler on the backside once when he was crying hysterically and I needed to get his attention. But even that probably wasn't a good idea. Spanking isn't usually about what the kids need. It's more about parental domination and revenge for the child's bad behavior. If you have to spank your kids all the time, you've already lost control. I heard tough guys in the Navy justify the way they punished their kids by saying 'my old lady beat the tar out of me, and look how I turned out.' Most of these guys were big bullies and blowhards, and I just thought to myself, 'yeah, just look how you turned out,'" offered Wells sarcastically.

"Did you set a curfew for your sons when they were teenagers?" asked Zimmerman.

"Sure, but it was flexible. If they had some legitimate reason to be out late, we would negotiate until we agreed on another zero hour. If they couldn't make it, they could always call. Basically, I trusted them," Wells said quietly, reflecting on his parental past.

"If someone asked you what kids need most from their dads, what would you say?" Zimmerman inquired.

"I'd say they need the one thing a lot of dads find it hardest to give. They need quality time with their dad. We work, or we follow our hobbies, or we split from mom, or we're tired - the list of excuses goes on and on. And then one day our kids are grown and gone and we don't even know who they are. Fathering is just like anything else in life. If it's important to you, you make the time for it."

"So let's go back to you and Scott," Zimmerman suggested. "How did you feel when you heard about his kidnapping?"

"Empty, hurt, afraid, like I'd lost something very precious," Wells mused as he rose and paced.

"And that made you do whatever it was you did to bring him safely back home?" Zimmerman pressed.

"It's like you said on the phone, Maury. There is no line I wouldn't have crossed to save him. And if it had been his brother instead, the same would have applied," Wells answered, looking the reporter straight in the eye.

The question and answer sessions persisted for five days. When Maury Zimmerman thought he had all he needed, he thanked Curt Wells, packed his bags and headed home to New York, promising Wells a look at the finished manuscript before it was submitted for publication. Three months later, he would deliver as promised.

A Safe House Outside Wilsonville, Oregon

Yusuf Ali Atef was as hard, as experienced and as embittered as any twenty-five-year-old could possibly be. Errant American bombs wiped out his whole family in one day in Afghanistan. The only reason he didn't die with them is that he was staging with the Taliban for a raid on an American military outpost near Kabul. He became hardcore al Qaeda, and the leader of an American- based terror network on the West coast. He laughed out loud when he first heard about Anan Barghouti's plan to kill Curt Wells and his family, and now listened skeptically, staring at him across a large tabletop as Barghouti detailed his aspirations.

What Barghouti lacked in field experience, he compensated for in enthusiasm. A college friend, Muhammad Isfahan, accompanied him on this night. Isfahan, whose real name was Artis Cleaver, had done a stretch in prison for selling crack cocaine. There, he converted to Islam, and his hatred for authority made him an easy recruit for the terrorists.

The more Atef listened, the closer he came to believing that these two green *jihadis* might just be able to pull off the proposed assassination. He finally interrupted Barghouti.

"And what would you require of me, brother, to undertake your *jihad*?"

"Six of your best soldiers, automatic weapons for us all, and a vehicle to make our escape. Oh, uh, yes, and some hand grenades," Barghouti effused.

"Do you even know how to use a hand grenade?" scoffed Atef.

"Of course I do," Barghouti remonstrated. "I was trained in Pakistan just as you were in Afghanistan."

"It is one thing to speak of brave deeds, and quite another to perform them," Atef reminded him. "When the gunfire starts, the knees become weak and the spirit feeble."

"But with Allah on our side we cannot fail. Our surprise will be complete. They will be fat and dull with food and drink and unarmed, or poorly armed. We will overwhelm and kill them quickly," Barghouti promised confidently.

"If you do this thing, the two of you must then leave America. Are you prepared to do that?" Atef quizzed them. "I cannot afford to bring the American FBI down upon us all in their search for you."

Barghouti and Isfahan quickly assured him that they would do as he wished, and then Atef spoke again.

"I will give you my decision in one week's time. There are others with whom I must consult," he said, rising to signify that their audience was at an end.

CHAPTER TWENTY

Whispering Ridge, Tuesday Before Thanksgiving

Curt and Molly Wells sat in the living room of the main house in front of a blazing fire. The nights were colder now, and Curt's arthritis had been acting up. The warmth of the hearth seemed to help, and he edged closer, rubbing his hands together near the brightly flaming logs.

"Where are we going to put all of these people this weekend, Mother?" he asked Molly with a grin.

"Well, the boys have their own rooms, and we can put Alex and Mary in the main guest room and Callie in the other. Marty and the younger Logan boy can sleep on the day beds in the sun room, if you think that'll be okay," she replied.

"You think Callie will want a room of her own?" Curt asked impishly, purposely looking away.

"Just what are you implying, Curtis Wells?" Molly demanded in righteous indignation. "I hope you're not suggesting that we sponsor Tyler and Callie sleeping together before they get married."

"Oh come on, Mom. They're adults and they can do what they want," he said, pretending to busy himself with a menial chore. "Younger people tend to think differently now about these things nowadays."

"Of course they're adults," she responded, clearly peeved. "But they're *young* adults, and there's a difference between our meddling in their sex life and just presuming that they're already sleeping together. They've only known each other for a little while. Thank God for engagements. I guess I'm just old-fashioned."

Wheeling and sweeping her up in his arms, Curt said, "Yes, you are, and I love you just that way."

Most disagreements between Curt and Molly Wells were whimsical, good-natured bartering sessions like this one, and ended similarly. But this brave man who'd unflinchingly faced down enemy guns, knew that when Molly's ire was kindled, the prudent course of action was usually strategic retreat. In such cases he did not view retreat as defeat, so much as it was the purposeful surrender of love and mutual respect.

An NSA Communications Array Near Yuma, Arizona

As the monster dishes outside mined the spinning satellites above for every shred of information they could yield, an army of analysts buried deep under the desert sorted and deciphered their chaotic feeds. Amy Lassiter sat at her desk, watching a dozen monitors at the same time and eavesdropping intently on a conversation between an unidentified party in the northwestern United States and a familiar voice from the mountains in eastern Pakistan.

An honors graduate of Duke University, Amy's unique talent was that she could understand, read and write Arabic, Pashtu and Pharsi as though they were her first languages. What she heard through her headset on this night caused her brow to furrow and her stomach to churn. Although she was taping the conversation, she nevertheless scribbled away furiously on the notepad beside her keyboard, not wanting to miss the slightest nuance of meaning. When the palaver was done, she swiftly gulped down the last swallow of her lukewarm coffee, stood, straightened her clothing and marched intently toward her supervisor's office.

Jack Slater, a middle-aged National Security Agency gatekeeper looked up and smiled as she entered. Amy was one of his very best people, and he was always eager to hear what she had to say. Tonight, he saw the lines of deep concern etched on her face, and put down the document he was reading when she closed the door behind her.

"What is it?" Slater asked.

"We just picked up part of a conversation in Pashtu between a man in the Portland area calling himself 'Atef' and someone in Pakistan whom Atef repeatedly called 'The Teacher.'"

"The Teacher?" Slater sought confirmation, leaning back in his chair. "Isn't that a euphemism for …?"

"Ayman Alzawahiri," Amy finished the sentence for him.

"So what was on the old Egyptian eye doctor's pathological mind this evening?" Slater quipped.

"Nothing good," Amy shook her head. "As nearly as I could make it out he was approving some kind of mission that this Atef had inquired about."

"What kind of mission?" Slater pursued, now turning his chair to face her directly.

"Unknown," she replied. "I taped it and within a few minutes you'll have the tape and a transcript of everything we heard.'

'That's good," Slater mused, staring vaguely off into space. "Amy, you are very good at picking up on what these characters aren't saying, as well as what they are saying. What does that sixth sense of yours tell you about this? Are they planning a big attack?"

"Some kind of attack, probably. But big? I doubt it. There was no talk about logistics or support. Atef made some vague reference to 'the *fatwa*,'" she responded.

"What *fatwa*?" Slater wondered aloud.

"Again, unknown," she answered. "The only *fatwa* on the radical websites has been the open contract on that guy in Oregon who rescued his son from those kidnappers in Saudi."

"Yeah," Slater mused, "and killed a hell of a lot of them in the process, as I recall. What was that guy's name?"

"Wells, Curtis Wells," she said, retrieving the bit of information effortlessly from her extraordinary memory banks.

"And you say the U.S. caller was somewhere in the northwest?" Slater followed up, wincing a bit as Amy nodded.

"This may be nothing at all," Slater remarked casually, "but then again, somebody probably ought to give this Wells a heads up. I have to drive over to the backup generator station to look at a maintenance issue. When I get back, I think I'll give Washington a call on this one and let them make the decision," he said. "Good work Amy, as usual."

Slater waited for the transcript of the intercept to appear on his computer screen, then read it carefully and printed it out. This was by no means the first time they overheard al Qaeda bigwigs commiserating with their stateside minions. But Slater's own gut told him something was different about the synchronicity of the *fatwa*, Atef, Alzawahiri and Wells, and that set off the alarm bells in his crowded mind. Yes, he'd call the office of the director of national intelligence in Washington right after running his errand, and together they would decide what to do. He laid the two-sheet printout on the desk beside his computer, slipped on a black windbreaker and headed for the parking lot.

A communications array as big as this one required a lot of electrical power to operate. And because they dealt with a fair amount of sensitive data, they couldn't simply "go down" in case of a power outage. They ran on their own massive generator system and, a quarter of a mile away, an equally formidable bank of back-up generators stood ready in case the primaries should fail. In good weather, Slater might well enjoy the long walk. But the high desert wind had developed a chilly bite, so he climbed into his Toyota 4-Runner to drive over.

Jerry Skelton, the maintenance supervisor for the facility patiently awaited Slater's sign-off on the installation of some more modern equipment. It had been on site for several days now, and the replacement process was nearly complete. Jack Slater just had to give it a cursory once over, scrawl his initials on a government issue form attached to a clipboard, and that would be that.

What Slater didn't count on was a chance meeting with Joshua Miller. Joshua, a twenty-one-year-old hometown boy gone nowhere worked two part-time jobs in Yuma. By day he drove a delivery truck for a small electrical supply company and four nights a week he tended bar at Gulliver's, a waterhole with a dependable, if somewhat seedy clientele. He was on his way back from visiting his sometime girlfriend, Marla Cook, at her aunt's country boarding house. After smoking a couple of joints, and downing three or four beers with her, he said goodnight and headed back into Yuma on his way to Gulliver's. He could have, and should have gone the long way, around the government reservation and the signs that clearly said "U.S. Government Property, Keep Out." But during the course of his late night assignations with Marla, Miller learned that the road leading past the communications station was ten minutes quicker and never patrolled. There was no real reason for traffic enforcement on the road. The array itself is completely surrounded by a ten-foot electrified steel fence set in solid concrete, and is posed no significant threat by the occasional misguided motorist who got somehow off the beaten track.

Joshua Miller gunned the powerful engine of his blue Ford pick-up, and glanced at his watch to see just how late he was running. The fog from the pot and brew clouded his vision and thinking, causing him to weave erratically on the narrow and deserted roadway, often crossing the center line.

Jack Slater saw him coming more than a half-mile away as he pulled his Toyota out onto the road. Miller, paying scant attention to his driving, got out a cell phone and punched in some numbers, concentrating more on the lighted keypad than on the road ahead. Suddenly he looked up and jerked the steering wheel, momentarily blinded by the lights of the Toyota. Miscalculating and slow to react due to his stuporous condition, he struck the smaller SUV a glancing blow on the left front fender, causing it to careen out of control, slew over onto the passenger side and slide with frightening force into a concrete abutment in a nearby drainage ditch.

Jamming on his brakes and sliding to a screeching stop, Miller jerked the truck into park and sprinted back to where the 4-Runner lay on its side, the front end badly damaged but one headlight still boring a bright golden hole into the pitch dark desert night. Looking inside, he saw Jack Slater, unconscious and bleeding from a nasty head wound. He should do something. He should call somebody, he knew. But then there would be questions, so many questions. Why had he been on this road in the first place? How did the accident happen? How many beers did he drink? And was that marijuana they smelled in his truck?

Backing away from the disabled SUV and gripped by uncertainty and panic, Joshua Miller decided. He got back into his truck and drove away. He was never here, and this accident never happened. He hoped the man in the car would get help in time, but it wouldn't be coming from him. He supposed he'd just have to live with that.

Jack Slater's desk was situated directly under an air vent, perpendicular to the door and facing a row of bookcases. As the chill of night cooled the facility and the forced air heating system kicked on, the breeze from the vent ruffled the papers on the desk. Two sheets lying next to the computer stirred, then lifted gently off the surface and drifted soundlessly to the floor between the end of the desk and the wall. And as they flew away, so did any hope that Curt Wells and his family would receive advance warning of Anan Barghouti's murderous mission.

Slater lay unconscious in the ditch for another twenty minutes, before being discovered by security officers who became concerned when he did not arrive at the back-up power station. They rushed him to a hospital in Yuma for emergency medical aid, but his injuries were serious and he did not immediately regain consciousness. NSA analysts worked four ten-hour days on, with three days off each week. Amy Lassiter, blissfully oblivious to Slater's plight, had long since shut off the light and closed down her workstation, not scheduled to work again until after the Thanksgiving holiday.

Portland - The Day Before Thanksgiving

Callie and Brett Logan journeyed home to Denver from their respective halls of higher learning, and Marty flew in from Dallas to join them, his father Alex and stepmother Mary for the trip to the coast. The Willamette Valley to which they were headed was enjoying an uncharacteristically sunny late November, although the temperatures remained brisk. The flight from Denver passed smoothly, and the Logans disembarked at gate D-1, close to both security and baggage claim. As they rode down the escalator to claim their baggage, Callie caught sight of Tyler and Scott Wells and waved, smiling broadly.

Shortly, the luggage carousel began to spin and the bags were lifted smoothly off. At the curb, Carlos waited with the nine-passenger VIP van that was often used to host visiting wine aficionados for customized tours of Whispering Ridge Cellars. The happy group helped load the bags, then got aboard, with Callie and Tyler cuddled close together in the rear seat. Because it was the day before a major holiday, airport traffic was snarled and even the roadways headed south were heavily traveled. The trip to Whispering Ridge took them over an hour.

Molly was waiting on the front porch, and embraced each of the guests while Curt, Tyler, Brett and Marty carted luggage to the various guest rooms. When they drifted back to the main living area, luscious smells emanated from Molly's kitchen as the pumpkin and apple pies were baked to taste. In the dining room, trays heaped with finger sandwiches, bowls of chips and a larger bowl filled with a festive holiday punch invited the hungry travelers to a late lunch. As the women drifted into the kitchen, Curt Wells and Alex Logan loaded plates and retired to the two leather chairs facing each other and nearest the fireplace.

"We never really had a chance to talk after the rescue," Alex said. "What you went through over there must have been just awful, and I'm not even going to ask about it. I just want you to know, man to man, how incredibly grateful I am for the life of my son Marty."

"So am I, for all three of the boys," Wells responded. "It was dicey, and I was lucky to get out in one piece. I guess God was looking over my shoulder yet one more time."

"You know, when we were here before we were so concerned about our kids and preoccupied with planning that I never got to see how the winery works," Logan changed the subject.

"Would you like the twenty-five cent tour?" Wells asked, grinning from ear to ear.

Logan nodded eagerly, and as both men emptied their plates and glasses Curt led the way out onto the porch, down the stairs and toward the main winery building.

"My late father-in-law was fond of southern Europe, and had these buildings styled as authentic replicas of some old world wineries in Italy," he observed. "That's the appearance, anyway. But inside they are fully modernized, with all the bells and whistles that enable us to produce Oregon's finest wines in quantity."

As he swung the massive oaken door ajar, one might have expected to be stepping back into another century. Ignoring the door on the left that led to the aging cellar, Wells struck out for the main ground level operations center.

"We harvest our grapes here in October," he said. "We grow mostly *pinot noir, pinot gris,* and some of the finest Riesling grapes in the United States. The harvesting baskets are emptied onto that conveyor belt, where the grapes go through an extensive washing process. Then they go into these machines over here to be squeezed and mashed for their yield of juice. The juice and smaller pieces of pulp go through a filter, like this one," he said, reaching for and holding up a coarse metal grate.

"You let some of the pulp go through?" an amazed Logan inquired.

"Yes," Wells answered animatedly, "we call it the 'must,' and it stays with the juice through the initial part of fermentation. It's what ultimately gives the wine its color."

"Where does the fermentation happen?" Logan wondered aloud.

Do you see those eight big tanks over there?" Wells asked, pointing across the floor of the operations center. "They're over nine feet tall, and each one holds nearly a thousand liters. The juice is put in there along with several kinds of yeast to complete fermentation. Want to take a look inside?" he asked with a mischievous grin.

Logan nodded and Wells led the way up a moveable steel ladder that was attached to one of the tanks by four metal clips. At the top of the ladder was a platform just big enough for two men. Wells opened a small door in the top of the tank, and Logan peered in.

"Not what I expected," Logan said. "It looks like it has a head on it."

"We call that the 'cap,'" Wells explained.

"Some of the pulp and extraneous matter floats to the top during fermentation, and is useful because it keeps everything underneath it covered and busily fermenting. Eventually it is drained away. You don't actually drink that, if that's what you were worried about," Wells joked.

"Then what happens?" Logan asked over his shoulder as he made his way down the ladder.

"The fermentation process is carefully monitored by our enologist, Fritz Emswiler. I think you met him when you were here before," Wells offered, Logan nodding assent.

"At exactly the right time, the wine is drained through another filter at the bottom of the tank, and the pure, fermented juice is evacuated through these spigots," Wells said, pointing to the small tap at the bottom of one of the tanks. "Then it goes into barrels like the ones you see over there before being sent to the cellar for aging. We use two types of barrels here at Whispering Ridge. This one is French oak, literally imported from France. Those down there are Oregon live oak. The wood of the barrels contributes to the mellowness and flavor of each wine. The French oak yields a kind of smoky flavor, and the Oregon oak produces a somewhat sweeter taste."

"How long does the aging process take?" Logan asked.

"Here, we age most of our wines from four to twelve years, a few even longer," Wells said proudly.

"So you're now fermenting …?" Logan seemed confused.

"The wine we'll begin selling four or five years from now," Wells coached. "Let me show you the cellar."

He opened the heavy door and let Logan lead the way downstairs. In this particular building, the cellar was twice the size of the facility that stood atop it. Their eyes were greeted by rack after rack of casks stacked three high on steel shelves that extended in every direction.

"Wow," Logan exclaimed in awe. "I like wine, but I had no idea what actually went into making it. What happens to it after its appropriately aged?

"Do you see this conveyor belt?" Wells asked, pointing to a nearby flat apparatus that ran some forty feet in length before sloping gradually up and disappearing out of sight. "Barrels of aged wine are loaded and locked onto the belt one at a time, then carried up to the prep room that is just behind the wall where you saw the tanks. It is hand poured into another machine that precision-fills bottles one-by-one as they pass by on another automated system. Once filled, the bottles are corked and labeled, also automatically, then stored on shelves like the ones you see down here, only twice as high. It's all overseen by people who know exactly what they're doing, but the technology is state-of-the-art."

"I'm incredibly impressed. I suppose I should have expected as much," he said, paying Wells a compliment.

Just then, Carlos Gutierrez came sprinting up, out of breath.

"You have to see this," he said to Wells between gasps for air.

Wells looked at the sheet of paper and smiled.

"This, Alex, is the biggest single order ever received by Whispering Ridge Cellars. It's from a well-known restaurateur and resort owner up in Canada. Actually, he was at the tasting the evening before our little trip. The man wants 12,000 bottles of our finest."

"That's unusual?" Logan asked.

"Very," Carlos said, "A big order is usually 2,000 bottles."

"Let's skip the commercial carriers we usually use on this one, Carlos, and give the transport to Don Mackey and his boys. I don't want any screw-ups on this. Let's make this man a happy customer."

"You've got it, Chief," Carlos said, whistling happily as he walked away.

"Is the help usually so upbeat?" Alex Logan wanted to know.

"I have a very positive crew here," Wells confirmed, "but Carlos is a lot more than just 'help.' Six years ago I made him a minority owner, giving him a real stake in the success of the place. The same with Fritz. So an order like this one means dollars in their pockets as well. Both of the guys are like family to us."

"It's beautiful here," Logan observed as they emerged from the building. "But why 'Whispering Ridge?'"

You see that hill over there to the southwest?" Wells queried while pointing. "*That* is Whispering Ridge. In the evening, when the breeze blows gently in from the west through the trees on the hill, it makes a low, moaning sound, like someone talking in a stage whisper. Molly says she thinks it's God telling us that everything is going to be all right."

CHAPTER TWENTY-ONE

Portland, Oregon, Thanksgiving Day

While the buzz at Whispering Ridge focused on food, wine and the upcoming nuptial announcement, in a dimly lit rented warehouse in southwest Portland the topic was far more *macabre*. Yusuf Ali Atef gave the space to Barghouti on loan, along with those who would accompany him the following night. The poorly heated building was unpleasantly cold, dank and poorly lit, and the men sat on metal folding chairs around an impromptu table comprised of metal drums that had been moved together shivered in the autumn chill. Before them was a detailed map of the area surrounding Whispering Ridge. Atef pointed to a spot at the south end of the property where there was a narrow service road.

"There," he said emphatically, "there is where you must leave the vehicle. You will divide into four teams of two, and advance on foot through the vineyard. When you have surrounded the house you will enter and kill everyone inside. But you must leave one man outside to watch, in case of trouble. When the mighty deed is done, you will return on foot the way you came, driving south when you get to the main road. When you reach Salem, you must go to the address that I have written on this card. There, you will be provided with false identity papers, passports, bus tickets to either

Los Angeles or San Francisco and airline tickets taking you out of the country. Do you understand?"

"We understand," said Barghouti eagerly. "Will your men also be leaving?"

"No," Atef replied, "I need them here. They will remain at the safe house in Salem until it is safe to bring them back."

What Atef told the naive Barghouti was only part of the story. Like most Muslim radicals, Atef wanted to see Curt Wells and everyone he cared for dead. Barghouti might be a useful tool in accomplishing this. But both Barghouti and his friend Isfahan were too green, too inexperienced, too unproven. Should they be captured by the FBI, they would certainly break, exposing Atef and his entire cell. Of that he was quite certain. So before his six hardened terrorist soldiers were dispatched to the warehouse rendezvous the following evening, he planned to give them simple, deadly instructions. When Wells and his family were dead, the others must kill Barghouti and Isfahan as well. The loose ends would then all be tied off..

Whispering Ridge, Early Afternoon

Thanksgiving at the Wells home was nothing short of an Epicurean orgy. A good country breakfast was served early, and guests snacked throughout the day on a selection of cheeses and biscuits from all over the world and, of course, Whispering Ridge's fine wines. At two in the afternoon, Wells called the group together and informed them that the main event, stuffed wild turkey with all the trimmings, was about to be served. He invited them to join hands in a traditional blessing of the food, and when he had finished asked them to remain as they were for a moment.

"Thanksgiving is something we celebrate every year here. But this year we have so much more to be thankful for. We have Scott and Marty with us, and Aaron is no doubt celebrating with his parents in Connecticut. That's something to be extra thankful for this year. And through the events that occupied us earlier in the fall, Callie and Tyler somehow found each other. I think we can all be thankful for that, too. And so our two families are about to be bound together in joy, just as we were bound earlier in sorrow and worry. Let's hope that this is just the first chapter in a wonderful new book," he said.

They all applauded and then, seated around the generous dining table, began to consume what Molly Wells had prepared. Molly loved to cook, and she was very good at it. It gave her pleasure to please others, and she smiled incessantly as they all filled their plates to overflowing.

Watching them from afar, it would be difficult to imagine Tyler and Callie as political activists, Scott and Marty as bloodied hostages or Curt Wells as a ruthless killer. It all seemed so far away, so imaginary. And not one of them had an inkling of the wolves that yet lurked at their doorstep.

Yuma, the NSA Communications Facility

The National Security Agency doesn't take Thanksgiving off. Edith Navarro, a ten-year NSA veteran sat at Jack Slater's desk poring through his e-mails and the latest intercepts. She was the interim supervisor pending Slater's recovery and return.

She heard a knock on the door and said, "Come in."

Amy Lassiter opened the door and quietly entered the room. She heard belatedly about Jack Slater's accident, and the question of whether he had asked for or received comment from the DNI about the Atef/Alzawahiri intercept weighed heavily on her acute mind.

It took great courage for Amy to approach Navarro. The two didn't particularly like one another, having clashed openly in staff meetings over the significance of bits of information they had harvested. Navarro was senior to her in the agency, and her temporary superior. This would have to be handled very carefully.

"Good afternoon, Miss Navarro," she said in as cordial a tone as she could muster.

"Hello, Amy, I thought you were off until Saturday," Navarro said without looking up or making eye contact.

"Yes, I just came in to catch up on a few things. But I need to ask you a question," Amy said.

"What is it?" Navarro asked snappishly, peeved at the interruption.

"Night before last, before Jack, er, Mr. Slater had his accident, I brought him an intercept of what seemed to be a conversation between Ayman Alzawahiri and someone named Atef. Mr. Slater agreed that it should be passed on to the DNI, and I was wondering if he had either called them or sent if off by e-mail before the accident. Would you mind checking for me?" she asked as nicely as she could.

"I'm sure that if it was important he took care of it," Navarro intoned disinterestedly.

"We thought it might have something to do with a possible attack on a man in Oregon," Amy pressed anxiously.

"Look Amy, I'm very busy here," Navarro hissed, shooting her a hostile glare. "If it will make you feel better, I will go through Jack's sent items and see if he shipped it off, but *not* now!"

"Yes ma'am," Lassiter deferred. "Sorry to bother you."

Walking slowly back to her workstation Amy Lassiter was unconvinced that Edith Navarro would pursue the matter. Navarro's normal beat was deciphering communications between South American and Mexican drug lords and their stateside operatives. She considered the obsession with Islamic radicalism a bit hysterical, and didn't mind saying so in agency meetings. Her cavalier attitude was tolerated only because she was very good at her own specialty. The last thing she was likely to give credence to was some obscure chitchat between the *jihadis*, especially in view of the fact that no particulars were attached.

Amy sat in her darkened cubicle and wondered what to do. Then she decided. If she could lie low until Edith took a meal break and then go into Slater's office, she might be able to find out whether he actually contacted the DNI and whether they responded. It could mean her job if Navarro caught her at it. But if Curtis Wells got blindsided by terrorists because Jack Slater had an accident and Edith Navarro was too pigheaded to talk to the DNI, that was something Amy wouldn't be able to live with.

Two and a half hours dragged by before the light in Slater's office went off and Edith Navarro bustled out. No doubt she was on her way to dinner at the on site cafeteria. That meant she wouldn't be gone more than thirty minutes. Five of those were spent waiting to be sure Edith wouldn't return to retrieve something she'd forgotten. When she didn't, Amy slipped out of her loafers and padded down the hall. The door was not locked.

Switching on the desk lamp, she slid in behind Slater's keyboard. She knew his password, "Mindy." It was his daughter's name, and although Slater was divorced and the little girl lived with her mother in Los Angeles, she was always on Slater's mind. He told Amy that "Mindy" was his password because it helped him to remember her face.

His e-mail opened smoothly and she quickly went into the sent items directory and scrolled back to the day of the accident. Sure enough, there was a single e-mail addressed to Warren Chapman with the DNI. She began to breathe easier as she opened the e-mail. But her hopes were dashed when she saw that it contained nothing at all about her intercept. She scrolled on until she was sure there had been no other relevant communication about the matter. Shutting down the e-mail program, she logged out, looking around to be sure no one was watching.

She rose and began to search the office. Scouring the desktop, she took great pains to replace everything just as she found it. As she was about to walk over to a gray bank of four-drawer files, she happened to glance at the small area of carpeted floor between the end of the desk and the wall. There, she saw two sheets of paper. She couldn't get at them without moving the desk, so she went to the coat closet, found a wire coat hanger and, straightening it out, managed to hook the two sheets one at a time and drag them from obscurity. Sure enough, they were Slater's printout of Amy's intercept. Folding them, she turned off the lamp and exited the office, closing the door softly behind her. The mangled coat hanger dangled loosely from one hand.

But answering that question just posed an incredible new series of dilemmas. If Slater failed to inform DNI and Navarro refused to do so, then who would call Curtis Wells? If she took it upon herself to call DNI after Navarro, her acting supervisor, declined to do it, her butt was likely to end up in a sling. She booted up her computer and opened the DNI e-mail directory. She needed to find out who Warren Chapman was, since he was the last man up there Slater communicated with. Sure enough, she found him. Warren Chapman was an assistant deputy director, assistant, that is, to Mitchell Starr, deputy director of intelligence. What would happen, she wondered, if she just e-mailed him the intercept herself? Probably the same thing as if she called him, she thought dejectedly.

Then it hit her. If she got back into Slater's office while Navarro was away, she could find the document in which she originally sent the intercept to Slater in the first place, and send that to Chapman. The belated communication would only be traceable to Slater's system, and Navarro would never be able to prove that Amy sent it. Again she arose and slipped her shoes off. She almost reached the office, then heard Navarro making passing small talk with another analyst. It was too late.

Most of the analysts were billeted at the facility. Many of them also kept apartments in Yuma for their families and their off time. Some were commuters. Amy, who stayed at the station most of the time, went to one of the workout rooms and lathered up a good sweat, then showered and returned to her eight-foot by ten-foot sleeping quarters and drifted off into a troubled slumber.

At quarter after twelve she awoke and sat bolt upright in bed. This just wasn't working. She couldn't let it go. Navarro would have clocked out at midnight when her shift ended. They were operating shorthanded due to Slater's mishap, which meant that while there would be a floor supervisor on duty, it was unlikely that person would actually be in Slater's office. She pulled on light blue sweats, laced up her Nikes and headed to the elevator that was the gateway down into the operations center. Slipping her pass card into and then out of the black box near the elevator, she began the descent that would enable her to do what needed to be done.

They were supposed to clock in, again using their pass cards, whenever they were on duty. She hadn't done so before when she visited Navarro, and she surely wasn't going to do so now. If the floor supervisor caught her in Slater's office and not properly checked in to boot, there would be hell to pay. But that was a chance she was now committed to take.

Once again operating by the dim light from the desk lamp, she opened up Slater's system and located the original document she sent him. Going into e-mail, she attached the document typing in the address, and then hit the send button. The fat was in the fire.

She turned off the lamp and sat there in the dark, musing on what she had set in motion. What she failed to factor into the equation was the modern miracle of the BlackBerry. A small, hand held computer, the wonderful little gadgets allow busy people to monitor and respond to both their e-mails and telephone calls remotely, and around the clock. Warren Chapman's BlackBerry played the first few notes of Beethoven's Fifth Symphony. Tucson, Arizona is in the Mountain time zone, and so while it was quarter of two there, it was quarter of four in Virginia, where Chapman lived and worked. Chapman had the day after Thanksgiving off, but he was a chronic early riser who seldom slept past four-thirty in the morning, holiday or not. He realized his error in forgetting to mute the paging feature of his BlackBerry when the tone sounded. Bah-bah-bah-*bah*!

He sat up on the edge of the bed, wiping the sleep from his tired eyes and shaking the cobwebs from his foggy brain. Through bleary eyes he saw that he had an e-mail from Jack Slater of the NSA. He thought that for Slater to be sending it at this odd hour of the morning, it must be important. So he opened up the attachment and began to read Amy Lassiter's transcription of the sinister al Qaeda conversation.

Minutes later, as Amy was about to leave, Slater's phone rang. Could it be? The smart thing to do was probably to run, not walk out the door. But she was drawn to the ringing phone as if by an unseen magnet. She picked it up gingerly and spoke into the mouthpiece.

"Mr. Slater's office," she said timidly.

"Put me on with Slater, please. This is Chapman, DNI," rasped the gravelly, urgent voice on the other end.

"I'm sorry, sir, but Mr. Slater was injured in an accident, so he's not here just now," she offered.

"Then how in hell did he just send me an e-mail from there?" Chapman demanded impatiently.

"He didn't send it, sir. I did," she confessed, wincing.

"And exactly who are you?" Chapman wanted to know.

"I'm Amy Lassiter, an analyst on Mr. Slater's staff. I'm the one who taped the conversation and did the transcription," she said.

"Why in holy hell did you people wait so long to pass this up the chain? This thing is two days old." Chapman virtually shouted into the phone, clearly alarmed.

"Well, after Mr. Slater got hurt in an automobile accident I tried to convince my acting supervisor, Miss Navarro, that this might be important, but she didn't agree."

"So, you took it upon your own initiative to send me this?" he inquired in astonishment.

"Yes, sir. I hope I did the right thing," she said in a demure voice.

"You damned sure did, young lady. I just hope it's not too late. I'll be talking to the assistant director in five minutes and then probably to the director, the FBI and the CIA later this morning. Shoot a copy of the tape up to me electronically so our people here can scrutinize it. How can I reach you if I need to?" he insisted.

She gave him both her cell and desk numbers before hanging up, shutting down Slater's office and hurrying off to send Chapman a copy of the tape. She couldn't understand how she could, at the same time, feel both proud and guilty, but those were undeniably the feelings carrying out their little war within her.

Washington, D.C., Five Hours Later

Putting together a high level inter-agency meeting the day after a major holiday was not quite the milk run Warren Chapman had expected. His boss, retired Vice-Admiral Mitchell Starr, the former head of U.S. naval intelligence had been easy to reach. DNI John Baines, and FBI Director Alfred Kendrick were at their family homes in other states and had to be piped in by conference line. The CIA sent up its deputy director for intelligence, and Chapman had brought in a couple of other lower level DNI people to kibitz.

It had taken much longer than he would have liked. It was Deputy Director Starr who presided over the meeting and who turned to Chapman for enlightenment.

"All right, Warren, why don't you run down this intercept for us and tell us what you think it means," he said gruffly.

Each of them had a transcription of the intercept on the table top in front of them, so Chapman didn't waste time re-hashing the substance of it. Instead, he spoke directly to his concerns.

"As you can see," he began, "this is a transcription of a conversation between someone named Atef and one he referred to as 'Teacher.' We know that 'The Teacher' is what most of the *jihadis* call Ayman Alzawahiri. Atef is asking, here, for Alzawahiri's blessing on some mission having to do with a *fatwa*. The only *fatwa* we're aware of that could affect U.S. citizens directly is the one demanding the death of Curtis Wells in reprisal for the rescue in Saudi. It seems likely, then, that what Alzawahiri signed off on was an assassination to be carried out in the state of Oregon at some unspecified time."

"Do we know anything about this Atef?" Starr asked.

"There's a Yusuf Ali Atef on the terrorist watch list," the voice of Alfred Kendrick boomed from the speakerphone. "But if he is already in the United States we didn't know about it."

"Our people think he may have been here for some time, and may command a terror cell somewhere on the West coast," the DDCIA offered, trying to one-up the FBI.

"Nice of you to let us know," Kendrick shot back caustically.

For the better part of an hour they bandied back and forth bits and pieces of hard intelligence and supposition, each trying to appear more "in-the-know" than the rest. Finally, Mitchell Starr cut to the chase.

"Director Kendrick, I think it would be prudent to put your people in Oregon on alert, and I think we owe this Wells the courtesy of a heads up. We also need to let the White House in on this, don't you agree Mr. Director?" he asked, looking at the blue speakerphone.

"Yes, Mitchell, I do," came the strong voice of DNI John Baines, who was vacationing in Maine. "The president wouldn't like being kept out of this one."

It was agreed that the DNI would inform the president by telephone, and only when that had been done would Chapman call Curtis Wells.

Camp David, Maryland

The Catoctin Mountain reserve in Frederick County, Maryland, hosts the famous Camp David. The presidential retreat named after Dwight D. Eisenhower's grandson is frequented by presidents, presidential advisors and invited heads of state from all over the world. On this day, the day after Thanksgiving, Norman Sloan was deeply involved in a foreign policy workshop with his secretary of state and ambassador to the United Nations. He wasn't to be disturbed except in case of a national emergency. At least that is what his chief of staff, Kenneth Karns, told Director of National Intelligence John Baines.

"Well, when he has a break, please tell him that the combined intelligence services believe a reprisal attack on Curtis Wells may be imminent, and that we would like to give him some advance warning," the frustrated DNI said sharply.

Karns listened, then asked how they came by the information in question. Promising that he would pass the advisory along to the president as soon as possible, he thanked the DNI and hung up.

Karns was not a particularly thoughtful man. What he was good at was manipulating the president's harried schedule and, sometimes, manipulating the president. His reaction to the DNI's call was that it was paranoia based on the thinnest kind of evidence. He'd mention it to the president if and when the opportunity presented itself. Curt Wells already had caused this administration enough headaches, he reasoned, and he didn't much like the thought of rehearsing the past. So, he planned to sit on it, for now.

Just before dinner, five hours later, he finally reported the matter to Norman Sloan.

"When did Baines call, Ken?" the president inquired.

"Just after lunch, sir, but I didn't want to bother you with it," Karns replied lamely.

"I hope that's not a misjudgment we both live to regret," Sloan chided. "I tend to take it seriously and I think we should warn Wells by all means."

At six-thirty, Karns called the DNI back and said the president concurred that Curtis Wells should be alerted to the possible danger. Baines called Starr and Starr called Chapman. The clock was ticking. By the time Chapman got the phone number at Whispering Ridge and gathered himself to make the call, the Wells and their guests had departed for Fenouil, and the engagement celebration. Chapman's call was answered by a cheery holiday greeting recorded days earlier by Molly Wells. He left a short message and asked that Curt Wells return his call. It was too little, too late, and all to no avail. The clumsy, bungling bureaucracy of government had once again failed those who paid to keep it running.

But at least one civil servant wouldn't let it go. Amy Lassiter, not hearing back from Chapman, remained deeply concerned. She decided that she couldn't get in any deeper by ringing up Curtis Wells herself to be sure he had gotten the warning. When she did not find him listed in the normal telephone directories, she began searching online for the articles about him. Finding one, she was quickly reminded that he was the proprietor of Whispering Ridge Cellars, and there was a listing for the winery. Alas, when she dialed no one on the other end picked up. She left a short message requesting a return call, and hung up.

Portland's Pearl District, Fenouil

When the Wells party arrived, Brett Logan was not among them. He was obligated to return to campus on an afternoon flight for a mandatory football team practice. Saturday night would mark his team's last conference game of the season. But four of the Wells and three of the Logans, plus Carlos and Fritz, approached the evening's chosen venue in high spirits. Curt Wells, their host for the event, held the door for the others as he looked back across the adjoining bricked plaza at the fountain gurgling there.

There were "oohs" and "ahs" from the Logans when they saw the restaurant for the first time. On the right crackled a welcoming hearth. Spiraling above it was a wrought iron staircase festooned with bright twinkling lights to signal the onset of the holiday season. Muted violins played in the background as the string quintet hired by Curt Wells for the evening played in one corner of the spacious upper level dining area. They were shown to a large table that, in reality, was several tables pulled end to end and then covered by a long linen tablecloth. The remainder of their section had been cleared of other tables to guarantee their privacy and make room for the wine steward and waiters who would soon ply them with Chef Henri's finest food and drink.

As the wine was poured and the appetizers were being served, Henri himself emerged to meet and greet the entourage, gallantly kissing the hand of a blushing Callie Logan. A magnificent off-the-menu seven-course meal soon followed, and it was entirely memorable. That, thought Wells, was normal for Henri and Fenouil.

As they were finishing dessert, he rose to make a toast.

"As the prospective father-in-law of the bride to be, and the father of the man she's going to marry, I want to say just a few words. Molly and I have always hoped that when our sons decided to marry, they would find women from fine, respectable families. Tyler has beaten his brother to the punch, and Callie, I want to say how delighted we are to embrace you as our first daughter-in-law, and to contemplate this joining of the Wells and Logan clans. Here's to you and Tyler, a long and happy married life."

"And lots of babies," Molly added in an unsubtle whisper that brought laughter from all.

Then it was Alex Logan's turn.

"Mary and I, likewise, have always wanted the very best for our little girl. Then one day we woke up and she wasn't a little girl anymore. She had become a beautiful young woman. While I'm sure we all regret some of the events that brought Callie and Tyler together, their love turns out to the bonus on top of getting our boys back safely. We have already toasted the special couple, and now I want to propose a toast to one of the finest and bravest men

I have ever known. If it weren't for his courageous actions against all odds, we probably wouldn't be celebrating here tonight - Curt Wells," he offered, raising his glass.

Cheers and the sound of clanking wine goblets followed. Then Tyler rose and knelt beside his chair and in front of Callie.

"Callie Logan, I love you with all my heart and soul, and I believe that you love me, too. Will you marry me?" he asked, re-enacting his proposal for the well-wishers.

"Oh, yes I will, Tyler Wells. And I do love you, too," she said, tears of joy glimmering in her blue eyes.

With that, he placed a large diamond ring in a stunning platinum setting on the third finger of her left hand, and the celebrating began in earnest. By nine-thirty the happy group was well spent, and Molly suggested that they return to Whispering Ridge to continue the reveling. At twenty minutes past ten, they pulled off the main road and entered the winding drive up to the house.

CHAPTER TWENTY-TWO

Whispering Ridge, 10:45 PM

A wispy gray blanket of patchy fog had descended over Whispering Ridge, lending the lights outside a ghostly, ethereal aura. From the service road to the south the assassins, parked with their lights out, observed the big stretch van returning from the party. Soon it would be time.

Anan Barghouti insisted that they wait until everyone had a chance to relax and mellow down for the night. Twenty minutes later, on his signal, they silently exited the van, checked their weapons and climbed easily over the split rail cedar fence at the vineyard's boundary. Dividing into teams of two, they began moving toward the house. The westernmost team's job was to cut electrical power and phone lines to the house before bringing up the rear. The intruders would spread out and surround the house, then move in for the kill.

Curt Wells, preoccupied as he was with the joy of the evening, did not notice the flashing message light on his telephone. Not, at least, until it rang. He considered letting the machine take it, but since he could now see that there were already two messages waiting, he thought it might be important and picked up. "Hello," he said into the receiver.

Long time Whispering Ridge employee Jacob McCaskill

and his black Doberman, Satan, observed the same ritual every evening just before bedtime. They would stroll together through the vineyard and up the hill, usually to the south, and all the way to the fence line. There, the dog would relieve himself, and then the two would meander back to the apartment they shared above the rear section of the winery complex. Tonight was no exception. But tonight it was their misfortune to run into Anan Barghouti and Muhammad Isfahan. Not sure just what to do, Barghouti hesitated as they stared at each other through the fog and darkness. Isfahan, the least experienced of the intruders, did not. Raising his AK-47 he fired a three-round burst straight into McCaskill's chest, killing him instantly. As the anguished dog charged, another three rounds dispatched him as well.

"Stop firing, brother," shouted Barghouti anxiously. "You will alert them all to our presence."

Curt Wells was adept at processing a number of external stimuli at the same time, as most present and former field operatives are. The short bursts of automatic rifle fire registered with his subconscious even as the voice on the other end spoke.

"Is this Curtis Wells?" a female caller inquired.

"Yes, it is. Who are you?" he demanded, while trying to quell the silent alarm in his head.

"Mr. Wells, I'm Amy Lassiter with the NSA, the National Security Agency. Based on a recent telephone intercept we believe you may be in terrible . . ."

The phone went dead at the same moment the lights all went out. The word "danger" had been spoken on her end, but not heard on his. The whole thing came together for him instantly like an onrushing freight train.

"What happened to the lights?" Molly asked in puzzlement as he returned to the family room.

"We are all in harm's way," he said urgently.

"Some men are here to kill me in reprisal for Al B'ir. I should have seen it coming. Scott, right now Carlos will be putting his boots on and heading out to fire up the generator. Use my cell phone here – he's auto dial number 1. Call him and tell him to stay put. We'll be safer in the dark. Tell him to get his varmint gun and go to the tunnel entrance. I'm sending you all through. You'll be safe there."

The original owner of the winery didn't particularly like walking in the rain, and it rained often in Oregon, sometimes every day for weeks at a time. So he had built a tunnel, spacious enough for humans to walk through comfortably from the main house to the wine cellar. The Wells never used it. But they would tonight.

Withdrawing a small penlight and a string of keys from his pocket, Wells opened the gun case and slid out his Winchester 30-30 deer rifle, along with a box of ammunition.

"What are you going to do, Dad?" asked Scott with alarm.

"I'm going to go out there and try to kill them before they come in here and kill us," Curt replied, the calm in his voice a ruse. "I want you and Tyler to lead the others through the tunnel and then I want you to barricade yourselves in the wine cellar until this is over."

"No way," chimed Scott and Tyler in unison.

"We're not letting you go out there alone," Scott spoke for them both. "Thanks to you, we can both shoot, too."

Curt wanted desperately to argue with them, to persuade them that combat is different from hunting because the quarry can shoot back. But he knew they were already on borrowed time and there was none left for a debate.

"All right, Sunny, take the Mossberg and load it up with deer slugs. Ty, you take the other 30-30. I want you both to find places of cover where you can see the house, but can't be seen. If you have to shoot, aim carefully, then fire and move right away, because they'll fire back at your muzzle flash and they've got automatics. And for God's sake let's be careful that we don't shoot each other."

Turning to Alex he said, "Do you know how to use this?" handing him his Colt .45 semi-automatic pistol.

"Yes," confirmed Logan, "if I have to."

"Well don't, unless you have to. I'm counting on you, Carlos and Fritz to protect the women," he added.

Jerking open the door to an elongated coat closet, he moved quickly to the back and undid the latch to the tunnel door, then handed Logan a powerful hand held lantern.

"There won't be any other light in the tunnel with the power out," he reminded him. "Take six steps down the ladder and you'll reach the bottom. Help the others down and close the door. Then lead everyone through. Carlos and Fritz will be waiting at the other end."

As Logan nodded and began herding the rest into the closet, Wells opened the fireplace cleanout and grabbed a generous handful of soot and ashes, spilling part of it on the floor. The rest he rubbed all over his face. He was already wearing a black turtleneck and slacks, and now he would be very difficult to spot in the fog and darkness.

"What are you going to do?" Tyler asked fearfully.

"I'm going hunting. You two get outside and keep your heads down. If I get shot, stay down. Maybe they'll be satisfied. No use in all of us getting killed."

With that, he opened the side door, and without further conversation they all moved, staying low, out into the thick darkness of night.

Alex, Callie, Mary and Molly all descended the ladder and started down the tunnel. Molly, bringing up the rear, hung back. Finally she let the others move on without her, took a small flashlight from her pants pocket and turned back in the direction of the ladder. She'd forgotten something that might come in handy. In a closet near the pantry, Curt always kept a fully loaded, sawed off, double-barreled Winchester Defender. The Defender was no hunting weapon. It had one purpose only, and that was to protect the family from bodily harm in case of a home invasion. Making her way as quietly as possible up the ladder and pushing up the hatch, she moved silently back through the closet. Gingerly retrieving the weapon from an upper shelf, she checked to be sure it was loaded. It was.

Just then, she looked up and saw the menacing figure of Muhammad Isfahan peering through the window in the kitchen door. Because of where she was standing, she was certain he could not see her. Her first thought was to slip quietly back into the closet and down into the tunnel with her prize, when suddenly she heard the shattering of glass and splintering of wood as Isfahan viciously kicked in the door.

Molly Wells had few character flaws, but she did have a temper. Just now the emotion she felt was a nearly uncontrollable rage. Peeking back around the corner she could see Isfahan standing there, just inside the doorway, sweeping his automatic rifle from side to side, seeking a living target. As he swung away from her, the rage, the sense of violation boiled through her and she stepped into the doorway to the kitchen and discharged both barrels in his direction with a loud roar. The recoil hurt her shoulder and drove her backwards, but that was nothing compared to what the twin load of double-ought buckshot did to the intruder.

What Molly did not fully see as she staggered backward, was the blast from her weapon lifting Isfahan literally off the floor and hurling him back out the door and over the porch railing, dead before he hit the ground below. Quickly, she ejected the spent shells and scurried for the tunnel carrying the extra shells in her pocket. As she climbed nimbly back down the ladder she muttered out loud, to no one in particular, "That'll teach you to come into *my* kitchen, you son of a bitch."

Barghouti, who had strongly urged caution upon Isfahan, saw him fall, and scuttled quickly to his lifeless body. Finding him quite dead, he retreated into the shadows and linked up with another twosome, who had also heard the shotgun blast. Now, they knew there was armed resistance in the house, and were unsure how to proceed. This was supposed to be a slaughter of unarmed civilians.

Curt Wells also heard the commotion, and used it as a diversion to get behind the three and slightly uphill. There would be no such thing as a good, clean shot in this fog, but he was able to make out just the protruding head of the tallest man. He took a deep breath and let it out, trained his iron sites as best he could on the head and squeezed the trigger.

The instant scream of pain told him that he had hit his target, but probably not with a kill shot. He was lucky to have hit him at all under these conditions. The heavy slug struck the man considerably lower than intended, entering at the shoulder blade and shattering

Abdul Retif's left clavicle. He could no longer hold a weapon, and was now quite useless to the others who, fearing for their own lives, crawled away leaving him to whimper and writhe in pain.

Inside the winery cellar, the refugees were busily rolling heavy casks of wine against the doors as barricades. Fritz was on his cell phone with Ted Peale, the Yamhill county sheriff, begging for help. No, he could not say how many assailants there were, who they were or how they were armed. But the help was needed both urgently and immediately. In the cellar, reception was garbled, and Fritz hoped against hope that Peale and his dispatcher had understood.

Amy Lassiter was busy, too. When the phone went dead she tried to call back, only to be informed that it was suddenly out of order. Fearing the worst, she alerted the Portland FBI who immediately mustered a waiting S.W.A.T team for action. It was too foggy to fly, but they swiftly loaded into two black SUVs and roared southbound at emergency speed with red and blue wigwags flashing.

In the vineyard above, about a hundred yards south of the house, Curtis Wells slithered on his belly, stopping periodically to look and listen for signs of the two men he was tracking. As he waited alertly, he detected a low buzz, two male voices in animated conversation and about fifty yards to his left. Crawling again, he made his way slowly down the hill toward them. His strategy was to draw them out and isolate one from the other. Then they would be his.

Finding a good-sized rock, he lobbed it high over his shoulder. When it fell with a crash some thirty feet up the hill, he saw one of the men rise and begin firing wildly toward the sound. Raising himself to one knee, he sighted in the Winchester and fired. The man went down like a tree, making no sound. This was a clean kill.

Now alone and on the defensive, Anan Barghouti's courage and bravado were ebbing quickly away. He knew for sure that he had two dead and one wounded. But he had no idea where the rest of his soldiers were by now, and he also knew that he was being hunted by one who had already proven himself an expert.

Up on the service road, Hakim Mansour waited nervously behind the wheel of the escape vehicle. With the windows open he heard the intermittent firing going on below. Since not all of it was coming from automatics, he also knew that the *jihadis* had run into an unexpected fight. Leaning across the seat, he craned his neck to see what was going on. It was at just that moment that he felt Sheriff Ted Peale's nine millimeter Sig Sauer jammed into his left ear, and heard the command to put both hands on the steering wheel, or else.

The two killers who cut the power made their way, now, back down toward the house. Tyler Wells, perched silently in the loft of the barn, watched them throughout their stealthy approach. When they were less than fifty yards away, he sighted in his own 30-30 and put a round right between the shoulder blades of the nearest man, who fell forward on his face and did not move. But his comrade, quickly deducing the source of the deadly shot whirled, spraying the upper half of the barn with automatic fire. As Tyler rolled away, the spray of bullets seemed to track him, shredding wood in their wake. When the shooting stopped, his enraged attacker slammed in another magazine and took off for the barn on the run. He meant to find out who was in that loft and put an end to his miserable existence.

His headlong path took him, however, within twenty yards of Scott Wells who was wedged into the support above the emergency generator at the corner of the winery building and about ten feet off the ground. Seeing the man running wildly and understanding full well his deadly mission, Scott aimed the heavy Mossberg shotgun and, when the man was at his nearest point, fired. The shotgun slug, designed to kill a deer, hit the man in the shoulder and spun him around toward Scott. Methodically, he dropped another shell into the chamber, aimed and fired again. This second shot hit the man in the left hip, dropping him to his knees and leaving him flailing desperately in the dirt. As he sought to lift the weapon with his one good arm, yet another shotgun blast leveled him, and this time he lay very still.

Moments later Scott and Tyler met in front of the barn and spoke in hushed voices.

"How many of them do you think there are?" Tyler wondered.

"Your guess is as good as mine, brother, but I don't think we should stand around out here and make ourselves targets for them."

"Right, I'm going to head around the barn to the right, and take cover behind that stone wall," Tyler said.

"Okay, I'll circle left and try to find somewhere else to hide," answered Scott. "Have you seen dad?"

"No, but the last shot I heard from the east was definitely his 30-30, so I think he's still giving 'em hell," Tyler remarked with a grim smile.

As the two went their separate directions, red and blue flashing lights appeared to the west, on the main road, and more were apparent up on the hill, near the service road. Help had finally arrived.

Special Agent Shelby Joiner assumed custody of Hakim Mansour from Sheriff Peale, and was now deploying his S.W.A.T unit in a skirmish line at twenty-yard intervals.

"Move north, toward the house," he instructed. "But be careful who you shoot. Wells and his two sons are supposed to be out there too, if they're still alive."

Slowly the black clad commandos moved off into the vineyard, staying low and sweeping the area with alert eyes. They hadn't gone far before they found themselves in the firefight of their lives. The two remaining intruders were headed back to the waiting van, bent on escape. Both were veterans of the conflict in Afghanistan and had fought with the Taliban against the invading coalition forces. They knew how to fight, and seriously wounded two of the S.W.A.T team members before suppressing fire drove them to the ground. For ten minutes they continued to put up spirited resistance, but the numbers game was working against them. Eventually an agent armed with an M-16A automatic got behind them, and it was over quick and ugly.

Seeing the lights, and hearing the furious battle in progress out in the vineyard, Tyler Wells concluded that since the cavalry had arrived it was all over but the shouting. Resting the Winchester momentarily against the wall, he turned to look in the direction of the main road. It was then that Anan Barghouti stepped from the shadows, his AK-47 leveled, and pure malice etched in the twisted lines of his swarthy face.

"Turn around and face me," he hissed hatefully through tightly clenched teeth. "If I cannot kill the father, perhaps at least I shall kill the son. You will die, never having known the pleasures of the woman you sought to marry," he smiled. "*Allahu akbar!*"

As he raised his weapon to execute Tyler Wells, a confluence of events occurred which could have best been viewed in stop action. Curt Wells, who had been tracking Barghouti for over fifteen minutes, suddenly rounded the corner of the barn.

Seeing what was about to happen he shouted "*No!*" at the top of his lungs, and lunged headfirst, hurling himself between Tyler and Barghouti as the latter squeezed off a long burst of deadly fire. At the same moment, Scott Wells stepped from the shadows on the other side and cut Barghouti down with a point blank blast from the Mossberg. Oblivious to the fact that Barghouti was already dead, Scott kept advancing and firing, ramming in round after round until the chamber was empty and the descending hammer rendered only empty clicks.

Picking himself up off the ground, where the impact of his father's lunge had thrown him, Tyler ran to Scott's side, putting one hand on his shoulder and another, momentarily, on the smoldering barrel of the gun.

"It's over, Sunny. It's all over. You can stop now," he said softly.

For a moment the brothers stood there, gripping one another by the upper arms, grateful that their nightmare had finally ended. Then Scott spoke. "Where's dad?"

They turned as one, and seeing Curt Wells propped up against the stone wall, they ran to his side. There was blood gushing from his left side, and some of it had splattered onto his face, nearly hidden by the mask of ashes and soot.

"My God, he's been hit," Tyler gasped in anguish.

Almost instinctively Scott whipped out the cell phone Curt had given him before they left the house. Quickly he auto dialed Carlos.

"Carlos, it's over. We need help up here. Dad's been shot,"

he said quickly, not staying on the line to answer the inevitable questions.

Almost immediately, Carlos dialed 911 and told the dispatcher to contact the sheriff with his number. In less than a minute Ted Peale was on the line.

"It's over down here, but Curt Wells has been wounded. We need medical assistance, and we need it right now," Carlos shouted into the phone in an urgent voice.

"On the way," said Peale, motioning to the ambulance driver who made a quick u-turn and sped down the graveled drive toward the house.

"Don't try to talk, Dad," Tyler said lovingly as he laid Curt Wells flat on the ground, cradling his head in his strong arms.

Suddenly, he noticed that his father had the hint of a smile on his face.

"What's funny?" Tyler asked in bewilderment.

"Not funny, ironic," Curt said, coughing between phrases.

"I made it through twenty-one SEAL missions and all that mayhem in Saudi last month, and now I'm shot in my own front yard?"

'You're going to be okay, Dad, you're going to be all right. Do you hear me?" Tyler demanded, trying desperately to convince himself that it was so.

Then the paramedics were there, pushing the sons aside and ministering to Curt Wells.

"I've got fluctuating BP and low, unsteady respiration. I count four bullet holes, but only two exit wounds. This man's carrying lead, so we have to be careful when we move him. Let's get him on oxygen and start a Ringer's drip," one of them said urgently as they began to slide the wounded Wells gently onto a gurney.

As they were loading him into the ambulance, Scott turned and spoke to his brother decisively, but in low and measured tones.

"I'm going with dad to the hospital. You gather up mom and get there as quickly as you can. We got into this as a family, and we're going to get through it as a family. Do you hear me, Tyler?"

Tyler, all color long-since drained from his face, simply nodded before turning and running as fast as he could toward the group now emerging from the winery building.

CHAPTER TWENTY-THREE

Highway 99 Northbound

The siren's harsh shriek tore through the black night as the ambulance hurtled along highway 99, headed for the Newberg High School parking lot and a waiting "life flight" helicopter whose pilots had braved the fog on a rescue mission of their own. Their ultimate destination was the Rose City Medical Center in south Portland. On the radio, the medics carried on a continuous patter with hospital emergency personnel, updating Curt Wells' condition and vital signs. Scott Wells was no medical expert, but what he could make out didn't sound encouraging.

Curt Wells' breathing was labored, and he continued to lose blood in spite of all the paramedics could do. Scott moved close and spoke quietly.

"Hold on, Dad, we're almost there. You have to hold on."

Locking his son's hand in a vise grip, Curt brushed the oxygen mask aside and replied, "If I don't beat this, you have to promise me you'll look after your mother."

His sentence was cut short by a violent coughing spell.

"I don't want to hear that, Dad. There is no *if*," Scott said emphatically. "You are going to make it," he promised as they rolled up on the waiting helicopter.

When the chopper finally arrived at its destination and came gently to rest on the helipad atop the emergency receiving area, medical personnel streamed from the hospital, swarming around the gurney as they swiftly moved Curt Wells inside. Scott, who arrived twenty minutes later with the ambulance, was told he would have to take a seat in the waiting area. But he could not sit. Instead, he paced nervously, awaiting the arrival of his brother and mother and wondering what he needed to say to them, what he could say to them.

In another fifteen minutes, Tyler, Callie, Alex, Marty and Mary Logan and Molly Wells also arrived. Carlos Gutierrez and Fritz Emswiler were close behind. When they had assembled in a corner, Scott spoke quietly to the group.

"I don't know anything yet," he confessed. "They've got him in the emergency room. He was bleeding and coughing a lot. They said they'd let us know as soon as they stabilized him."

Surprisingly, Molly was the calmest one of all. Wiping the tears from her eyes she said, "We have to think positively. Your father is a tough old bird who has been in a lot of scrapes before, and he's always found a way to come through them. I have to believe he'll do it one more time."

With little left to say, they dispersed to various parts of the waiting room, while Scott and Tyler went outside to get some air.

"It's my fault, you know," Tyler remarked bitterly. "If I hadn't stood up out there in the open like some silly deer in the headlights, I'd have gotten the drop on that guy you shot, instead of the other way around. Dad took bullets that were meant for me, Sunny."

"Do you think he would have wanted it any other way?" Scott answered thoughtfully.

"Do you think for even half a second he'd rather it was you in the emergency room fighting for life? Do you have any idea the risks that man took to save *my* life? It's a miracle that he didn't get killed in Saudi."

"Greater love has no man than this," boomed a deep, resonant voice from somewhere in the nearby shadows, "that he lay down his life for his friends. It's in the gospel according to Saint John."

Father Donovan O'Riley, the priest at the parish to which the

Wells belonged had come, called by the hospital in case last rites needed to be administered.

"Hello, Father," Scott Wells said. "I guess that's right, we are his sons but we are also his friends."

"You have really said something, there," the priest remarked. "Most sons think of their fathers as just that, their fathers. For the two of you to call your father 'friend,' well, that's something very special. It's a testimony to the man."

"Our dad is the best of the best, Father" Tyler responded. "It's just not right for him to die like this."

"You believe in God, don't you, my boy?" the priest asked solemnly.

"Of course," Tyler responded instantly.

"Then I think this would be the right time to trust Him, and to ask for your father's life," the priest counseled.

Just then the door to the waiting room burst open, and a nurse said, "Father, they're calling for you in emergency."

As the priest hurried off, Tyler and Scott Wells, surmising what the urgent call for Father O'Riley probably meant, stood there in the damp, chilly night, feeling terribly powerless and stricken with grief. Silently, they prayed.

Walking through the swinging double doors of the emergency room, O'Riley passed through a preparation area that hung heavy with the odor of antiseptic, then into a smaller chamber where three men and three women worked feverishly on Curt Wells, who appeared to be unconscious.

Approaching the table on which Wells lay, but trying to stay out of the way, O'Riley began the familiar litany, "*En nomini patri, et filii, et spiritu sancti ...*" when he was cut off abruptly..

"Go away, Father. I'm not going to die just yet," croaked Curt Wells through the respirator mask, never opening his eyes.

Encouraged by this sign of will, the doctors waved the priest out and continued their healing errand. By now they had him hooked up to heart and blood pressure monitors, as well as a respirator to help him breathe. They had already begun typing and cross-matching him for a transfusion.

Another ninety minutes passed as Father O'Riley comforted

Molly and the others in the emergency waiting room. Finally, a medic in surgical scrubs waved to them to follow, and showed them all into a private conference room. He addressed himself to Molly Wells.

"Mrs. Wells, I'm Doctor Angelo Petrakis, the head of emergency medicine here at RCMC. We have temporarily stabilized your husband, but he is a long way from being out of the woods. He took four large caliber bullets. One passed through the fleshy part of his right side causing minimal damage. One broke a rib, then caromed off and lodged near his left armpit. We have already removed that one. Number three slammed into his left shoulder, breaking it, then exited through his neck, narrowly missing his carotid artery. The problem is the fourth one."

"Tell me," Molly said, grasping the physician by the arm.

"The fourth bullet fragmented upon impact. One part of it nicked his left lung, causing it to collapse. That's why he's having trouble breathing. But the biggest fragment, the one we're most concerned about, is lodged right next to the main coronary artery. If it moves, and penetrates the left aorta, whether we could save him by surgical means is problematic. He might bleed to death internally," Petrakis reported candidly.

"So what do you propose to do?" Scott Wells moved in close to his mother, putting his arm around her and posing the question to the physician.

"We have already intubated the lung, trying to re-inflate it. Then, we need to open him up and try to remove that big fragment close to his heart. But we'll need your signed consent," the doctor finished.

"Of course," Molly said willingly.

"You said 'try to remove' the fragment," Tyler had now flanked his mother on the other side with a question of his own. "Just what does that mean?"

"In plain English, it means that we could save him or, if the procedure causes the fragment to move in the wrong direction prematurely, we could kill him," Petrakis responded directly.

"Give us a minute, Doc," Scott said, pulling his mother and brother to the side.

"I don't think we have a great menu of choices here, folks," he said.

"This is the best hospital in the city. This doctor seems to know what he's doing, so I think you should sign the papers mom, and let them do their stuff. Then we trust the rest to God, and to the fact that dad is one tough son of a gun who won't give up."

Molly and Tyler both nodded silent assent, and then they turned back to the doctor.

"Go ahead and do what has to be done," Molly said soberly. "Where do I go to sign the release?"

"I'll have it brought to you here," Petrakis answered. "If you'll excuse me, I'll page the cardio-vascular surgical team and get ready to scrub in for the procedure."

The Portland FBI Field Office

Special Agent Shelby Joiner sat at one end of a long conference table, with Special Agent In Charge Gordon Blatt on his left, and United States Attorney Peter Bledsoe on his right. In the middle of the table was a black speakerphone. On the line were FBI Director Alfred Kendrick, National Security Advisor Ethan Ellis, Deputy Director of Intelligence Mitchell Starr and Homeland Security Director Andrew Benton. It was five AM, Portland time.

"We're all here," said Blatt, confirming that all the relevant connections had been made.

"Thank you Gordon," said Kendrick. "Please give us a rundown on exactly what happened out there last night."

"This is Special Agent Joiner. I was the supervisor on the scene, Director. It seems that nine Islamic terrorists descended on the winery at Whispering Ridge with the intent of assassinating Curtis Wells along with his family and some holiday guests he was entertaining. They cut the power to the house, but when they closed in for the kill Wells, his two sons and his wife had armed themselves with hunting weapons and fought back. Five of the intruders were KIA by the Wells clan, and another seriously wounded. Our S.W.A.T unit took out two more, and a local sheriff captured another one without a fight. Two of mine were wounded, one is in serious condition. Curtis Wells was also wounded and is in critical condition at the Rose City Medical Center. Oh, and there was one more casualty, a winery employee by the name of Jacob McCaskill. He apparently made first contact with the intruders and they shot him and his dog. As it turns out, the local vet says the dog is going to make it. McCaskill was DOA at the hospital," Joiner finished.

"God, how can this have happened on our own soil?" Ellis, the national security advisor wondered aloud.

"More to the point, how can we keep it from happening again?" the director of homeland security lamented.

"Have you secured the Wells place?" Kendrick inquired.

"Yes sir," came Joiner's response.

"Good. We'll send suitably armed U.S. marshals to replace your people in case there is a follow-up attack. They will stay until further notice. Have you interrogated the two prisoners?" asked Kendrick.

"We have, sir," Blatt answered. "They are a man, a kid actually, who identifies himself only as 'Mansour,' and a Salim Abdul Retif, whom we believe Curtis Wells shot."

"What did they tell us?" Kendrick persisted.

"Retif wouldn't give us anything but his name, and demanded an attorney. But Mansour sang like a bird. He confirmed that the purpose of the mission was to kill the whole Wells family, and gave up the mastermind, Ali Yusuf Atef, along with the location of a house outside Wilsonville where he believed Atef to be," Blatt said proudly.

"And have we acted on that information?" Kendrick followed up eagerly.

"We raided the house about two hours ago. There were three men inside. They fired and we returned fire. Two are dead, and one went to ground on foot in the surrounding countryside. We believe that was Atef," Blatt reported.

"So, we've lost him?" the national security advisor asked with disappointment.

"Not exactly, sir. We've cordoned off a twenty-square-mile area using our people, local law enforcement and Oregon state police.

There's no way he can get through that net. We'll have him within hours," Blatt promised.

"See that you do," Kendrick barked. "Have we identified any of the dead?"

"Yes sir," Blatt said.

"One was a Portland State University student named Anan Barghouti, a Pakistani. Mansour said Barghouti was in command of the mission. The older Wells boy cut him up pretty badly with a Mossberg full of deer slugs. I doubt even his own mother could identify the remains. But before they got him, he's definitely the one who shot Curtis Wells."

"Go on," ordered Kendrick.

"Another body was that of Artis M. Cleaver, also known as Muhammad Isfahan. Cleaver was an American who did hard time in Walla Walla for selling drugs. While he was in prison he converted to Islam, and when he got out, enrolled as a part-time student at Portland State where he met Barghouti. Cleaver, or Isfahan, apparently penetrated the house. Details are sketchy but it looks as though he confronted Mrs. Wells in the kitchen, and she let him have both barrels of a sawed-off Winchester in the chest, blew him right out the door," Joiner picked up the narrative. "The other five dead had no identification on them, and we're still trying to run that information down."

"What about Wells? Is he going to make it?" Mitchell Starr inquired.

"Fifty-fifty at present, sir," Blatt answered.

"To your knowledge, did the Wells receive any advance warning, Gordon?" Starr followed up.

"I'll answer that, if I may, Sir," piped up Shelby Joiner. "We don't think he ever got a warning. An NSA analyst by the name of Amy Lassiter was on the line trying to warn him when the line went dead. We think that's when the power to the house was cut. There was a message on Wells' recorder from Warren Chapman of your office asking Wells to call back immediately, but the message didn't specify what the call was about. So we don't think he knew till the lights went out and McCaskill was shot."

"If it hadn't been for this Amy Lassiter putting two and two together and calling us, we wouldn't have known either."

"Ugh!" Starr groaned. "I think we're going to have to do a complete review of our communications and response scenarios, and I think a shift supervisor named Navarro at the NSA's Yuma facility has some serious explaining to do."

"How are you going to charge the two in custody, Peter?" Kendrick directed his question to the U.S. attorney.

"Murder, attempted capital murder, conspiracy to commit murder and a boatload of illegal firearms charges," came the response.

"Mansour has already agreed to a plea bargain deal in exchange for his testimony, and since he wasn't one of the shooters, we agreed to ten years hard time. Retif will fry! He emptied half a clip into the house after Isfahan went down. When we catch Atef he'll go down on murder, conspiracy and terrorism charges. All three are also in the country illegally," Bledsoe said.

"That'll play well in the media," the secretary of homeland security groaned.

"All right Gordon, Shelby, good job. Please call me as soon as you have Atef." Kendrick concluded.

"Yes sir," Blatt answered before terminating the connection.

Rose City Medical Center, Emergency Waiting

Scott Wells paced aimlessly. Tyler, too exhausted to do otherwise slept, his head cradled in Callie Logan's lap. Molly put down her cup of stale coffee, rose and touched Scott gently on the arm.

"What do you suppose is taking so long?" she asked. "It's been more than two hours now."

At that moment a door opened, and a tall, dark-haired doctor wearing a surgical mask pulled back onto his sweaty forehead and blue surgical scrubs said, "Mrs. Wells?

"That's me," Molly responded, anticipation in her tone.

She followed the doctor obediently with Scott, a groggy Tyler and Callie in hot pursuit. They went into a small, brightly lit interior conference room with a table and chairs and sat down.

"I'm Michael Dillon," the doctor said, extending his hand first to Molly and then to the others. "I'm a cardiovascular surgeon who is working with Dr. Petrakis and others on your husband, and I wanted to give you a quick update. The collapsed lung has not, as yet, re-inflated, but we think that it will do so shortly. And, your husband has a very strong constitution. He's holding his own."

"And the bad news?" Scott queried, sure that there was some.

"The bad news is that the large fragment has moved, only a millimeter or so, but it has moved and is now snuggled right up against the aorta. If the fragment penetrates that artery, or causes it to spasm, we're concerned that in his weakened condition Mr. Wells might well bleed out, or go into complete cardiac failure," he said in an even, but urgent monotone.

"But we think we can save him from further damage if, and I emphasize *if* there are no unforeseen complications," Dillon offered cautiously.

"What kind of complications are we talking about?" Tyler asked innocently.

"Well, complete cardiovascular failure is possible. Your father is not a young man, and although he appears strong now, his system has already been through a lot. And with any kind of surgery, plus the lead he's still carrying, a secondary infection is possible, and in his condition that could kill him just as easily," Dillon replied. "It's not an enviable choice we're faced with, but our recommendation is to go after that fragment right now. If you agree, you can go up to surgical waiting and we'll try to keep you updated on his condition."

"Curtis is in your hands and God's, Doctor. I know you will do your best," Molly said tearfully.

CHAPTER TWENTY-FOUR

Bandon Beach, Near Coquille, Oregon

A solitary figure sat on a sand hill and watched the massive, tempestuous breakers roll in, spending themselves in a headlong, frothy, crashing assault on the desolate stretch of beach. Ali Yusuf Atef was alone with his thoughts. Contrary to the glowing predictions of the FBI about his imminent capture, he had managed to elude their dragnet and make his way to the coast. His mood, however, was hardly one of elation.

He had managed to pick up a copy of the Portland daily paper, along with one of USA Today. Both detailed the shootout at Whispering Ridge and the subsequent raid at Wilsonville. Both also carried slightly outdated photos of him, and named him at the top of the FBI's most wanted list. His usefulness to al Qaeda in America was at an end. His network was a shambles, with nine dead and two captured. The news stories were explicit about one of the captives who traded information for leniency. To make matters worse, now Atef could not show his face anywhere in public. Like so many others, he had underestimated Curtis Wells, and it had cost him dearly. The only consolation was that Wells himself appeared to be near death.

Atef resolved to stay, temporarily, with a Muslim brother in this coastal Oregon city, and when things calmed down, he would make his way south to California where he could secure help and safe passage out of the country. But how was he going to explain this dismal failure to "The Teacher?"

Portland, the Rose City Medical Center

Molly Wells was physically and emotionally spent. Scott prudently rented a room in a motel near the hospital where they could alternate shifts sleeping and standing by in surgical waiting. Communicating in person when they could, and by cell phone when they had to, they took turns encouraging one another with words of hope. The mayor of Newberg, along with a half-dozen city councilmen came by to see Molly and to wish Curt well. Virtually every church in the little Oregon community was conducting a round the clock prayer vigil.

Unlike other professionals, hospital emergency surgical personnel don't always get to take Sunday off. Today, the hospital corridors were abuzz with the thrum of activity preceding an important, life-saving medical intervention. Most of the doctors and nurses didn't know Curt Wells personally. But they had all heard the media surmises and talk show whispers about the man behind the daring rescue in Saudi Arabia, and they knew they were treating an honest to God American hero. He wasn't going to die on their watch. Not if they could help it.

Surgical theaters are typically both chilly and brightly lit. Curt Wells was wheeled through the swinging double doors of the operating room in a semiconscious state, and for just a moment the bright lights made him think he was back in An Nafud, under the merciless sun. Except that he was aware of being cold, so very cold. And from some unknown source he could hear strains of surreal electronic music playing. Desperately he fought for consciousness, awareness, control. But the harder he fought, the more clarity eluded him, until finally the uniform gray faded to black and he fell away into uncomprehending darkness.

Deftly the surgical team opened his chest cavity. The bullet fragment was visible to the naked eye, but they took no chances, employing the precise magnification of microsurgery and working with infinite care, so as not to jostle the foreign object inside him or inadvertently puncture the coronary artery with their own surgical instruments. In less than thirty minutes they completed the critical extraction, but concern for the patient's vacillating vital signs remained.

"Let's close him up and get him out of here," Dillon barked. "He's going to need another unit of blood, and I want monitoring of his brain activity as well as his heart, lungs and functional internal organs."

Later, he emerged at the door of surgical waiting once again, where Molly had returned with a cup of black coffee. Tyler, asleep on a wooden bench, roused at the commotion and sleepily followed his mother into the hall.

"We've done everything we can, for now," Dillon reported. "We got the fragment, but it left a nasty bruise on the artery. That should heal in time, if there are no follow-up complications. The lung has mostly re-inflated, and the next twenty-four hours will be decisive. He's going to need at least one more unit of type A blood, so if you know any potential donors ..."

"I'm type A," Tyler announced proudly, glad to be able to contribute something to the life saving effort in progress.

"Me too," came the voice of Scott, arriving belatedly from his nap at the motel. "Just show us where to go, and we'll both donate right now."

Dillon pointed down the hall, but a nurse in blue scrubs had already grabbed both men gently by the arm and begun to guide them in the right direction.

In a sterile room Tyler and Scott Wells lay on separate tables across from one another, needles inserted into their arms and the red, life-giving fluid draining into clear glass receptacles suspended on metal frameworks.

"Do you remember when we were both young, and dad took us on our first real fishing trip up in the mountains?" Tyler asked.

"Like it was yesterday," Scott responded without hesitation.

"And that big thunderstorm came up, and lighting was flashing everywhere and trees were falling all around us from the wind?" Tyler continued.

"Yeah, and I remember how dad tucked us under an old fallen log, and covered us with his own body until the storm let up. I remember it all," Scott reminisced.

"I was just thinking how much I wish we could cover him up and protect him right now," Tyler mused wistfully.

"Right Ty, I love him too," Scott said with a gentle, knowing smile.

Later, the brothers went back to the motel to rest, but Molly refused to leave until she had seen Curt. In the recovery room, consciousness was returning to Curt Wells, and with it an unwelcome dose of pain and general discomfort. He felt the sharpest pain in his chest and shoulder, and his breathing was still labored and irregular. But his neck was also howling from the position in which they had propped him to expose his chest for the procedure. He couldn't remember being this uncomfortable. In fact, he couldn't remember much at all.

"Nurse," he croaked in a quiet, strained voice.

"Yes, Mr. Wells, welcome back," came the disgustingly cheerful response.

"Could we please get on with whatever it is we're going to do here?" he pleaded pathetically. "I'm uncomfortable as hell."

"The procedure is over Mr. Wells. It's time for you to wake up," she said.

"Water?" he asked hopefully.

"Not yet, but I'll brush your lips with a wet cloth, and maybe that will help," she offered.

Then there was more activity, with nurses and recovery room personnel buzzing around him like a hive of worker bees, checking his vital signs, shining lights in his eyes, trying to make small talk to test his lucidity. Finally, satisfied that he was coming out of it, they wheeled him, still connected to the monitors, into a more private area where they pulled a green curtain to isolate him from others in the recovery room.

"Molly?" he inquired.

"She's right outside," the cheery voice assured him. "In a few minutes we'll let her come in, but just for a short while. Please, try to rest."

Why don't *you* try to rest, he thought dourly to himself, with *your* chest and shoulder on fire and *your* neck all out of joint. The whimsical testiness was returning, a very good sign indeed.

About a half hour later, Molly Wells was shown into the curtained area of recovery where she stood over his bed.

"Oh, thank God, I've died and gone to heaven," he said upon opening his eyes. "It must be, because I see an angel."

With tears welling in her green eyes and spilling liberally down her cheeks, she moved to him and took his weathered hand between her own.

"You gave us a real scare, old man," she quipped with just the hint of a smile.

"Too old, too nasty, too mean to die," he rasped the partial sentence through parched lips.

"You have no idea, Curtis, how many people have been supporting us and praying for you," she said softly.

"Must be good people, 'cause the man upstairs seems to have listened," he said.

"You just rest now," she added, patting him lovingly. "The boys will be in as soon as the docs say it's okay."

"How are they?" he asked.

"Fine, just worried about you," she responded.

He smiled, shrugged and closed his weary eyes.

CHAPTER TWENTY-FIVE

Coquille, Oregon, Tuesday Morning

Dan Masters was a career postman. For twenty years he'd driven and walked around the seaside resort town delivering the mail. Repeatedly he declined supervisory positions just so he could keep on doing what he loved to do, carrying letters and packages in a timely manner to his long-time friends and neighbors. Almost everybody in town knew Dan, and they all liked and respected him.

Just now, his generous brow was wrinkled and his face screwed up in a frustrated frown because he just couldn't quite squeeze the awkward little package into the unremarkable metal mailbox in front of the small white frame house at twenty-four Carson Avenue. He delivered a lot of mail here during the past year, but never recalled seeing the home's occupant, a Mr. A. Majid. Well, no matter. Today he would just have to go up to the door, knock and hand deliver the package that didn't fit in the mailbox. Deliberately, he opened the creaky gate in the white picket fence and moved on up the sidewalk between the flowerbeds on his well-meaning errand.

Ali Majid was not at home. But his houseguest was, and scrambled with alarm as he saw Dan Masters begin his approach to the house. Ali Yusuf Atef was, so far, anonymous in this little

277

Oregon community, but killing a mailman would quickly change all that. No, he would play it straight, pretend to be a relative of Majid and see what the postman wanted. But he also stuck the Beretta nine millimeter in the waistband at the back of his trousers, just in case.

"Yes," he said abruptly, opening the door before Masters could knock.

"Mr., uh, Majid?" Masters queried.

"No, I am his cousin. Can I help?" Atef replied.

"Well, uh, sure, I guess so," Masters allowed. "This here package didn't quite fit in the box out front, so I thought ..."

"It is all right. Give it to me and I will tell my cousin it came," Atef barked, trying to cut the conversation short and get this unwelcome stranger off the porch.

"I guess that'll be okay, then," Masters said, handing him the package, tipping his cap and turning to walk away.

The door closed behind him, but not this particular chapter. One thing about small town postal people is that they trade on knowing everyone, on recognizing and responding to friendly faces. And there was something about the face he had just seen that was decidedly out of place here, very wrong. He walked on, busy about his work, but the uneasiness nagged him throughout the morning.

At the Beachcomber, an unremarkable local eatery with dog-eared menus and white plastic furniture, Masters paused for an early lunch break. A petite, fifty-something waitress soon approached his table.

"You want the special today, Dan?" she asked. "It's the open faced roast beef sandwich."

"Sure, the special's good with me," Masters replied with a good-natured grin, "and black coffee, if you please."

On a nearby table lay an already well-perused copy of the *Portland Times*. The Beachcomber not being known for its speed of service, Masters decided that he might as well read to pass the time, so reached over and picked up the paper. After chortling through the mindless cartoons, he flipped the paper over and there, on the front page, was a sight that caused the hair on the back of his neck to prickle. It was a picture of Ali Yusuf Atef, the man to whom he had just delivered a package.

Putting on his reading glasses - Masters was just vain enough that he didn't like to wear them in public - he read the whole sordid story about the recent gun battles at Whispering Ridge and Wilsonville. He thought for a moment about what to do, and when the waitress, Lily Snyder, approached with his lunch, he asked her to phone the police chief requesting that an officer come by. Fifteen minutes later, as the last bite of his roast beef sandwich was disappearing, a uniformed officer strode through the Beachcomber's front door and headed straight for his table.

"He's here," Masters said without preamble.

"Who's here?" asked four-year patrolman Todd Henning.

"Him!" exclaimed Masters pushing the newspaper picture over in front of the lawman.

"How do you know?" queried Henning skeptically.

"I know, son," Masters intoned patronizingly, "because not an hour ago I handed him a package over at twenty-four Carson Avenue."

"No way!" replied the uncomprehending police officer.

"No shit!" replied Masters. "So what are you gonna do about it?"

"Uh ...uh, the first thing I'm going to do is call the chief," Henning said, clutching the paper, rising and heading for the door at a much faster pace than that at which he had entered.

Chief E. D. Cosby, the 'E' standing for Elvis, was not one of the more astute lawmen in the American west. But neither was he a fool. And when Todd Henning shared the Masters' revelation with him, he was savvy enough to know that if an FBI S.W.A.T unit had failed to take Atef down earlier at Wilsonville, it was unlikely that his small-town, under-equipped, short-on-experience police force would fare any better now.

He called in another deskbound officer and ordered him, along with Henning, to change into street clothes while he called the FBI office in Portland. When he identified himself and stated his business, he was swiftly patched through to Special Agent In Charge Gordon Blatt.

After ascertaining the time of the sighting and credibility of the witness, Blatt asked Cosby to place the house on Carson Avenue under *very* discreet surveillance, and to call in for further instructions if Atef attempted to leave it. Before hanging up, he told the chief, who was suddenly reveling in self-importance, that appropriate units of the FBI would be dispatched immediately by helicopter to deal with the situation.

Quietly, Cosby huddled with Henning and the other officer, Ken Beene, and explained exactly how to position themselves so they could keep watch on the Carson Avenue sanctuary without being seen. Then he sent them packing, with orders to call in immediately if Atef started to move. Inside, he was hoping to hell that the I.D. provided by Dan Masters was solid, and that he would not later have to explain to the mayor why his department was wearing a generous helping of egg all over its face.

Portland, the Rose City Medical Center

Curtis Wells was moved out of critical care, although his condition was still listed as serious but stable. His powers of recuperation seemed near miraculous. Doctors and nurses still hovered, regularly checking his pulse, respiration and heartbeat, ever alert for any sign of secondary infection. While still spending most of each day at the hospital, Molly now went home at night to sleep in her own bed. Tyler and Scott, however, kept the motel room, and one or both of them showed up every time that visitors were allowed.

Scott arrived right after lunch to find his dad awake and in good spirits. The bed was cranked up so that Curt Wells could watch television and enjoy the many flowers sent by a myriad of well-wishers, including the president and first lady of the United States.

"How's the pain today?" Scott asked.

"A little better. They say I'm going to hurt for a while, but the stuff they give me for it makes me sleepy, so I only take it when I just have to. How are you, your brother and mom getting along?" he responded.

"We're fine. Better now that we see you're going to pull through," came the reply. "But I want to talk to you about something else."

Interested, Curt Wells switched off the TV and turned full attention to his oldest son, who clearly had something serious on his mind.

"I've decided to leave Halvarson, Dad," Scott said slowly. "My life and my heart are here in the Pacific Northwest. I've been offered a partnership track position in the intellectual property division at Burnside, Biddle, Coppage and Fitch right here in Lake Oswego, and I'm going to take it."

"I hope you're not doing this because of me," Curt began, before being waved into silence.

"It's partly about being near the family I almost lost, I won't deny it. What happened over there in Saudi changed me in ways I can't even begin to explain. Mostly it's about me. All we've been through has led me to reflect on what I really want in life, and the truth is that I'd like to have more time to enjoy you, mom and Ty. And at some point I'd like to find as nice a girl as Ty has, and raise a family of my own. Oregon is where I want to do that," he offered thoughtfully.

Laying his tiring head back on the pillow, Curt Wells smiled and said, "I guess we can find a room for you somewhere."

Visitors were limited to one at a time, and Scott knew that Tyler was waiting his turn. He touched his father supportively on the arm and rose to leave. Halfway to the door he remembered something else.

"Oh, I forgot to ask, do you know some woman named Amy Lassiter?"

"Name sounds familiar, but I can't place it," Curt Wells answered.

"She's with the National Security Agency – said she was on the phone with you when the lights went out the other night," Scott followed up.

"Sure enough," Curt said, "that's where I heard the name."

"She blames herself a little that we didn't get a warning sooner," Scott added. "She wants to come out some weekend after you're better and meet us all."

"You're saying the feds knew about the attack in advance?" Curt Wells could hardly believe his ears.

"Hard to fathom," Scott concurred, "but it would seem so."

Coquille, City Police Headquarters

Special Agent Shelby Joiner sat on one side of the table in an interview room with career postman Dan Masters on the other. Joiner's purpose was to evaluate Masters' credibility as a witness and learn anything he could to help him capture Ali Yusuf Atef. He first showed Masters a series of pictures that constituted a veritable rogues gallery of terrorists believed to be in the United States. Repeatedly he shuffled the tabletop lineup, and every time Masters picked out Atef.

"That's the man I saw, I tell you. I'm sure of it. I don't know much, but I do know people, and that's the guy who took the package from me," Masters insisted.

Unable to shake Masters' certainty, Joiner was now faced with the task of taking Atef into custody without shooting up the quiet little seaside community of Coquille. The three big black helicopters with "FBI" emblazoned in gold on the side had swept in from the east and landed near the eastern edge of town, well away from the Carson Avenue house where Atef was believed to be holed up. A direct daylight assault would almost surely result in a lot of shooting, while waiting till nightfall risked losing the terrorist in the dark. Further complicating the situation was the fact that sometime in the early afternoon, Ali Majid returned home. So now there were two subjects in there instead of one.

When he was through with Dan Masters, Joiner summoned Chief Cosby. A plan was slowly coming together in his mind.

"Chief, the last thing I want to do is get into a shoot-out with these fellows in a nice, peaceful neighborhood. So we're going to do our dead level best to take them without a fight. Who do you know in this neck of the woods with a bulldozer?"

"Well, uh, Fred Haynes has all kinds of heavy equipment on the construction site where they're building the new boat repair yard. I'll bet he's either got one or can get one in a hurry," Cosby speculated.

"Good! Please call Mr. Haynes up and get him down here right away. Tell him it's an emergency. Tell him whatever you have to, but don't tell him what it's about," Joiner instructed. "And then I want to evacuate all the houses and businesses within two blocks of the suspect house. Notify people by phone. Ask them to move quickly, but not make a stir when they go. Tell them there's a gas leak, or something."

"Where are we gonna put all those people ... I mean ..." Cosby was scratching his head.

"What would you use for an emergency shelter if there was a natural disaster of some kind?" Joiner asked astutely.

"Probably the high school gym, or one of the churches," Cosby was quick with the answer.

"Either of those'll do," Joiner said. "Just please don't let anyone know the real reason for the evacuation. I don't want any spectators, heroes or bystanders to get in the way."

"I'll get on it right away," the chief promised, bustling off.

Next, Joiner sat down with his S.W.A.T team leaders, Agents Cassidy and Walston.

"Here's the plan, men. We'll wait until late tonight, when the subjects turn out all the lights and retire. I've got thermal imaging gear on the way that will show us what rooms they're in. Once they zone out, we're going to make silent entry, just four men, and then ram a bulldozer or backhoe right through the wall of the bedroom where one of them is sleeping. Their first inclination will be to run away from the 'dozer, and when they do, our guys will be waiting in the main part of the house to take them down. I want them alive, so no shooting unless there's no choice."

"And if they get away?" Cassidy asked with concern.

"I've already contacted the Oregon State Police, and a half-hour before we go in, they'll close every road in and out of town, nobody in, nobody out until the suspects are in custody," Joiner assured him.

"What about local law enforcement?" Walston followed up.

"They'll back us up, but they're going to be busy with traffic control and keeping our target area clear. This is our op all the way, so we have to make it work," Shelby replied.

Joiner had previously asked Cosby to run down what the locals knew about Ali Majid, and the chief had obliged by bringing in Dale and Maggie Nettles, from whom Majid was renting the Carson Avenue house. The Nettles' figured to be Joiner's hardest sell, since their property was about to be damaged. But to his delight, he found them cooperative and understanding, made more so by his solemn promise that the United States government would stand good for full repairs. Maggie Nettles told him that Ali Majid was a truck driver for Western Lumber, hauling logs from south and central Oregon to processing plants near Salem, Portland and as far north as Tacoma, Washington. He was often on the road for two or three days at a time, didn't speak very good English, was quiet and kept to himself. He had never been late with the rent or caused any problems at all. Joiner did not tell them that his own background check revealed that Majid was in the country illegally and must, therefore, be working here on the basis of forged documents.

Fred Haynes, as it turned out, did in fact have a bulldozer, a big one. And he was thrilled to accommodate the FBI. He even offered to drive it himself, an offer Joiner tactfully declined for liability reasons. Now came the hardest part, and that was the long, nervous wait.

Whispering Ridge, Late Afternoon

Carlos Gutierrez was busily making permanent repairs to the Wells' kitchen door that had been first kicked in by Muhammad Isfahan and then decimated when Molly Wells' shotgun blast propelled him back through it. Carlos had teased her about protecting her kitchen and said with tongue in cheek that he'd always knock before entering.

For her part, Molly was all smiles. Doctors said that barring unforeseen complications, Curt could come home by the week's end, although his activities would be restricted for some time. She was spending time with her two sons every day, and her world was about to attain perfect symmetry once again.

Carlos and Fritz were running the business like two mother hens clucking over their new hatchlings, and raving about how well the processing was moving along and how sweet the grapes were.

Tyler and Callie set a June wedding date, Scott told Molly about his new job and the sound of her whistle and the radiance of her smile were signs that the Wells family was on the road to restoration.

As the sun began its inevitable descent behind Whispering Ridge, these happy people were entirely innocent of the drama playing out over on the coast.

Coquille, Eleven-Thirty-Five PM

Finally, the last lamp inside the house at twenty-four Carson Avenue went out. Joiner's vaunted thermal imaging equipment arrived as promised, and by coupling its heat signature recognition capacity with random window sightings by unobserved watchers who had taken up stations in neighboring homes, the S.W.A.T team now knew beyond a shadow of doubt which room contained Majid, and which Atef. The evacuation was deliberate, efficient and innocuous. Temporary shelter was arranged in the high school gymnasium at the far end of town, where people thought they were waiting out repairs to a broken gas main. Heavily armed state troopers closed all highways in and out. It was time.

Black clad S.W.A.T teamers glided in total silence to positions outside a rear window. Soundlessly the glass was cut and removed by the use of large suction cups. Carefully, quietly, the four men made entry. In seconds they transmitted the electronic code signifying that they were in position.

Most bulldozers have big diesel-powered engines, and so they are not very quiet. This one was no exception, and had been fired up over a block away. It made significant noise, nonetheless, as it rumbled onto the property. Fortunately, it had less than twenty feet to travel before making thunderous contact with the wall of the room in which Ali Yusuf Atef slept. As glass, wood frame and plaster disintegrated all around him, showering him with debris, Atef grabbed the nine millimeter Beretta from under his pillow and scrambled to flee the destruction in progress. As he emerged from the bedroom doorway, one agent swept his legs out from under him while another jumped directly on top of him, pinning his arms to the floor and separating him from his weapon. In seconds they rolled him over, cuffed his hands behind him and jerked him roughly to his feet, dragging him outside where spotlights and automatic weapons were trained on him.

The scene was duplicated down the hall when a terrified Ali Majid ran, half asleep and in his underwear, straight into the other two FBI agents in the house. Now the two heavily bearded men stood in public view, manacled, only partially clothed and shivering in the cold night air.

"Ali Yusuf Atef, you are under arrest for murder, conspiracy to commit murder and flight to escape prosecution. Ali Majid, you are under arrest for illegally entering this country, and for harboring a federal fugitive," Shelby Joiner said with a broad smile on his face.

"But at least that son of a pig Wells is dead or dying," spat Atef defiantly.

"Oh, I'm afraid you're a little behind the times, bucko," Joiner chided. "Curt Wells is alive and kicking, and just now his prospects for a long and happy life are a great deal brighter than your own. And, if you're keeping score, you have nine dead and four in federal custody, and God knows how many dead across the pond. You fellas screwed with the wrong old sailor this time. You see, your favorite saying 'God is great' is undeniably true. Only the way this all turned out, it looks to me like He's on our side instead of yours."

"Please, take these two scumbags out of my sight," Joiner said to one of his men, jerking a thumb decisively toward the waiting armored prisoner transport vehicle.

EPILOGUE

A Month Later, Whispering Ridge

Molly Wells was confused about just who Amy Lassiter was, or how she fit into the bewildering series of events that had overtaken the Wells family. But, ever the gracious lady of the manse, she warmly invited Amy, who called from the Portland airport, to come on out for a visit. About an hour later, the taxi pulled off the main road and wound its way over the tree-lined venue leading up to the winery.

Scott Wells, clad in faded blue jeans and an Oregon State University sweatshirt, was just exiting the main winery building where he was helping Fritz and Carlos to fill a big order. One good look at Amy Lassiter stopped him dead in his tracks. She was a tall, willowy brunette with misty gray eyes and a figure just buxom enough to snugly, but modestly fill out her elegant frame. When the cabbie hoisted her small suitcase out of the trunk, Scott almost tripped over his feet, or maybe his tongue, in haste to introduce himself and offer assistance with her luggage. Curt was sitting on the front porch in his wooden rocker, enjoying the sunset, when Amy approached and introduced herself.

"NSA, eh?" he said, a bit distantly. "And you're the one I was talking to when all hell broke loose here?"

"I'm afraid so," she confessed. "It really wasn't supposed to happen that way."

He invited her to sit in the other rocker opposite him, and she poured out the whole sordid story of the bureaucratic snafu that prevented the Wells' from knowing about the impending attempt on their lives, and her own desperate campaign to cut through the red tape.

"It sounds to me like you did all you could, and probably a hell of a lot more than was safe for you," Wells remarked when she finished.

"I guess so," she shrugged, "but I wasn't the one who got in trouble for it. I think repercussions are still coming down all the way from the White House."

"Well, let me explain something to you, Amy," Wells offered philosophically. "Screwing up is what government bureaucracies are good for. It's a wonder that they even have enough common sense to hire good people with initiative, people like you."

At this point in the conversation, Curt Wells became aware that his eldest son was hovering just behind his chair.

"Can I do something for you, Son?" he asked, not immediately catching on to the courtship ritual that had already begun.

"No, but mom wants to know if Amy has a room for the night, and if she would like to stay for dinner?" Scott said, smiling from ear to ear.

"Mom wants to know, huh?" Curt Wells smirked as the full scenario sank in. "Well, what about it young lady?"

"The answers are no, I haven't located a room yet, and yes, I'd be honored to have dinner with you," she said, inadvertently looking Scott up and down.

The fates were kind, and Molly and Amy hit it off famously. Dinner led to an invitation to spend the weekend, and Scott Wells' parents laughed together later about how he and Amy couldn't keep their eyes off one another.

In the dusk of evening, the younger couple walked, already arm in arm, up the hill into the green arbors. Scott had offered to show their guest around. Later, he announced that he planned to spend the following weekend in Yuma.

As the dusk set in and the gentle breeze rustling through the trees on Whispering Ridge turned cooler, Curt Wells sat in his old wooden rocker, gently stroking the ears of the late Jacob McCaskill's Doberman. Satan had adopted him completely, and now rarely left his side.

As Wells watched his son and new love interest walk off into the evening, he scratched the dog's ears and said aloud, "Satan, wherever old Jacob is tonight, he's probably looking down at the two us right now and figuring that you and I have two things in common. One, our pups have all grown up, and two, we're both salty old dogs that are awfully damned hard to kill."

THE END